I0651606

Moonrise Forest

Malcolm Hughes

Domilo

First Published 2008

Domilo Publishers

31 Molyneux Drive Wallasey Wirral CH45 1JS

ISBN 978-0-9556901-0-5

A long time ago, when our kids were *still* kids, my mate Billy swore to me that he wasn't on anything when he dreamt about a monkey, a red squirrel and some foxes in a clearing in a forest...and he pestered me to write him a short story he could read to his kids.

Well, it took a long time to get from there to here—some of our kids have kids of their own and the short story turned into a long one. But my mate Billy still likes it and it's still for the kids, however old they are.

So that's alright then...

And cheers, mate; without you, I'd never've learned to type!

Chapter One

As he stepped off the turtle's back and onto the marshy ground at the edge of the lake, the monkey cast a nervous glance over his shoulder and twitched his nose.

"It's alright," the turtle said in a slow and bubbling voice. "They won't have left the road yet."

The monkey looked down at the wet, glistening face of the turtle. "Who?" His voice was slightly breathless, pitched high.

"The circus men. And their dogs. The one's you're running away from." The turtle smiled and waddled a short distance towards the trees. "But, to make sure, why don't you get a bit further into the forest?"

The monkey hesitated a moment and then followed the turtle, choosing a young willow to sit behind. His eyes seemed to be looking everywhere at once and he scratched nervously at his chest.

"How did you know about that? I didn't tell you anything about the circus or the men or the dogs and how does a turtle know about circuses and men and dogs anyway and what makes you think I'm running away from them and what is this place you've brought me to anyway—"

"Whoa, monkey, my nervous friend." The bubbling voice was calming, pleasant, almost hypnotic. The monkey found himself settling on his haunches, relaxing a little. "One question at a time," the turtle went on. "When I picked you up on the far side of the lake, you were as jumpy as a flea on a scratching dog and you kept looking over your shoulder. Just like you're doing now. It seems obvious that you're trying to get away from something. I might be a bit slow and awkward out of water but my hearing and eyes are very good. I heard the dogs and the men shouting on the road and I'd seen the bright colours of the wagons and caravans of the circus earlier today. As for this place, it's Moonrise Forest and this lake is Sunset Lake. As for knowing about circuses…well, let's just say I wasn't always a turtle."

This made the monkey jump up, his eyes bright but wary, his front paws bunched into fists at his sides. "Oh yes? And what does that mean? Eh, what does it mean, when you say you weren't always a turtle? Eh?"

"Dear me, you're an inquisitive monkey, aren't you? So many questions. No wonder you're breathless all the time." The slow smile returned to the turtle's face and the pleasant ebb and flow of his words, so like the gentle slap of the lake, held no obvious threat to the monkey who relaxed again.

"I'd still like to know what you mean," the monkey said, the nervous edge gone from his voice. He squatted again, scratched his chest and then, almost to himself, he said, "It's my nature, I suppose."

"Yes, I suppose it is," the turtle replied. "And I suppose it would be unkind if I didn't explain, now that I've made you curious. Well, you lean back against that tree and I'll tell you a story. You might or might not believe it but, whatever, it's true."

The monkey smiled, almost a grin, and leaned back against the tree. He plucked a long stem of grass from the ground and popped it quickly into his mouth to chew on.

The turtle nodded his head once and said, "A little less than a year ago, I was walking along the bank of this lake. Over there." He turned his head so that he was looking over to the left, his neck wrinkling even more. "Can you see that cottage?"

The monkey looked, shielding his eyes against the low, golden rays of the setting sun, which looked as if it were actually setting into the lake.

Such a huge lake, he thought. *I wonder if...*

"Can you?"

"What? Oh yes, I can see it. I was just wondering…"

"Yes, I'm sure you were but, for now, save your wondering until I've finished my story." When the monkey lowered his paw and looked at him, the turtle went on. "So, I was walking by the cottage and, as I got nearer, I could see somebody sitting on the front step. It was very hot that day, a lot like today, but whoever it was wore a thick black dress, and a hooded cape over their shoulders but at least the hood was down. Still, strange as this looked, it wasn't the oddest thing. Now that I was nearer, I could see that the person was a woman. And she was smoking a long-stemmed pipe, sending perfect little smoke-rings up from the bowl. I leaned on the small gate at the end of the path leading to her front door and—"

"Wait a minute," the monkey interrupted. "How could a turtle lean on a gate?"

"I told you, I wasn't always a turtle. Now, are you going to listen or do I just waddle back to the lake?"

"Sorry." The monkey lowered his head and put his front paws in his lap. He scratched the sole of his right rear paw with the nail of his left front paw.

"Good. So, there I was, leaning on the gate, already warm and feeling warmer by the minute just looking at all her clothes. 'Well?' She said to me. 'What're you staring at, then? And who gave you permission to lean on my gate?' The question startled me and I laughed and said, 'I'm staring at you, who else?' She took her pipe out of her mouth and frowned. 'Oh? And what's so funny about me, you arrogant young peacock?' She tapped her teeth with the stem of her pipe. I said, 'Surely you must know how funny you look. All bundled up for winter and blowing those smoke-rings from your pipe.'"

The monkey stared at the turtle. He had a feeling he knew what had happened then.

"She didn't say anything to me, just stared at me, still tapping her teeth. So I said, 'You're dressed as if it's cold and wet instead of a glorious, hot summer's day.' She nodded and said, 'Cold, is it? Wet is it? Well, you shall know what it means to be cold and wet my laughing young…turtle.' She pointed her pipe at me and, well, you can see what happened." The turtle finished his story and rested his head on the springy turf.

"Oh. Er, well, I mean, er I...oh my fur and tail, I don't know what to say. Or think."

The turtle raised his head slowly. "Don't worry, little friend, I've said and thought enough about what the old woman did. Even after she changed me, I tried to explain that I hadn't meant to offend her but she refused to listen. She just told me that I would stay a turtle until I changed my arrogant ways and learned that there were as many different ways in the world as there were things and creatures. I asked her how long, and she just turned her back and went inside her cottage. I've thought long and hard these last months and, now, I think I understand what she was saying. And what she said is true. But now, she never seems to be sitting on her front step so I can't tell her what I've learned."

"Well, look, listen, why don't I just go over there and knock on her door and tell her how kind you've been? I could tell her that you've learned your lesson and she'll turn you back. What d'you think? Eh? Mmm?" The monkey was standing now and he suddenly began a hilarious dance, jumping up and down and hopping from one paw to another, clapping his front paws. His mouth was wide in a teeth-filled grin, obviously filled with joy at the idea of returning the turtle's favour.

The turtle smiled at his antics and at that the fact that this furry bundle of noise and questions wanted so much to help. He looked longingly towards the cottage, which was now shrouded in mist and mottled shadow as the last of the sunlight filtered through the trees. Beyond the cottage's roof, the turtle saw that some of those shadows were moving.

"Sshh," the turtle hissed.

The monkey was doing back flips and making a high squeaking noise, which was clearly building to a loud and insistent shriek.

"Eek chee chee...what?"

"Sshh," the turtle repeated and took two waddling steps to his left, peering into the gloaming, his hidden ears straining for any noise that might come from those moving shadows.

Both animals heard it at the same time; the sharp, guttural sound of a dog barking. It was followed by a man coughing and then the piercing tone of a whistle.

"Oh my tail and fur! They'll find me for sure! Oh no, oh dear me no!"

"What's all this?" The turtle asked, looking back at the monkey. "They're still a long way off. Just calm down and let me think." His head drew back into his shell a little and he closed his eyes. After a few moments, he said, "Mmm, just the ticket. The forest. That's where you should go. It's a very big forest with many hiding places."

"But if I go in there, I won't be able to speak to the old woman and you'll still be a turtle and that's not fair, eh?"

"Don't worry about me. The important thing is to get you hidden and the forest's the only place. Now, go."

The monkey dropped his head and chewed at a nail but finally nodded. "I'm sorry, you're right." He lifted his head. "But I won't forget what you did for me. I promise I'll come back as soon as I can." He grinned again. "And I'll tell you my story then." He turned and began to pad into the trees, his front paws curled into fists, knuckles almost scraping the ground, his long tail held high in the air behind him.

"There is one thing you could do now."

The monkey turned his head. "Oh yes? What? Eh?"

The turtle smiled his slow smile. "You could tell me your name."

"Oh yes! My name! My name's Chatter," the monkey told him and clapped his paws.

"Of course. What else could it be? Now, off you go and take care. You'll be safe in the forest. It's a good place. Nothing bad ever happens in Moonrise Forest."

The monkey padded into the trees and the turtle saw him reach for a low branch, pulling himself up effortlessly. Then he was lost among the branches.

"I hope you can keep your promise one day little chatterbox," the turtle whispered to himself and waddled back into the lake, glancing up at the early moon that looked like a fingernail in the deep blue of the sky.

"But nothing unusual ever happens in Moonrise Forest. Everybody knows that," said a young squirrel at the back of the clearing. His voice was a mixture of worry and wonder. A low murmuring from the other squirrels agreed with him.

"Well, *something* strange is going on *now*!" Rolf shouted to get everybody's attention. He was squatting on the ground, his red fur puffed up and shiny. His eyes sparkled with a fierce intensity and his bushy tail moved from side to side behind him.

"Now, let me say it again so we all understand. Our winter-store is dwindling and we don't know how or why. It's just coming into real autumn after a very hot summer and you can feel by the air that it's likely to be a hard winter. We can't afford to lose our store. If we do, it'll mean going outside the forest to find food. And we know what's beyond the forest." He didn't have to say what was beyond the forest because they all knew. Foxes. Nobody spoke but an uneasy shuffling replaced the murmuring.

Finally, the Elder Squirrel spoke. His voice was quiet but it managed to carry to every squirrel there.

"Yes, Rolf, you make your point well if a little loudly. But you're young and full of the rashness of youth. The years will add experience. Still, you're right. The winter will be hard and we need a large store. Now, tell us how long you think this dwindling has been going on and what your plan is to stop it. I see in your eyes that you have a plan."

He's done it again. He's managed to tell me off for trying to wake these half-asleep nits up and made me feel good because he knows I have a plan. Will I ever learn or know enough to be Elder Squirrel in this forest?

Rolf shook off the thought and raised himself on his rear legs, rubbed his protruding front teeth and, as evenly as he could, said, "We think it's been happening for about six weeks but we knew for certain just a week ago. Scamper saw that a large hazelnut he had put in himself was missing. Nobody had heard anything or seen anything. We've taken a tally every two days since and there's a definite dwindling. There's no sign round the tree or on the ground. No scratches, nothing."

"Thought you had a plan, big mouth? You talk a good fight but I haven't heard anything about how you plan to stop it."

This came from somewhere near the back of the gathering but nobody stood up to identify himself. It was a bully's voice, full of bravado and petulance but some of the other squirrels muttered in agreement.

Rolf tensed, fuming and trying to control his anger.

I know who that was. Chestnut. He's got a cheek, telling me I talk a good fight when he won't even stand up so we can see him. I'll...

The Elder Squirrel put a paw gently on Rolf's flank and the younger squirrel relaxed but he was still angry.

"Easy, Rolf. We still have to hear your plan and that will quieten them and be enough to silence any bully-boys."

Rolf turned to look at Saltpepper and nodded. Saltpepper raised himself on his back legs and spoke to the gathering and, this time, his voice had a harder edge to it, not much louder but everybody heard that edge.

"This is an official meeting," Saltpepper began. "Called by me and led by me. And we will have order. If there are questions, they will be asked at the end of the meeting and they will be asked properly. Not shouted from the back by somebody who is afraid to be seen. Is that understood?"

The silence showed that it was and Rolf took the time to collect his thoughts before telling them all what he had in mind.

"We've arranged to meet the birds later today and then with the badgers. We want their help in keeping a watch on the store. We want to watch the store-tree every minute. In my opinion, whoever is taking the food is getting into the tree from above, somehow. We're going to ask the birds to watch the very top of the tree and ask the badgers to keep an eye on the ground. I'll be with others, climbing up and down the branches. That way, we should be able to catch this, this...treepocket."

Rolf looked around the gathering, expecting somebody to ask him who he thought the thief might be. The truth was that he had no idea. The thing was that, in Moonrise Forest, the long years of peace and stability and safety had led to interdependence between the animals who lived there. The squirrels collected most of the food for the winters but most of the other animals helped at some time. Except the badgers, of course. The badgers kept to themselves mostly because their food was available anywhere in the forest. Given all of this, it was hard to believe that it was one of the forest animals stealing the store.

"Any questions?" Saltpepper asked quietly. "No? Not even from those who thought that Rolf didn't have a plan?" He looked pointedly towards the rear of the gathering but not a sound came from Chestnut or any other squirrel. "Well, can I take this to mean that we accept Rolf's plan?" There were mumbled 'yeses'. "Good. Then this meeting is closed until Rolf catches this... treepocket. Not quite the right word but it gets the idea across well. Thank you for coming to the meeting today."

When the clearing was empty apart from them, Saltpepper turned to Rolf and smiled. "You did well, young Rolf. Taking what that braggart Chestnut said and keeping your temper won you many admirers today. You have it in you to be a fine leader. Life and years will smooth out the rough edges. Now, you go and meet the birds and badgers to arrange your trap. And, if you'll take a little piece of advice, put somebody *inside* the tree." Saltpepper winked one black eye and left Rolf staring at his back.

Rolf squatted on the floor of the forest, thinking that Saltpepper knew or suspected more than he was letting on. Saltpepper had been Elder Squirrel for a long, long time and had seen a lot and Rolf wished he had that experience.

Eventually, Rolf left the clearing and headed for the meeting he had arranged with the birds. The sun was still quite high and its heat pleasant but there was a smell to the air and a feel to the breeze that hinted at frost later in the night. It wouldn't be long before winter came in on autumn's heels and the sooner this tree-pocket was caught the better for everybody.

Among the high boughs of a chestnut tree a good way from where Rolf had outlined his plan, the high, cheerful voice of an animal filled the air.

"Up it goes, in the air, watch it drop and catch it here! Crunch, mmm, lovely."

Chatter munched happily on the nut and followed it with a juicy berry from a pile he held in his left hand. He was lying on his back, unconcerned about how loud his song might be; he was in a part of the forest where few other animals came or went. Chatter was feeling rather pleased with himself. He had escaped from the circus with the turtle's help and had found a nice quiet spot with an ideal tree where he had made his home. The tree was a huge, gnarled oak, older than anything Chatter had ever seen, even older than Methuselah, the elephant who had been his friend in the circus. Yes, finding the ancient oak was wonderful but there was something even more wonderful.

Chatter had found a tree that had, inside its deep hollow, a mound of food. Just lying there, berries and nuts in a huge mound.

"Funny that," Chatter said round a mouthful of berry.

It was about a week after he had first entered the forest. He was abroad one evening, swinging from branch to branch, high above the forest floor when he landed on a thick branch that was obviously dead but not cracked or fallen. He stepped gently off the branch onto another, firmer branch and peered through a hole in the body of the tree. It was dark inside the hole but Chatter's nose twitched as he caught the faint but unmistakable smell of food. Looking down towards the base of the tree, he tried to see if there was anything or anybody there but he was too high and the evening was drawing in fast.

The smell of the food, faint though it was, started his stomach rumbling and his mouth watered so he took his courage in his paws and squirmed inside the hollow tree.

Climbing down was the most frightening experience of his life. The almost silent darkness of the inside of the tree was eerie, broken only by the sound of his nails as he lowered himself down, and by the occasional faint light showing through a place where a branch had broken off and the bark fallen away. All the way down, he was convinced that somebody or something was inside the tree with him, following him down or waiting for him below. His heart seemed to take up residence in his throat and ears. His mouth, so recently watering, dried up and his tongue stuck to its roof.

Sitting on his branch now, Chatter shifted uneasily at the memory. He thought, instead, of his arrival at the bottom of the hollow tree and finding the very large mound of fruit and nuts. Just the thought of all that food made him feel better and he tossed another berry in the air and caught it in his mouth, singing his little song to celebrate. The song had become something close to an incantation, a spell to enhance the taste and, maybe, a superstitious way of keeping out all bad thoughts, all uneasy memories.

After eating his fill of the food that first time, he had sat on top of the mound, letting his stomach digest what he'd eaten, not thinking about what the food meant, only happy that he'd found it. Finally, he began to climb back up towards the hole he'd entered by, not frightened now but still going carefully because, he was beginning to think about things properly.

Something told him that the food had not arrived inside the tree by accident and, as he came closer to the opening, the fear of something or somebody waiting or following him was replaced by a fear of being caught by whoever had collected the food. When he finally clambered out into the air again, it was full dark and thin cloud had covered the moon so he was in almost total darkness. He had listened for sounds of anything close to the tree but the forest was quiet and all he could hear was his own breathing.

The following night, Chatter had gone to the tree again and, again undisturbed, had eaten his fill. It convinced him the tree was safe but he decided that, in future he would always visit the tree after evening had fallen and he would not to eat more than he needed.

That was what he had done and he was still free and still well-fed.

"Funny that though," he repeated as he finished the last of his little snack. "It's times like this," he went on softly. "That I miss the circus."

Yes, at times like this he missed the circus. Not much, oh no, but it would be nice to have somebody to talk to, to ask questions; like who collected the food and put it into the tree?

Chatter was a bright, clever monkey with a quick brain and he had learned a lot in the circus. But, because he spent all of his life in the circus with other circus animals and with people, he had almost lost the most important thing any truly wild animal possesses—instinct.

There was a smattering of it, buried deep down in an older part of his brain. It was this smattering that had told him that the food he'd found hadn't arrived in the tree by accident and it had told him to be careful about eating or taking too much of that food. Still, it was not the full-grown thing it should have been. There had been little use for it in the circus. In the circus, he had never needed to worry about where his next meal came from or where he would sleep that night and everything he had needed to make him warm and comfortable had been available, just when he needed it. Finding the old oak tree had been a bit like the circus; it was comfortable and safe. These last few nights, though, the air had been a little sharper and he had added a few more leaves to his cover. It hadn't crossed his mind that the red and gold and yellow leaves he found wherever he looked might soon be gone; the passing seasons were things Chatter had only really watched from behind the bars of his circus cage.

So, his instinct wasn't functioning the way it should and he had no idea how severe the coming winter was likely to be, the signs around him were things he missed altogether.

Chatter was a bright, clever monkey but he still had a lot to learn.

That same late afternoon, as Chatter made his way back to his new-found home, Saltpepper was in his drey. Saltpepper's home, too, was in an oak tree but it was much more gnarled and far older than even Chatter's ancient oak.

The Elder Squirrel lay with his nose between his front paws, his black eyes hidden behind closed lids, looking for all the world as if he were asleep. His breathing was shallow and hardly disturbed his winter-heavy coat of silver and faded red. He was old now and sometimes weary but his mind and his instinct were as sharp as ever. Saltpepper's instinct had been honed to a sharp edge but there were times when he thought it might be more than just a highly developed sense. When he was younger and learning from his own master, Whitefur, he had heard a word that touched something deep inside. Whitefur had used the word himself when he explained some of the history of Moonrise Forest and the duties owed by the Elder Squirrel.

"Saltpepper," Whitefur had said in his thin, wavery voice. "Time you learned about your heritage, don't you know?

"Long, long ago, when there were more trees than there are now and Sunset Lake was not much more than a large pool, our ancestors lived here in Moonrise Forest. Back then, they weren't really organised, they didn't spend all summer collecting for the store and they didn't live so close to each other. And, more importantly, there were other animals who were easier to catch than squirrels. Back then, squirrels knew the land well, knew where the food could be found even when the snow fell. They didn't worry about being out and about during the cold days or the dark nights, don't you know? Foxes, then, weren't a problem, d'you see? But the years passed and the forest grew thinner and the lake grew larger and the foxes...well, they became a problem. They began to move closer to our ancestors' dreys.

"With no need for proper organisation, there was no need for an Elder Squirrel. Until, one winter when the winds blew angrily and the skies were always heavy and grey, filled with snow, one young squirrel was killed while out searching for food. Two other squirrels who had been looking for him found the ripped and torn remains.

"Now, young Saltpepper, can you imagine the shock, the chilling fear such a discovery must have caused?"

Whitefur had given Saltpepper a piercing look and it seemed to go deep inside the young squirrel so that he was sure he could imagine exactly how the finding of that ripped and torn squirrel must have chilled the forest squirrels. Saltpepper had nodded, feeling sick and cold.

"Mmm," Whitefur had said softly. "I can see that you can. Well, what were they to do? A meeting was called and all the squirrels arrived in a large clearing, the very one we use today. They talked and talked and decided that *something* needed to be done. There were calls to leave the forest and others wanted somebody to pay for the two squirrels while a small number claimed that the two squirrels had been taken by The High Ones as sacrifice. These few squirrels demanded that, in future, the squirrels themselves should make sacrifices willingly to make

The High Ones look kindly on them. Oh yes, the talk was much and many and going nowhere sensible until, finally, the meeting was ended by a fierce snowstorm which lasted until late the following morning. That afternoon, two more squirrels were found dead, torn to shreds.

"This time, there was no need to call a meeting. Their grief and terror brought them together, the need to share and to be with others brought them, struggling over the deep snow in ones and twos. They all gathered in the clearing and sat on the hard-packed snow beneath a pale moon and they waited as the bitter night swallowed the afternoon. It was almost as if they were waiting for something. Or someone. Our clearing must have been an eerie place that long-ago winter's night."

Whitefur had paused then and Saltpepper had stared at him without seeing him. He was seeing the clearing as it had been all those years ago, so vivid he felt he was actually there, feeling the snow beneath him and the sorrow all around him. Then Whitefur had spoken again.

"Finally, as night began to give way to the first hesitant light of the dawn, there came into the clearing a squirrel alone."

Saltpepper had known by the tone of Whitefur's voice and the words he used that this was some of the secret lore, handed down from Elder Squirrel to Elder Squirrel through the years.

"Nobody had seen this squirrel before. He was a big one with piercing eyes and a thick, gleaming coat of Autumn Red. His front teeth were as white as the snow on which he stood, as sharp as the winter wind. He stood on his hind legs and pawed the air three times. The silence in the clearing deepened. Then he spoke.

"'I am sent to help you in your time of need. I am sent to bring you counsel and to show you the way. The High Ones did not take the four dead squirrels as sacrifice. They were killed by foxes. The foxes have watched you down the years and seen how safety has made you complacent. They have watched you go out alone in the midwinter, unwary of danger and they have laughed. Now, they have moved their dens closer to the forest and closer to you. They look at you and see food at the entrances to their dens. You must awake from your long sleep of safety and prepare to defend yourselves. You must listen and learn and nevermore put yourself at risk when the winter winds wail and the snow shrouds the forest.'

"So, our ancestors learned that they should gather as much of their food as they could during the safe days of summer and early autumn and store it. They learned that all animals of the forest were vulnerable and that there was a need for co-operation amongst all who lived in Moonrise Forest.

"Now, young Saltpepper, I see you have a question."

"Master," Saltpepper had said respectfully. "Where did the squirrel come from? What was his name?"

"He did not say and I doubt anybody asked. It was enough that he had come in their hour of need. What you need to remember, Saltpepper, is that the Autumn Red squirrel lived among our ancestors for a long, long time. He led them, advised them on how to defend themselves when necessary, especially in the collecting and storing of food. And, so, he gave us our future."

Saltpepper needed more, needed to see beyond the legend, to know the origin of the Autumn Red squirrel. "Master, was he one of The High Ones, d'you think?"

Whitefur had reared up on his hind legs and, for an instant, Saltpepper was afraid but when his master spoke, it was with his normal voice and the younger squirrel let out a long, relieved breath.

"Do you think The High Ones come down to play with squirrels because they are *bored*? No, I don't think so. What I think, *think*, mark you, is that the Autumn Red squirrel was not one of The High Ones. But…I believe he was sent by them in the squirrels' hour of need. I think he was mortal for all his long years, but I believe he was more. I believe, like my old master before me, that he was given more than just a long life. I think The High Ones gave him some of their power so that they did not have to give all of their time to the animals of Moonrise Forest. There are many other creatures in the world who need the husbandry of The High Ones. It is said in our lore that since the Autumn Red squirrel dwelt among us, each Elder Squirrel has been his true descendant that something in each chosen squirrel comes from him and makes it natural for each Elder Squirrel to be chosen." Whitefur paused then and closed his eyes, thinking, then he nodded and looked again at Saltpepper. "I believe that what each Elder Squirrel has is a remnant of the Autumn Red squirrel, like an ember of fire perhaps, which sometimes flares to life in some Elder Squirrels. You know about our heroes and wise ones of the past and I believe it flared in them. While in others it remained only an ember. As it does in me and in you, Saltpepper. A flame or power, or magic, if you like."

Saltpepper, a lot older now but still as sharp as ever, nodded to himself as he remembered that long ago conversation with his old master. Magic, Whitefur had said and it had rung true to the young Saltpepper. It still rang as true today.

Saltpepper knew that he only had the ember and not the flaring flame but, even so, he knew that it had sharpened his instinct to a fine thing. And his instinct, his faint ember of the flame, his tiny magic was now telling him that all the long, peaceful years of his leadership were coming to an end. A great change was coming to Moonrise Forest. Saltpepper did not know what it might be or exactly when it would come but he felt it strongly. He could feel it in the air, almost taste and smell it.

"Change," he murmured to himself. "Does anybody truly like the idea of change?"

No, Saltpepper did not think so. Wasn't change a sign of mortality? Ah well, whatever it was, Rolf must be told because it surely involved him.

Saltpepper left the warmth of his drey to meet with Rolf and hear if the birds and badgers were going to help. As he stepped onto the branch, which reached across, to a smaller tree, Saltpepper looked up through the gap in the leaves and saw the sky filled with stars. As he turned his head, he saw a shooting star. He wished upon it.

"Well, Stripe, will you help?" Rolf asked in what he hoped was a respectful tone. All the time had been speaking, none of the badgers had said a word. It had been easier with the birds; at least they had asked questions and sounded interested. And, of course, they had offered their help. These badgers, well, it seemed that they might be asleep.

"Harumph, now then, Golf is it?"

"Rolf! Rolf!"

"Yes, yes, Rolf. Now then, you say the birds will help?

By the lake! I think he was asleep! Rolf thought but he said, "Yes, they will help. Weren't you listening?"

"Now then, a little civility please. Just needed to make sure. Harumph! Well, if the birds are willing to help, then there can't be much wrong with your plan. Right then, we'll sniff around the tree. Tomorrow, yes? We'll make a start then. Humph!" And the badger walked away, followed by the other two badgers, who hadn't said a word.

Rolf felt foolish. He shook his head and rubbed his teeth; it was time he got back to Saltpepper and report. He scampered across Badgers Hollow where there were no trees for him to use. The ground was covered in fallen leaves and Rolf's paws made them snap and crackle as he headed towards the trees.

It was a long way back to Saltpepper's drey and Rolf would pass the store tree. Since the birds and badgers were not beginning their watches until tomorrow, Rolf decided it would be a good idea to check the tree; you never knew he might even catch the thief in the act.

Two thirds of the way back to the tree, Rolf froze on the low branches of the tree he was on. His nose twitched madly and his ears strained at every whisper of sound. There was...*something*, close by. There was no smell or sound that he knew, but there was definitely *something.*

This part of the forest was dense with trees and there was still thick leaf and branch cover overhead. The moonlight was struggling to get through and Rolf couldn't see clearly but he felt it. He stood still on the branch, his body taut.

Then it was gone.

Rolf waited for a moment to make sure and then he relaxed. As he waited for his heart to stop pounding in his ears and for his breath to slow, he considered what had happened. And he realised that he hadn't felt threatened at all. Oh, it had been something unknown, mysterious and that should have been enough for him to warn every living thing in the forest but...it hadn't. He had felt no malice in whatever it had been. What he had felt was, more than anything, a sort of innocent mischievousness.

"But I'll tell Saltpepper," Rolf told himself and then continued on his way.

The store tree stood to the east of the clearing. It didn't grow there; it was dead, struck by lightning long years before the Autumn Squirrel had come to the forest. Over the years, as the number of squirrels increased, the need for more food had meant that the tree had been hollowed out more and more. Now, as Rolf approached the tree, it was probably as close to being completely hollow as it could be without collapsing.

The entrance to the tree faced west, towards the clearing and was about the size of two adult squirrels. The bark around the entrance had been scratched and worn away so that, now, when the moonlight shone on it, it seemed to glow. The tree and its entrance had always felt safe to the forest animals and many of them would stop here simply to pass the time of day. There was another hole in the trunk of the tree about six feet above the entrance, used to pile more food on the store and the animals knew it was there. However, because there had never been a need to go further up the tree, nobody knew that, almost at the top of the tree, was another large hole, which gave entrance to the tree. Not knowing this meant that the squirrels didn't know that the thief could find a way in without worrying about being seen.

Chatter was inching through his private entrance, one front paw and his face already inside, when he heard the sound below. It was a steady thump-thump approaching from the east. He froze.

It was getting closer. He edged back out, his tail wrapped round a branch above him, and peered down. The thumping noise ceased and, for a moment, Chatter wondered if he had only heard his pounding heart, but then the scuffling at the base of the tree left him in no doubt that it hadn't been his heart in his ears. He looked down, hoping to make out what it was but all he could see was a vague shadow, bobbing right to left. Chatter followed this movement, gripping the branch tighter with his tail to keep his balance.

The sound of the creaking branch seemed the loudest thing he had ever heard.

Oh my tail and fur! That's torn it! Whatever's down there will know I'm here and it'll charge up the tree and that'll be that and oh why did I ever leave the circus?

The panic was rampant in him, so much so that he was unable to move. He just clung on, waiting for the inevitable capture.

Below, Rolf stopped moving. He heard something but, what to Chatter had been the sound of the tree cracking and falling in some wild winter storm was just a creak as a dead branch moved in the light breeze. It wasn't really the sound that made Rolf stop but that same feeling he'd had not far from Badgers Hollow. Once again, Rolf became an animal of almost pure sensory input.

He reached out with his ears and eyes and nose, the fur prickling on his back but there was nothing there, no threat. He poked his head inside the tree but there was only the smell of food and no sign of any thief. He pulled his head out and peered upwards before climbing to the smaller hole six feet above him. Clinging with his claws in the dry bark, he could still sense something above him but there was still no sense of danger.

"Snow and hail! What is it?" He turned and made his way to the floor of the forest again, knowing that there was something strange going on, knowing that he had to tell Saltpepper. And soon.

Once he was back on the ground again, he peered up once more but the moon was behind a bank of cloud and he could see nothing in the darkness. He ran towards the low branch on the next closest tree, his eyes bright, ears flattened against the side of his head, tail high in the air.

High in the store-tree, Chatter watched with wide-eyed relief as the bobbing shadow left. He suddenly realised that he was holding his breath and let it out in a noisy rush, which scared him all over again.

"Oh dear, oh dear me, what was that? Got to get away from here, got to get away to my comfy tree but I'm so hungry. It was only one of whatever it was, wasn't it? Yes, it was. I could just..."

He pushed into the tree, darted down to the store, grabbed a handful of food and pushed it into his mouth, grabbed another handful and darted back up the inside of the tree. Once outside, he almost flew back through the trees to his own oak tree. His heart beat wildly as he made his way home and his mind kept telling him that he had to be careful, had to be careful next time, just take enough and leave, don't hang around to eat.

Chapter Two

Chestnut was sitting on his haunches, his tail curled round his body to rest on his paws, his back against the inside of his drey in the beech tree. He was gnawing a hazelnut, occasionally taking big bites and crunching the nut into white slivers. He liked the sound of the nut as he crunched and it broke. To tell the truth, he liked the sound of *anything* breaking.

Two other squirrels sat in front of him, chewing their own food. Both were younger and smaller than Chestnut and he was their hero. Chestnut wasn't afraid to tell the older squirrels what he thought. Even now, as he gave vent to his anger and spite, their eyes were bright with something very close to worship.

"Not from anybody who doubted there was a plan?'" Chestnut said in a mocking imitation of Saltpepper's question earlier that day. "Stupid old fuddy. Time he left this part of the forest and found somewhere to lie down and die." He spat a piece of shell out.

The two younger squirrels looked sideways at each other and then quickly looked at their paws; what Chestnut had said was a bit too close to the bone. They'd been taught to believe in the office of Elder Squirrel even if they thought the actual squirrel was an old duffer who was too old-fashioned. But they were in Chestnut's drey and eating food he had given them and, anyway, he was too big to cross in the confines of his own drey. Better to let their hero get it off his chest and then they could think about tomorrow and what tricks they could get up to with the old stick-in-the-muds.

"I'll get my own back, see if I don't. Making me look small in front of everybody and siding with Rolf." Chestnut snarled as he said Rolf's name and spat out another piece of shell. "I'll get him, too. Bigheaded bugger. One day, I'll get him and then he'll know what a fight is. I'll do him over good and proper. Shut him up for good. I'll break him. I'll bite and gouge him and scratch and scar him. Crunch him like a hazelnut!" The nut in his mouth shattered into a dozen pieces and the noise it made as it broke apart was very loud in the small space.

The two younger squirrels jumped but knew better than to say anything or make any movement to try to leave the drey. They tried to look everywhere but at the awful light in their hero's eyes as he went on with his diatribe.

"Hope the badgers tell him to take a running jump and the birds leave their droppings all over him. Ha! That'd take him down a peg or two. What's he got anyway? To make him so high and mighty, what's he got? Don't see as how he's better than me. Should be me talking at meetings and making plans and getting ready to take over when the old duffer pops off. Me! Should be me! Me! Me!"

He was on his hind legs now, his mouth open, teeth glinting wickedly in the thin light coming from outside the drey. He reared up higher and swung a vicious punch at the inside of the tree. It made a terrible screeching noise and the other squirrels covered their ears. They winced and cringed at the sight of Chestnut in his anger.

"It should be me!" He roared again. "I wish I was a fox. Then I'd sort them all out. Yes, a fox." He stopped and a queer gleam replaced the wild light in his eyes.

If the two squirrels in the drey had ever seen a fox, they would have recognised that gleam as cunning. And they would have been even more afraid. But, of course, none of the forest squirrels had ever seen a fox; the power of the Autumn Red squirrel had kept the forest safe from foxes for a long, long time.

Later, when the other squirrels had left, Chestnut was settling himself down for the night, a slow smile working the corners of his mouth. After his thunderous outburst, he had remained very calm, talking about tricks and other unimportant things. His mind, though, had been working furiously while his two younger friends had talked about which females to scare or which older squirrels to give cheek to. Before today, Chestnut would have joined in with a will but, now, his mind was set on bigger things, more audacious plots. And, he cautioned himself, more dangerous.

Something that had been hidden deep in Chestnut's mind had been disturbed, brought angrily to life when he had vented his anger and his spite and bitterness.

It was evil, an evil that only surfaced once in perhaps two or three generations. It might lie dormant in every generation, maybe even in every squirrel but, like the flame that burned fiercely in only some of the Elder Squirrels, this evil could burn as fiercely. Perhaps great evil needed great good before it could appear to work its horror.

While Good was around all the time, in the sky and the ground, in the leaves and the air, perhaps evil was too often thought of as nothing but bad luck; when a beech tree is hit by lightning and felled, killing its occupants and destroys a burrow or a sett; or the summer sun stops being a life-giver and becomes, instead, a life-taker, when all the water dries up and the food rots. These things may be considered bad luck, something to be accepted and borne because it is something *natural.*

Moonrise Forest had not known Evil as the animals thought of it, for seasons beyond count. Only the old ones, the historians of the forest knew that there had been occasions in the past when Evil had marched through the forest, a time when Good had become Great Good to combat the Evil. But the forest was always in the throes of Good and Evil and it had its own way of warning the forest animals if they cared to pay attention. But it had been so long and, like Chatter's instinct, the forest animals' ability to heed the warnings had faded.

One of those warnings had been when Saltpepper had taken up the office of Elder Squirrel. The very day he made his oath, the stream that fed Sunset Lake had, fuelled by the torrents pouring down from the mountains, flooded the lake. It had overflowed its banks close to Badger Hollow, leaving a marshy area, which always smelled and felt unwholesome, where colonies of midges buzzed and hummed in clouds. The squirrels stayed away if they could. Of course, it had just been bad luck.

Many seasons later, there had been a great loss of trees to the north west of the forest. The destruction was caused by a terrible storm that had killed many animals and made many more homeless. Just bad luck, of course. And nobody had made the connection between this event and the arrival in the forest of a squirrel called Chestnut.

A year later, a disease had killed almost all of the newborn animals of the forest. And, though the squirrels didn't know, the same disease had killed many of the animals who lived outside the forest.

One of the surviving squirrels was named Rolf. One of the surviving animals outside the forest was a fox cub called Slink.

The forest itself knew these things for what they were; preludes to a great event, like the first far-off mutterings of thunder before the storm arrives. The forest knew that what was considered bad luck were the first skirmishes in a war between Good and Evil. A war that would require courage and sorrow and loss. And love.

Saltpepper heard him before he saw him. The sound of crackling leaves and bending boughs and breaking twigs was audible a long time before Rolf came panting into the clearing. He began to speak before he had all his breath back and Saltpepper had to tell him to stop and start again.

Rolf nodded and took in long gulps of air and then told Saltpepper everything, from his talk with the birds and the badgers to the feeling he had when he had reached the store tree.

"I felt him, Saltpepper. Or it."

Saltpepper nodded but he was looking back towards the store-tree, as if he could see through the early night and its shadows and see what it was that was stealing the food.

"What was it?" Rolf asked. "What *was* it, Saltpepper?" Rolf's voice had an edge of frustration; he had been so close. It rankled that, now, he was still as far away as ever from catching the thief.

Saltpepper turned to him and smiled slowly. "Such a small question, eh Rolf? And how can I, who has not felt it as you have, how can I answer it?"

"Because…well, because you are the Elder Squirrel. You know things!"

"But not everything. Not by a long way. But perhaps I can make a guess. Mmm?" And he laughed.

Rolf could not remember Saltpepper ever laughing before. He looked closely at his master and saw that, while the laughter was real, something in Saltpepper's eyes was also, almost…sad. "Please," he said, all his frustration gone now. "Make a guess, Saltpepper. I feel…oh, lost almost. Like the ground's changed places with the sky and I don't know where I am anymore."

"Do you? Do you really, Rolf? Well, perhaps it has, perhaps it has. Come on, Rolf. Come to my drey. It's time you learned something of your heritage, don't'cher'know."

The following day dawned bright and cold in Moonrise Forest. There had been a frost in the early hours of the morning and it sparkled fitfully in the grass and trees as the early sunlight filtered through the leaves. Rolf's head ached. His mind was full of the things Saltpepper had told him and he felt in turmoil. History, legends, Autumn Red Squirrels and heroes, hidden fire and magic (mustn't forget that). What did it all mean?

And what did it all have to do with the treepocket, with the thief? And with Rolf himself? Rolf had no idea. At least, he thought he had no idea but a part of him seemed to be insisting that, if he really thought about everything he had heard then the answer was there.

"D'you know what a catalyst is?" Saltpepper had asked just before Rolf left for his own drey last night.

"Er…something that er, makes something happen? Isn't it?"

"Near enough, Rolf. Well, I don't know exactly who or what our thief is but I think he might be a catalyst."

"For what? What's going to happen?"

"That, I don't know. But remember everything you have heard tonight. Don't think about it too much and, when the time comes, you will know what you need to know."

Don't think about it too much.

Well, that would be easy because every time he *did* think about it, his head ached. What he needed was a good scamper round the forest so he would be fit and ready for tonight's watch on the store-tree.

"I won't just feel you tonight," Rolf muttered as he left the drey. "Tonight, I'll *catch* you."

But he didn't catch him that night.

That same morning, Chatter kept the promise he had made himself the night before when he had finally, breathlessly reached the oak tree where he had made his home; he tried to find food somewhere other than the store-tree. Last night, when he finally lay down along the two, intertwined wide boughs of the tree, he shook so hard that he nearly fell off. He was hot and cold alternately and he was so panicked that he simply couldn't think straight. He just lay on the boughs and stared at the moon as it flitted across the sky, arcing calmly until it disappeared from his view and he had finally felt calm enough himself to think. And to talk to himself.

"Oh my gracious, oh my what a fright. Years on me, it put years on me. What was it? Must've been a man, yes a man from the circus. Nearly caught me, yes he did. Oh my tail and fur! I'll never sleep now, oh no, not ever again."

Of course, he did sleep. He slept deeply and didn't dream but he woke early, feeling cold and hungry. He ate the few nuts and berries he had left while the air warmed around him and the sun rose over the treeline.

"I won't go back," he told himself. "No, I won't go back tonight. If it was a man and he knows I go there, I'll fool him. Oh yes I will, I'll fool him and won't go back tonight. I'll look for food somewhere close by. That's the ticket, oh my yes, somewhere close by."

That was the ticket. In fact, the best thing would be never to go back to the hollow tree. Unfortunately, looking and finding were two different things. Although the day was like early summer in its warmth and sunlight, it was still well into autumn and there just wasn't much food lying around the forest or on the trees.

That first day, he padded west and came to the very edge of the forest where it bordered a huge, ploughed field. He didn't go into the field because he would have felt too exposed, too vulnerable to watching eyes, to men. He picked around the long grass and became more dispirited as he realised that there was little chance of finding any food here. He worked his way north, still following the edge of the forest until he came to a wide pathway where the grass was so beaten down, the earth showed through, hard and rutted. And he finally found something.

As he wondered if he should cross the path or stay beneath the tree-cover when a slight shift in the soft breeze brought a scent to him. It was a scent he thought he knew but he couldn't remember where from. Still, wherever it he knew it from, whatever it was, it was making his mouth water. And that made his mind up.

"Chee chee!" Chatter shouted and did a back-flip, the thing he'd found held in his front paw.

He'd had something like this one day when he was in the circus. A little girl in a bright pink dress with a matching ribbon in her yellow hair had held it out to him through the bars of his cage. It had been made of something dark brown and so full of sweetness that it almost made his tongue cramp. This one lying on the path was half-eaten but it was still food and it smelled wonderful.

"Oh my, oh yes, better than nuts. Oh yes!"

It was gone in three bites and cheered him no end. He decided that it was a good sign, a sign that he would find plenty of food if he just kept looking. He continued north, still keeping to the tree line along the path. Deep down, he was hoping that he would come across another tree with food inside but, as the day wore on and he found nothing to stop his stomach rumbling, the hope faded. He was about ready to return to his tree when he saw an apple beneath a withered willow. Obviously, somebody had dropped it because it was far from any apple tree and it had teeth marks but it made a satisfying crunch when he bit into it. The apple would have disappeared as quickly as the chocolate except that a large grey hare, which came bounding out of the trees to his right, startled him.

For a moment, both animals were so stunned that they simply stood and stared at each other, eyes wide, the hare's long ears laid flat against the side of its head, Chatter's tail held straight up in the air behind his stiff back. Both of them were still and silent, as if the rest of the world did not exist. Then, the world came back in a rush to them both at the same time.

"Cheee chee chee!" Chatter screeched and jumped straight up in the air, the apple still held in his paw, his other front paw held up to grab the branch of the tree close to him. If the branch hadn't been there, he probably would have kept on going until he grabbed a star.

"Squee squee squeee!" The hare propelled himself forward off his hind legs, almost reaching the same height as Chatter had reached. He kept going, not caring if his front paws touched the ground ever again, just as long as he escaped whatever animal it was that was behind him. It would be a snowy day in August, the hare told himself, before he set paw in this part of the forest again.

"Oh my tail and fur, oh my tail and fur," Chatter repeated over and over as he hung from the branch and watched the other animal bound away. What was it? A kangaroo? He'd seen one at the circus once but this one, which had half-frightened him to death, seemed very small. The ache in the monkey's arm reminded him that he was still hanging from the branch. He dropped down onto the ground.

"I'll get home and finish this," he said, looking at the apple. "Oh yes, get home and finish it…or maybe keep it, save it in case…" He didn't finish saying what he was thinking; that he might not find any more food for a while.

He padded back towards the oak tree, trying to ignore the smell of the apple and the way his mouth was watering, telling himself that he needed save it. Even so, he finished the apple before he fell asleep that night, covered by the extra leaves he pulled over himself because the night had turned chilly. He slept with his thumb stuck firmly in his mouth and dreamed of finding food closer to home.

But the following day was worse for Chatter. There were no more sudden shocks to make his heart stagger in his chest but there was no food either. He kept his promise to himself and searched closer to home, venturing only as far as the small creek that burbled half a mile from the base of the oak tree. As the day wore on, he returned to the creek, trying unsuccessfully to fool his stomach into believing the water he drank was food. His stomach still rumbled.

The day began as cool as the day before and, just like yesterday, had become pleasantly warm in the afternoon but as the sun sank into the lake, the air chilled again and a thin mist curdled up from the water of the lake. The mist soaked him and made him feel even colder.

"All I need," he moaned. "Oh yes, that's all I need. Cold and wet and hungry!" He flung a small branch into the water and was rewarded by being splashed on his face. "Pachew! Ach! Bloody thing!"

There was nothing left but to go home, back to the tree, still hungry. The mist thickened until it became a real fog and still there was worse to come. When he finally got home, he saw that the small breeze that had blown for an hour earlier in the day had blown his makeshift home away.

"More trouble, more work," he mumbled as he looked forlornly at the bare boughs he called home. He glanced around and saw that there were no more leaves lying around for him to replace the ones that had blown away. Even the few leaves on the ground were small and brittle and cracked or shredded when he tried to pick them up. He sat on the flat crutch where the two boughs met and rested his paws on his drawn-up knees. He shivered and muttered for almost two hours until the forest was dark and silent. Finally, he surfaced from his self-pity, moaned and winced at the stiffness in his joints and heard his stomach still rumbling.

"What am I going to do?" Chatter asked but the forest did not answer.

It's been two days.

The thought came suddenly.

Two days now. Maybe whatever was at the tree has gone?

"Maybe," Chatter murmured.

Yes, maybe it had, whatever or whoever it had been. Maybe he or it had waited for him to come back but Chatter hadn't and, well, nobody would wait two days and *still* be there. Would they? Chatter nodded; he could go back. The fog would help keep him hidden. He could go back and get some food. And it would be warm and dry inside the tree, too.

"Oh yes, I think so. Warm and dry. And food!"

Chatter reached across and grabbed the branch above him and then on to the next tree. And the next. All the way to the store-tree.

Rolf was just leaving for the store-tree when Saltpepper called him back.

"I know," the old squirrel sad as he reached Rolf. "You're off on guard duty. I won't keep you long. I know you saw or heard nothing last night and I know it's disheartened you. But think about this, Rolf. At least nothing else was taken from the tree. Who knows, perhaps the fog will give our thief some idea that he'll be safe, mmm? Well, off you go and if you catch him tonight, bring him to me first. I want to see him before we call a meeting."

Rolf nodded and set off for the tree.

Saltpepper waited until Rolf had disappeared into the fog and turned towards home again.

"Bbrr, wet and cold. I'm getting old," he said and then chuckled. "Ah well, there it is."

He stopped on the branch he was on and stood stock-still.

"Something? The thief?" Saltpepper wondered and then shook his head. No, whatever it was he felt moving through the forest it was not the thief. This felt like squirrel but he could not feel *which* squirrel. It was way off to the north but he was positive that it was not the thief.

"And not fox, either," he muttered and rubbed at his teeth and then shivered. "That wasn't from the cold or the damp," he told himself.

No, the shiver that had shaken his body and ruffled his fur wasn’t caused by the fog or the cold night. It was caused by the squirrel he felt moving in the forest off to the north and, though it was undoubtedly a squirrel, it felt *worse* than a fox. Whatever walked the forest this night felt dark and cold, almost black. It felt…noisome, like fruit that had gone over and rotted. It felt...

"Evil," Saltpepper whispered and didn’t know he was whispering, as if whatever he felt could hear him. "Dark and festering and rotten. Deep down in its heart." He bowed his head as he said the words and, still with his head bowed, he went on. "Am I afraid? Yes, I think am. But what is coming will come whether I am scared or not. Ah Rolf, be careful. You are yet young but I am old. And I am afraid."

Saltpepper made his way slowly to his drey, his shoulders rounded, head down as if carrying a great weight.

Chestnut flitted from tree to tree, from cover to cover like a shadow. Shadow-silent, hidden by the cover of the trees and the fog, Chestnut made his way eastwards, thoughts filling his mind as he went.

When I'm Elder...no, that's the old way. When I'm Chief *Squirrel, they'll know it. Oh yes, I'll teach them to cock a snoot at me. Soon, very soon, I'll have a special friend and then...well, then I'll teach them a thing or two.*

These warm thoughts kept out the cold and damp as he passed the meeting clearing and turned north. He was soon past Badger Hollow and on towards the edge of the forest.

And Rolf. Ah yes, favoured Rolf, learning the tricks of the trade. Well, not long now and I'll show him tricks that'll make his fur stand on end.

He turned east again at the stand of birch trees and passed the marshy land, his body hidden and his eyes, even in the fog, glinting with cunning.

"So, Stripe, a nice night for it, eh?" Rolf attempted to sound cheerful because, since talking to Saltpepper just before leaving, there seemed to have been a cloud hanging over him. It made him feel depressed.

"Humph. Too damp, too damp, humph!" Stripe sounded as miserable as the weather.

"Well," Rolf said slowly. "Maybe tomorrow will be better. Have you seen Blinkwink at all?"

"Hoo hoo here I am."

Rolf looked up but the fog was too thick for him to make out anything up in the branches of the store-tree. He waited until the owl came down to the lower branches.

"Right, I just wanted to make sure we all know what we're doing," Rolf told the badger and the owl.

"Humph! You only told us last night. D'you think we're all fools?"

"No no, it's just—"

"Hoo hoo hold on badger," Blinkwink said. "No harm in making sure."

Rolf nodded at the owl and went over the plan again. It was simple enough. Rolf would be inside the tree, Stripe would patrol round the base of the tree and Blinkwink would be in the topmost branches. The other birds and badgers would spread out around the tree to give early-warning of the thief's approach. But they would do it as quietly as possible because they wanted to have the thief inside the tree. That was important. Only then could Rolf be sure of catching and holding the thief. Once the thief was inside, Stripe would block the ground entrance to the tree and Blinkwink would seal any holes toward the top of the tree. It was a good plan as far as it went. All they could do now was hope that it worked.

At night, when there was no moon, even those who knew it well could find the forest a strange, unnerving place. Sound seemed to carry further at night and so made the forest actually seem and feel smaller than it was while, *at the same time,* the darkness seemed to make it feel larger. Tonight, though, gripped by the fog as it was, the forest seemed even stranger, almost eerie. Stripe felt it as he lay behind the tree, snout resting on his massive front paws. The fog somehow seemed to befuddle his sense of smell so that sniffing the air gave him no sense of any approaching animal. High in the tree, Blinkwink found that his wonderfully sharp eyes failed to penetrate the fog and his marvellous hearing was affected as well; if anything came tonight, the owl knew that it would have to be almost upon them before they knew it.

Inside the tree, Rolf sat in the dark but he could still sense the change in the forest. It was almost as if the fog were passing *through* the tree and, yes that made it feel eerie. But, deep inside, he felt calm, almost serene because he felt sure that, tonight, the thief would come again.

And I'll have him.

Chatter was arguing with himself as he made his way to the tree.

"Let's go back, eh? Let's just go home. It's too late and too dark and too foggy, oh yes."

It's good that it's dark and foggy.

"I don't like it, oh no, not a bit. I'm cold and wet and it's…scary."

No, not scary. Helpful. Nobody's going to be at the tree on a night like this. Just think of all that lovely food. And it'll be warm inside. Besides, you're closer to the tree than going back home.

It was true; the food-tree was closer. He nodded once and set off again. Two trees later, he was only three trees away from the food-tree and he stopped again. He strained every sense, listening for any sound, peering ahead to see anything that might be seen by the tree. Nothing. All he could hear was his heart beating heavily in his ears and all he could see were the shadow-shapes of the trees in the fog.

If you can't see or hear anything, his mind told him. *Then nobody can see or hear you.*

Chatter gave in to his mind's voice or perhaps he just gave in to his hunger. He swung easily through the trees until he was outside his own private entrance. He paused and listened but he could still hear nothing, either inside the tree or out in the open forest. He poked his head inside the hole and then the rest of his body followed

Below him, Rolf smiled in the darkness

Come on thief. Here I am, waiting. I'm Rolf.

Above Chatter, Blinkwink waited until he could see nothing of the animal he had watched approach the tree. Then the owl glided down to the branch above the hole in the tree.

Hoo hoo who are you, little thief? Well, soo soon we'll know.

When Blinkwink heard the thief's voice, he stepped carefully onto the rim of the hole and waited.

"Oh, lovely food, here I come. Oh my tail and fur, it's lovely and warm in here. Oh my, oh yes," Chatter said cheerfully as he began to climb down the inside of the tree. His mouth was watering.

Rolf tapped lightly on the inside of the base of the tree and Stripe heard the tap by his right ear. He moved round the tree slowly and noiselessly.

Chatter was a quarter of the way down now and the rumbling of his stomach seemed very loud to him but he didn't care. He was inside the tree and nobody had seen him or heard him. He was safe.

Half-way down and grinning in the blackness...

Blackness?

Chatter came to a sudden stop, clinging to the inside of the tree with all four paws, his back taut, tail curled beneath his body. The word screamed inside his head again.

Blackness!

There should be some light. Even when the moon had been hidden on the other nights he'd been here, there had been some light, some faint starlight creeping inside the tree from the small holes in its bark. There should be *some* light.

The thought broke free from his mind then and ran riot all through Chatter's body. All the fears and wild imaginings he'd had the first time he found the tree came back. This time, oh this time, he *knew* there was something here, something waiting for him in the tree, in the darkness. *In the blackness.* Oh yes, he knew. It was probably huge and black with long teeth.

Chatter began to scramble back up the tree, back towards his private entrance. Back towards the foggy light. Back to freedom.

He reached up with his right forepaw and gripped. He gripped with his left rear paw. He reached with his left forepaw. And missed his grip. He slid back further than he had climbed and the panic, the fear was a live thing in his chest, hammering to be let out.

"Oohh, now it'll catch me! Oh my, oh my, help!" Chatter thought he screamed it out loud but he could hear nothing. It felt like there was a stone lodged in his throat. The panic was still wild inside him and he reached up with his right forepaw and felt it grip. His mouth opened in a manic grin and, this time, he managed to say what he was thinking. "Oh thank you, oh my, free!"

Hoo hoo here I am. Blinkwink thought and leaned forward, his beak pointing downwards.

Chatter was reaching up with his other paw when something bit his right paw.

"Chee chee chee! Teeth! Oh its teeth! Its teeth have got me now!"

He let go. He felt himself falling and tried to catch onto the inside of the tree as he fell but he was moving too fast. Then the voice in his mind, the one that had told him that he would be safe if he came tonight, hidden by the fog, that voice told him its final lie.

If it's at the top, it can't be at the bottom. Just let yourself fall and you'll be free.

Chatter, believing, let himself fall.

But the thing, the animal that had bitten his paw, was at the bottom of the tree, too.

Rolf heard the cry of the thief and then the sound of something falling and he smiled to himself. When the thief hit the pile of stored food, Rolf pounced.

"Claws in me!" Chatter screamed. "Oh its claws in me, all over me, oh my, how big is it? How big?!"

Rolf was strong but the thief, this tree-pocket, was all squirming limbs and sinews. Rolf knew he would be hard-pressed to keep hold of the thief for long. He needed help. If he managed to get it outside where Stripe was, then... the thief lurched again and Rolf lost his grip so he did the only thing he could think of; he bit down with his front teeth.

"Cheeeoow! Oh more teeth, more teeth, how big is it!"

This time, Chatter's scream seemed to fill the night as it soared up the inside of the tree and out of all the tiny and larger holes and into the night. The anguish in the scream shocked all of the three forest animals. Blinkwink fluttered out of the tree and perched on a lower branch. Stripe stepped away from the entrance to the store-tree.

Chatter heard his own scream but, in the terrible nightmare he seemed to be living, he thought it was the screech of the huge animal that had caught him and, thinking that it was all over for him, he simply lay down and waited for the final, killing bite.

The thief's agonised howl sent the adrenaline rushing through Rolf's body even faster than it had and he bit down harder. Chatter felt the increased pain and decided that this was the final bite. He fainted, convinced that he was dead.

"Killed him?" Rolf wondered aloud. "But...that bite wouldn't've broken a nut."

The squirrel released his grip and began to try to haul the thief out of the tree. It was hard but, because the thief was on the food, lying on the stored nuts, Rolf actually managed because, as he pushed and pulled, the nuts moved beneath the thief's body and rolled him towards the entrance. As he pulled the thief's shoulders through, Blinkwink fluttered to the ground next to him.

"Hoo hoo had me worried there, Rolf. Thought it was you screaming."

"Humph," Stripe grumbled as he moved towards Rolf. "Terrible noise, terrible. Dead is it?"

"I..." Rolf had to take a deep breath before he could say anything else. "Don't know. Can you help me get him out?"

Stripe moved behind the thief's body and leaned into its back with one big, strong shoulder. Stripe shoved and the body of the thief shot out of the hole, almost smothering Rolf.

For a long moment, the three animals simply stared at the body between them. None of them spoke but they all had the same thought; *what is it?* At last, Blinkwink broke the thoughtful silence.

"Noo noo now what, Rolf? You've caught your thief but how are you going to get him to Saltpepper? Too big to carry or drag."

Rolf shrugged. "I don't know. Let me think."

"Harumph," Stripe muttered and nodded at the body on the ground. "Better make it quick. When it realises it's not dead, it's going to try to get away."

Rolf rubbed at his front teeth. Finally, he looked at the owl. "Blinkwink, could you get…say three other birds? No, make it four? And, Stripe, two badgers?"

"S'pose so," Stripe said. "Why?"

"Well, if we sort of…surround him. You know, if two badgers are behind him and Blinkwink perches on his head and a bird on each shoulder and you and me in front of him…well, I think we could walk him back. If he tried to escape, he'd either be pecked or he'd fall."

"That might work, Rolf."

Rolf smiled and looked at Stripe.

"If the owl thinks it'll work, then, humph, it probably will." He turned and trundled off as Blinkwink flew into the forest.

Rolf was left alone with his prisoner. "Well, Saltpepper," he said. "I've got him, whatever he is. He still doesn't *feel* bad, though. Even when I was fighting with him. Oh well, time enough to find out about him I suppose." He sat down close to the thief's head and waited.

"D'you understand me, tree-pocket?"

Rolf was standing in front of the monkey who was still in a state of shock.

Tree-pocket? Chatter thought. *Is that what I am? Funny, still feel like a monkey. Must have something to do with being dead. I better answer this, whatever it is.*

"Yuh…yes. Walk slowly and follow you. If I try to get away, the birds will peck me and…the badgers will trip me up. Oh my, oh dear, yes."

Rolf nodded and set off, his tail high in the air, pleased to be on the move and pleased with himself that his plan had worked so well.

So, through the fog-shrouded forest, this strange procession made its way to Saltpepper's drey. If they thought that this was the end of things, they were wrong. And they would find out how wrong very soon. Saltpepper already knew this as he sat in his drey feeling old and not a little scared.

The fox had been scavenging around the downs on the eastern edge of the forest for over an hour. When he'd left his den and seen the fog, he'd thought it would help, keep him hidden from his prey. Instead, it had been a hindrance. His sense of smell seemed dampened by the fog and when he'd finally caught the scent of a rabbit and given chase, he had lost it in the blasted fog. Now, he muttered angrily to himself as he slowly worked his way back towards the edge of the forest.

"Aarrgh, hungry again. Bloody place is empty. Ggrr, where do they all go in the winter? And the forest…ggrr. I *know* there's food in there but it never comes out and we can't get in."

Worst of all, the fox knew that the coming winter would be the worst in living memory. Something needed to be done. The rest of the foxes expected him to come up with the plans and why not? He was their leader, after all. He'd spent a lot of time forcing them to accept his ideas and orders. He'd fought them and bullied them and now they would want him to come up with something to make sure they didn't all die in the coming winter.

The forest.

He knew, all the foxes knew, that there was food beyond the trees but they all knew that something, who knew what? kept them from getting any further inside than the marsh. It wasn't the stink of the marsh or the biting insects there, which kept them from going further in. It was something else, something that could not be seen or heard or smelled. You felt it, inside you, deep in your heart. It was strong and powerful and…hot. Yes, it was hot the way it felt when one of the humans on the farms pointed a firestick at you when you were trying to get inside the chicken coop. But the thing in the forest was even hotter than a firestick. You knew that, if it wanted to, it could swallow you whole and alive and howling and it would burn you up from the inside.

"But there's *food* in there!"

Oh without a doubt, there was. If he could just break past the marsh and into the real forest, all the whingers in the pack would know how strong he was. They'd all know that Slink was a real leader. Still, if he couldn't come up with something soon, some fox was going to suggest he wasn't up to the job and maybe he should move over and let somebody else try.

Slink slid down the slope towards the marsh, still muttering about the whingers. He slithered to a stop and his snout twitched as it always did here. The smell was terrible but at least the fog kept the insects away tonight and he didn't have to put up with the humming and stinging. He hated the humming, that horrible buzz that made your eyes water and hurt your ears.

He stood still and thought again about how some fox was bound to suggest it was time he moved on. He consoled himself with the thought of how he would answer that suggestion, how he would bite and gouge and rip. Slink loved to fight, to break and crunch and snap and he loved to kill most of all.

With such thoughts to keep him warm, he idly stepped towards the forest and then halted. He didn't want to stop, he was made to; the hot scent, the hot *feel* of whatever lived in the forest forced his feet to stop. He growled deep in his throat and began to turn away. That was when he scented it. Not the hot thing but something different, something exactly opposite.

Cold. Very, very cold.

Slink sniffed again and thought he almost recognised this coldness. When? Where? He dropped his head and moved it from side to side, thinking, trying to remember.

Ah yes. When he was small, a pup, out exploring, he'd gone to the northern edge of the forest and caught the scent of something far off, something he'd never scented before. Curious, he'd started to go in search of it when his mother found him. She scolded him for wandering so far from the den but then she, too, scented it and Slink has asked her what it was.

"Smells like squirrel," she had told him. "Far off. Very young by the feel. They never come out and we can't get in. Now, come on home before I nip your paws like you deserve."

Yes, that's what this was like. Was it squirrel then? This thing coming through the fog, was it squirrel? Well, if one of them had suddenly forgotten that they never left the forest, there was one very hungry and very angry fox who would welcome it.

Slink backed away from the edge of the marsh, settled behind a clump of hawthorn, and waited. It was a good fifteen minutes before it was close enough for him to think about pouncing. When he thought it was close enough, he began to ready himself, looking forward to the pounce, to the biting, to the killing. And now, it was close enough to…

The animal, the squirrel if that was what it was, had stopped. Just far enough away so that Slink could scent it properly but too far for him to think about attacking. Slink settled into a crouch, waiting for the thing to begin to move again. And it spoke. Its voice made Slink's hackles rise.

"Is that a *fox*? I know it's something, I can feel you. Yes, feels like a fox. Strong and sharp and sure. *Are* you a fox?"

Slink stiffened; if this was squirrel, it was nothing like his mother had described. Oh, it sounded wary but it didn't sound timid or afraid. There was something else, too. As well as the coldness, Slink sensed something shadowy, something that smelled even worse than the marsh. Slink kept still and kept his silence.

"You probably know I'm a squirrel. From what I've heard, foxes are clever." Slink, even wary as he was, warmed to the flattery in this. "Well, if you are a fox, then I'm looking for you. I'm not coming any closer and if you move towards me, I'll be off into the fog and trees. If I do, you'll miss out on something very interesting, very helpful. Are you going to listen?"

Slink thought about it. What could a squirrel have that would be interesting or helpful to him? As far as Slink knew, squirrels and foxes were enemies; they didn't swap useful hints and tips. Still, what harm could it do to listen? While the squirrel was talking, Slink could make his careful way towards it and, if it was just talking rubbish, at least he'd be able to eat squirrel tonight.

"I'm listening."

"Good. Now, are you hungry? Are your friends hungry? Is the coming winter something you'd rather not think about? No answer? Well, never mind, I think I'm right. I think you'll thank me when you've heard me out. You'll probably want to do something for me. To say thank you. And it won't be much, not a big thing. Not for a strong, sharp fox like you."

"I haven't heard anything interesting yet. Ggrrr, not yet."

"Just as long as I have your attention. Now…"

And Chestnut told Slink something very interesting, something Slink would find very helpful. And what the squirrel asked for in return was not much, not really.

When Chestnut had finished and he and Slink had made their plans, the fox trotted back to his den. Just before he reached home, he came across a starling that had fallen from its nest and broken its wing. Slink grinned and ate it. He took it as a good sign, one that meant things would go his way.

He was right. Up to a point. But he was also wrong.

Chapter Three

"Hoo hoo hello Saltpepper," Blinkwink said.

"Hello Blinkwink. It's been a long time since we talked. We're grateful for your help. You too, Stripe."

"Harumph, welcome. No problem."

They were standing outside Saltpepper's drey. Chatter stared at the Elder Squirrel, still half-convinced he was dead despite hearing Rolf tell him that he was alive. His arm just below his elbow throbbed dully where Rolf had bitten down and, somewhere in his bewildered mind, Chatter had an idea that this meant that he was, indeed, alive. Now, the squirrel he'd been told was the Elder Squirrel, was talking to him.

"…have we here? I've never seen anything like this tree-pocket, Rolf. Strange indeed. All arms and legs. No wonder you had such a fight to catch him. I imagine he squirmed like a fish." Saltpepper laughed.

Chatter's eyes widened; it seemed such a strange sound to come from this furry animal.

"So, thief, what are you?" Saltpepper asked.

"A monkey. I'm not what you called me, oh my no, not a tree-pocket. I'm a monkey. From the circus. At least, I was but I'm not now. Oh dear me, no. I'm a monkey."

"Well, you might be a monkey," Saltpepper agreed. "But you are also a thief. What Rolf calls a tree-pocket. You were caught in the act."

"But I'm not," Chatter said in a squeaky voice. "My tail and fur, no, not a thief. Not really." He looked at Rolf and saw how angry the squirrel was and gulped.

"How can you deny it?" Rolf demanded. "We caught you robbing the food, taking it from our mouths." Rolf had to struggle to hold down the anger that made him want to bite this ... this monkey again.

"Oh. But, oh dear, I didn't *know*," Chatter said and wrung his hands together. "If I'd known it belonged to anybody, I wouldn't've taken it, oh no, not really." He paused, part of him remembering how his mind had wondered about how the food had just been there, in the tree, as if it had been collected for a reason. "If…oh dear, if I'd known there was somebody to ask, I would've asked. My tail and fur, I would have. Promise." And he realised that he was telling the truth.

"Well, let's leave that for a moment," Saltpepper told him gently. "I'm more interested in finding out what a circus is and why you aren't in it anymore. So, since the fog is lifting and it's not so damp, tell us your story."

Chatter blinked and wrung his hands some more, he swallowed hard and looked at Rolf who, the monkey could see, was still angry. Chatter looked back at the Elder Squirrel who had least spoken kindly to him, and told his story.

Chatter was born in the back of a large, travelling cage whose floor was covered in straw. The cage belonged to Professor Trimbull's Travelling Circus and was pulled, as were all the wagons and caravans, by two large horses. As he grew older, Chatter became part of the show. He was never a star attraction but the children loved him and he made them laugh with his antics. He would carry things into the Big Top and stand on top of the barrel organ with his tin cup held out for money when the crowds queued to enter the Big Top.

At first, not knowing anything else, Chatter was happy enough. Deep down, though, he had a restless urge to be doing something else, something different. Travelling only fed this urge and he was always asking questions of the other animals, the older ones who had been to more places and seen more things. It was this constant questioning that earned him his name among the other animals. He found that most of the animals were resigned to their fate and a lot of the time, they scolded him for asking so many questions. All except one, the oldest animal in the menagerie; the huge bull elephant, Methuselah.

In a strange way, Chatter reminded the old elephant of himself; anxious to learn new things, eager to hear whatever was told. He took a liking to Chatter and told him about the many different things he had seen during his long, long life.

It was on a gloriously sunny day, with the sky a blameless blue and the breeze a soft, scented stirring in the grass, that Chatter's deep-seated urge to be free and able to explore was finally released. It was Methuselah who broke the chains.

"You know, little chatterbox," the elephant said in a wistful tone that Chatter had never heard from him before. "I remember a time some, oh, twenty years ago, when we stopped at one of the larger towns. It was near a river and had a big, arched bridge over it that led to the large green where we pitched the tent. The people flooded over the bridge to see the circus and the children ran everywhere, chattering and laughing. Just like you. There was one small boy who came to see the menagerie before the show. He was with his father and he asked his father so many questions. His dad smiled and tried his best to answer them all but the little lad always had one more question. Finally, his dad put his big hand on his son's head and ruffled the brown curls and told him that his dad only knew so much, that he couldn't answer all the questions and that the best he could do was to say that his son, when he was older, should go out into the world and find out for himself." The elephant cocked his massive head at Chatter then and crinkled the deeply lined skin of his face in what was a wink. "I think you have too many questions, just like that little lad, and I don't have all the answers."

"Oh," Chatter said. "D'you think I could? Mmm, oh my, d'you think I could do that? Get out and see, well, *everything*?"

"Well, I think that, if I was younger and had the chance…mmm, I think I'd be off to see what I could see. Tricks and shows are all very well but they're not real life. Are they?"

Chatter nodded his head hard. "Oh right, oh yes, right. I know that. Tricks are so boring and they make me feel so…so useless! But if I got out, what would I do? Oh, that's a question, isn't it? Oh my tail and fur, it is."

"That, little chatterbox," Methuselah said slowly. "Is what you'd find out. Just another question to find an answer to."

So, one night when there was no moon and cloud covered the stars, Chatter worked at the leather thong that held the cage shut until it finally fell away. Then he skipped off into the night, whispering good night to his old friend Methuselah, heading for the real world and all its questions and all its answers.

The forest animals stood or sat silently, watching Chatter as he stared down at his clenched hands resting in his lap after he had finished telling them his story. His mind so full of memories, he had forgotten that he was captured.

All the forest animals were thinking the same thing; when you took away all the dazzle and sparkle and colours of the circus, what you were left with was a cage. *A cage.* The idea that they could not come and go as and when they pleased was something that made them tremble a little inside.

Then there seemed to be an unspoken agreement between the forest animals and Chatter was no longer penned in. Blinkwink flapped away to stand on the ground beside Saltpepper while the other two birds flew onto low branches. Stripe and his fellow badgers moved away and, finally, Rolf stepped back alongside Saltpepper and the owl. In that moment, Chatter could have fled away into the forest and nobody would have tried to stop him or followed him. But that unspoken agreement also seemed to have included the monkey and so he only sat on his haunches and looked up to face the others.

"Not free to roam? Not free to come and go, stop and drink, to play? In a cage? Why didn't you escape sooner? How could you stand not being free?" Rolf was angry again, not with Chatter, not really. He was angry at the idea that an animal could be imprisoned.

"He knew no different, Rolf. What did he have to compare it with, how could he know there was something different?" Saltpepper put his paw on Rolf's shoulder and felt the tension, the anger in the body. Anger was not necessarily a bad thing. As long as it was controlled.

Chatter blinked stupidly, flicking his gaze from one animal to the next. Eventually, he spoke, his voice cracking. "Oh my yes. That's right, I didn't know. Never dreamed. And now look at me! Lost and alone and my heart going skippity-bop and bobbity-skip and caught and..."

"Now, Chatter, be calm. Look around you. You're not a prisoner anymore. Still, you did steal our food and it belongs to all the forest animals if they want it. Those animals must hear your story and make up their own minds," Saltpepper told him kindly. "We'll have a meeting tomorrow. I have no wish to keep you prisoner and, if you decide to run off, there'll be nobody who'll stop you. But I'd like you to stay and tell your story to the rest. Will you?"

Saltpepper's voice struck a chord in Chatter and made him feel a strange sort of homesickness and nostalgia. For what? Maybe for something as simple as a friend. So he nodded and said, "Oh yes, I'll stay. I'll tell my story but I'll be a bit frightened. Oh dear me, yes."

"Noo noo no reason to, Chatter," Blinkwink said. “We won't eat you." The owl came as close as he could to a chuckle and even Stripe's lips curled a little.

As the little group broke up, Saltpepper felt again that cold, black shadow he had felt going east earlier in the night. This time, it seemed to be returning. But the Elder Squirrel pulled his fear into himself and said, "Good. Now, let's get home and get some sleep. If you want, Chatter, you can stay with me in my drey. It's in the old oak over there."

"Oh, an oak," Chatter said and clapped his hands. "I lived in an oak tree when I arrived in the forest. Oh yes please!" He did a back-flip.

The others stared at him for a moment and then they all laughed.

"Tomorrow then," Rolf said as he turned to leave for his own home. "I'll pass the word."

"Goodnight, Rolf."

"Goodnight," Chatter said. "I'm sorry for all the…trouble I caused."

Rolf smiled and nodded and left.

Behind a holly bush, not far from where Chatter told his story, two black, glinting eyes watched as the little meeting broke up. The owl and the badger passed very close to the bush.

"Well, humph, what d'you think will happen tomorrow? At the meeting?"

"What Saltpepper thinks but didn't say," Blinkwink said. "The monkey's story will make the others feel woo woo what we feel. I think the forest will have another animal to feed this winter." And then the owl flew off to his nest.

Stripe nodded. "Harumph, well strange things happen these days and I suppose…" Stripe paused as a chill passed through him. He was pretty sure it had nothing to do with the thinning fog. "Cold, very cold. And not friendly. Time to get home, Stripe. Time to get home."

Behind the bush, Chestnut pressed himself flat on the ground; this was no time to be spotted by anybody. No, the plan required Chestnut to be a solid member of the forest for a little time yet. He smiled. Time would show how solid he could be. How hard and solid, how unyielding. Yes, they'd all see. In the meantime, he needed to think about how this…monkey affected his plans. It took him only a few minutes to decide he could use it for his own ends.

When the old duffer of a badger had passed by and was long-gone, Chestnut made his way home.

Slink was wide-awake. His long black snout rested on his front paws. His mind was full of thoughts, as it had been since the talk with the squirrel who didn't really feel or sound like a squirrel should. But that didn't matter. All that mattered was that Slink could be King of the foxes.

The foxes would see how he'd provided all the food they needed and they would know he was a true leader, a true King. The forest animals would cower before him when they saw how cruel and quick he could be if they didn't. Ah, the blood. Yes, the blood he would taste when he finally padded beyond the marsh and into the forest.

For now, though, Slink needed to prepare his speech for the foxes and then he would have to organise them for the raid so that they would be in and out as quickly as possible. It would happen at what the fog-squirrel called a store-tree. Slink would have the foxes form a fan-shape, with a sharp point made up of Slink and his lieutenant, Slygo. Any squirrels at the tree would be soon disposed of and then the foxes would scatter the food like autumn leaves. Once the food was scattered, their secret known, the morale of the forest animals would be destroyed. They'd know that they'd have to be abroad in the forest during the winter and the foxes, allowed into the forest by a squirrel, would be able to pick all the food they wanted.

It was a good plan. Slink couldn't find a flaw in it. And all made possible by a squirrel. And what did he want in return?

"He wants to be Chief Squirrel, Boss Bushy Tail, King Cruncher."

Slink chuckled; well, for a while, perhaps. Until Slink was ready to kill him in his turn.

"And then I'll be Supreme Ruler of Moonrise Forest. Grrooowwooo!"

The howl was long and ululating, rising up towards the moon that was now a silvery-blue in the sky as the last of the fog tattered and blew away.

Blinkwink, perched high in a tall beech, had given up any serious search for food over the downs. Instead, he drifted along with his thoughts. They were thoughts, which, for some reason, unsettled him.

Stripe, too, had settled down for the night but his thoughts also disturbed him. The badger, though, knew exactly what disturbed him—it was that coldness he'd felt on the way home.

Rolf slept but his dreams made his paws twitch.

Chatter slept a warm, dreamless sleep.

Saltpepper was wide-awake. He followed his own thoughts along what were, by now, well-worn paths. Ever since he had felt that coldness, his thoughts had always been the same. And they all amounted to the same thing; something was coming that would change the forest forever.

Still, knowing this, Saltpepper could not decide if the changes would be for better or worse.

But not good for you, old squirrel. No, not for you.

Ah yes, that thought was always the same and hard as he had tried, he could not push it away.

Chestnut shivered and shook in his drey, like a willow in a storm. Part of it was reaction after his meeting with the fox; part of it was almost being spotted by that old duffer of a badger. Most of it, though, was excitement at how close he was to becoming Chief Squirrel.

One way or another, the new day would bring many things, many changes.

Dawn came bright and shining and cold. The animals' breath puffed when they spoke and they all knew that winter was very close now.

Saltpepper had met with Rolf before the sun rose, outside the Elder Squirrel's drey where Chatter slept on. Rolf was all for telling the meeting that they should forgive the monkey for his theft but Saltpepper told him to simply tell them all how he had captured the monkey.

"It's their forest, Rolf and it was their food. They have the right to decide about Chatter. I know you and I both think Chatter's story is reason enough for what he did but it is not our decision alone. This is a lesson you must learn if you are to be Elder Squirrel after me."

After Chatter told his story to a lot more animals than he had the first time (and with many more oh dears and oh mys), the debate ranged back and forth, for and against. Rolf wanted to say what was in his heart but the presence of Saltpepper next to him kept him silent. The more he listened, the more Rolf was convinced that Chatter was going to lose the argument but Saltpepper put his paw on the younger squirrel's shoulder and said, quietly:

"Patience. Another voice will be heard soon."

One of the younger squirrels who had been in Chestnut's drey the night he had crossed the threshold to evil, said what he thought Chestnut would be thinking. By saying it, he hoped to show his loyalty to Chestnut.

"A thief's a thief. I'm sure we're all sorry for the monkey's troubles but he should be punished."

There were loud shouts of agreement from the meeting and the young squirrel who had spoken looked around to see Chestnut smiling and he felt sure he had pleased his hero.

Chestnut was smiling for another reason; the door was open now. He waited for the noise to subside, then he spoke, making sure Rolf and Saltpepper could not see him.

"I'd like to say something on this strange matter."

The voice sounded reasonable and calm and Rolf thought there might be somebody on Chatter's side after all. Saltpepper gave no hint of what he was thinking.

Chestnut continued. "I can understand your anger and, truth to tell, I felt it too when I learned how our food had been stolen. But think for a moment. Compared to the whole store, not much was taken and most of it's been replaced."

Rolf wondered who the speaker was because he'd never heard a squirrel speak so moderately before, not about something as serious as this. Saltpepper also wondered and he wasn't sure he liked these syrupy-sweet tones.

"This creature, this Chatter, meant no real harm. He was lost and afraid and hungry, a stranger in a strange place. Who among us would not have done the same thing in the same circumstances? Surely the forest is big enough to share with one more animal? I'm sure he'd help us gather more food. Will we turn away an animal who needs help, needs food and shelter from the coming winter? Can't we find room in the forest and in our hearts for one orphan?"

There were several moments of silence and then the cold air was filled with cheers and shouts of 'welcome' and 'friend' and Chatter was almost smothered by all the animals who wanted to touch him and shake his paw. Rolf cheered with the rest but, when he looked at Saltpepper, he saw that his master was shivering slightly.

"What's the matter? It's what we wanted, isn't it?"

"Yes," Saltpepper agreed. "Yes it is. But who gave that speech? Look, at the back, d'you see who isn't cheering and clapping with the rest?"

Rolf stood on his hind legs and looked hard towards the back of the clearing. "It's Chestnut. It must've been him who made that speech. Well, wonders will never cease!"

"Have you *ever* heard Chestnut talk like that? So…calm and collected?"

"Well, no but you said that Chatter's tale would touch a lot of hearts."

Saltpepper sighed. "Yes, I did." He rubbed his front teeth. "You'd better go and rescue the new family member before he gets crushed or dies of fright."

Rolf moved into the melee around Chatter but Saltpepper continued to watch Chestnut. When Chestnut moved quietly, almost furtively, out of the clearing, Saltpepper's eyes widened and his heart missed a beat.

Where's he going? And what's he up to?

Saltpepper had no answers for the questions. What he did have was the same sense of fear he had the night he'd felt the cold shadow in the fog. There had been no sense of coldness or blackness in Chestnut's sweet words but those words had not rung true to Saltpepper's ears.

"Ggrr I'm not interested in your little debate or your speech. Just tell me where the tree is or I might just decide to take my chances with the winter and have you for my dinner now."

"No, you won't, fox. And you know it."

Slink knew the squirrel was right but he didn't need to hear it from the squirrel. The tone of voice the bloody squirrel used was nothing like one that should have been used by an animal, which, by rights, should have been a trembling mess. "Don't tell me what I will or won't do! Now, where and when?"

"Now, if you like. If you're ready."

The squirrel's tone of voice had changed. Now it was almost mocking. The idea that this might not really be a squirrel crossed Slink's mind. As it did, that coldness he'd felt the first time tickled some ancient part of his fox-brain and that part almost screamed at him to forget it, *right now*, and get away as far and fast as he could. Then the younger part of Slink reminded him that the winter was going to be hard and there was plenty of food just waiting beyond the trees of the forest. Did he really want to give all that up? No, he didn't.

"Right, good, let's go then," the fox said.

"First, our bargain, Slink the fox."

How did he know his name? Slink hadn't told him.

The coldness came back, stronger than ever but Slink forced it back and away.

"Ah yes. You want to be Chief Squirrel and rule over the puny little animals and you want me to stay around to make sure they do what they're told." Slink's tongue lolled from his mouth as he sneered at the squirrel but it was more to make himself feel better than to intimidate the squirrel.

Chestnut simply smiled. "More or less. Now, is it a bargain, Slink the fox?"

Something about the way this bloody squirrel put his name and the animal he was, together, really irritated Slink. There was contempt there and Slink knew he should just kill the thing and have done with it but he also knew that the bloody thing was right; Slink wouldn't kill him. "We have a bargain," he said angrily. "Just get on with it."

"Follow me," Chestnut told him and turned his back.

I'll kill you, Slink thought as he followed the squirrel. *I'll eat your steaming guts and you'll watch me do it.*

The afternoon was like the morning; sharp and bright but the sunshine mellowed as it filtered through the trees and laid a somehow-old, golden light that lent no warmth. Every animal knew that, tonight, there would be a hard frost.

Slink had mustered the foxes about four hundred yards from the tree Chestnut had pointed out. Slink himself had scouted the area to make sure there were no perimeter guards and saw that the bloody squirrel was right; now that they had their thief, there were no defences at all. There was an almost carefree air in the forest and it made him smile as he thought about what was going to happen very soon.

Chestnut had insisted that the attack be made late in the afternoon to give him time to be well away from the tree and so free from any suspicion. It was late afternoon now and Slink felt the time was perfect; the light was beginning to fade and the shadows were deepening. The foxes knew the plan and their anticipation was almost palpable as they realised how close they were to finally ending the long years of hunger and frustration.

Slink nodded to himself and then gave the signal for the others to follow him.

Saltpepper was in his drey but he was restless. A half-gnawed nut lay between his paws. He'd been like this since the meeting, since hearing those oh-so-sweet-words of Chestnut. And, he admitted, *that* was reason enough for him to be restless but there was something more.

"Come on, old fellah," he said aloud. "Get some air, take a stroll, settle yourself down. Let's see who there is out and about and wants to pass the time with an old squirrel."

Rolf, now that the matter of Chatter was settled, was doing what he liked doing the most in the autumn afternoons; strolling through the forest and talking with anybody he met. He loved taking his time, stopping here to investigate a pile of leaves in case there was a nut there, breathing the sharp air and smelling the faint hint of frost, talking to some friends about families and other old friends. This was *his* forest, his home and his friends. Oh, there were times when they drove him to distraction with their antics and stubbornness but he loved them and their faults because they were the same faults he had himself.

He stopped by a fallen branch and considered this idea and realised it was what Saltpepper called an insight. Rolf felt a little throb of pride that he at last seemed to be seeing himself as others must see him. Perhaps he was actually on the way to being like Saltpepper, to being the Elder Squirrel.

This, for some reason, brought to mind Chestnut's eloquent speech and, now that the chaos and hubbub of the monkey's acceptance was over, Rolf had to admit that he couldn't really reconcile the Chestnut he had known all his life with the animal who had made that speech.

Almost without thinking, Rolf stepped over the fallen branch and made for the store-tree.

Chatter was in his element. He, too, was roaming the forest and everywhere he went, there was animal who wanted to talk to him. They all wanted to hear more of his life in the circus and the journey he'd made to cross the lake to reach the forest. Chatter was happy to oblige and, in return, he asked many questions and they were all answered.

Without realising he was doing it, he had scribed an almost perfect circle round Saltpepper's oak tree and now he was at the very limit of that circle. He was very close to the point where the turtle had set him ashore and a very long way from the store-tree. Another thing he didn't know was that, for a long time now, he'd had a shadow.

Chestnut had decided on the perfect alibi for when the foxes attacked. He waited for a pause in the conversation between the monkey and the old squirrel who seemed to like to answer questions as much as the monkey loved to ask them. When the old duffer paused for breath, Chestnut padded out from behind the birch tree and up to the monkey.

"Well, well, I've been looking for you, Chatter," he said and smiled broadly at the monkey and the older squirrel.

Chatter looked at the newcomer and frowned. Then he recognised Chestnut and grinned. "It's you! The one who changed everything at the meeting. Oh my, and I never thanked you."

Chestnut shrugged, still smiling. "Oh, no need for that," he said cheerfully; he still found this new talent of *niceness* a little disconcerting but he knew it was just one of the new talents he would need when his plan succeeded. "I thought we could have a talk and you could tell me about your life in the, what was it? Circus? And I thought you could show me where the…turtle?...brought you ashore?" He turned to the older squirrel. "You don't mind, do you grandfather?" It was hard not to call the old duffer 'pops' or 'granddad' as he wanted to.

"Not a bit of it. This young fellah has just about worn me out with all his questions. It's time I was getting inside before the chill gets to these old bones of mine."

Just don't forget this when the others want to know who was where and when, Chestnut thought as the old duffer padded away.

"Thanks grandfather," Chatter said to the old squirrel. "Oh my, right then, just down here it was, where the turtle dropped me off. Oh yes, just here."

Chestnut nodded and walked alongside Chatter as they headed to the lake.

The foxes were waiting for the signal from Slink. Slink was inching closer to the tree to make sure there were still only the two squirrels there. They weren't really guarding the tree, just sort of sitting outside the entrance and talking about something called a monkey. This suited Slink even if he was a little disappointed that there weren't more squirrels he could actually kill. He was about to the give the signal when he heard the sound of approaching voices.

Slink crouched flat on the ground so he was hidden by the bracken and leaves and narrowed his black, glinting eyes. When he saw two more squirrels drop down from the young beech tree to the left of the store-tree, the fox grinned widely, already tasting the sharp tang of the blood when he led the attack.

The two newcomers stopped at the tree and began to talk with the others. Slink eased himself up from the crouch and his shoulders bunched in tight, muscular knots. His back legs braced against the ground, pushing his backside up while his front legs tensed ahead of his lowered head.

He gave the signal to raid the store-tree.

Rolf and Saltpepper had met not far from the tree and had paused on the branches of a thick birch to talk. During the talk, as Rolf described how he'd been unable to reconcile what seemed like two different Chestnuts, Saltpepper realised that the fresh air and his walk had done nothing to calm his own restlessness. And, as Rolf talked, that restlessness increased.

The monkey and the store-tree and Chestnut. Saltpepper thought. *And they all go together with that awful cold darkness I felt in the fog.*

"I think we need to get to the store-tree, Rolf. Something..."

Rolf frowned as the Elder Squirrel stopped talking and looked upwards, as if searching for some answer in the sky. "Saltpepper?"

Saltpepper shook himself and looked back at his young pupil. "I think we should get there quickly."

Rolf needed no second telling and the two squirrels darted across the branches and finally down onto the ground in front of the store-tree. The two squirrels who were supposed to be guarding the tree were pleased to have the Elder Squirrel and his pupil join them and were already asking questions when Saltpepper raised his left forepaw to silence them.

"Rolf, there's something...something very wrong here. Terribly, terribly—"

Slink gave his signal.

A howl, long and ululating split the late-afternoon air.

For Rolf, the howl seemed to galvanise his mind and body into a whole that somehow sharpened his instinct. It was as if some race-memory finally came to the surface. It took over and made Rolf act the way he needed to act to survive.

He looked around for the source or at least the direction of the terrible howl so he could take off in the opposite direction.

The two guards simply stood where they were, rooted to the spot. They seemed to be waiting for the death the howl seemed to promise.

Time stood still for Saltpepper. All his thoughts, his memories and his long years of learning crystallised in his eyes. In those two black, sparkling eyes there was no sign of fear or indecision; this was the point to which all of his life had been leading. It seemed so obvious to him now and he felt a little stupid for not recognising it sooner. Which of course was stupid in itself; no amount of foreknowledge could have altered this moment because it was fated.

"Saltpepper! We have to run! Now!" Rolf almost screamed; the forest seemed to have come alive with noise, barks and yips and the thudding of paws vibrating through the ground.

"No, Rolf. We stay." Saltpepper's voice was very calm.

"*What*? Saltpepper, it must be foxes! How can we stay? We'll die!"

"Perhaps but we *will* stay. If it means we must fight, then we will fight." He turned to the two rooted squirrels. "You are meant to be guards and guards you will be. Turn to face the trees. Do it now!"

Here was a tone they'd never heard from the Elder Squirrel before. Its imperative left no room for doubt or disobedience and both turned to face the trees. Rolf had already done this and now Saltpepper joined him. It was rank stupidity of course; four squirrels to face who knew how many foxes? But they were doing it.

The foxes broke through into the small store-tree clearing.

Slink came out of the trees opposite Saltpepper and barely paused as he bounded towards him, building up speed, ready to spring and to crush, to break and to bite. The bloodlust filled his mind.

Saltpepper braced his hindquarters and waited.

The two guard-squirrels faced in opposite directions, their bodies quivering with fear but doing what the Elder Squirrel had ordered. Although facing opposite directions they both saw the same sight--foxes pouring out of the trees. The sight froze the squirrels again, any thought of fight gone with the sight of the lolling tongues and huge teeth. They died almost painlessly as they were torn apart, their blood spattering the ground.

Rolf saw foxes. Wherever he looked, he saw foxes. Hearing the howl and feeling for the first time that instinct to flee and *then* hearing Saltpepper tell them they would stand and fight—that was bad enough. Seeing the foxes, the actuality of them, the black eyes, the lolling tongues and the teeth—worse, so much worse.

Rolf's heart seemed to lurch up into his throat and then it almost stopped altogether before beating again at twice its normal speed. Bright spots danced across his eyes and his fur, *all* his fur stood on end.

Slink could already taste the blood of the old squirrel. It filled his mouth as he leapt through the air and his ears could hear the sound of bones breaking. When he landed, though, the squirrel wasn't beneath him. Slink sprawled on the ground, his front legs splayed, his mind confused and disbelieving.

Saltpepper waited until the last second before swaying to his left. He felt the wind of the fox passing and heard the click of closing teeth as the fox bit down on what he expected to be the throat of the squirrel. Instead, they bit down on themselves. When the fox hit the ground, Saltpepper settled himself on his hind legs and faced the next fox. He had no real thought as he did this; instinct reaching further back than his actual memory simply made it happen.

The next fox was neither as large nor as fast as the first and Saltpepper took half a step forward as the fox sprang. As the fox passed overhead, the Elder Squirrel bit down hard and connected with fox's snout. The fox screamed in agony and rolled away to land solidly on the back of the first fox, knocking the wind out of both of them.

Rolf, realising that there was no place to run or to hide, decided that he wasn't going to die without some sort of fight. He darted between and around the foxes, nipping where he could and slashing with his front paws when he got the chance. The howls of pain and surprise from the foxes made Rolf grin. He did very well. Three foxes suffered long rips down their legs that would take all winter to heal properly and which, he hoped, would come back every year to remind them of the price they had paid for their attack on the store-tree. He was actually warming to the work, to feel exhilarated when he was caught.

He was darting to the right, his mouth already open and aiming for the first joint on the fox's rear leg, when he felt a searing pain scorch down his back from a point just below his left ear. The blow lifted him up and flung him down in a crumpled heap. He was aware of the warm trickle of blood on his left haunch as he struggled to right himself. This only made the pain flare gigantically in his back and his head. The world turned grey, like the colour of the lake during January except, with each beat of his heart, a redness marched across his eyes. He inched his way forward, wanting only to find somewhere to rest and to be quiet, perhaps even to sleep for a while so that this agony would stop. For a long moment, he thought he might actually succeed in this and then another, sharper and deeper pain flowered in his right hindquarter. The grey disappeared in a deep crimson band and then it, too, faded into black. In the blackness, Rolf found a place to rest and perhaps to sleep.

Saltpepper was tiring. He could sense that, behind him, the food from the store was being scattered all over the place but he needed to watch the trees where there were more foxes. More than that, the lead fox was still uninjured. Saltpepper knew that five foxes were now out of action but while the leader was still unharmed, the rest would keep coming. Besides, Saltpepper knew that, while scattering the food was the aim of the attack, the leader was really out for blood and that meant that, sooner or later, he would be back for Saltpepper.

The squirrel tried to take in as much air as he could, hoping it would give him more strength but part of him knew that he was wasting his time.

Saltpepper was no longer looking at charging foxes in front of him. They had all stopped and were simply watching him. No, that wasn't right; they were watching something behind him. Saltpepper turned slowly, feeling his own breath in his throat like a piece of bark he had swallowed. His fur was damp with what might have been early evening mist but was blood. He felt very tired.

Slink had shrugged off the fox that had landed on him and was now back on all fours. He took one look and saw the food scattered for yards around, much of it turned into pulp or covered in blood and urine. Good, the first aim was achieved. Now.

He had watched the old squirrel fight, using his swaying body to dodge the foxes coming for him. The old bugger had actually lamed five foxes and suffered nothing more than a scratch down one flank. Yes, it was this old squirrel Slink had to deal with and now the old bugger was turning slowly to face him. Well, he would never complete that turn.

Saltpepper was three-quarters turned round when the leader hit him with both front paws. The little breath he had left came out of Saltpepper in a whoosh and he fell onto his left side. The fox swiped at a front leg and Saltpepper heard a tendon snap but what should have been a scorching agony seemed to be nothing more than a slow, pulsing ache. And this was diminishing by the second.

Saltpepper's eyes began to close and a fog swirled in front of him. A squirrel appeared in the fog. The biggest, strongest squirrel Saltpepper had ever seen and he was saying something to Saltpepper. In his agony and weariness, Saltpepper thought it must be Rolf, putting the size and strength down to the pain and his fading awareness. Saltpepper smiled.

"Ah Rolf, such a day, such a time to have to leave. Be strong, Rolf and look for the good in them. Lead them well." Saltpepper closed his eyes but he still heard the other squirrel saying something and, finally, he could understand what was being said.

"*Welcome, Saltpepper. Welcome.*"

Saltpepper opened his eyes and tried to move closer to this squirrel so he could hear better but the fox growled deep in his throat and Saltpepper heard nothing more.

Slink lowered his head, opened his mouth and buried his teeth in the squirrel's neck. He lifted him up and shook the body from side to side. Saliva dripped in strings from Slink's mouth and mingled with the squirrel's blood.

Slink was still growling and shaking the dead squirrel, his mind blank except for the single word—*kill*—when his lieutenant, Slygo, spoke urgently to him.

"Be done, Slink. We've scattered their food to the wind and gone. Be done and let's go."

Slink gave no sign that he heard anything at all and kept ragging the body and growling.

Slygo had had enough. He bit Slink in the brush, just where it joined the muscular backside. "Slink, the sun's almost in the lake and it sounds as if the whole forest is about to come down around our ears! Leave it and let's get out of here!"

The pain in his tail brought Slink back to himself and he could hear the sound of animals pounding the ground, coming towards them, could hear the sound of bending branches and falling leaves as more animals sped through the trees towards them. He knew that his anger and bloodlust had almost lost him this game on the first throw. And there was something else; this thing, this dead and broken squirrel in his mouth tasted like rotted mulch. He spat it out and spat again, trying to clear his mouth of that horrible taste. He spat once more to rid his mouth of fur and flesh and then nodded at Slygo.

"Gggrright, let's go."

The foxes bounded away, heading for their dens beyond the forest. Slink led them, knowing that he had succeeded in doing what he'd wanted to do, knowing that the future was his. But he couldn't seem to rid his mouth of the taste of the dead squirrel.

Chatter talked incessantly all the way to the lake's edge but Chestnut hardly heard him. His mind was too full of the thought that it would not be long now. When they reached the lakeside, they sat and the monkey told again the story of the circus and the ride on the turtle's back and Chestnut waited.

"It was just here," Chatter said. "Oh my, yes, just here when he told me about—"

Chestnut felt it then. A sudden knowledge that he had to be away from here, had to leave the thief (Rolf had got that right, at least) and be somewhere else. Yes, his alibi was set and he could now use the monkey, *the thief*, to lay the next, possibly the last, stone in the foundation of the rule of Chief Squirrel Chestnut.

"Chatter, my friend," he said and smiled at the monkey. "I'm sorry but I've just remembered that I promised to do a favour for my neighbour. You understand, don't you? A promise is a promise."

"Oh dear me, yes, of course. A promise is a promise. You go, don't mind me. I'll just sit here for a while and watch the water."

"I knew you'd understand. Don't be too long, though. The sun will be in the lake soon." Chestnut smiled again and padded back into the forest. About ten trees into the forest, he met another squirrel and stopped to talk for a while, cementing his alibi and the rest of his plan.

At the same time, Slink the fox was waiting for the exact moment to give the signal and Rolf and Saltpepper were hurrying to reach the store-tree.

After watching Chestnut disappear into the trees, Chatter turned back to the lake. He felt a deep contentment, a sense of belonging. He dipped one finger into the water and idly swirled it round and round. For once, his mind wasn't filled with questions and his body didn't feel the urge to be up and doing. He'd found a place where he felt part of everything, where he had the time and freedom to ask as many questions as he wanted or simply sit and be still.

He sighed and looked across the huge lake. A slight breeze rippled the water and the sun turned the ripples a dusky pink as the light faded.

"Oh turtle," he said quietly to the air. "Oh dear me, I wish you were here. I could tell you my story now but, oh dear, it would be a longer one now. Oh yes, so many new friends and—"

A long way from the water's edge, Slink gave the signal to begin the attack.

And Chatter could say no more. His body seemed to shrink and his stomach did horrible flips and flops. All his nerve endings crawled and the strength drained from his legs. This was worse than being caught in the store-tree. This was worse than thinking you were dead. This was like being dead but not being allowed to simply die. You had to stay alive long enough for all the monsters of your nightmares to arrive so they could torment you forever.

All Chatter's happiness and contentment died in the middle of that long, blood-freezing howl.

Chatter was penned-in again but, this time, his captors weren't Rolf and Saltpepper, Blinkwink and Stripe. None of those animals were in the crowd that faced the monkey. Chatter had searched the crowd for them and, not seeing them, only felt more fear.

His mind seemed to have given up trying to work out what had happened since that terrible howl. He'd been cowering by the lake when the forest seemed to come alive with the snap and rustle of twigs and leaves and the calls of the other animals. He stayed where he was, not even turning when they arrived at his back. They'd fired questions at him but he had no answers to give them about how long he'd been there, how did the foxes know where the store-tree was, when did he make the plan with them? And, the worst; what was to be his reward for his treachery?

Finally, getting no sense from the monkey, they had forced him back to the small clearing where the store-tree stood. Now, here he was, penned-in and scared half to death.

Suddenly, the murmuring and angry calls ceased and a horrible tension took its place. The monkey tried to see beyond the crowd of animals but the heads of the animals obstructed his view as they turned to see the newcomer to the meeting.

The crowd parted and a path formed that led directly to Chatter's feet. The tension increased, Chatter's mouth dried, and his body trembled. He looked ahead and saw the newcomer approaching.

And the fear left him as he saw Chestnut padding steadily towards him.

"Oh my, oh dear, oh now you can tell them that's it's all a terrible mistake," Chatter said. He was tempted to do a back-flip in celebration but, when Chestnut spoke, the fear came back in huge waves.

"So," Chestnut said slowly. "We have the thief back. Good. Let's get on with it and rid ourselves of this treacherous monkey once and for all. I have to apologise to you all for persuading you to accept him in the forest. I have no excuses other than I thought what I was doing was right. I was fooled and misled. I'm sorry but, now we know his true nature, we can deal with him as he deserves. He must pay for the death of our beloved Elder Squirrel and for the death of our future Elder Squirrel, Rolf."

An angry, guttural sound went up from the animals and the squirrels who were guarding him bit him viciously round his fingers and toes. But it was the shock at what Chestnut had said rather than the pain that made Chatter cry out; Saltpepper and Rolf dead?

Chatter understood that this was a nightmare that wasn't going to fade when he woke up. He *was* awake. This was real. He was going to be killed.

Chapter Four

"Dead? So, this is dead? Well, it wasn't so bad, was it? I mean, it could've been a lot worse. It didn't hurt that much. Not really. And I got in a few good nips and swipes before they got me. But it wouldn't have held them for long. There were too many of them...*ow!*"

The sudden, bright flowering of pain that bloomed in his shoulder choked off not just the words but also the thought behind them. Only the pain mattered, only the pain was real.

The squirrel, who had begun to push himself onto his paws, now slowly eased himself back to his original position, hoping that this would stop the pain. It worked up to a point but the pain only retreated slowly and didn't fade completely. It left a gnawing ache in his shoulder but at least he could think again. He began to make an inventory of his body for more injuries.

He felt various scratches that he knew were no more than those he suffered when he was foraging amongst the brambles for food. Along his right rear flank, there was a deeper one but it wasn't bleeding very much. And his jaws ached so he knew the few nips he'd managed must have been good ones and…

how can I still feel pain if I'm dead?

This new thought filled him with a stomach-churning hope that he was still alive but then logic flooded back and with it the idea that, wherever he was, it must be the place you went before you passed on to the final place. This was clearly the answer because there was no way that he could have survived an attack by so many foxes. No, most definitely, he was dead.

With his mind settled, albeit reluctantly, he tried again to raise himself up but the pain crashed back in on him and the deep wound in his rear flank began to bleed again. He lay on his left side and wondered how long he would have to wait here before he could move to the next, the final place.

He dozed. The pain faded again. When he opened his eyes properly, he tried again to move and, this time, he managed to inch himself onto his front paws, dragging his stomach along the ground. The pain only throbbed so he moved a bit more, just to that long tuft of grass round that tree.

He eased himself into the lush springiness of the grass and let out a long breath. Then the pain came back. This time, it came on a sickening wave and he could smell as well as feel the blood flow from his wound. It was not just blood he smelled, either; there was an acrid whiff that he didn't like at all. Still, it was nothing to worry about too much. He was, after all, dead. He couldn't die again, even from infection.

Lying against the bole of the tree, his head cushioned by the deep grass, he looked down the aisle of trees in front of him and thought it was very like one he used to know in Moonrise Forest. Ridiculous, of course; that was when he was alive, before this...wherever it was. Even so, the sight of the aisle brought on a sudden nostalgia and the trees blurred as he found himself crying for the things he had lost, the animals and the places and...he closed his eyes against the blurred scene and then opened them again as a fresh wave of pain made him moan. And saw something other than an aisle of trees.

It was a squirrel. A squirrel he recognised. Never mind, it didn't matter, just another memory, just another part of the homesickness.

Even if the squirrel *was* talking to him.

"Rolf! Rolf, snap out of it! Now!"

"Just a dream," the injured squirrel murmured.

"It's not a dream, Rolf!"

And the dream-squirrel reached out and put a paw under Rolf's chin and raised his head so that their eyes met.

"Rolf, you have to pull yourself together and listen to me."

"Hello, Saltpepper. D'you know where this place is? I didn't know you had to wait before you moved on to the final place."

"Rolf, pay attention. You. Are. Not. Dead. At least, not yet. I'm dead. You, though, are still alive. Do you understand?"

Rolf tried to keep his eyes closed in the hope that he would fall asleep but Saltpepper wouldn't let him alone. Rolf finally had to open his eyes and look at the Elder Squirrel again.

"I know it's hard but you have to listen. I'm dead but, for this short time, I can talk to you. You aren't dead but you are badly hurt. This is still Moonrise Forest. Quite close to the Midge Marsh. Are you still listening?"

Rolf nodded; the idea that he was alive seemed to have blown away all thoughts of death and left just the pain. The pain seemed to make him more aware of everything and he found himself, ridiculous as it seemed, actually understanding that this was *really* Saltpepper. Dead but real.

"Ah," Saltpepper said and nodded. "Good. Right, I know you have questions and before you *truly* accept what I am and what I say, I'll have to answer them. So. The foxes have killed me and they thought they'd killed you. The food is scattered but, more importantly, it will reek of fox, as will the tree. That stench will be so strong that no squirrel will be able to regather any of that food."

Rolf nodded slowly and then his eyes widened with a sudden realisation.

"Ah, I see the question has occurred to you. I think you have to answer this one yourself Rolf. It is part of everything, I think."

"The foxes must've been told where the tree was. They must've had help to get into the forest, to get past the power that has kept them out for so long. To do that, it couldn't have been just *any* animal…It had to have been a squirrel. Do you know which one?"

Saltpepper heard the edge in Rolf's voice and was glad but he had to be careful; what he told Rolf could work against as well as for Saltpepper's purpose. And he had so *little* time. Already he could feel the pull, the tugging at his mind, trying to take him away completely and finally. Still, he had to say it so he must say it straight out.

"Yes," Saltpepper said. "But before I tell you, I have to tell you this; not only has the food been scattered but the animals' sense of unity has also been scattered. It is your responsibility to bring it back. I believe that this is the reason for your survival against all the odds. You have in you more of the fire we spoke of, the fire that was handed down from the Autumn Squirrel. You have to use that fire now. Not only for squirrels but for all the forest animals. In fact, you will need to find other animals than squirrels to help you begin. The squirrels will not be ready for you yet. They will have many problems now. You must find Blinkwink as soon as you can. Do not fail in your task Rolf.

"Do not hide from your fate or betray the fire that burns in you."

These last words did not seem to either squirrel to have been spoken by Saltpepper. To Rolf, it seemed that the voice came from everywhere, from the trees and the grass, from the shadows, from the very air. Saltpepper heard himself speak the words but his voice sounded very like the voice of the squirrel he had heard when the fox had killed him, the red squirrel who had welcomed him as his life dwindled away.

"Saltpepper, look," Rolf said, the pain etched in his face as he struggled to breathe. "I don't really understand much of what you've said and my wounds seem to be worsening. I don't know what you mean about a fire inside me but I do know that you still haven't told me who the traitor is."

"Chestnut," Saltpepper told him. "It was Chestnut." He wanted to tell Rolf that he must fight the idea that trying to save the squirrels from whatever fate awaited was a waste of time, but the tugging in his mind was stronger and he knew he did not have time. "Rolf, you must do what I've told you. Leave the squirrels and Chestnut until the time is right. Rolf, you *must* follow your destiny."

"What about my treepocket? What about Chatter?" Rolf's voice was almost wistful.

"What? I…I don't—"

"A guess?"

"At a guess, I would say that he will be blamed, somehow, by Chestnut. But I don't *know*. Perhaps he is still wandering the forest and is safe. I don't know. Rolf, promise me you will not fail. Rolf, do not fail."

"Probably dead," Rolf said, apparently to himself. "That's it. Probably dead."

"I don't know! Rolf, promise me! Promise me! Do not fail!" Saltpepper felt the great tug then and his voice was fading.

Rolf watched as Saltpepper's body faded and finally vanished as his old master died completely. Still, in the air, there was the sound of those last words.

promise me…don't fail

Rolf moaned as the pain wracked his body and then a pulsating darkness overtook him.

Slygo watched Slink prowl back and forth outside the entrance to his den. With each grunt and growl his leader made, Slygo felt his own hackles rise. It was no longer the aftermath of the raid that filled Slygo with tension but Slink.

Slink had been like this since their return. The sun had sunk into the lake and the moon cast a flat silver light across the downs but Slink was still prowling and growling. Slygo could stand it no longer; he was tired and his body still ached and stung where he'd been bitten by the other squirrel. When he spoke, he felt better for simply releasing some of the tension.

"Slink, I..."

"Ggrr, back off, Slygo. Just back off."

"No. You can fight me if you want. The way I feel now, it might even be a relief but I *am* going to speak to you."

Slink's hackles rose higher and he planted his front paws and tensed his hindquarters as if about to spring.

"We did it," Slygo said. "We scattered their winter food, we went into the forest and did it. We've never been further than the marsh before and we still got out. We'll be able to get in any time, just like you thought. We'll have food all winter, you shut all the moaners and whingers up and proved yourself, proved that you're our leader. Not only that, you killed *their* leader. So..."

Slink howled. It was the worst howl Slygo had ever heard. There was death in it and he wondered if this was going to be his last night alive. "What?" Slygo demanded through his fright. "What's wrong?"

"That old squirrel. Oh, he was their leader, never doubt it. He never flinched, not once. He didn't freeze or bolt, he stood there and fought. Why didn't he run?"

"His mistake," Slygo said, relieved now because he knew wasn't going to die after all. "He's dead."

"Yeah, I killed him but I couldn't *eat* him. I wanted to rip his guts out and eat them but I couldn't. Not a single mouthful. It was like…he felt, his body felt hot but it tasted rotten." He growled deep in his throat again. "There's no way to describe it. It was fresh meat so you tell me how it could taste so bad?"

Slygo shrugged. "What does it matter? If he tasted and smelled that bad, it's as well you didn't eat it. You'd've got sick and we couldn't afford that. We need you fit and well. He was old. Maybe he was diseased? Who knows, who cares? He's dead and we've got to a way into the forest and we'll get through the winter."

Slink thought about it and eventually nodded. "You're right. He was old and sick and it doesn't matter. And you're right about getting through the winter." He lowered himself onto his belly and grinned. "With him gone, it means the squirrels won't have a leader. I won't have to push too hard now to make sure that bloody Chestnut gets what he wants. He should be able to get himself elected without too much trouble."

"You mean you were *really* going to help him?" Slygo asked.

"Oh, I was going to help him. Still will. I've got a feeling that that squirrel can provide us with food not just for this winter but for a few good generations down the line." He grinned again.

The grin made Slygo growl; for a moment, that grin looked as if it might go all the way round Slink's head and then the top of his head would just fall off. The image was so vivid, that Slygo had to growl to keep the laughter away. Slink, fortunately, took it as a growl of approval.

"There's something about that bloody squirrel..." Slink said thoughtfully. "I think he's probably craftier and nastier than most of our crew put together. This winter won't be hard on the forest animals just because we scattered their food. I think that damn Chestnut will give them a lot more problems than that. You know, I really don't like him."

"Oh," Slygo said doubtfully.

"Oh, I'm not scared of him. I think he's dangerous but more to his own than to us. It's that craftiness I don't like. Still, he'll do for now. When I'm ready, I'll bite and break and crunch him. When the forest's ours, I'll have him then." He closed his eyes for a moment but the grin remained. Then he opened his eyes and said, "I feel better now, old mate. Let's get some sleep. We've got a whole forest to explore tomorrow."

Slygo nodded and headed back to his own den. As he reached it, he glanced up at the moon and just as quickly glanced down again; for a moment, he thought he saw a face in the moon and that face had looked like a huge squirrel.

Inside his den, Slygo tried to sleep but the unease he felt kept sleep at bay. The worst thing was that he had no real idea why he felt uneasy but it was undeniable; something was not right. He struggled for a moment, trying to get a grip on it but he couldn't and finally told himself to fix his mind on the morning, when he and Slink could roam through the forest. Finally, after what seemed like an age, he fell asleep.

And dreamed.

He was deep in the forest, late morning, and it was cold. By the coop, it was cold. The moisture from his nose ran freely until the air hit it and then it seemed to freeze round his nostrils. His winter coat was thick but the cold still got through. The snow was almost up to his underbelly. He looked around and saw no sign of any other animal; the snow was untouched and startlingly white.

Yet, for all of this, he felt that he wasn't alone.

Still, he moved forward and, as he did, he noticed that things were slightly wrong, slightly awry; like the apple tree to his right that showed bright blossom and one single fruit. In the winter? Then there was the evergreen to the left, which had no leaves at all. An evergreen with no leaves? And the trees all around him made an arch of their branches and the snow on them blocked out the sight of the sky. Yet there was his shadow, as dark and sharp as if he were walking beneath a hot summer sun. And it was silent. Deeply silent. Slygo didn't like the silence, it unnerved him. Even his own movement, his breathing, made no noise. Slygo decided that he would make some noise, if only to prove that he was there.

"Bbrroow!"

In the dream and to his relief, he heard himself. Then, right at the end of the howl, instead of resonating as it should have done, the howl choked off. It was as though he'd howled into a den-hole blocked by something bare inches inside its entrance. It was as if the howl had been *swallowed* by something.

Slygo looked around but the snow was still unmarked and the tree still had its single fruit and the evergreen still had no leaves. Ahead of him, he looked down an aisle of trees that seemed endless. He looked down the aisle and didn't like it but something inside him made him want to walk there.

He padded forward and the silence became heavier. Slygo pushed on, glancing up to the arch of the trees occasionally but mostly simply staring ahead. After what he thought had been five minutes, he looked back. He could not see the entrance to the aisle. He looked forward and could not see an end.

The trees groaned.

The noise was so unexpected that he fell forward in surprise, his head hitting the snow and forcing his mouth closed. His teeth bit on his tongue and the pain was as sharp as the cold. As he struggled up, snow fell from the trees and covered him.

The panic was worse than the pain in his tongue and he fought madly to push himself up through the snow. On trembling legs, he looked around and saw that, not only were the trees still groaning, they were shaking, as if getting ready to drop every last inch of snow on him. Slygo ran forward.

He seemed to run for a long time but he never once thought of stopping because the trees were still making that terrible sound and still moving. Slygo ran and his chest heaved and pained him as he struggled for breath and still he kept running.

Then everything changed.

The snow disappeared, not even murky brown slush remained. The trees were free of snow, too. In fact, the trees were all now in full bloom and in fruit. And the smell was wonderful, a mixture of every smell Slygo thought of as good. The silence, though, remained.

There were no arched trees here, no aisle. It was a glade, a perfectly circular clearing. The surrounding trees were a mass of colours that almost hurt his eyes to look at. It seemed that he was looking at them and seeing them for the first time ever, as if he were the first animal to see them. The sight took his breath away. And there was peace here. It was a peace deeper than any peace Slygo had even considered. He tried to compare it to something in his experience but it was pointless; there was nothing in his experience to compare it with. He just settled back on his haunches and let the peace and the colour sink into him.

"This is...well, it's enough for me, for everything. Certainly enough for this fox."

It was. Right up to when it all...went.

The colours and the textures and the smell. And, with them, went the peace.

Slygo's body tensed, his nerves and muscles twitched and sang, his mind overloaded with everything he had seen, both in this dream and in his waking life. And, stamped over all this overload of sensory input was his own awareness of himself.

Fox. Fox, fox, fox. I am a *fox*.

A roaring wind and the crashing of thunder and the blue-white flash of lightning replaced the blankness. The ground shuddered beneath him. The trees shrieked. Slygo chased his tail madly, howling and barking, yelping and yipping. Saliva frothed at his mouth and then the dizziness hit him and he collapsed. He landed on his right flank and his eyes stared at the opening to the glade, staring back down the aisle of trees through which he had come.

Something was coming towards him. Something huge was coming towards him and it was *hot*. Slygo could feel the heat throbbing towards him as the thing marched down the aisle of trees. No, the thing was not marching towards him, the thing was marching *for* him.

The thing got closer and it was no longer a huge thing, it was a huge, hot *squirrel*.

Slygo whimpered and the whimper became a scream and the scream woke him up.

"A dream," Slygo murmured, shaking in his den. "A bad dream, that's all, just a—"

"You alright, Slygo?"

Slygo shook violently and almost screamed again until his overtaxed mind informed him that it was only Rusty, just Rusty, outside, wanting to know if he was all right.

"Yeah, fine. I'm okay, Rusty. Just dreaming about…chasing squirrels."

"Oh. Right. Good dream, eh?" Rusty said and then made his way home.

Slygo settled deeper into his den and knew he wouldn't get any more sleep. But he did and, if he dreamed, he didn't remember when he woke.

Slink and Slygo stood on the edge of Midge Marsh and looked towards the trees. Slink's mouth was watering and his tongue lolled from it like a long, thick leaf. Slygo was just staring at the trees and at the ground. Winter had come to Moonrise Forest in the night.

Snow lay thick everywhere and, while it looked fresh and clean and almost beautiful, Slygo couldn't help but think of the terrifying dream he'd had last night.

"Well," Slink said and Slygo blinked and looked at him, glad to be rid of his memory of the dream. "Can you smell it?"

Slygo frowned and then shrugged his broad shoulders.

"Food, my old mate. Lots of it." Slink grinned and then cocked his head, sniffing the air. "And nothing else but the snow."

"What?" Slygo asked, curious about the odd tone in his leader's voice.

"There was always a hot scent in the forest. I think it was part of what kept foxes out for so long. But not now. At least, it's there but not as strong, like it's fading or something." He nodded his head. "Yeah. You know what I think? I think it was in that old squirrel, something to do with him being their leader. But he's dead and gone and the scent's going, too."

Slygo sniffed at the air and agreed with Slink. Then something else occurred to him. "What about this Chestnut? He's going to be their leader. Has he got it, this hot scent?"

Slink shook his head. "No, not even a little bit," he said but he didn't tell Slygo about how the bloody squirrel seemed to smell, to *feel* almost exactly the opposite. Chestnut felt and smelled cold, very cold. And dark. But that was nothing to talk about. Not now, not when the whole forest was there, waiting for them. "Come on, let's get breakfast."

Midmorning found them down by the creek. Breakfast had been everything they had expected and not just the actual eating of the food. The chase had been good, too. There had been three squirrels, young but plump and totally unprepared for foxes in the forest. Slink could still smell their shock and fear when he and Slygo chased them. Now, he was licking his lips, tasting the last of the blood. This done, he bent his head and took a drink from the creek.

The water was so cold it made him catch his breath and he withdrew his mouth in a hurry, coughing and spluttering. Slygo laughed. He couldn't help himself. Slink got over the coughing fit and growled at him but it was only a mock-growl. Then he burst out laughing, too. They pretended to fight each other, something neither had done since they were cubs. They rolled about in the deep, blood-spattered snow and laughed.

As the winter drew on and each day's events seemed eager to pluck his sanity from him, Slygo often thought back to that first morning and the fight by the creek; it felt, later, like the last time that things seemed right, the last time he felt good and whole.

Rusty joined them a little later and the three foxes followed the creek until it emptied into the lake and then they turned and began to head for home. They heard the growls of hunting foxes and the sharp cry of a squirrel dying and, once, saw the end of one chase just to their right.

The temperature dropped as the afternoon wore on and there was a breeze coming from the far-distant mountains, smelling of ice and more snow. As they reached the edge of the trees, the first big flakes began to fall and seemed to shine silver in the last light of the pale, dying sun.

None of the three foxes knew that, high above them, wheeling and soaring on the air, an owl watched them with bright, glinting eyes and an ache in his heart.

Blinkwink watched until the three foxes decided it was time to eat supper and cornered two squirrels in a tight group of young birch. He banked to his left when he heard the first growls; he'd seen enough killing today to last a lifetime. He'd lost count of the number of animals he'd seen killed and eaten. The forest seemed full of foxes. The noise was terrible; the barking and yipping and growling, the anguished squeals of the squirrels. Blinkwink was a hunter and he fed on other animals but there was a difference; he always killed quickly, almost immediately. These foxes seemed to enjoy the sight and sounds of slow death almost as much as they enjoyed actually eating.

And then there was the laughter. That, somehow, was the worst. Blinkwink heard the laughter and knew that Moonrise Forest was now the domain of the foxes. The inhabitants of the forest had no idea how to cope with this threat; they'd lived so long without any threat that they simply had no idea how to react. Instead, they died. Slowly and in terrible agony.

Blinkwink alighted in his nest, high in a silver birch far to the north of where the foxes made their dens. He folded his wings and puffed out his feathers. He watched the snow falling outside, thick and fast, telling everybody and everything that winter was here and it was going to be a bad one. Which, of course, meant more trouble for the forest animals; with the store gone, they would have to look for any food they wanted and that would leave them wide-open to attack by the foxes. In his mind, Blinkwink saw the forest under a thick covering of snow that was slowly but surely stained red by blood.

The owl shuffled further back into his nest. The remains of the field mouse he had caught earlier on the downs littered the nest. He tossed them out and then settled down to do what, apart from flying, he did best. Blinkwink began to think.

Saltpepper was dead.

Oh, it hurt to think that but it was vital that he accept that fact. Without Saltpepper, most if not all the organisation was gone. Rolf? Blinkwink didn't know. He'd flown to the store-tree soon after the carnage must have taken place and had seen Saltpepper's torn and bloodied body. The owl had seen the remains of the two guards' bodies but there was no sign of Rolf. After a long ground search, Blinkwink had come across a trail of bloodspots leading away from the death scene and he'd followed it until they simply faded into the ground. He'd found no other sign and had finally flown back to the squirrel's meeting place at the clearing.

He landed on a branch low enough for him to hear but hidden enough so he could not be seen and waited.

Blinkwink had expected the commotion, which he heard a good while before he actually arrived overhead. But when he was in sight of the clearing, what he saw happening wasn't something he'd been expecting at all.

Chestnut accepted as Chief Squirrel (Chestnut's own words)? The *monkey*, Chatter, a prisoner accused of treachery and collusion with the foxes?

Blinkwink didn't know who had betrayed the forest to the foxes but, in his heart, he was sure that it hadn't been the monkey. The more he listened, the less he liked what he heard, particularly the way Chestnut was suggesting that they should kill the monkey.

Oh, the squirrel wasn't saying it outright but Blinkwink knew that it was what his oh-so-reasonable voice and words meant. When the point arrived, as it was always going to, and the mob began to call for Chatter's death, Blinkwink decided enough was enough.

The owl dropped from the high branch like a falling stone. His wings thundered as he reached the shouting crowd of squirrels, scattering them all, including the ones guarding the monkey.

"Roo roo run, monkey! Run and climb, whatever you have to do to escape! Doo doo do it now!"

The monkey had needed no second urging. In seconds, he was up amongst the highest branches of the nearest trees and then he was gone. Blinkwink had flapped his wings and stared at the squirrels. The light in his eyes brooked no argument but Chestnut spoke anyway. And what he said confirmed the owl's half-formed suspicions.

"The owl too, then. We'll have the owl, too. Kill him," Chestnut said, his voice not loud, almost conversational.

Blinkwink battered at the air with his wings and barely raised himself off the ground before the first claw swiped at him.

Still, once he was up, he was away. As he flew, he heard Chestnut shouting at him.

"For now, owl! But only for now! You won't escape me for long! I have more than one group of animals with me now!"

Now, as he sat in his nest, Blinkwink recalled those words and began to consider what Chestnut could have meant. More than one group of animals? More than squirrels? Well, of course, he had the other forest animals now that he was Elder—*Chief* Squirrel, but Blinkwink was relatively certain that none of the other animals could face him unless they were in force. Besides, none but other birds could come near him when he was flying and, whatever else happened, the birds would still respect him as leader of all the birds. So, what other animals could Chestnut mean?

Blinkwink then used a trick he had perfected over the years, a trick that helped him when he came across a problem he couldn't immediately solve. He picked a spot in the nest to focus on, stared at the spot and thought of nothing. With his concentration fixed and his conscious mind switched off, his body relaxed by degrees until he became almost part of his nest. His breathing became deeper and slower. Time dwindled down a tunnel, the sounds of the forest and his own breathing followed time down that tunnel. Blinkwink was nothing and yet everything. Nothing and yet everything flowed to him and from him.

Outside, snow came down thick and fast as the wind from the mountains began to blow steadily and strongly. The forest was being slowly buried beneath winter, a corpse being laid to rest by Nature until Nature herself called the body back to life in the spring.

Inside his nest, Blinkwink, too, died a little as the answer to his question returned down the tunnel he had created and filled his body and mind with its terrible certainty.

The foxes.

So obvious. The other group of animals Chestnut referred to was the foxes. So hideously obvious. The renegade squirrel had, somehow, made a bargain with the foxes. This was a vile and terrifying betrayal. The foxes had been paid by being allowed into the forest to kill and eat the animals. What had Chestnut received in return? Oh, just that the foxes helped him remain Chief Squirrel. Chestnut would need no help to *become* Chief Squirrel; the death of Saltpepper and the disappearance, the probable death of Rolf, left a hole that the squirrels in their fear and shock, would gladly fill with Chestnut. But Chestnut knew he'd need help to remain in power.

Rolf?

The name almost shouted in Blinkwink's mind.

There was no body. Was he dead? Had the foxes simply dragged him off so they could eat him later?

Blinkwink opened the tunnel wider, seeking the answer to this new question. The answer, when it came, came with a fuller understanding of what Chestnut wanted.

Chestnut wanted control. Not just of the squirrels but of the whole forest and he wanted that control to be total. How would he gain such control? With fear. With the blood of any who went against him.

Blinkwink came back to himself with a jerk.

"It cannot be allowed. And the only way to make sure it doesn't happen is to stand against Chestnut. There is only one animal who could do this. Rolf. The High Ones know everything and they will know this and so…"

Rolf was not dead. He was probably dreadfully wounded but alive. Blinkwink was sure of it and he would have to find him. It might be a long search and he would need to be rested.

"So," the owl said. "Time to sleep, then."

Blinkwink searched right through the following day until late afternoon. He began at the store-tee clearing where the bloodtrail had been two days earlier. He flew high above the forest, buffeted by the bitter winds, his view often obscured by flying snow, and saw nothing. He flew north to where the snow lay thickest and found nothing. He flew west to the meadow and found no sign of anything. He banked east and saw it just under cover of the first trees.

The owl's sharp eyes saw a squirrel who was clearly injured and, for a moment, his heart filled with hope. When he flew closer, though, Blinkwink saw that it wasn't Rolf. He saw, too, that this squirrel was not going to live much longer.

Blinkwink was used to death but what this squirrel had suffered and was suffering was terrible. His body was broken and there were several, large wounds that bled freely. He'd lost one ear and the white fur on his chest was stained blood red.

Blinkwink landed in front of the mauled squirrel and sighed deeply, his large eyes even larger as he wondered how the poor squirrel had survived this long.

"Who did this? Foxes?"

The squirrel moved his head once from side to side. "Nuh…no," he said and a line of blood ran down his chin. Blinkwink tried to hush him but the squirrel forced himself to finish. "It was…Chu…Chestnut."

"Woo woo *what*? Why?" Blinkwink thought the squirrel was delirious with the pain and shock; a squirrel did this to another squirrel?

"Discipline. I…questioned an order. He's mad now. He's not…a squirrel now, not really. He's sending squirrels out…looking for food, knowing the…foxes are abroad. He knows what…will happen. He's using the foxes to…threaten, to get his own way." He stopped and the owl thought he'd finally died but the squirrel stirred himself one final time. "I've been…looking for you Blinkwink. You have to stop…to stop Chestnut. You *must*. Ah…Blinkwink, I'm…dying but the…the pain is so bad and I'm not brave. Blinkwink, please, a mercy? Please?"

Not brave? Blinkwink thought. *To have stood up to Chestnut at all and then to have this happen and still to search for me? Not brave?*

The owl nodded, knowing that it would be a mercy; the High Ones would see and understand. "I will and I will not leave you out in the open," he said. "I will take you into the forest and hide you as best I can. The snow will cover you until the spring and by then your body will be safe from the foxes."

The squirrel nodded his thanks and closed his eyes. A small smile seemed to curl his bleeding mouth.

Blinkwink bent forward and, with his sharp beak, did the squirrel a final mercy.

When he finished hiding the body behind a clump of leaves next to a thick fallen branch, Blinkwink felt the first stirrings of hunger but, after what had happened, he couldn't face the thought of killing another animal. He would have to later on or tomorrow but not now. He hopped out from beneath the tree and into a small open area and then rose lazily into the sky above the forest.

It was almost night time now and still the snow swirled down from the darkening sky. As he banked towards the lake, he thought that, if nothing else, he'd had his ideas confirmed. But he was no closer to finding Rolf. If he wasn't dead and as the hours passed Blinkwink became even more convinced he wasn't, how could there be no sign of Rolf?

Blinkwink had overflown the forest three times and seen nothing but the one squirrel. The only place he hadn't flown over was the downs where the foxes had their earths.

"Woo woo well," Blinkwink said and flicked one wing and headed over the lake towards the downs.

He glanced down as he flew over the lake, which, amid the white of the snow, was black. Just seeing it, you knew that the water would be freezing and any animal unlucky enough to fall into it would surely die. Still, he was high above it and flying was what he did best.

He banked right, feeling the coldness radiating up from the mass of water and adjusted his wings to compensate. He descended, watching the downs carefully for any sign that the foxes had taken Rolf back to their homes. There were many foxes out and about, idly talking or ambling back from the forest. The atmosphere was relaxed and a deep, sudden and burning rage filled the owl—this calm, contented atmosphere had filled Moonrise Forest a bare three days ago, before Chestnut's treachery.

The anger burned inside him, hotter and hotter until the only thing in his mind was dropping down and killing a fox, maybe three foxes. The air currents around him meant nothing and, without realising it, he left his concentration on the cold currents and, for too long, forgot how to fly properly.

He plummeted down, heading for the hard-packed snow-covered ground and certain death. The thought of his broken body was not the only thing that brought him back to himself; he heard again the poor squirrel he'd killed pleading with him to stop Chestnut. Blinkwink could not do that if he was dead.

The anger blew out of him and his concentration returned. He forced his wings to batter at the air in a panicked attempt to stop the descent.

It slowed him down but came nowhere near stopping him.

The foxes heard the *whirr-snap* as the owl's wings beat at the air and they all looked up. It was obvious that whatever bird was falling from the sky, it was out of control and so posed no threat to them. Instead, what the foxes saw was food. One of them was Rusty and as he looked up, he saw that the falling bird was an owl.

Rusty shook his head. "First the forest is opened to us and now food falls from the sky. Good times for foxes," he said cheerfully.

Blinkwink landed, still flapping his wings, and stumbled forward, finally tipping over on his left wing. The foxes were at him immediately but not as savagely as they would've been before the forest became their domain and food was easy to come by. They could take their time with this owl, have some fun.

Blinkwink sensed this and used the seconds to get some of his wind back. He shifted his weight to free his flight feathers. If he could somehow manage to get himself out of this, it wasn't going to be without some pain so he prepared himself, determined that if he was fated to die here by fox-claw and fox-teeth, one or two of them would regret their part in his death.

The first fox took a lazy swing at Blinkwink's tail and the owl felt two feathers pull out but he didn't swing to face his attacker. He twitched his head a little and snapped at the air with his beak. The longer he could fool these foxes into thinking he was badly hurt, the more chance he had of actually getting out alive. He could hear their laughter as they egged each other on and he felt his anger returning but he forced it back; he needed his mind unclouded. The two foxes in front of him looked the most likely to lead the attack when the fooling had ended and Blinkwink made a careful study of them. And, all the time, the playful and not-so playful nips were increasing but he suffered no serious injury.

"Okay, you lot, playtime's over. Let me at my supper," Rusty said and laughed again. The other foxes stepped away.

Blinkwink watched the fox approach with his head lowered and the owl could almost read the fox's mind—nothing here to worry about, no need to pounce, a quick bite and it'll be all over. Blinkwink waited.

Rusty bent his head and raised his front paw towards the owl.

Blinkwink struck.

In a deafening, blinding thunder of wings, the owl raised himself upright. He threw his head forward and his beak raked across the fox's eyebrows and into the flesh of his ear. Blinkwink pulled back, tearing a piece of flesh away before letting it fall onto the snow. The suddenness of the attack stunned the other foxes and Blinkwink began to beat his wings again, readying for flight. It was the realisation of what the owl was doing that finally got through to the foxes and they sprang at him.

The first felt the full force of Blinkwink's talons in his face, losing one eye and having his lip split so that it looked like a second mouth. The fox fell, howling agony. Another fox felt a talon embed itself in his ear and no amount of twisting could dislodge it. He fell back onto the ground, pulling Blinkwink with him.

Blinkwink flapped his wings harder and faster, trying to free himself. There was a sharp pain in his back and then the first trickle of blood and he knew a good portion of his tail had been bent out of shape; if he didn't get out of here *right now*, he would be dead in seconds. He gave one final, straining yank on the leg caught in the fox's ear and felt the velvety fur and flesh rip away inside the ear. As his talon came loose, Blinkwink thrust up from the ground and, this time, nothing stopped him

Suddenly, wonderfully, he was up and away. His throat burned and his wings ached but he was free. The pain in his back was bad but, free or not, he knew the worst thing was the damage to his tail, to his flight feathers; he was still in danger if they failed him now.

He banked to his right and rose, searching for a pocket of warmer air so he could use the thermal to help him get away completely. He found one and rose several more feet. But it took him out over the lake. And the air above the lake was colder still.

Blinkwink felt the change in the air temperature and tried to fly out of its range but his tail feathers failed him. He began to fall again. Not back towards the forest but towards the water of the lake. And the freezing water would kill him just as efficiently as the foxes. Quicker, perhaps, but dead was dead.

Blinkwink hit the lake like a stone.

The water was as bitterly cold as he'd thought it would be. It filled his mouth and soaked his wings. He sank. The cold and the pain from his injured back stole his consciousness and his last dwindling thought was that he was sorry he hadn't done more damage to the foxes.

Chatter the monkey was squatting down by the edge of Sunset Lake, idly stirring the water with a long branch he'd picked up. Chatter's mind was, in a sense, idling, too.

It had been idling ever since he finally ran out of breath in his mad escape from the squirrels. He'd arrived high in a horse-chestnut tree and he thought that he'd managed to outrun any chasing squirrels. He stayed in the tree until the snow began to fall. Dithering, he'd looked around for shelter and ended up pushed hard up against a bramble bush. The bitter cold sank into his bones and he shivered until everything that had happened to him finally overtook him and he fell asleep.

He'd woken, still shivering and knew he needed to move or he'd become a permanent part of the tree. As quietly as he could, he'd inched down the tree until he could see the ground without any animal on the ground being able to see him. Finally, he'd put all four paws on the snow-covered ground and bounded away as fast as he could until he arrived at the lakeside.

Now, his mind felt empty. It felt better this way. He didn't want to think about anything to do with what had happened and had developed the knack of switching off whenever his mind showed him flashes of the squirrels calling for his death.

The water rippled as he moved the branch and he watched this for a while. The snow had stopped but the air felt hard and sharp and it turned his face numb, the way he liked his mind to feel. But his mind was an insistent thing and, even now, it wanted him to recall the calm, reasonable way Chestnut had announced Chatter's virtual death sentence.

This time, Chatter couldn't stop the memory. He raised the branch and smashed it down on the water, sending jagged ripples towards the centre of the lake. Large droplets of water rose into the air and landed all over him.

"Chee chee chee!"

The sudden shock brought him upright, shivering again.

Right. Well, if his mind refused to be still, Chatter himself would choose the memories. He would recall the good things; the sound of the children's laughter when they watched him do his tumbles and make his funny noises; the way the same children would throw him small pieces of food, like chocolate, like that piece of chocolate he had found in the forest…

No!

The forest had no good memories; he would not remember anything about the forest.

Bananas. Oh, how he loved bananas even if the smell of animal dung almost crowded out the sweet smell of the fruit. The dung used to smell warm and sickly-sweet but it wasn't as bad as the smell of the raw meat the big cats used to eat. No, it was better to think of the muddy, leathery smell of his old friend Methuselah the elephant. Oh my, what a good friend he'd been. Never too busy or tired to talk with the little chatterbox of a monkey and how Chatter missed him today, missed the twinkling eyes and the yellow tusks and the old, wrinkled skin. That skin was a wonderful thing and...

Chatter's eyes widened and he looked down at the lapping water of the lake.

It had been here, yes, just about here. This was the place where the turtle had dropped Chatter off that long-ago day. And the turtle had the same wrinkled skin as old Methuselah.

"But, oh dear me, Methuselah is a long way off and a long time ago," Chatter told himself. "But the turtle must still be in the lake. Mustn't he? Oh yes, I think so."

If he could find the turtle, maybe things wouldn't seem so bad. Oh, how he wished he could find the turtle again. Of course, wishing and getting were two different things. Still, what else did he have to do?

Chatter stretched and rubbed his palms together and then blew into them, liking the brief, small warmth he felt. Then he nodded to himself and set off down the bank to his left.

"I can look for him, oh yes. Don't know what I'll say if I find him but I can look."

The monkey padded almost cheerfully along the water's edge, eyes keen for any sign of the turtle in the water, not knowing that he would come across *two* animals, both of whom had recently saved his life.

It was strange the way you didn't feel wet even though you'd drowned. He felt a little damp, yes, and he could still feel droplets of water in his nostrils but mostly, he felt as if he hadn't fallen into the lake at all. The other thing that surprised him was that he could feel the pain from the wound he'd received in the fight with the foxes. That didn't seem right, still feeling pain when you were dead. Well, maybe he would understand if he opened his eyes and had a good look round. When he opened his eyes, Blinkwink's heart lurched in his chest.

"Ah, hello Mr Owl. How d'you feel?"

The question burbled and sounded as if it came from the bottom of the lake. Of course, being drowned probably explained the sound but not even being drowned could explain what Blinkwink saw.

He raised himself, wincing at the stiffness in his body and the pain in his back but he straightened himself and this new position did nothing to alter what he was looking at.

This…thing in front of him was very big and its head was wrinkled like a walnut shell. The eyes were black and beady but weren't hard like the beady eyes of the foxes; there was something there, some light that made Blinkwink feel…well, warm. The body behind the head had no fur or feathers and was something Blinkwink just couldn't explain because he had nothing to compare it to. It was green/brown and had a sort of pattern and seemed, well, like a shell on a very large nut. Yes, that was what it looked like. A shell that covered the body, showing only the long, long neck and the four stubby feet. The neck and feet were as wrinkled as the head.

"Whoo whoo… er, what are you?"

"Well, I'm a turtle. Who I am is something else but it's not important at the moment. What is important is how you feel."

There was no threat in the burbling voice of this…turtle? Blinkwink felt no need to get away. Besides, if he was dead, it didn't matter anyway. "I…I feel sore. All over. And the wound in my back hurts more. And it woo woo wasn't what I was expecting. Being dead." Blinkwink was startled to hear what was obviously laughter coming from the wrinkled mouth of the turtle.

"I'm sorry," the turtle told him softly. "I meant no offence. But, you see, you're not dead. Oh, you most certainly would have been but I was quite near when you fell into the lake and I was able to push you up and out of the water. No, you're not dead."

"Then this is still Moo Moo Moonrise Forest?"

"Yes."

"Then I owe you my life," Blinkwink told him. "I don't know what I could do for you in return but, if there's anything and I can manage it, I'll doo doo do it gladly."

"Well, Mr Owl, there are one or two things and I'm sure you'll be able to manage both of them. First, though, let's get you somewhere warmer. There's a small break in the trees where there are several holly bushes that should be fine. Not a nest but it should do." He saw the worried look on the owl's face and smiled slowly. "Don't worry, I may look awkward and the water is my element but I can manage short distances on land."

Blinkwink nodded and hopped, testing his legs and body and, when both seemed ready to hold him up, headed away from the lake.

The turtle did manage well over the short distance to the holly bushes and Blinkwink nodded; the shelter was good enough. And a lot warmer than outside. He took some moments to check his injuries and was pleased that it didn't seem likely that the damage was permanent. The most worrying was his tail and the flight feathers there. Still, drying out and rest would help and this place seemed as good as any until he could make it back to his own nest.

"Noo noo now then, turtle, what are the things I can do for you?"

"Oh, they're easy. What is your name and how did you manage to crash down from the air and into the lake? I've never known a bird miscalculate so badly so close to water."

"My name is Blinkwink," the owl told him.

"A fine name."

"But to explain how I came to fall into the lake, I'd have to tell you a story a lot longer. And it is not a pleasant tale, either."

The turtle saw a look cross the owl's face and something in those large eyes spoke of pain and sadness and he knew that he would listen no matter how long or unpleasant the tale. "Tell me," he said simply.

As he finished the story, Blinkwink's voice cracked a little with dryness and emotion. It was almost morning and he felt the need for rest. The snow had stopped but the air was still sharp, bitterly cold and there was that deep quiet that comes to all things in winter when the snow is thick and covers everything. The turtle, too, was silent. In fact, he'd only spoken once during the telling of Blinkwink's story; when the owl had mentioned Chatter the monkey.

"Chatter? Chatter the monkey? I know him!" The turtle had shaken his head at the look on Blinkwink's face. "I'll tell you but finish your story, Blinkwink."

Now, it was told and it was Blinkwink's turn to listen as the turtle told him about his own meeting with Chatter the monkey and how it had been the turtle's idea for Chatter to live in the forest. When he finished, there was no mistaking the sadness in the turtle's wrinkled face.

"Woo woo why so sad, turtle?"

"It seems I may have started all the forest's troubles. All the strangeness and all the death. My fault. I should never have told him to live in Moonrise Forest."

"Now, turtle, I don't think you had much to do with what happened. Listen now, I've had time to think about things and I believe that everything was meant to happen. I think Chestnut would become what he's become sooner or later. The monkey made it happen sooner but it *would* have happened. There is some greater purpose behind all of this. How else could I have escaped the foxes and be found and saved by you? Not only that but you also know Chatter. Can't you see how it is all linked?"

The turtle thought about it for a few moments and then slowly nodded his head, moving his long neck up and down inside the shell. "Perhaps you are right but, even so, I still feel responsible for a lot of it."

"Woo woo, well but it's done now. Things are the way they are and we must deal with them as they are. Now, I am tired and sore and I need to rest. I am not well enough to try to reach my nest. Can you stay out of the water long? Long enough to watch over me while I sleep? When I wake, I must try again to find Rolf."

"Of course I can," the turtle said but then smiled as he realised that Blinkwink had already fallen asleep. While the owl slept, the turtle thought over everything he had heard.

He felt there was a great change in the offing and, as Blinkwink had hinted, perhaps he was going to be a part of it. He had crossed the witch and become an animal. That animal had met and helped a monkey and that monkey had set off a chain of events in the forest. It was too much to lie at the door of coincidence, wasn't it? Oh yes, he thought so. So, what part could he, as a turtle, play?

This squirrel named Rolf seemed to be important, almost vital. Assuming he was still alive. But Blinkwink seemed positive of that and the turtle thought the owl was probably right; the bird was more than two wings and a sharp beak. Yes, this Rolf was certainly the lynchpin in any plan to save the forest and its animals. The thing was, though, what could a turtle do to help? He certainly couldn't roam through the forest searching because he could only stay out of the water for a short time.

"Ah, Chatter, what did I do?" The turtle pulled his head inside his shell, hoping to think of a way he could help in the search for Rolf. Then he popped his head out again. He was smiling. "Chatter," he said.

Yes, Chatter, who was still alive. The monkey was still out there in the forest. The turtle felt in a part of him that he knew was more animal than human that Chatter still had a part to play in all of this.

As the winter morning drew on, the turtle began to see a little light at the end of his own particular tunnel.

Chapter Five

It was cold in the Chief Squirrel's drey, despite the number of squirrels in and outside the opening. Chestnut didn't mind the cold; it helped him in his strategy. Most of the squirrels here were too cold, too busy stamping feet and rubbing paws, to offer much argument as he outlined his latest orders. Not that he worried about arguments anyway. Not now. After Chestnut himself had dealt with that first dissenter after what he called the coup, the rest knew who was in charge. Now, he could leave any reprimands to his five lieutenants and they never needed to be more than heavy cuffs or nips. No, there were no more dissenters and the rest gathered each day to hear their Chief's orders. The orders were generally the same every day.

"You and you towards the lake, you and you towards the northern edge, you and you to the old store-tree."

The last one was the one Chestnut enjoyed giving the most. Going to the old store-tree meant going eastwards, towards the downs, where the foxes lived. Seeing the horror in the eyes of the squirrels he told to search for food in that direction was wonderful. The sheer terror in them was almost like food to him.

This morning, though, he had other things on his mind and was anxious to get the daily orders out of the way; he had his own errand to run and could not delegate it to anybody else.

Chestnut moved forward to the opening of his drey and stood between the two guards. He stood on his hind legs, his eyes bright, looking from one squirrel to another as he took in the numbers gathered to hear his orders. As his eyes made contact, the squirrel he looked at found something incredibly interesting to look at by his own feet; to hold the Chief Squirrel's gaze was a sure way of incurring his wrath.

Chestnut yelled out his orders in a hoarse voice and used one open-clawed paw to point. His lieutenants moved through the crowd and pushed the chosen squirrels off in designated chosen directions. When he had finished, Chestnut said simply, "Same time tomorrow." and the rest dispersed without a sound, only eager to get away.

"Watch the usual ones you two," he told two of his lieutenants and the other three were left to guard his drey. "I'm going for a walk. Alone."

"But Chief, don't you—"

"Alone. Nobody's going to bother me. This is my forest now, remember. Expect me when you see me."

Chestnut headed off in a westerly direction, his paws leaving prints in the snow. He padded slowly, tail up, looking completely at ease. When he reached the stand of old beeches that offered the first real cover, he passed between then, climbed one and moved quickly north before turning east.

After twenty minutes, he stopped on a low hanging branch and, five minutes later, noise ahead brought him to all fours, eyes wide, ears stiff and up. The noise increased as the approaching animals moved towards him and the realisation that there were more than one excited him but he was still in total control of himself.

There were two of them. Their leader and probably his second-in-command. Not that it mattered. One, two or the whole crew, it didn't matter; Chestnut the Chief Squirrel was in total control. Of everything.

Even so, his mind twitched, a question forming there.

He was here, waiting for Slink the fox and it was right that he should be here but ... how did Chestnut *know* he had to be here at this time? And what was it that they had to talk about?

Well, obviously it was...naturally it was to...it was simply...oh Lake and Forest, he just *did*!

Chestnut relaxed a little, breathing deeply but regularly. He felt the tension fade and ... then it was back, stronger than before as another stray thought invaded his mind.

If you don't know exactly how and why, does that mean you might not be in total control after all?

Nonsense! Of course he was in control

Totally?

Lakeslime!

For a moment, Chestnut was unsure whether he had said that aloud but he didn't sense any change in the mood of the approaching foxes, so that was alright. But the question still wanted an answer so he thought back over the previous days and, no matter how hard he tried to make it not so, he could not deny that perhaps it might not have been all his own work. He chewed on this the way he would chew on a tough kernel but nothing came to him, no bright lights in his mind to light up all answers.

It doesn't matter, he told himself.

And it didn't. Perhaps he wasn't in total control but *something* was and, since whatever that something was had chosen Chestnut, it must be on his side. Something was...driving him. Yes, driving him towards...something. What? Never mind, that was for later. The foxes were here now.

"Is that a fox?" Chestnut called out. "Feels like fox. Strong and sharp and sure. Or two foxes? Yes, two. But I want to speak to *my* fox. The other can wait or go, I don't care. But he will not come closer. Do you hear me?"

As soon as he heard the squirrel speak, Slink's hackles rose and he suddenly wanted, not to fight but to run. He knew he would not run; whatever the squirrel wanted to say, Slink would stay and listen. He turned to Slygo and saw a look on his old friend's face that he understood even as it sickened him. Quite simply, Slygo looked terrified. Knowing that he was apparently terrified by a squirrel's voice made it all the worse for Slygo.

"Wait here, old mate," Slink said kindly. "D'you hear me? Wait here."

"What?" It was almost a whisper. "What d'you mean? If you're going, then so am I." But there was no conviction in his voice.

"Are you? You really want to come?" Slink asked and got no answer. "No, best you stay here. Or go for a ramble or a good run. Yeah, run it off."

Slygo watched his leader walk away and noticed that Slink's brush was down, almost to the ground, very close to curling between his back legs. In a way, it was seeing this that made Slygo pad away. He purposely kept his mind blank until he reached the very edge of the forest and passed out of the trees and into the meadow. There, he ran and ran. Slygo ran until a large part of meadow was no longer an expanse of white but a churned mess of slushy brown. He ran until his breath hurt in his chest and then finally rolled around in a patch of undisturbed snow to cool himself off. Then he trotted back into the forest and lay down in the lee of a large elm, not feeling terrified any more, just exercised and tired.

In a way that he did not quite understand, Slygo knew he was different from his peers. He used his mind more and acted less on impulse. Not too much—he was still a fox and lived on his wits because that was how a fox survived. Still, he also knew that, somehow, he used his mind in a different way to Slink and because he did, he understood exactly why the squirrel's voice and its words had terrified him.

The voice and its words had settled on Slygo like the cold of the snow itself. Colder. It had felt to Slygo that the words…no, the *mind* behind the words was colder than the bitter air and it was this that had terrified him. And the fact that the voice had belonged to a squirrel only made it worse; a squirrel was supposed to run from a fox but Slygo had scented nothing like fear coming from the owner of the voice. So, when he was dismissed by both the squirrel and by Slink, Slygo had felt relief. He thought now that he knew why he had felt relief.

Slygo had missed death by a whisker. It was that simple. He had felt and still felt that death had cast a glance towards him and then decided to let him alone, perhaps to save him for another day.

The thought of death, of being so close to death, made Slygo aware of everything more sharply than ever before. Mostly, it made him aware of himself, a feeling that he was part of everything and everything was part of him. It was a sense that all living things were bound together in some way, a circle of life that was only really completed when death occurred.

The thing that had summoned Slink and dismissed Slygo, though...no, that thing was not part of the cycle or the circle, not bound in any way to every other living thing.

Yes, that was the real reason for Slygo's terror. The thing was alien and did not belong. Yet it was here. Why?

To destroy

The thought hit Slygo hard enough to make him shudder. If it was true and he knew instinctively that it was, where did that leave him? Trying to explain something like this to Slink would be impossible, a waste of time because, after the first meeting between what he supposed he had to call a squirrel and Slink, the forest had been opened to the foxes. And Slink didn't seem to have any problems dealing with the squirrel anyway. So what was Slygo to do with his thoughts, with the feeling he had that the squirrel wasn't really a squirrel but a thing intent on destruction?

Slygo got up and shook himself and then, rather than head back to where he had left Slink, he headed back through the forest, heading for the downs. As he walked, he thought about his feeling, seeking an answer to what he could do with the feeling. Eventually, he decided that, perhaps, there was no answer. Other than to watch and wait.

He was close to the point where he needed to head right to approach Midge Marsh and ultimately his own earth. He had to push his way between two trees, one of which leaned and twisted away from him while the other twisted the other way. A heavy growth of bramble had grown in the gap, covered in snow, as were the trees. As he pushed through the snow at the entrance of this little grove, he suddenly came across what felt like the smooth contours of a chicken coop; regular and flat and nothing like the way brambles should have felt. He frowned, about to back out, when his mind threw another question at him.

What? You think maybe two branches fall and split in exactly the right way to make something like a chicken coop wall in the middle of a pile of brambles?

"Oh, shut up," Slygo told the voice in his mind. "I've got enough to think about. Who cares if I have to go round? It's nothing to worry about."

So he moved round the small blockage and made his way home. Slink would probably already be at the earths now and Slygo wasn't sure if he was looking forward to meeting with his old friend.

"The owl and the monkey too and a brown/green turtle they both knew."

The words had a singsong rhythm that kept Blinkwink from opening his eyes because it lulled him so much that he did not know if he was awake or still asleep. The words repeated once more and then stopped and the owl finally opened his eyes. For a second, he wondered where he was and then he saw the turtle's shell and it all came back to him.

It was late afternoon but the clouds still hung low in the small area of sky Blinkwink could see above the top of the turtle's head. The owl fluffed his feathers and spread his wings as wide as he could in the confines of the holly bushes. The turtle showed no sign of having heard Blinkwink but continued to stare away from the bushes at something the owl could not see or sense.

"Doo doo do you see anything?"

Watching the turtle turn was strange because it looked such a slow and ungainly manoeuvre. It started with the turtle's neck and then the feet waddled, as if trying to catch up until the turtle finally faced the owl. The eyes in that wrinkled face looked like deep holes but the voice was warm and friendly.

"Hello again, Blinkwink. How d'you feel?"

"Stiff but better. *Do* you see anything out there?"

"I see the snow and the trees and I know the lake is out there but nothing else. You slept a long time, Blinkwink."

"I flew too much during daylight. I'm not used to it. Night is my time and noo noo now my body's trying to catch up with itself. Still, I think I'll have more daylight flying to do if I'm to find Rolf."

"Mmm. While you slept, I've been thinking. When I said I saw nothing but the snow and the trees," the turtle said slowly. "It was true but only really half-right. I *felt* that there was something out there and very close-by. I'm not used to feelings, Blinkwink because...well, you know what I was before. Still, there is no denying that this feeling is very strong."

Blinkwink nodded his head wisely. "Feelings are always important, turtle. Right now, I think they might be the *most* important thing we have. There is such strangeness in the forest now that any sensations which feel strong and true should not surprise us."

The owl was right. Of course the owl was right and, since the turtle was an animal to all intents and purposes, why shouldn't that strangeness touch him, too? "You're right, Blinkwink," the turtle said, nodding his head so that his neck seemed to sag in the middle. "I think I should go and try to find out what is out there. Will you be alright on your own?" The turtle did not intend to leave the owl on his own if there was the slightest chance that the bird would be unable to protect himself.

Blinkwink said nothing but he hopped forward until he was outside the shelter of the bushes. He extended his wings to their full reach and raised them twice slowly, checking the damage he had suffered in the fight with the foxes and the fall into the lake. The flight feathers in his tail were the main problem and they still felt less than perfect. They might get him off the ground but he knew they would not serve him well if he had to fly out over the lake again. He cocked his head, listening for anything that sounded like foxes but there was nothing and, more, he did not sense anything out there in the forest that felt dangerous. But, like the turtle, he *did* sense something out there but there was no threat in it.

"Goo goo go, turtle," he said. "I can sense something out there and my feeling about it is that it is not dangerous to me. I also feel it needs to be investigated. So go. I'll be here when you return."

The turtle nodded slowly, watching the owl carefully, looking for anything that hinted that Blinkwink was playing down any injury or fear he had. Finally, he said, "I'll go but promise me you'll stay out of sight." The bird nodded and hopped back inside the cover of the bushes. The turtle moved off towards the lake.

When he reached the water, he glided into it smoothly, feeling the ice in it and he knew that the only thing stopping the lake from freezing over was its constant movement. He turned right, facing west and a sudden ray of setting sun stabbed through a break in the heavy overcast; a last defiant gesture by the sun before it sank into the lake. The turtle had an almost undeniable thought that it would be a long, long time before the forest saw the sun again.

As the night settled over the lake and the forest, the turtle moved silently and effortlessly through the water, looking for whatever he might find, certain that he would hear anything long before he saw it and could simply dip below the surface if it felt dangerous or unfriendly.

When he heard a sound, though, there was no need to disappear below the lake. Instead, he trod water with what he imagined was a rather stupid grin on his face.

Of course, he knew the voice but, still, there was something different about it, something that he only understood when the owner of the voice was close enough for the turtle to make out the words.

He's speaking slower, the turtle thought to himself. *And there aren't so many oh dears and oh mys.*

This thought saddened the turtle; the monkey had grown up it seemed but he had had to grow up very fast and the experience had not been kind. The turtle also knew that if he didn't prepare the monkey somehow, as soon as the turtle spoke, it was likely to make Chatter vanish into the trees never to be seen again.

"Oh, used and abused," Chatter murmured to himself. "Better off in the circus. If I'd stayed in the—" He stopped and held his breath, cocking his head to one side. There was a gentle splashing in the lake to his right.

All of Chatter's muscles tensed, ready to spring into the forest away from whatever was here. The spring never happened because Chatter suddenly recognised the splashing, remembered it from when he had first arrived in Moonrise Forest.

"The turtle," he said and clapped his hands. "Oh yes, oh my, it's the turtle!" He ran towards the sound, skipping and clapping his hands. "A friend! Oh a friend at last!"

A friend at last and one who would not turn on him, the only friend in this terrible place.

What about the owl? And the two squirrels who are dead?

Chatter stopped skipping and stopped clapping, suddenly ashamed by this last thought.

"Oh they were my friends, yes. But I won't be seeing them again, oh no. Not even the owl because this forest is his place and I want to get away from here. Oh my, as far and as fast as I can."

"I think I hear a monkey," a slow burbling voice said from the darkness. "I knew a monkey called Chatter but I don't suppose it's him."

"Oh yes! Oh dear me, yes! Here I am, turtle, here I am!" Chatter nearly ran into the lake in his excitement.

"Well, well, well," the turtle said and climbed out of the water and onto the snowy ground next to Chatter.

"Oh turtle, oh my, I'm so glad you remembered me," Chatter said and almost collapsed onto his haunches.

The emotion in the monkey's voice told the turtle exactly how much Chatter's experiences had changed him. If he had been naive when the turtle carried him over the lake, Chatter was no longer naive. The turtle was sad but he also thought that some good might come from it, too. If this Rolf was still alive, then he would need all the help he could get and Chatter was a good animal at heart. The problem might be that Chatter would not want to help animals he probably thought had turned against him, forced him to be alone and scared. Ah well.

"I'm so glad I'm not alone," Chatter told the turtle but still did not look at him, only at his own hands.

"No, you're not alone and it isn't just me, Chatter. There's an owl who will be glad to see you."

Chatter's head came up quickly and even in faint light of the moon, the turtle saw how wide the monkey's eyes were. "What?" Chatter said. "An owl? Oh dear, you don't mean...not..."

"Yes, his name is Blinkwink. If you don't mind having another ride on my back, we'll go and see him, eh?"

Chatter almost jumped on the turtle's back. "Oh yes, oh my yes! Let's go and see Blinkwink!"

The happy sound of the monkey on his back made the turtle smile, glad that not all of the old Chatter had been buried by the terrible things that had happened lately in Moonrise Forest.

Somewhere deep inside himself, Rolf knew that he had come very close to never again having to worry about his pain or his hurts or his grief or even his life. Deep inside, he knew that the animal that had started to push its way into wherever Rolf was now, had been a fox. But, for some reason, the fox had decided against going through and had gone around. Rolf had no idea how long ago this had happened (in fact it had been almost twenty-four hours ago) but he found he didn't really care anyway. It was gone.

But it's gone and it doesn't matter. Not now, not never, no way, hey hey, wait until another day and it's so cold but I'm so hot, why am I so hot? Doesn't matter, don't care, oh my no, oh dear me....

His incoherent thoughts trailed off but something about them had tingled in Rolf's mind. Something familiar, something...

Chatter!

The word echoed loudly in his mind and, though the sound was croaky, he actually spoke aloud.

"Ah, dear Chatter. I liked him. But he'll be dead now, won't he? Chestnut will have seen to that. Used him, yes. That's what he would've done."

How do you know?

"What? I...well, I...he couldn't've got away, that's why? Could he?"

He stayed out of your reach for a good while, didn't he? But there's something more important here, don't you think?

Rolf waited but his mind had stopped talking to him, as if it expected him to do some thinking of his own. Rolf almost laughed at that; how could he think when he was so sick, so hot in the freezing cold, so...

"Wait," he told himself and tried to think, tried to forget for a moment how ill he was and to think.

That was it. Of course, that was it. If he could think, if his mind could ask questions and if Rolf could try to answer them, then...

Yes. You might not be as sick as you thought or wanted to be. And there's something else, too. What about your promise to Saltpepper? You promised to find Blinkwink.

Rolf's body moved, apparently of its own accord. The more he argued with himself, with the mind-voice, the more movement his body made. It was testing itself, in much the same way that his mind was testing itself, testing Rolf. And the results of the tests were that, yes, his wounds were bad and they really did hurt but they were not yet mortal. There was fever and infection and the beginnings of a rattle in his chest and all of these could prove mortal if he stayed out in the open for much longer but…

But you're not dying yet and you can move.

"Yes," Rolf agreed with his mind-voice and with his own body.

He lifted his left hind leg and it hurt, as if a long splinter of wood was driven in it, and it felt as if it had begun to bleed again. But it took his weight, as did his other legs and he was standing, albeit gingerly, on all fours.

"Yes, I can stand but I'm still hurt and this infection could still kill me. I can't just go out into the forest like this," Rolf muttered. "Even if I did, how am I supposed to find Blinkwink? I don't even know where *I* am."

All of which was true and it sounded and felt like there was another storm blowing out there beyond the cover of these brambles. Well, maybe he should sleep out the storm and maybe he would feel stronger when he woke and maybe then he would be able to try to keep his promise to Saltpepper.

"Bloody squirrel! Damn his fur!"

"Yes, but it doesn't really help us much, Stripe."

"Humph. What?!"

"Cursing the squirrel doesn't help much," Bumper said quietly.

"Harumph, well, what I do know is that there is no way we're helping that bloodydamn squirrel with his night-sentry duty or whatever he calls it."

"But what about the foxes, Stripe?" The question came from a younger badger and his voice betrayed his worry at what was going on in the forest.

"Who's that? And what about them?"

"Er, it's Peaty," the young badger almost squeaked. "The foxes are on the squirrel's side. D'you think it's a good idea not, er...co-operating with that bloodydamn squirrel?"

"That's enough, son. You don't argue with Stripe. You're not too big yet for a cuff around the head," said Peaty's father and Peaty nodded but he didn't look particularly worried about being cuffed.

"Since when have we been worried about any fox?" Stripe asked, his voice gruffer, angry now.

"But it's not just one fox," Bumper said, still softly. "It's their whole crew now. The forest's as much their forest now as Chestnut's. That's a big problem, Stripe."

"Harumph! You telling me that white stripe of yours is turning yellow, Bumper?" Stripe's anger was clear now, the more so because he and Bumper had been friends for a long, long time; he hadn't expected this sort of talk from his trusted lieutenant.

"Now, you hold back your gruff, you old battle-grouch. You know me well enough to know I'm no coward."

The other badgers were quiet now, the tension between the two old friends palpable in the freezing air. Peaty felt it and it made his stomach churn and his head ache. He thought their leader, Stripe, would get so angry that he might fight Bumper. But Stripe didn't speak and when Bumper spoke, the tension in the air lessened.

"Listen to us," Bumper said, shaking his broad head. "We should be talking about sorting out that bloodydamn squirrel and, instead, he's got us arguing amongst ourselves. If he knew, he'd laugh himself silly."

"You're right, my old friend. That squirrel is poisoning everything and everybody in the forest. Still, humph, I meant it about not helping him with his night-watch. What's he want it for anyway?"

Bumper shrugged. "All I know is that there's nobody more afraid of being robbed than a thief and that's all that blackheart is when you get down to it."

The badgers all agreed with that but, while the others grumbled and growled about that bloodydamn squirrel, Stripe was already thinking about other things. Mostly about Rolf and Blinkwink. When he called for order, he got it immediately; they all knew who their leader was.

"Right, first, if there's any badger here who fancies that his or her life would be easier by helping this Chestnut, say so now and then leave. You won't be bothered by anybody here but you better stay out of my way if you do go." He squinted at the gathering and saw nobody who even looked like they were thinking about leaving to join Chestnut. "Good. Now, why does Chestnut need guards at night when he's got all the squirrels scared to death with the threat of the foxes? Mm? I think

Bumper's right, I think that squirrel is scared, worried anyway. Who's he worried about? Saltpepper's dead and it seems likely that Rolf is, too. Who's left?"

"Blinkwink?"

"What? Speak up whoever you are."

"Er, it's me, Peaty...maybe he's worried about Blinkwink?" Peaty didn't sound very sure but his uncertainty was because he was speaking at a proper meeting for the first time in his young life. Still, as far as Chestnut and Blinkwink were concerned, he was almost positive he was right.

"Humph," Stripe grumbled but he smiled and nodded. "Yes, youngun, I think you're right. Anything else in that quick mind of yours?"

Peaty felt his body thrill at the compliment and almost stood on his hind legs but that would have been too much, too soon. Instead, he shook his head slowly.

"I'd like to know what happened to that monkey," Bumper said. "I know he got away because I heard some squirrels whispering about it. It sounded like it was Blinkwink helped him escape. But there's been no sight or sound of either since."

"I can see you've been thinking about all of this for a while, eh my old friend? Well, any ideas? We need to do *something* about that bloodydamn squirrel in a hurry."

"Yes," Bumper agreed. "But I don't want to put it to this meeting till I've thought about it a bit more. Besides, there's a storm coming. Let's all get to our setts and maybe you and me can talk about this idea I've got?"

When they got to Bumper's sett, Stripe hadn't even settled himself properly before his old friend got him angry all over again.

"I think we should stand Chestnut's night-watch for him."

"What? Harrumph! There better be more to it than that, Bumper."

Bumper smiled. "Oh there is. See, if we agree to be his night-watch guards, we could *learn things*. Stuff he wouldn't tell us and we wouldn't find out if we stayed here, out of the way. The sort of stuff that might help us, stuff we could use against him when the time was right." He raised his large eyebrows and left the idea in the air for the very simple reason that he knew his limitations. Oh, he could think and he could come up with ideas but they needed fleshing out. Bumper's ideas were thin, skeletal things, made of gristle and some sinew but which a good wind would demolish easily. Stripe was the leader because he could take ideas and make them tough and strong, he could think them through and see snags and find ways of removing them. If this idea of Bumper's felt right to Stripe, he would make it a workable plan.

Stripe nodded and frowned and mumbled to himself for a while and then raised his head slowly. Bumper smiled at the gleam he saw in his leader's dark eyes. "It feels right, Bumper. Humph, yes it does. *But* it's got to feel right to Chestnut, too. He'll sniff out anything that doesn't feel genuine. Okay, he'll get his guards but he won't get *me*. No, that'd be too unlikely, wouldn't it? See, if this, humph, gruff, bad-tempered badger was to be run-off, displaced or, maybe even killed...with some convincing proof mind...well, that would look good to him. That would make him take the badgers at their word, eh? You'd have to be the leader, Bumper and you'd have to make sure he doesn't think he can order badgers about. I won't have that. Even if..." He grinned. "Even if I'm dead. And no punishment duty. No badger's going to get involved in any bloodletting for that bloodydamn squirrel. You listen and find out what we need to know. He'll want reports from you, about what's happening in the forest. Now, he'll probably have you spied on so make sure your reports are right. Yes, haruff, that should work, I think."

"What about you?"

"Ah, well, I'll be dead, won't I? I reckon I can snout around without being seen, eh? Maybe I'll find some other animals to help us when it's time to sort out that squirrel."

"The owl and the monkey?" Bumper asked softly, smiling. "You're going to look for them, aren't you?"

"And Rolf, if he's still alive."

"D'you really think he might be?"

"Well, humph, I hope so, Bumper. Even if we can get something going to clear out the stink that's in this forest now, we're not going to keep it out for long without some half-decent squirrel to take old Saltpepper's place."

Bumper nodded. "Well, what about this proof I'm supposed to show Chestnut?"

"Blood," Stripe said simply. "That'd work. It's the sort of, humph, thing he likes, I bet. You get some blood on your snout and paws, maybe some fur in your claws. Then you go and see that bloodydamn squirrel tonight."

Bumper stared at his old friend, not making any move toward him. So Stripe cuffed his old friend on the side of his head. It startled Bumper and he reacted without thinking, striking Stripe on the snout and swiped him on the foreleg.

"Humph! Well, that was a bit harder than I expected but it did the trick, Bumper. Now," he said gently. "Tug a bit of fur out of my back and smear that bit of blood on the rest of your claws."

Bumper did what he was told and then looked at Stripe.

"Humph, yes, that looks right. Now, you get straight to Chestnut. You'll smell of me and my blood. Take...yes, take young Peaty with you. You can tell him on the way and I'll explain to the rest while you're gone. Make sure Peaty understands that I'm dead. Not missing or gone off, dead."

"When will I see you again?"

"Badger Hollow still belongs to the badgers," Stripe said. "I can get in and out better than anybody else in the forest. Don't expect me till you see me and then we'll swap what information we've got. Mind, I don't think I'll be back for a while."

"Where will you start?"

"*Who*," Stripe told him. "Not where but who. I think I'll try to find Blinkwink first. Now, get off before that blood goes too cold and smells stale."

"You take care, you old battle-grouch," Bumper said gruffly and then raised his front right paw. Stripe nodded and raised his own right forepaw. They placed their paws against each other and then went their separate ways.

Chestnut was alone in his drey. His fur was puffed out and he was warm inside his well-insulated home. Outside, the snowstorm piled drifts high throughout the forest but it could have been midsummer in his drey. Here he sat, Chief Squirrel, lord of all he surveyed.

"Including the foxes," Chestnut said quietly and the words made him feel warm, inside as well as outside.

He puffed out his fur even more and began to plan his next few days; who to point to and send to the old store-tree; who to send to the lake to freeze perhaps; who to send eastwards towards the foxes; who to beat. Ah, yes, perhaps there should be another beating, just to keep them honest.

He didn't even have to close his eyes to be able to see the terror in the eyes of the squirrel he would punish; he could see the way the animal's nose twitched with fear and then with pain, could see the blood and smell the blood. Ah, such sights would keep him warm right through this hard winter.

"Chief? There's a badger here to see you?"

"What?" Chestnut's reverie was broken. "A badger? What the lake is he doing here now? It's late and I'm tired. Tell him to badger off back to his hollow."

On the branch outside, the guard said, "Alright, you two, badger off back home like the Chief said." He rapped his tail on the branch, wishing these badgers to the lake and gone so he could get back to just being a guard. If the Chief decided to see these badgers, then the guard would have to get very close to The Chief to keep him protected. The guard didn't like being close to The Chief. He'd prefer to stay here, cold and shivering on this branch than down there on the ground and within cuffing or even biting distance of Chestnut. Yeah, it would be better if this blood-spattered badger and his young friend just badgered off home. "You two deaf or something? He wants you to make an appointment. Now go!"

"We've come to see your chief and that's what we're going to do. He asked us for help and we're here to give him his answer. Now. Tonight." Bumper pushed forward to the base of the tree and looked upwards towards the guard. Peaty stood beside him but kept quiet; he'd heard the voice of that bloodydamn squirrel and, despite his pride in being part of the big plan, the sound of that voice had made Peaty wonder if going home, right now, might not be a really good idea. When Bumper growled, Peaty had to work very hard at keeping the shudder from shaking his whole body.

The guard caught his breath when he heard the badger growl; he didn't fancy his chances if the badger decided to pull him down and fight. But then, he didn't really know how bad a badger's bite was while he knew *exactly* how bad Chief Chestnut's bite was.

"Wait," Chestnut said from inside his drey and smiled when he saw how that one word made the guard stiffen. "Did he say he had an answer for me?"

"Er...that's what he said, Chief."

Chestnut came out onto the branch and looked down. "Is that blood I can see?"

"Yes," Bumper told him. "Now, do we get inside the hollow bottom of this tree or do we just go home and you find somebody else to do your night-watch?"

Chestnut cocked his head. Whatever made him...whatever he had become, was thrumming inside him. It was a cold thrumming but it was also very sharp at sniffing out anything that might go against Chestnut's plans. This time, Chestnut sensed nothing to worry about. "The hole is round the other side. I'll meet you at the bottom."

The guard closed his eyes and followed the Chief Squirrel inside and then down the inside of the tree to its base where the two badgers were already waiting.

As soon as Chestnut arrived at the bottom of the tree, the two badgers both noticed the change. It was cold inside the hollow base of the tree, just as it was outside. When Chestnut arrived to stand in front of them, the cold deepened and they could feel it almost gnaw at their bones. Bumper had to tell himself that he was a badger and this was just a squirrel and, if he had to, he could kill the bloodydamn thing with one swipe of his paw. Peaty was simply stunned, so cowed that he did not even try to remind himself that he was a badger. Peaty *knew*, the way he knew that spring followed winter that this squirrel could kill anything he chose to kill.

Chestnut saw the young badger's fear in his eyes and smiled to himself. "So," he said. "You have an answer for me? I take it by the blood on your snout and claws and by the fur, that not everybody agreed with you?"

"Just the one," Bumper said and was surprised at how level his voice was. "And he won't be arguing with anybody else. Ever."

"Chief Squirrel! You call him Chief Squirrel," the guard growled because it was expected of him.

Bumper went on as if the guard had not spoken. "We'll stand your night-watch. I'd just like to know what it is we'll be guarding."

"Chief Squi—"

"Oh shut up!" Chestnut yelled. The guard's teeth clicked loudly as he shut his mouth. "Tell me...what's your name by the way?"

"Bumper."

"A good, solid name. And you?" Chestnut looked at the other badger.

Peaty tried to speak but his throat had closed. He blinked and swallowed and tried again and still could not speak.

"His name is—" Bumper began but the squirrel held up a paw and cut him off.

"Oh, I'm sure he'll be able to tell me himself." Chestnut stared at the young badger.

Peaty could feel the panic gnawing at the edges of his mind and he wished he was anywhere but there with this...mad, yes this squirrel was mad. Oh, by the Lake Peaty wished he was *in* the lake.

All you have to do is give him your name. Your name is Peaty. You can say that. Say 'My name is Peaty.' Say it and Bumper will find out what you'll be guarding and then you'll be able to leave. Just say 'My name's Peaty.'

Peaty took another long, deep breath and filled his lungs and then he pushed it out as hard and as fast as he could and he could feel it coming all the way up from his stomach and into his throat and onto to his tongue and, *thank the Lake*, out of his mouth.

"Peaty! My name is Peaty and can I leave now!"

The other three animals inside the tree jumped as if something with very big teeth had nipped their tails. The guard banged his head on the side of the tree and Chestnut had to sit on his haunches to stop himself falling backwards. Bumper swallowed back a sudden urge to bark.

When the sound of Peaty's answer had stopped echoing inside the hollow tree-base, Chestnut turned to Bumper and asked, "Is he simple or what?"

Although the words came out soft, Bumper sensed the anger the squirrel was working hard to bank down. "Mostly, he's just young," the older badger said. "It's his first time on something so...important, Chief Squirrel. Now, what will we be guarding?"

Chestnut smiled. "The blood? Whose is it?"

"Stripe's," Bumper replied without missing a beat. "He's dead."

The Chief Squirrel turned to Peaty. "Is this true, young Peaty?" He stared at the badger and, when Peaty nodded, he turned back to Bumper. He moved closer and sniffed at the blood; yes, it was quite fresh.

"Fine. You will be guarding the forest, of course. Keeping an eye out for anything that looks out of place in my forest."

"How are we supposed to know what looks out of place? To badgers, the foxes look out of place in this forest."

"Well, not to me, badger, not to me. Let's say, oh, a monkey? Yes, a monkey would look out of place and maybe a squirrel who is probably dead but might not be. Let's say *that* squirrel would look out of place."

"Rolf, you mean?" Bumper asked innocently.

Chestnut rubbed his teeth. "No names, eh? Now, you just send the badgers who are to stand the duty to me in the early evening and—"

Bumper shook his head once. "No. Only badgers order badgers. Right now, that means they take their orders from me. And they'll give any report to me. I'll come and tell you anything we find that's...out of place." Bumper waited to see if the anger he could feel in the squirrel would come boiling out. For a second, it looked like it might but, slowly, Chestnut got himself under control.

"Yes, yes." The squirrel took a breath and let it out slowly. "I'll...*talk* to you and *you* can order your badgers. Oh, yes, I almost forgot. If you see anything or hear anything, *anything at all*, of the owl, I want to know. Any news at all of Blinkwink, I want to know *immediately*." He rubbed his teeth again and blew out another breath. "Now, I think that's all. Don't you? Yes, fine. Goodnight then." He clambered up the inside of the tree and was gone. The guard waited a few moments until the badgers had left and then he followed his chief. But he went up the *outside* of the tree.

The storm had abated and only brief flurries blew across their path as they made their way home. Half way back to the Hollow, Peaty finally spoke.

"I'm sorry, Bumper. I let you down, didn't I?" His voice sounded very small to his own ears.

Bumper chuckled. "No, Peaty, not even a little bit. You did just fine. That bloodydamn squirrel is convinced that Stripe is dead. He thought you were so scared of him that you couldn't lie to him to save his life."

"He might be right," Peaty said but his voice did not sound so small now. "He really is scary."

"Yes," Bumper agreed. "But don't you fret about it, lad. He's not as in control of things as he wants everybody to believe. No, his grip on things isn't unbreakable. He's worried about Rolf and the monkey and about Blinkwink. He's worried that the three of them, *if* Rolf's alive, might be able to break his grip on the forest. Anyway, Stripe's got the hard part now. Finding any of them in this weather is going to be a job and a half."

"D'you think he'll be able to do it?"

"If any badger can do it, Stripe can. Now, let's get home. We've got some sorting out to do with the others."

Slink had eaten well and was curled round himself in his den. The storm had died now and only the occasional gust of wind hooted round the forest. The cold, though, was deep and constant. Slink had no doubt that the cold would be with them for a long time, possibly even right through to the spring. Well, that was fine with him; finding food when the ground was bone hard would be no easy task for the squirrels and *that* would mean easier hunting for the foxes.

And he, Slink, had made it all possible.

Oh? All by yourself?

Slink growled. "Oh, lake and forest! Can't you leave it?"

The voice in his head seemed to be with him all the time now. When he was out hunting, he could keep it quiet but when he was alone and fed, it kept asking him questions he had no desire to hear let alone answer. Maybe he should go and see Slygo? Talking might keep the voice quiet. That said, Slygo might not want to talk with Slink. Since the afternoon that bloody squirrel had dismissed him, Slygo hadn't seemed to want to spend much time with Slink. And, really, Slink didn't blame him but Slink needed somebody to talk to.

By the time he reached Slygo's earth, Slink was bone-cold and wet and didn't even wait to be invited in. He pushed down into the den, already shouting for Slygo.

"Oy, Slygo, you old brush-biter! You asleep?"

Slygo woke to the sound and scent of another animal inside his home and struggled to wake up enough to defend himself. His hackles were high and his paws digging into the loose earth. When he recognised Slink he growled with released tension.

"What the coop are you doing? I might've ripped your bloody throat out, you idiot!"

"I'm cold and wet and need some company and I was yelling well before I got inside."

Slygo let out a breath and settled back into a comfortable position. "Well, what d'you want to talk about?"

"Aach, nothing special, just a talk, you know."

"Come off it," Slink said. "You didn't come here in the wet and cold to talk about nothing special. What's up?"

"You know," Slink settled himself down on his belly and snorted air from his nostrils. Then, comfortable at last, he said, "When I was a pup, my mother used to tell me all sorts of stories. You know, about raiding chicken coops and racing away with the bird before the farmer got his firestick out. Stuff pups love to hear. But she never told me any stories about raiding Moonrise Forest. I never heard the forest mentioned except once when she caught me close to it and dragged me away, telling me it wasn't a place to go. Now, we've raided the forest and we've got food for as long as we want it." He stopped and stared at his old friend.

"So? We both know it's because that squirrel let us in. You've got a thing, a…some arrangement with him and it gets us food. He gets to be Boss Nutcruncher. Everybody's happy so what's to talk about?"

"Don't try to kid a kidder, my old mate," Slink said and smiled but the smile didn't really look real. "I know you've been thinking about that bloody squirrel ever since he sent you away. So have I. Now, listen to this and tell me what you think because it's driving me round the bend."

Slygo nodded and let out a long breath.

"Okay, you know what he wanted to know when I went to meet him? He wanted to know what happened to the fourth squirrel when we made the raid. I told him he was dead, what else? So he asks me where the body is. I shrugged because who cares, right? But he asks me again and I have a think and couldn't come up with any pictures in my head about that other squirrel, you know? So I tell King Cruncher that one of us must've eaten the bugger. He looks at me for a long minute and then changes the subject. At least, that's what I thought he did because he wanted to know if we'd come across the monkey."

"What the coop is a monkey?" Slygo asked.

"Exactly what I said and he says it's a bit like a young dog but with fur and long arms and a long tail that he uses to hold onto branches when he climbs trees. This monkey can climb trees better even than squirrels. Anyway, I told him no, never seen anything like that so he tells me to keep a look out for this monkey and to tell him if anybody even hears about anything that even sounds like what he'd just described. *Right away*, he says.

"I'd had enough so I told him if that was all, I was on my way because I was freezing. He says no, the main reason he wanted to see me was so we could agree how many squirrels we took during the winter."

Slygo blinked and his ears went up. "What? And you told him to stick it where he sticks his nuts, right?"

Slink frowned. "No," he said and looked at his front paws. "Oh, I asked him what was stopping us taking however many we liked and then he explained it and, well, it made sense."

"Oh?"

"See, he reckons if most of them get eaten, there won't be enough to mate and that'd mean there'd be no new squirrels and that'd mean—"

Slygo was nodding. "Yeah, I can see that. But I don't see how we can keep a check on the numbers. If a fox sees a squirrel and the fox is hungry..."

"He'd already thought of that. He's gonna send so many squirrels out each day and only to certain parts of the forest. We make sure the foxes only prowl those parts of the forest."

"Yeah, okay, seems like he's got a good mind for organisation. I still don't see what the problem is, what's driving you round the bend," Slygo said but he thought he had an idea.

"He...he called me back after I'd agreed and started to leave." Slink looked at his paws again and didn't look up when he went on. "I...I didn't want to go back, Slygo. I...I couldn't help myself."

Slygo nodded; that was the problem. Of course that was the problem. King Cruncher was a puny squirrel who was, theoretically, two bites and three swallows of breakfast but, somehow, he managed to make the leader of the foxes turn and come to heel. "What else did he have to say?"

"He told me again to make sure we keep on the lookout for the other squirrel, just in case it's alive, and for the monkey. Then he tells me to watch out for some owl. I wasn't paying much notice then. I was more bothered about not being able to keep on walking when he called me back." He growled deep in his throat.

Slygo wanted to comfort his old friend but you didn't do that with Slink so he waited until his old friend was simply breathing instead of growling. Then he told him what Rusty had said about the owl that had fallen into the lake.

Slink brought his head up and grinned. "Really? Well, that'll shut that cold nutcruncher's mouth with a snap. I'll enjoy telling him that because he had the cheek to tell me to make sure no fox or foxes toyed with the owl, just killed him. Thought the owl might be a bit too quick and tough for us. Hah, wait'll I tell him that we didn't just toy with the owl but we drowned it in the lake."

"When d'you see him again?"

Slink lowered his head and bared his teeth. "There's no set times," he told Slygo. "I'm not that far gone. He's cold, somehow, and it bothers me that he called me back but I'm not so far gone that he thinks he owns me."

"Fine, Slink, fine. Calm down. I know he doesn't own you but it's worrying, isn't it? The way he is? I mean, he's not what you'd call normal."

"No, you're right. But...well, I think he is still a squirrel, deep down and that means that he's still food, right? Anyway, I'll be seeing him soon just so I can rub his snout in it about the owl."

Slygo nodded and then almost surprised himself into a heart attack. He said, "Well, I'd like to be there when you do." He blinked and then grinned. "Yes, I'd really like to be there."

Slink nodded. They said little else before Slink went back home.

When he was alone again, Slygo wondered at how he had told Slink he wanted to be there when the squirrel found out about the owl. After all, that one time he'd seen the squirrel had been enough. At least, he'd thought so at the time. But there was no denying he *did* want to go with Slink next time he saw King Cruncher. It was a puzzle and it played on his mind until, finally, sleep overtook him.

Rolf had a problem. Well, he had two or three but, right now, he had one *main* problem.

When he woke up and still wasn't dead, he knew he would have to get out of wherever he was. It was still freezing cold and he still felt feverish so those problems remained but the deep wound in his left rear leg had stopped bleeding so that was something. But, he still had to get out of this place and, each time he thought about that, he remembered the fox that had not been able to get inside to where the sick Rolf lay.

Rolf had another good look at the odd place where he was and it still looked exactly the same and exactly as difficult to get out of for him.

This space seemed to consist mainly of brambles that twined round the boles of two wide trees. The branches of the trees hung very low and the brambles had twined among these, too, forming a canopy. The heavy snow covered the canopy and when he first noticed this, Rolf just didn't believe it; there seemed to be so much snow up there that the weight of it should have just forced the brambles to give way and all that snow should have buried Rolf during the time he was unconscious. But the snow did not fall and, so, the ground on which Rolf lay and now sat was dry. Bone hard but dry.

Rolf had thought about the fox and how he had obviously tried to push through the brambles but, when he couldn't, the fox *hadn't* pushed harder but simply walked away. If the fox had given up trying to get in, how could Rolf get out? And, even if he managed it, how was he supposed to find Blinkwink when he could only limp?

Getting out is the first thing. After that, well, why not head for Blinkwink's tree?

That sounded reasonable enough but he still had to get out.

Look, nothing about this little hidey-hole looks natural so maybe just walking into the largest gap you can see will work?

Well, he had to get out so he might as well give it a try.

Rolf limped right up to the widest break in the brambles and pushed gently with his right forepaw, not expecting anything more than a small fall of snow. But a whole section of brambles simply moved sideways and he was suddenly staring at the forest.

Rolf blinked and then shuffled through the gap and stood on the deep, packed snow outside. He glanced back over his shoulder and, for a moment, the gap was still there. It showed him the dry, snowless ground he had slept on. To Rolf it looked like something in a tale of myth and magic Saltpepper might once have told him. Then the brambles moved back and it was once again a packed mesh of bramble and branch. Rolf blinked again, wondering if he had imagined it and then the weight of the snow collapsed the whole thing, sending swirling clouds of snow into the air.

Rolf shook his head and turned back to face the forest. He looked up and saw a billion points of dazzling brightness in the endless sky. Even the moon had broken free of the clouds and Rolf thought he had never seen it look so beautiful.

"Let's see if I can find Blinkwink," he murmured and began to limp away through the trees.

Stripe had not seen or scented any foxes or squirrels since leaving the Hollow. It didn't surprise him really; since that bloodydamn squirrel had taken over, Stripe imagined that the squirrels stayed in their dreys as much as possible. Besides, something told him that there was an arrangement between that bloody Chestnut and the foxes, one that probably meant that squirrels were out in the daylight, searching for food and so prey to the foxes.

"Bloodydamn squirrel, humph!"

Striped pushed forward through the snow, his feet and most of his legs unfeeling, almost as if they weren't part of him anymore. It was a long way to Blinkwink's tree and Stripe just hoped that his legs would keep him going long enough to get there.

Half an hour after the moon sailed from behind the last of the flying clouds, Stripe reached the base of Blinkwink's tree.

"You home, owl?" Stripe called.

No answer, not a sound from anywhere. Stripe trudged round the tree, hoping for a scent of Blinkwink but his snout had no better luck than his ears or his voice.

"Humph. Now what? At least when I left the Hollow, I had a place to go. Now, I've got nowhere to go. Can't go home and put every badger in danger so now what?"

What about the monkey?

Yes, he supposed he could look for the little chatterbox but...

Stripe stopped thinking and stopped moving. There was a sound out there. He cocked his head in the direction from which the sound was coming. It was the sound of squeaking snow, as if somebody was walking on it and, with this sound was a noise like harsh breathing. It was still a fair way off and Stripe couldn't scent what was making the sounds but it was getting closer.

Stripe moved back to the other side of the tree and pushed himself down into the mound of snow; it wasn't perfect but it would give him some element of surprise when the animal finally arrived.

The sound came closer and, as it did, Stripe realised that whatever animal this was, it was injured; there were three footfalls and then a sort of shuffling, which hinted at a limp. This made Stripe feel better because the less energy he had to expend fighting and killing this animal, the better. Then all thoughts of fighting and killing vanished from the badger's mind.

"Oh, *please* be home, Blinkwink."

Stripe almost fell over his own paws as he scrambled round the tree. When he saw Rolf crawling over the snow, so many things filled his mind that he found it impossible to say anything.

It must be his ghost. The badger told himself and then shook his head. *No, no ghost would breathe like that. Or even breathe at all. It is Rolf. And he's sick.*

Rolf was at the end of his strength. Actually, he had passed that point a while ago. He had come this far on sheer willpower and the constant thought in his head—*promise to keep, blinkwink to find, promise to keep, blinkwink to find*—and now he was dragging himself forward, his eyes closed, head barely above the snow and, oh Lake and Forest, now something was in his way and stopping him from...

Rolf pulled in a deep, painful breath and raised his head to see what was in his way, to call out for Blinkwink to help him if he could.

"Rolf!"

For a moment, Rolf was amazed at how strongly he had managed to shout, even if he'd only managed to say his own name and, Moon, but he was doing it again.

"Rolf! By the Lake, I thought you were dead!"

Rolf blinked and stared.

"It's me, Rolf. Harrumph, me, old Stripe."

A brief flash of panic tinged with despair ran through Stripe and then he half-dragged, half-carried the squirrel round the base of the tree where he laid him against the snow. When he was sure Rolf was still breathing, Stripe began to dig at the heaped snow against the bole of the tree, hoping there was a hole there where he could get Rolf out of the open.

Stripe growled with relief when he saw the broken bark and felt the sponginess of it and he began to use his long, strong claws to widen the hole. When he judged it large enough, he turned back to Rolf.

"Right, lad, come on. Humph, let's get you inside," he said gently and, just as gently, eased Rolf inside the hole in the tree.

Rolf groaned and blinked his eyes open. He saw Stripe and smiled. "Real," he muttered. "Thank you. Nick of time. Thanks, Stripe. Love you, you old gruff-grouch." Then he lay on his right flank and closed his eyes again.

Stripe pushed himself against Rolf, wrapping his front paws round him, giving him as much of his own heat as possible. There was a lump in the badger's throat and, although he told himself that it was just tiredness, it was probably tears, which moistened his eyes. When he was sure that Rolf was breathing regularly if shallowly, Stripe, too, fell asleep.

While Stripe and Rolf had been trudging towards each other, Blinkwink had been telling a wide-eyed Chatter what had happened after the owl had helped the monkey escape. Now, the shelter where they were was quiet and so was the forest beyond the holly bushes. The turtle was just inside the shelter watching the other two animals. When the owl had told his story to Chatter, the turtle had watched the monkey carefully; he watched to see if the monkey reacted to the story as the turtle hoped he would. In fact, Chatter had not reacted at all. There was no shock, no doubt, not even any sadness when Blinkwink told him about Saltpepper's death.

Blinkwink had sensed the change in the monkey almost as soon as Chatter had finished saying hello. It was something about the way Chatter spoke now; slow and without so many oh mys and oh dears. Now, with the story told, Blinkwink was resting, his tail feathers splayed out on the ground around him. Resting, but waiting to see what Chatter said.

Chatter said nothing. Blinkwink riffled his feathers three times and still the monkey said nothing. Finally, the owl ran out of patience.

"Woo woo well? Have you nothing to say, monkey?"

Chatter blinked and then looked at his hands in his lap. "A sad, terrible story," he said and then fell silent again.

"That's all?" The turtle lifted his head so that his eyes were on a level with Chatter's head.

"Sad? A sad story?" Blinkwink asked in a loud voice. "Saltpepper is dead and *that's all you have to say*?" The owl's voice filled the little space and seemed as loud as the wind had sounded at the height of the blizzard.

Chatter squeaked and jumped up, already heading for the gap in the bushes but the turtle blocked the way. Chatter sat down on his haunches and his hands squirmed in his lap.

"Oh dear me, oh my, everybody's against me now, everybody."

"Oh stop that babbling," the turtle demanded. "We're not against you. Stop being so selfish!"

"The turtle is right," Blinkwink said in a quieter voice. "This isn't about you, monkey. Noo noo now, are going to help us? Mmm? Lend a hand?"

Chatter looked up and saw that both animals were staring at him. Not angry now, just waiting and the monkey realised how selfish he must have sounded. How selfish *he had been.* "Oh dear me," he said softly. "I am selfish. You helped me and I let you down. Oh yes, oh dear." He rubbed at his eyes and snuffled back a few tears. "Yes, I'd like to help but...what can I do?"

"Woo woo well, we don't know yet but now we can at least think about it properly." He nodded at Chatter and got a smile in return.

The turtle nodded his wrinkled head. "Yes, there must be something we can do."

The three animals fell silent again, thinking about what they could do. Occasionally, one would clear his throat as if he had thought of something but then would shake his head and say nothing. Blinkwink was thinking hard, his eyes open, trying to use his old trick of concentration but it wasn't working; this wasn't his nest and he was used to being in his nest. The more he tried, the more this fact loomed large in his mind— he wasn't at home, wasn't in his own nest...wasn't in his own nest...

"Woo woo wait!" Blinkwink flapped his wings and rose up on his feet, as if trying to fly.

"What have you thought of?" The turtle moved further inside.

"Rolf is alive. Don't ask me how I can be so certain but I am. Now," Blinkwink relaxed again, spreading his tail feathers on the ground. "If you were hurt, badly hurt and if you knew or assumed that your old teacher was dead, killed by foxes...what would you do?"

Chatter frowned and his fingers twisted together as he imagined how Rolf could have felt; it wasn't hard because Chatter had felt like that when Chestnut called for his death.

"Probably the first thing," the turtle said slowly, still thinking it through. "Would be finding somewhere safe from the foxes."

"Oh yes," Chatter agreed. "Somewhere safe where he could get over his hurts? But then what?"

"Well, assuming you didn't die from the wounds, once the foxes had gone, you'd probably hope to find some help. You'd hope to find a friend."

"And if yoo yoo you knew a bird who was a friend and you knew where he lived—"

"You'd go there! Oh yes, oh my yes!" Chatter clapped his hands, glad to have worked it out.

Blinkwink nodded. "Yes, but I'm not there. He'd only find an empty nest."

"Would he wait?" The turtle closed his eyes and then shook his head. "No, I don't think so."

"Noo noo no, so what would he do? Would he just turn back into the forest and wait to die?"

"Oh no," Chatter pleaded. "No, don't say that. Oh dear me, what can we do? What..." He stopped and his eyes widened and then he grinned. "I could try to find him. Yes? I could, couldn't I? I'm not hurt like you, Blinkwink and I don't have to stay by the water like you turtle. I could...oh yes, I could look for him. I could go to your tree and find him and if he's not there, I could search between your tree and where those terrible foxes killed Saltpepper. Couldn't I?"

The turtle smiled; Chatter was no longer thinking about harshly he'd been treated. Now, he was thinking about how Rolf and Saltpepper and Blinkwink had helped him. "Yes, Chatter, I think you could."

"Oh yes. You better tell me where your tree is then Blinkwink."

Blinkwink nodded, his eyes bright and his beak open in a smile. "Thoo thoo thank you, Chatter. I thought you might decide not to help, find a place where it was quiet and where there was no trouble. I'm glad you want to help. Noo noo now, listen..."

The owl explained how to get to his tree and, if necessary, how to get to Badger Hollow because Blinkwink believed that if Rolf failed to find the owl at his nest, the squirrel would look for Stripe.

"Right," Chatter said eagerly and then looked out through the gap between the bushes. The moon was high now and shone a cold, blue light over everything. Then, in a gesture that the turtle had always considered human, Chatter blew into his hands and rubbed them together. "Oh my, but it's so very cold."

"Yes, so the quicker you get there and find Rolf, the better," the turtle said.

"You'll both still be here when I get back?" Chatter asked quietly.

"Doo doo don't you worry, Chatter. We'll be here."

Chatter nodded, satisfied and then left them. He climbed into the trees and set off for Blinkwink's tree.

Now that he was on his way, all his doubts faded and he simply wanted to find Rolf and, he realised, he also wanted the chance to pay back a couple of the animals who had turned out not to be his friends after all. The further he went, the stronger this idea grew in his mind. It made him feel warm, somehow, and helped him move from tree to tree with ease. Even when one of the branches he was gripping gave an ominous crack and then broke, the falling monkey felt no fear. He reached out with a long arm and his prehensile tail and finally grabbed another branch just before he hit the snow on the ground below. He let himself down slowly onto the packed snow and took a breather, the reaction to the fall still making his stomach churn but he was grinning anyway.

He waited until he got his breath back and then climbed back into the close-knit trees. This time, he was more careful and, a bare five minutes later, he was glad of it. He heard the sound of animals just ahead and he knew they were not squirrels.

Foxes.

Chatter nodded and snuggled into the crotch formed by three large boughs on the tree where he had stopped. He had to wait ten more minutes until the foxes moved off and he was glad they hadn't heard his heartbeat because it seemed as loud as thunder to Chatter himself.

It was about mid-morning when Chatter recognised the small stand of trees Blinkwink had told him about. Beyond these trees, the owl had said, was a small clearing, just a hop skip and jump for the monkey. On the far side of the clearing and another skip to the right and Chatter would be at Blinkwink's tree.

Chatter swung across to the closest stand of trees and then sat on his haunches on a wide branch and looked at the clearing, making sure the foxes he had seen earlier had not decided to look for food here. He watched and listened for a good five minutes and then, taking a deep breath, dropped onto the ground and hopped and skipped and jumped across the clearing. He looked to his right and saw Blinkwink's tree. He grinned and almost clapped his hands but then remembered the foxes again and rubbed them together instead. Then, still with one eye fixed on Blinkwink's huge silver birch, Chatter climbed up the bole of the tree next to it.

He climbed high and then swung across to Blinkwink's tree, right next to the nest. He peeked inside and saw nothing and then called himself an idiot.

What did you expect, monkey? Oh dear me, Rolf's injured and you expect him to climb all the way up here? Oh dear me.

Chatter tutted and began the long climb down to the foot of the tree. Paw over paw, he moved closer to the ground, ears pricked for any sound but heard nothing, not even the chirp of another bird.

On the ground, Chatter stopped muttered to himself. "Oh dear, oh my, not here. I'll have to go and—" His voice dried up and his throat closed and his heart skipped a beat when a voice spoke to him from the other side of the tree.

Stripe had woken with the dawn but Rolf had slept on, his breathing a rattle in his chest. That rattle worried Stripe and he really didn't want to stay here inside the bole of this tree. He wanted to get Rolf somewhere really safe, somewhere he would be safe until that rattle went away. But the squirrel needed rest and warmth and, since Blinkwink hadn't come home, Stripe decided to wait until Rolf woke. Maybe the owl would be back by then.

By the Lake, how the time dragged and still there was no sign of the owl and still no sign that Rolf was about to wake up. Stripe's eyes began to feel gritty and his body ached with being in the same position for so long. If he closed his eyes for a moment, he could blink away that grittiness and then he could ease his body into another position, yes just like that, that was better and now he'd be able to stay awake and wouldn't miss...

Stripe dozed and then woke with a start, which made his body jolt, and brought a moan from the disturbed Rolf.

Something, somebody was round the other side of the tree and that was bad enough. Bad enough that Stripe had fallen asleep when he was supposed to be on guard but not only was the animal on the other side of the tree, it was also muttering about finding Rolf and going to Badger Hollow to look for Stripe and that could only mean Chestnut had seen through the plan so Stripe needed to get out of this tree and kill whoever was on the other side. Right now.

Stripe came out of the hole carefully, making sure the animal hadn't come round the tree and, seeing nothing, eased himself slowly and silently round the bole of the tree. When he saw the animal who was muttering about Rolf and Blinkwink, the tension in the badger's body drained away so quickly, he felt a little light-headed. He took a long breath of the cold air and then, in as gruff a voice as he could manage and still smile, said to the animal's back:

"Harumph! Now then, why would a monkey want to go to Badger Hollow? Mmm? Humph, eh?"

Chatter stopped muttering and stopped moving so suddenly and so completely that he might have been turned into an ice-statue. Stripe waited for the monkey to realise who he was. And waited. And waited until, understanding that Chatter could probably die if he didn't take another breath, Stripe moved forward and cuffed the monkey's tail.

"Cheee cheeeit!" Chatter squeaked and jumped straight up in the air with his arm held high above his head, just as he had done the day he had met the hare. There had been a branch that day; there had *always* been a branch. This time, there was no branch.

Chatter went up and up and then came down and landed in a heap in front of Stripe. Snow billowed up and covered them both.

"Humph!" Stripe blew air through his nose to clear his face of snow. "Chatter, it's me, Stripe."

Chatter looked up, wiping snow off his face and his hands. "Oh dear me, Stripe. You gave me such a fright! I thought it was the foxes, oh dear me yes, I thought mmmf."

Stripe put a heavy paw over the monkey's mouth. "Enough. We've made enough noise. We'll have those foxes or one of that bloodydamn squirrel's spies down on us. Hush."

Chatter nodded, his eyes wide and Stripe took his paw away and beckoned the monkey to follow him.

Inside the tree, Chatter looked down at Rolf and shook his head. He could feel the tears in his eyes and he wiped at them with one long finger. The squirrel trembled in his sleep and his breath rattled in his chest and Chatter wanted to reach out and take away the illness from Rolf, take it into himself. He reached down slowly and put his arms round Rolf and then just hugged him gently, staring up at Stripe with huge, tear-filled eyes. Stripe lay down next to them and put his big paws round them both. And, still trembling, Rolf slept.

Outside, the sun moved westward, leaving the sky behind it a pale, pale blue. To the north, though, more clouds massed, dark and heavy with snow, moving once more towards Moonrise Forest.

Chatter told Stripe everything that had happened to him and about the turtle and Blinkwink and how they were waiting for him to return to the holly bushes.

"Humph, well, yes, but what about Rolf? And while you can go swinging through the trees, I have to plod across the snow."

"Oh dear," Chatter said miserably. "I...maybe...d'you think you could carry him?"

"Carry...? What?"

Stripe and Chatter looked at Rolf whose eyes were open and staring at them.

"Rolf! You're awake," Chatter said and clapped his hands.

"Chatter? Am I dead then after all?"

"Humph, not unless we all are," Stripe said. "He's real Rolf and he wants me to carry you to a place where Blinkwink is."

Rolf coughed and shook his head. "Blinkwink? Oh, yes, promises to keep, yes. Carry? Whuh..." Another fit of coughing sent dark spots flashing across his vision. When the coughing eased off, he asked Chatter to tell him where Blinkwink was and what else had happened.

When the monkey had finished, Rolf nodded and closed his eyes, thinking. "Well, Stripe, d'you think you could carry me?"

"Humph, well, I suppose I could but that's not the real problem, is it?"

"No," Rolf agreed.

"What? What's the problem, then? Oh dear, but we have to get back to the owl and the turtle."

"Yes, but we'd be out in the open," Rolf told him. "I can't climb and neither can Stripe."

"Oh," Chatter said and then sighed deeply. "Oh why couldn't we have wings? We could all fly then. I wish we had wings."

"Wishing is no good, monkey. And we still have to get there."

Chatter looked at Stripe, feeling that he'd been given a telling off he hadn't deserved.

Rolf thought so, too, and chided the badger who nodded and said he was sorry.

"Harumph, yes, well, but we *do* still have to get you there, Rolf."

Rolf nodded. "Well, maybe there's a way. I can walk. I'm not as bad as I was when I set out for this tree and that was a long way. The rest has made me feel a bit better and I could walk on my own. Now, if Chatter goes through the trees and watches for any danger, then we could hide and wait for it to pass. If we left late, when there's plenty of shadow, we could stay in the shadows and that would help, too." He looked at Stripe.

Stripe gave the squirrel a look that Rolf thought meant the badger didn't think much of the plan. Stripe, though, thought the plan was a good one and, more to the point, he thought that Saltpepper had known what he was doing when he chose Rolf as his successor. "I think it could work," he said slowly. "And, if you get tired, I could carry you for a while."

"Oh good! Oh yes, let's go then, eh?" Chatter clapped his hands.

Rolf laughed and then another fit of coughing doubled him up. Chatter stopped clapping and called himself a stupid monkey for making Rolf cough again.

Rolf got over the fit and smiled, shaking his head. "Oh, don't apologise, Chatter. It feels good to laugh. I didn't think I'd ever laugh again so it was worth a cough. But we'll wait a while. Till the sun sets in the lake. Then we'll see. It'll take a long time, I think but at least we'll be on the move.

While they waited, Stripe made Chatter describe the route he had taken. Chatter told them and the badger and squirrel memorised the reference points. It was an hour before they felt it was dark enough to set out.

"Off you go, Chatter," Rolf said and the monkey left them.

Chatter went about a hundred yards into the forest and saw nothing to worry him. The light in the trees was a dark purple but where the sun was setting, the sky was a dark orange. Chatter looked north and saw the heavy clouds and he knew they would hide the moon tonight and that was good. He thought it was about as fair and hopeful a beginning as they could hope for and hurried back to the tree.

Rolf went in front with Stripe following behind so he could see when the squirrel began to tire. Chatter padded alongside Rolf until they reached the place where he had stopped on his first check. While Chatter went into the trees again, the other two waited close to the wide bole of an ash tree

Rolf felt quite good. Oh, his legs were trembling and his wounds pulled and itched at him but he thought that might be a good thing, a sign they might be healing. Breathing was difficult but he still felt he could walk a fair way.

"Harumph, well so far so good," Stripe said as the monkey left them. "And the forest thickens up from here and that's good." He relaxed against the tree, waiting for Chatter.

Chatter was back and above Stripe before the badger was even of aware of his approach. Despite his surprise, Stripe was pleased; Chatter had learned to be careful and quiet.

Chatter told them that there were some sounds ahead but not on the path they would be taking. He thought they might be foxes because the noises were gruff but Stripe shook his head.

"More likely some of my badgers, doing whatever that bloodydamn squirrel wants. Humph, night-guard."

This made the three animals feel a lot better; if there were badgers out there, there wouldn't be foxes and the chances of getting a good distance without problems were better. They set off again.

They passed the second checkpoint and kept going. Chatter went ahead and he was thinking that this trek was turning into more of an evening stroll. Still, he was careful and he knew he was being careful and this made him feel rather proud. When he thought back to how he had been when he first arrived he realised he had been too harem-scarem, even scatty. Now, he was more grown up and responsible and it pleased him that he was going to get Rolf back to where the turtle and Blinkwink waited. What happened then, well, he didn't know and it didn't really matter. Not yet. His job now was to make sure the path was clear.

So they went on for what seemed like an age. Rolf felt the time more than the other two. His illness and injuries meant he was putting the badger and the monkey in danger for too long but each time he tried to quicken his pace, he ended up breathless and had to rest for a longer period. Stripe finally lost his temper and told Rolf that he was doing exactly the opposite of what he wanted because trying to go faster actually slowed them down. Chatter agreed but in a gentler voice, and pointed out that they were actually half-way and the sun was still an hour from rising so they had done well.

When they reached the next of Blinkwink's reference points, Stripe called a halt even though Chatter had spied out another trouble-free hundred yards. They were in a small clearing in an otherwise dense part of the forest and the place felt safe.

Rolf didn't argue because he was bone-tired. He nodded and lay down under the thick tangle of bush and Stripe placed himself next to him. Chatter climbed a tall tree on the edge of the clearing because it offered him a long forward sight of their path.

"I'm not tired at all, oh no. I'll keep watch while you rest. Oh, we're getting along this journey really well, aren't we?" Chatter said and then climbed the tree.

Rolf was soon asleep and Stripe dozed next to him. Chatter didn't feel tired but he felt relaxed and pleased and the path ahead was clear of anything but the spreading light of the new day. The clearing was safe and the path was safe and the clearing smelled wonderful, clean and fresh and, most of all, *safe* and Chatter didn't notice that his eyes were closing and his head was nodding. He wasn't really asleep but he wasn't fully awake, either.

The noise seemed to be coming from every direction when it finally imposed itself in Chatter's mind. His eyes opened wide and he turned his head urgently, trying to locate the right direction.

Oh asleep on duty! Asleep on watch! Stupid stupid stupid!

He shook his head to clear his thoughts and his stupidity, his *crime* came home to him with a sickening thud that made his stomach roll.

Two foxes were sniffing round the back of the bush were Rolf and Stripe were sleeping.

Chatter moved as quickly as he could without making a noise. If he could get down without the foxes hearing him, he might still be able to make amends. If he could get down and then across the clearing before the foxes actually decided to attack the bush, then they might be surprised. Chatter could charge them, making as much noise as possible and that would wake up Stripe. And Chatter had the feeling that Stripe was not an animal to mess with when he came out fighting.

He landed silently on the ground and grinned when he saw a thick branch lying on top of the snow. He picked it up and hefted it in both hands, grinning at its weight. He took a deep breath and then padded towards the foxes.

The bush exploded with a deep growling noise and Stripe came out with his paws showing wickedly sharp claws.

"Chatter! Harumph, come on now!" Stripe yelled and swiped at the nearest fox, taking out its left eye.

Chatter screeched and galloped across the clearing. He swung the branch over his right shoulder.

The unhurt fox howled and then growled at the badger. "Gggrr I'm going to kill you badger."

"Come on then," Stripe told him, one eyes watching the charging monkey.

The fox tensed all his muscles, ready to spring.

Chatter reached the fox and brought the branch down. Hard. It connected with the side of the fox's head and blood spurted from the fox's ear. The connection thudded all the way up Chatter's arm and it felt just fine, oh dear me, *yes!*

The fox crumpled and then its eyes closed and everything was blackness.

Stripe dismissed the fox and turned on the first fox, ripping into the animal's face and throat. The fox tried to howl but it was impossible with the agony in its face and then everything faded, faded and was black.

Chatter hit his fox again, this time on the back of its head and then dropped the branch. He grabbed the fox around the head and yanked hard, twisting to his right. The crack of the fox's neck breaking seemed very loud.

Finally, Stripe stood away from his dead fox and Chatter grinned at him. They were both breathing hard but they knew they had won and neither could stop grinning.

"Stripe? Stripe, Chatter, will somebody answer me for Lake's sake!" Rolf's voice was harsh and then he was coughing hard.

"Humph, it's fine, Rolf. Everything's fine. Come on out now."

Rolf emerged from the bush and then gaped at the two dead foxes. "Dead? You killed them both?"

"Oh dear me, yes," Chatter told him, still grinning. He picked up the branch. "This and Stripe's claws were too good for them."

Rolf shook his head. "Well," he said and then shook his head again.

"Harumph, the monkey knows how to fight," Stripe said and patted Chatter's shoulder. "Suppose we should hide the bodies, eh?"

Rolf shook his head. "No, I don't think so. I think if we leave them, it might help us. A mystery to keep them guessing and stop them from hunting us. But we should get away from here right now."

"There could be any number of reasons for them being late," the turtle said when he waddled back to the holly bushes after another fruitless look to see if Chatter was back.

"Yoo yoo yes," Blinkwink agreed. "If Chatter found Rolf, it would certainly make them late. Rolf must be hurt and they won't be able to travel quickly."

All true but it didn't make either Blinkwink or the turtle feel any better.

The turtle nodded and for a while, neither animal spoke. Blinkwink ruffled his feathers again and they felt no better than the one time he had left the shelter. He had tested his flight feathers and the test had only confirmed what he knew—they were not yet right and definitely not up to any long flights. While he was outside, he had caught some food. A water rat had strayed too far from the bank and the owl's talons had done their job. Blinkwink had eaten it but without much relish and now all he could do was sit and wait. Like the turtle.

The turtle was restless, worried about what could have happened to Chatter. Waiting was hard, not knowing was harder to take; it left too much to the turtle's imagination.

"Blinkwink, I'm going into the lake. I've been out of water too long and I feel the need of it. Will you be alright?"

"I'm dry and fed and over all but my most serious injuries. I'm also worried about Chatter and Rolf and that means if anything threatens me, they'll find an owl who is fit enough and angry enough to make them regret it. Yoo yoo you go and find the water, turtle."

Before he got to water, the turtle had to cross a lot of ice. The winter was going to be very hard and didn't need any help to make the forest animals' lives miserable. But there was more trouble, wasn't there? The foxes and the renegade squirrel.

The turtle glided into the water and began to swim as fast as he could, relishing the feel of the water on his shell and in his face. The movement of the water against him and the almost mindless way in which he swam, his eyes seeing nothing but water and his ears hearing nothing but the low swoosh of the water's movement, helped ease his restlessness and the worry he felt for Chatter.

It was as he turned back towards the shore, some hundred yards west of the holly bushes where Blinkwink was, that the turtle's ears heard something other than the sound of the moving water. He stopped swimming and paddled the water with his large flippers. He stared towards the shore and there, lit by the fading light of the day, was a figure whose arms were waving.

"And there's only one animal in Moonrise Forest who looks like a monkey," the turtle burbled and then grinned as he stroked towards the waving Chatter.

"Oh hurry, turtle! Oh dear me, hurry!"

By the time Stripe, annoyingly 'helped' by Chatter, had told the owl and the turtle what had happened, the early evening had become the late night and, finally, the early hours of the morning. The space between the holly bushes had narrowed down to a crack as all the animals crowded together. The turtle had taken his usual place at the entrance.

"Woo woo well, here we all are," Blinkwink said. "Quite good, really. Considering that three of us are supposed to be dead. Noo noo now we have to decide what needs to be done and what we can do."

"Humph, that's easy. We need to get rid of that bloodydamn squirrel," Stripe told them and nodded his broad, flat head.

The turtle smiled; the badger was never going to be one who beat around the bush.

"Yes," Blinkwink agreed. "But it is easier said than done."

"Humph."

Chatter looked as if he were thinking very hard, trying to sort out something in his mind before saying anything. Rolf was, at best, in a light doze. It was while he looked at Rolf that the turtle changed the point of the discussion completely.

"You're right, Stripe. About the bloodydamn squirrel but, first, I think we have to decide what we can do about *this* squirrel. He's ill and from what I've heard, he will be the one who leads any opposition against this Chestnut. Rolf needs to be well before he can do that. He needs rest but he needs something done about the infection he's got. And I've no idea what we can do about that."

The others looked at Rolf, knowing that what the turtle had said was true and knowing that they had no answers either. The turtle looked from one animal to other and wondered if any of them had any idea what herbs or plants might help Rolf. Or, if they didn't, whether they knew any other animal here in the forest who did. He was about to ask this when his mind seemed to light up. He closed his mouth and tried to work out what it was his mind seemed to be hinting at. If he failed to grasp whatever had flared for that second in his mind, he had the feeling that he could end up being witness to the death of the animal they all knew was their only real hope in beating Chestnut the renegade squirrel. While he thought about all of this, the turtle was aware of the other animals talking.

Blinkwink was asking Rolf how ill he felt and if he thought he might recover on his own. Stripe, meanwhile, was talking to Chatter, probably about some new battle-plan. The turtle could sense a mutual respect between the badger and the monkey, no doubt the result of the small battle they had fought and won together. Yes, it took all sorts. The turtle had learnt that many times since the witch had cast her spell and...

The witch.

Yes, that was what his mind was trying to tell him. The two words echoed loudly in his head and, finally, they echoed too loudly to be kept inside his mind so he let them out.

"The witch!"

The others turned sharply to look at him. Chatter actually got to his back legs, the branch, which he had brought with him, held in his hands.

"Oh no, not here, not now," the monkey said, eyes wide, head twisting as he tried to see the witch.

"No, no," the turtle said to Chatter. "Not here. Hush now."

"Woo woo what's a witch?" Blinkwink asked.

The turtle explained by telling them the story he had told Chatter all those months ago. When he finished, there was a disbelieving silence and the turtle could not blame them for that. He understood that disbelief but he really thought the witch was Rolf's only hope.

Rolf, even though he seemed to have been asleep, had listened to the story and accepted it without condition. He had no idea why but he accepted this, too.

"Well," Rolf began and then had to wait for another bout of coughing to subside. "Well, you better explain why you think she can help or even why she should care what happens here in the forest." He coughed again.

"Whether she'll help or not, I don't know," the turtle agreed. "But she will certainly know *how* to help. And I don't think we have any other ideas."

"Harumph, she turns you into a turtle and leaves you to paddle around in the cold and wet and you expect us to pad over to her cottage and hand Rolf over?" Stripe shook his head and grumbled. "As if we haven't got enough trouble with that bloodydamn squirrel and the foxes."

"Oh dear, turtle but he's right." Chatter shrugged, sorry for doubting his friend but there it was.

"What about you, owl? D'you think I'm mad to even think it?"

Blinkwink ruffled his feathers and cocked his head to one side. "I think you believe what you say but..."

The turtle nodded and looked down at the ground. The quiet was very heavy and seemed to last a lot longer than the minute it actually did. When it was broken, they were all surprised that it was Rolf who spoke.

"You know," the squirrel said slowly, waiting for the coughing to begin. When it didn't, he continued. "When I heard your story, I thought, well, forgive me if it sounds ungrateful...but it sounded like you brought it on yourself." He took a careful breath.

"No, no you're not wrong, Rolf."

Rolf nodded. "Ah. Well, I think that this witch might be a little like Saltpepper. What she did was harsh but Saltpepper taught me many things and sometimes he had to be harsh to make me see. I fought against that harshness a lot of the time but now, now I see that, even when he was hard with me, he was right." Rolf blinked away the tears as he remembered his old master. "I'm grateful for those lessons now and I think you might feel a little that way, too?"

The turtle nodded and smiled.

"Right," Rolf said and nodded. "Then I think we should go to see this witch."

"I think Rolf's right," Blinkwink said.

"I'll do what everybody else wants to do," Chatter said quietly. "But, oh my, I hope she doesn't turn me into a turtle."

"Humph, well, we're all in this together, I suppose," Stripe said doubtfully. "And I suppose I can see where it might help Rolf but..."

"Thoo thoo there is another reason," Blinkwink said, mostly to Stripe. "Moonrise Forest is no longer a safe place for you or me and definitely not for Rolf." He turned to the turtle. "D'you think the witch's nest will be big enough for all of us?"

The turtle smiled at the owl's small joke and nodded. When Stripe asked how they were all going to get there, the turtle smiled again and said he was going to see what the weather was like.

Outside the holly shelter, the afternoon was fading fast and the turtle could see by the sky that there would be no moonlight tonight; he doubted there would be any sunlight tomorrow. The clouds over both the forest and the lake were very heavy and the air felt full of sharp teeth. Still, there was no wind and that was something. He turned back and told the others, looking mostly at Stripe, that he thought he could get them all across to the cottage safe and sound.

"I'll explain it all in the morning," he said. "I'll spend tonight in the water." He looked at Stripe. "I hope the weather stays as it is now, Stripe," he said and burbled a laugh and left them for the night.

"Harumph, what was all that about?" Stripe wondered, looking at Chatter.

Chatter said nothing but he thought he had a good idea what that had been all about and he *definitely* didn't want to be the one to explain it to the badger.

"You are *what*?"

Stripe sounded and, to the turtle and Chatter, looked, comical. His black eyes were wide and his whole face seemed to have gone slack. Surprise wasn't the right word but shock probably was.

"I'm going to give you a ride across the lake on my back. I'll land you as close to the cottage as I can. The weather is perfect for it this morning. There isn't any wind."

"Harumph! There is not a chance, absolutely not a single chance that I will—"

"If I didn't know you boo boo better," Blinkwink said softly. "I'd think you sounded scared. But that can't be right, can it?" He hoped he hadn't crossed the line and so made the badger angry enough to be stubborn. Or to fight.

"Humph, being scared has nothing to do with it," Stripe said indignantly. "This cottage is a ways from the place where I'll be meeting Bumper when it's time. Going round the shore's too dangerous."

"Stripe," the turtle said lightly. "I can carry you back any time you need to be here. Come on, it'll take a few minutes and you'll be over the water and where you need to be. I may be slow as a summer's afternoon on land but there's nothing quicker or surer in the water than me. I promise you, the breeze won't bother you and the water's as flat as the Midge Marsh in

August." He looked at Stripe and saw that he was at last considering the possibility but he still wasn't totally convinced. Then the turtle had an inspiration. "Tell you what, you can watch while I take Blinkwink across and you'll—" He was interrupted by the sound of wings flapping and a stammering noise coming from the owl who was settled at the front of the holly bushes.

"Woo woo wait a minute, turtle. Just hold on a minute. Nobody is taking me anywhere. I can fly across the lake to the cottage a lot faster than you can swim."

Chatter giggled. "Oh, chee chee, chachee!" He held his arms across his chest and collapsed to the ground where he rolled around.

The turtle gaped at him and then burbled his own laughter and even Stripe saw the funny side to all of this and began to chortle. Then he got control of himself.

"Blinkwink, think about what you're saying," the badger said as gently as the owl had talked to him. "Your flight feathers aren't up to a short hop across dry land and you're talking about risking another dunking in the lake."

The owl riffled his feathers and nodded. "Yoo yoo you're right, Stripe. And I'm a confounded idiot. The important thing is Rolf and we have to get him some help. Soo soo so, I'll be first across."

"Good, sense at last," the turtle said.

"Good!" Chatter said and clapped his hands as he got up. "And then I can have another ride with my friend. Oh yes, good, good."

The turtle smiled and thought that, if for no other reason than to keep their hearts light, they needed their chatterbox.

As the five of them made their way down to the water's edge, Chatter began to give what he thought was helpful advice about how to ride the turtle's back but a short 'humph!' from Stripe warned him off. Instead, he squatted next to Rolf and the badger and watched the turtle carry Blinkwink across the lake.

It was an hour past sunrise, though there was no sun to see, and a thin mist drifted across the water on the far side of the lake. The turtle moved into the mist and, for a few moments, they all lost sight of him and the owl on his back. Stripe fidgeted but Rolf stared straight ahead, a dreamy look in his eyes. Stripe breathed out when he saw Blinkwink appear on the other side of the bank of mist and finally alighted on dry land again. While he waited for the turtle to return, the badger mumbled to himself about there being nothing to worry about, nothing at all to worry about. Chatter only looked at him once and then concentrated on watching for the turtle to return.

For Blinkwink, the trip was an unexpected delight. The turtle moved fast and smoothly through the water and the wind generated by their crossing felt wonderful in the owl's feathers. He felt himself smiling as the mist touched his face and he felt truly alive again.

When the turtle arrived back, he looked at Stripe but the badger was still chunnering to himself and the turtle decided to leave him until the next time.

"Well, Rolf, are you ready?"

"I'm not sure ready is the right word but I'll go next. If Chatter can help me up."

Chatter eased Rolf onto the turtle's thick shell and waved as they set off. Rolf didn't look back or even forward; the journey was necessary and he treated it that way. He kept his eyes closed and lay on his belly, trying to be as flat as possible. The smooth, lulling movement was something he thought he might grow accustomed to if he wanted but it was soon over and he slid down onto the ground next to Blinkwink.

Once he was on the turtle's back, Stripe hung on with his claws like grim death. He muttered all the way across and almost growled when a small wavelet crossed their path and he felt his balance tilt. The turtle compensated quickly and the badger went back to muttering to himself until he clambered off onto dry land again. The turtle headed back across the lake, knowing that the badger would never accept the water even if circumstances forced him to do it again.

When the turtle got back, there was no sign of Chatter. He was loath to call out in case there were foxes nearby. He paddled a short way eastwards and then the same distance westward. He came out of the water at the setting off point and was about to call out anyway when the monkey dropped down from the tree he had been in.

"What're you doing?" There was an edge in the turtle's voice.

Chatter blinked at that edge and twisted his hands together. "Sorry, oh my. But I heard noises and went up to have a look. In case it was trouble."

"Was it?"

"No. Well, not really. When I was up in the tree and a bit closer, the noise sounded a bit like Stripe. All, you know, gruff and huff? So I think it's another badger and it's coming this way."

"You're sure it wasn't just gruff, like a fox?"

"Oh dear no. Stripe's gruff but you know how he sounds when he just doesn't want to let on that you're a friend or he's pleased with you? Like that."

The turtle nodded; the frightened monkey he sent into the forest was long gone now. Back then, the monkey would have just heard the gruff and bluster and been scared. Now, he didn't just see beyond the gruff and bluster but he could explain it, too; maybe the turtle hadn't done everybody a bad turn after all.

"I think it might be Stripe's friend, Bumper," the turtle said. "I'll go back into the water. He knows about you but not about me and I might just scare him off."

Chatter nodded and faced the trees again, waiting. He didn't have to wait long. Bumper padded out of the trees and right up to the monkey. He had been half-expecting to find the monkey after picking up Stripe's scent. Chatter explained everything that had happened and suggested that Bumper come and meet the turtle. The monkey was a little surprised at how quickly the badger agreed to this and how easily he seemed to take to the turtle when the turtle came out of the water. Bumper even laughed a little when the turtle told him about Stripe crossing the lake. Chatter noticed, though, that the look in Bumper's eyes when he looked at the water was the same as Stripe's had been.

"I just want him to know that it's so far so good. Tell him I don't expect to have much to report for a while. Say another cycle of the moon and I'll meet him here. D'you think that's a good idea?"

"I'm sure it is," the turtle told him. "And Stripe will think so, too. Anyway, it's time we got back across the lake and you should be away from here. Just in case a squirrel or fox wanders down here and wonders what you're doing here."

Bumper nodded. "This...witch? You're sure about it?"

"To be honest, I can't be absolutely sure, no. But Rolf is very sick and the forest's too dangerous and I can't think of anything better. But knowing you're here and on our side makes me feel better."

"Thank you," Bumper said and dropped his eyes, a little embarrassed. "Rolf's very...important," he went on. "If she takes you in, this witch, d'you think she'll be...can she make him well?"

"The truthful answer is, I don't know. But...my heart says she can."

Bumper seemed satisfied with this and waited until the monkey had climbed on the turtle's back before saying goodbye. Bumper was grinning and shaking his head as he walked away; the monkey had hopped up as if he were climbing a tree instead of setting off across Sunset Lake.

"Thought you'd sunk," Stripe grumbled when they reached the shore.

"Sorry about that," apologised the turtle. "We have a good reason, though."

"Oh dear yes," Chatter agreed.

"Humph. What?"

So they told him and the others about Bumper and it cheered Stripe. Blinkwink seemed even more pleased.

"Woo woo we can give him messages," the owl said eagerly, riffling his wings. "He can give messages to the other animals who want to fight back against Chestnut."

"Humph, only one message I want to give," Stripe said and growled. "That Rolf's well and he's coming back to sort out that bloodydamn squirrel. That'll be a message and a half."

"Oh Stripe, will you listen?" Blinkwink blinked his large eyes and shook his head. "It will take time for Rolf to recover and we'll have plans to make. You can tell Bumper what those plans are and he can tell the other forest animals so everything will be ready when Rolf is well enough to cross the lake again. Birds will have steered clear of Chestnut and I'll have things for them to do. You can believe that."

Stripe reluctantly agreed and he and the owl, Chatter and the turtle were so busy discussing things that they all failed to hear Rolf who was trying to talk to them. Finally, running out of patience, Rolf did the only thing he could think of to get their attention. Chatter's tail was flicking from side to side excitedly so the squirrel took careful aim and caught it in his teeth as it passed him again.

"Cheeyit!" Chatter squeaked and jumped in the air. The others stopped talking and looked at Rolf with stunned expressions.

"At last," Rolf wheezed. "I'm glad you all think I'll soon be on the mend but, right now, I feel terrible. If we're going to see if this witch will help, can we please do it now?" He put his head on his front paws and tried to get his breath back.

They all apologised to Rolf and then the turtle raised a flipper and waved it to the right. "It's over there," he told them. "Chatter, d'you think you could carry Rolf?"

Chatter nodded and bent down to Rolf who apologised for nipping his tail and smiled. Chatter picked him up carefully and they all followed the turtle across the snow. Stripe walked with a wary look on his face but his eyes were determined. Blinkwink hopped and walked by turn, knowing that he still wasn't up to actually flying too far.

The ground beneath the deep snow rose away from the lakeside and Chatter was soon puffing with effort. He told them he needed to take a breather and they stopped for five minutes. Rolf sat on his haunches, his eyes dreamy, almost closed, wondering what awaited them when they finally reached this cottage. When Chatter picked him up again, the squirrel closed his eyes and decided that what would happen would happen and no amount of wondering would change things.

They saw the smoke before they saw the cottage because of the rise of the land and even Rolf opened his eyes for the last part of the journey. When they breasted the rise, they all stopped and looked at the cottage.

The cottage was plain brick and stone with no colour unless you counted dull grey a colour. Even the door seemed to be that same stone grey as the rest of the building. The door was in the centre of the building, a window on each side. The windows, too, were grey as they reflected the sky. The roof was steep and almost came down to touch the snow. Nothing marred the whiteness of the roof, not even a single bird track and the animals wondered if anybody living there could be on their side if not even flying birds paused to rest on the cottage. Between them and the door was a picket fence, which obviously ran all the way round the cottage.

Chatter put Rolf down and then all five animals stood and looked at the cottage. The silence was as deep as the snow and even the wind, which had begun to gust when they crested the rise, seemed to cease. Without a word, all four began to walk slowly towards the gate in the fence. When they reached the closed gate, they stopped again and stared at the windows, which showed no sign of life except for their own wavery images. It was Stripe who finally broke the heavy quiet.

"Harumph," he said and then coughed to clear his throat. "I...I think it's up to you, turtle."

"Yes," the turtle said quietly. "Chatter, you'll have to open the gate and knock at the door for me."

Chatter opened the gate and pushed it as far as it would go against the drift of snow behind it. He waited while the other four passed through and then he closed the gate behind them. He didn't know why he did this but it felt right. When they reached the door, Chatter looked at the knocker and a lion's head that gleamed even in the grey light of the winter's day looked back at him.

With a long sigh, Chatter took hold of the lion's head and lifted it slowly then, looking once at the turtle who nodded, he let it fall. It seemed to take a long, long time before the head made a dull clanking noise as it hit the plate.

The turtle, the monkey, the badger and the owl all stared at the door and all had the same thought; there was smoke so the witch was in but they did they really want her to answer the knock at her door?

Rolf smiled and did not really know why.

But the door remained closed until, without them hearing any noise or, it seemed, without anything at all happening, the door stood open. From beyond the open door, from inside the cottage, a voice spoke.

"So my Lord Turtle, you have come back. And with others, it seems. Well, come in and quickly. My door knows its place and is not fond of being out of it for long."

There was laughter then but it held no threat, only the gentle sound of amusement, which seemed to float out of the cottage and envelop the five animals at the door.

Rolf's smile turned into a grin and he was the first to enter the cottage. Seeing him limp inside, the others could only stare at his apparent eagerness.

"He is ill," the voice said. "Will you let him struggle so? And my door is beginning to think it is past time it was in its place."

The four animals followed Rolf into the cottage. Chatter turned to close the door and found that it was already closing. It closed gently but firmly with a sound like a whisper.

For better or worse, they had arrived.

Chapter Six

The afternoon had given way to twilight, which gave way to winter-night. The wind howled and hooted round the cottage, its sound enough to make your bones ache and your teeth click together. But in this cottage, the roaring fire in the ingle defeated the cold. It sent out waves of heat that the animals luxuriated in despite their wariness. To the right of the ingle was a door leading to a kitchen, and, as soon as she had made sure Rolf was only asleep and not unconscious, the witch had gone there and made them all food.

They were all surprised that the food she offered them was exactly what they would have chosen for themselves and all of them were sure that, somehow, the food had been ready and waiting for them to arrive, as if the witch had known they were coming. None of them doubted this was true. Despite the good food, Rolf had only been able to rouse himself enough to sip at some water before lapsing back into a doze.

While they ate, the witch said nothing, simply sat in the rocker close to the fire and puffed on a long-stemmed clay pipe which she lit using a taper from the brass vase in the hearth. She looked at the leaping flames of the fire and smoked the pipe, sending thin wreaths of blue-tinged smoke over her head. The rocker squeaked as she moved, a soft sound, almost a lullaby.

When they had all finished their food, the witch turned from and looked at each of them in turn. Then she spoke. "Now that you have all eaten and the warmth has eased your bodies, I'm sure you are all wondering again if it was such a good idea to come here." She smiled as they all seemed to sit up straighter. "Well, we'll see but, for warmth and food, I think there should be a price, don't you?"

Stripe stood up, foursquare, hackles rising, a deep thrumming in his chest that sounded like a low wind in the forest. He glared at the witch.

"Ah Stripe," she said quietly. "You believe all your doubts were justified?" She held his gaze for a moment and then turned back to the fire.

Stripe growled deeper but, even as he did so, he was trying hard to recall if he had told the witch his name. He could not remember at all but she had called him by his name. He began to get ready to fight.

"Relax, Stripe, you old gruff-grouch. My price will not be hard to pay. Not for any of you. It might be painful but that will not be my doing. All I want is to know how you all came to be here." She turned back to face them again. "Will you pay this price? It seems fair to me."

Chatter was sitting again, his tail curled round him, held by his left hand, which picked at the fur. When the witch caught his eye, he felt as if he were looking into the fire. He tried to look away but found he could only stare into those deep, burning eyes.

"Chatter, will you not tell me your story? It seems right. You did not start it all as you may think but you were there at its beginning. And," she said and smiled. "Doesn't it sound like a fine idea to talk and know that I will listen without interruption? Mmm? To be able to talk as much as you like and have nobody tell you to shush?"

Chatter sighed and, still looking into the witch's eyes, told her everything. He began with the circus and finished with his knock at her front door. She listened as she had promised, looking away from the monkey only to relight her pipe.

When Chatter had finished, Blinkwink told her everything he had seen and done. He needed no gentle persuasion because he sensed that there was no threat at all in the witch. Stripe, more reluctantly, told his tale. He told it in a straightforward way with little passion, a matter of reporting. Except when he mentioned that bloodydamn squirrel; then his voice was hard and his eyes blazed.

While the others talked, the turtle was watching the shadows thrown by the fire. They moved on the walls and in the corners but they held none of the fear shadows sometimes hold. Except, he noticed, when the others mentioned Chestnut; then, the shadows deepened and seemed to grow and become menacing. When it was his turn, the turtle told his story simply and quickly.

When the turtle finished, the witch nodded and stopped rocking in the chair. "Yes, and Saltpepper's heir shows the marks to prove how all your stories are intertwined."

The turtle nodded. "He is the reason we are all here but I believe you knew that even before we arrived. If the price for your help is a tale, perhaps you will not help him since he is unable to tell his own story. Is that how it is?"

"You want me to make him well, Lord Turtle? You ask nothing for yourself? Not one small favour for you?"

Chatter and Blinkwink and Stripe looked from the witch to the turtle; there was something here that they had forgotten for a while in their anxiousness for Rolf. The turtle was looking directly at the witch, barely breathing and not moving at all. The moment seemed to stretch the way an earthworm would stretch when it was pulled from the ground by a feeding animal. Finally, the turtle spoke again.

"We are here for Rolf..." He shook his head once. "No, we are for the *forest* and therefore we are here for Rolf. He is very ill and possibly getting worse. We ask your help to make him better or at least more comfortable. He has suffered a lot because of what has happened to him and to the forest. The forest is his home and the animals his family. The forest has been poisoned and maybe that poison is inside Rolf." He swallowed and looked at the floor. "As for myself, I feel I have a debt to pay but more than that, I believe these four deserve your help." He looked up into the witch's eyes once again. "Will you help Rolf and these others?"

Stripe and Blinkwink felt the turtle's speech and request was undeniable. Chatter, too, felt this but he also felt a deep pride in his friend the turtle.

The witch smiled. It was the type of smile they had all hoped for, even Stripe. It was slow and touched her eyes before it reached the corners of her mouth. That smile seemed to fill them all with a warmth to outdo even the roaring fire. On the floor, Rolf stirred and struggled to raise his head. He looked at the witch who looked down at him, still smiling. Then she left her chair and bent down to him.

"Ah Rolf," she said and lifted him up from the floor and cradled him in her arms. She sat down in the chair again. "Young master Rolf," she said.

And Rolf thought of Saltpepper who had called him by those same words. "I..." Rolf began and then wheezed a shallow breath. "I would be grateful for any help," he managed before having to take another breath. "I have a story and I will tell you if you want. At least...I will try."

The others saw tears in her eyes when the witch replied to Rolf. "I'm sure you have a story, young Rolf and I will hear it when you can tell it. But there will be no price for anything I do for you. I can make you comfortable but I can only *try* to heal you. There is little here that magic can touch, I'm afraid. Still, I have other skills and I will use them all. For now, close your eyes and I will sing to you." She stroked the top of his head and Rolf's eyes closed. "Think only of good things," she told him gently. "Of these four good friends who brought you here and of spring blossom and summer trees." She leaned back in the chair and began to rock gently as she sang her song.

Later, none of the animals could say whether it was watching her rock or the soft squeak of the chair that seemed to counterpoint the song or only the song itself, but they were all lulled by the melody and they were all soon asleep.

Chatter dreamed of his old friend the elephant. Stripe fought the song on principle but it soon overtook him and he dreamed of his old grandfather who had told him that a body's actions said more about them than a body's words. Blinkwink dreamed of high places and of a bird he had heard tell of once when he was an owlet. This bird, he was told, had wings that hid the sun from the ground. The turtle was beginning to drift off into his own dreams when the witch spoke to him.

"Before you take your rest, Lord Turtle, I think we should talk. Just you and I?"

The turtle blinked and nodded.

"The answer you gave me," she said softly. "I gladly accept it but, now that it is just the two of us, are you sure there is no favour you would ask of me? You must know that I would grant it now."

"Thank you," the turtle said and his eyes blinked slowly once again. "But no. It's hard to explain but...well, I'm an animal now, just like these others." His voice was light, almost carefree. "They are my friends and I believe that they and all they know are in great danger. What they have told me has filled me with great wonder and I feel honoured that I have, for some reason, been brought into it all. I want to do what I can for them. It's why I brought them here. If...I believe that I would not be able to help them if I were returned to my true form. I would lose my...place here."

"You don't think you could help them more if you were returned to your natural form?"

The turtle thought that the question had barbs in it as the witch looked deeply into his eyes but he answered it simply and as honestly as his animal heart told him to answer. "I don't believe I would be *allowed* to help in my true form."

The witch smiled and in that smile, the turtle understood that she knew he had found the true answer in his heart. She nodded and turned back to the fire. She lifted her hand off Rolf's head and lit her pipe once more and resumed her song. Soon, the turtle was asleep but if he dreamed, he could not remember them exactly when he woke, only that they had been of Rolf.

"You're positive he's not in the Hollow? If I find out later that he was there and you missed him, you'll be dealt with. You understand that, don't you?"

The Chief Squirrel's voice was light, almost cheerful and his madness was all the more terrible because of it. The squirrel who had brought the news was almost paralysed by that madness but with an enormous effort of will, he managed to nod and to say, "Positive, Chief."

Chestnut nodded and looked at his paws. "You followed them? When they left here? That...Bumper? And the young one, the simple one...Peaty? They made no contact with any other badgers?"

"No, Chief. They went straight to the Hollow and stayed there."

This was the truth as far as the squirrel knew but the badgers grubbed for food at night and seemed to stay in their setts most of the day; if the squirrel was to keep an eye on them, he needed to do the same. So, the squirrel had not seen Bumper make his trip to the lakeside.

Chestnut nodded again. "Good. That means the old grouch is dead and gone. Fine. All right, you can go. Leave off following Bumper, too. See the guard at the new store-tree and tell him you get enough food for two days."

When he was alone in his drey, Chestnut picked up a nut and cracked it and ate its fruit and smacked his lips. When he had finished, he rubbed his teeth and grinned at how good he felt, how alive and well-fed and warm.

"A walk," he said softly and left the drey.

The two guards stood to attention but he passed them without a word and they knew better than to do or say anything without his leave. They watched him scamper down the tree and head towards the creek and, when he was out of sight, they let out long breaths of relief and talked of mundane things. Foxes or their Chief's state of mind were not topics of discussion for the simple reason that neither trusted the other; there were spies everywhere.

Chestnut walked steadily across the snow, revelling in the fact that he *could* walk rather than climb and clamber through the trees. Of course, one of his new rules was that squirrels could only use trees for travel with his express permission. Chestnut could climb or walk as he pleased. Right now, he wanted to walk to the creek and he was walking. As he walked, he was aware of other squirrels out and about but he never saw them because they didn't want to be seen by him and this knowledge that his power was absolute made his grin wider.

The sky was heavy and the air frigid and he knew the winter would be even worse than everybody had expected. This pleased Chestnut because, after a long and bitter winter, his position would be completely unassailable and nothing, not even the foxes, would be able to threaten that position.

"Not even the foxes," Chestnut murmured as he sat beside the frozen creek. He chuckled. "Even now, when he no longer needs to be *allowed* into the forest, their Big Boss comes when I need to see him. I don't even have to send him a message." He was about to laugh aloud at this but his mind suddenly turned on him and his mouth turned down into a grimace.

How does he know when to come?

Chestnut squeezed his eyes closed and snapped his head from side to side. He let out a sound that was almost a growl. Then he opened his eyes and looked at the sky. "It doesn't matter," he hissed. "It's enough that he does. I am the Chief Squirrel and, with the others gone, this is *my* forest. That is all that matters!"

A snowflake landed on his snout and was melted by the hot breath he exhaled. He breathed deeply for a few minutes and then looked down at the frozen surface of the creek and watched more flakes land. He nodded.

"Yes, snow and snow and snow. Wild nights and freezing days. Days filled with fear. That's good, very good. Yes, Moonrise Forest is mine and after the winter it will be mine forever and nothing will take it from me. I will rule everything and everybody come spring."

This time, the laughter came and it was full of evil. As if on command, the snow began to fall thick and fast and Chestnut nodded; even the weather was his to rule. He was still chuckling when he arrived home. The two guards were stiff with cold but neither had moved from his post.

"Go and find some shelter," Chestnut told them absently as he went inside his drey. "Just stay within calling distance."

The two guards hurried through the driving snow to their own dreys in the trees either side of Chestnut's. Chestnut settled into the warmth of his nest and planned his rule.

The snow fell hard and heavy all night, driven by the wind that hooted and howled round and through the forest. Occasionally, even the wind's noise was punctuated by Chestnut's evil, gleeful laughter.

The snow fell for a long time and the wind howled. Eventually, the wind died but the snow continued to fall.

Moonrise Forest lay under snow that, daily, became more and more like a shroud. The layers of snow froze and the new snow froze on top of each layer. Under each layer were bodies that the white shroud covered.

Many of the bodies were animals caught out in the snow and the bitter temperatures and frozen to death. Others, mostly squirrels, were ripped and torn, victims of the rampant foxes or of Chestnut's increasing madness, killed by him in a fit of anger for no reason other than his madness told him to kill. Still, even in his madness, the renegade squirrel knew that he could not lose too many of the forest squirrels; there needed to be enough squirrels left to breed so that the agreement he had struck with the foxes would continue past this terrible winter.

Some squirrels even learned how to fight back, using stealth and working out what sort of fox to attack; the very young or the very old or the sick.

These few squirrels gravitated towards each other, away from the watching eyes of the guards but their meetings were few and far between. All of them knew instinctively that they needed to make some sort of contact with other forest animals, the badgers and the birds, because as few as they were, they needed to have what little courage they shared bolstered by the knowledge that there were others of a like mind.

It was a long-time friend of Rolf's who became the unelected leader of this small resistance group.

Beech had arrived late to the meeting where Chestnut had denounced Chatter, arriving just as Blinkwink had thundered down from the sky and scattered the meeting, freeing the monkey. The brutal way in which Chestnut had regained order that day was enough for Beech to know that he wanted no part of the new regime.

When he was young, Beech had been bold, often impetuous. He dared climbs nobody else contemplated and travelled far from his drey. He and Rolf had spent a lot of time together as they grew until Rolf's position as Elder-elect meant that Rolf had to spend more time with Saltpepper. They both regretted the lost time but their friendship had remained strong. In fact, it became stronger because Rolf would share much of what he learned with Beech.

Now, Rolf was dead.

Ah yes, he was dead. Everybody said so and there was nothing to suggest that they were wrong. Except...Beech was not totally convinced. His head, after searching for days for a sign of his friend, told Beech that Rolf must be dead. His heart, still close to his friend, was adamant that Rolf was alive. It was a belief that grew deeper and deeper, even as the snow fell.

It was a belief that, when the snow fell hard and fast, sent Beech out at night, searching for a sign of Rolf but as the blizzard raged, he knew what he was really searching for was a badger he could talk to. Beech knew that the badgers would have nothing but contempt for the foxes. Oh, they might be wary of them, especially when the foxes roamed in groups, but no badger would ever be afraid of a single fox or even two foxes.

It was on the third night after the snow began when Beech met Peaty just over the ridge of Badger Hollow. Beech had known Peaty for almost two years, had met him during one of those long journeys Beech made when he was younger. When he met Peaty that night and explained to the young badger why he was out alone, Peaty suggested Beech meet with the badger's new leader, Bumper. Beech met Bumper the following night, on the far side of the Hollow.

Bumper had listened to Beech and was pleased to hear that there were still squirrels prepared not to blindly follow Chestnut's madness, willing to fight if ever the chance came. By the end of the meeting, there was an agreement that *all* animals set against Chestnut would form a loose alliance, meeting as often as it was safe and sharing what little information they had. Even so, Bumper kept back the information that Stripe and Rolf were still alive; he thought that when Rolf and the others were ready to return would be time enough. Just in case, Bumper told himself, Beech wasn't as trustworthy as Peaty believed.

Any doubt Bumper had about Beech was completely removed two weeks into the blizzard.

Bumper and Peaty were on night-watch duty. The idea that anything would be out in the snow and wind was madness but, of course, Chestnut *was* mad and Bumper knew that some poor squirrel would be under orders to watch the badgers who were supposed to be on guard duty.

Bumper wasn't supposed to know that the badgers were being watched but he was too old a hand not have known all along. Tonight, he had the feeling that Chestnut was as sure as he was ever going to be about the badgers; there was only one squirrel watching them and, ah yes, now he was going home. Yes, Chestnut would call off the watchers after tonight; if the badgers were on duty in this weather, they could be trusted. That was how the renegade squirrel thought.

Peaty stamped all four feet alternately and muttered about the cold. They were standing in the lee of a huge beech tree, which cut most of the wind and snow. When Bumper nodded and told him that the squirrel who had been watching had left, Peaty asked if they could get back home now.

Peaty groaned when Bumper told him not yet. Then he crumpled to the ground with a grunt.

Bumper was so surprised that, for a moment, he only stood and stared at his young friend. There was a small, dark stain beginning to discolour Peaty's stripe. Bumper realised it was blood he was looking at and at last he reacted.

With a jerk, he looked round for whatever had hit Peaty but all he could see was snow and all he could hear was the wind and all he could scent was the sharp smell of the air. He looked down at Peaty who was still lying motionless but at least he was making a noise, albeit a groan. Bumper began to lower his head when something—a movement, a change in the air to his right made him twist his head and what he saw was enough to tell him everything.

Fox.

Bumper set himself solidly on the frozen snow.

"Ggggrrrr! Gotcha now badgers!"

Two more foxes joined the one who had knocked Peaty down. Bumper's instinct was to fight but given Peaty's condition and the fact that Bumper himself was the only link for Stripe and Rolf, he bit down the anger and spoke to the three foxes.

"Harumph," he growled. "We're on watch duty for that bloody...for Chestnut the Chief Squirrel and your leader's got an agreement with him. Just what the Lake d'you think you're doing attacking us?" Bumper looked at the foxes and knew, by the look on their faces, that they weren't interested in anything but trying to kill two badgers.

The largest of foxes growled softly, more of a chuckle. "King Cruncher and our boss have got something sorted about *squirrels* but we don't know nothing about badgers."

"Yeah," the smallest agreed. "And you bloody badgers owe us for Doggo and Denny. I don't know how a badger managed the two of them but there's only a badger could've done it, I know that."

Bumper didn't have the vaguest idea what he was talking about but it didn't really matter; all that mattered was that he and Peaty stay alive long enough to cause some damage.

"Ggrr, that's right," the final fox said and pounced.

Bumper stayed still until the fox was almost on him and then swayed sideways. He reared up on his hind legs and swiped at the fox as he went past. The badger's claws opened the fox's cheek wide and he went down with a howl. Bumper came down on the fox's back and dug his claws into the fox's face, close to the snout. He kicked his rear legs and felt his rear claws cut deep into the fox's back. As he began to turn, the oldest fox hit Bumper and his own breath came out of him in a whoosh. He felt teeth in his shoulder but the fox who was now trying to bite into his throat was the one to worry about.

Bumper pushed his face forward and bit down hard on the ear of the fox in front of him. When his teeth met through the velvety flesh, Bumper began to heave his body from side to side and the fox behind him fell off and onto his mate who was still howling loudly. It would have been a bonus but the falling fox's teeth ripped a long gash in Bumper's shoulder.

The fox whose ear Bumper was trying to amputate could smell blood and hear the howls of his friends and he growled even deeper and managed to get his head down, closer to the badger's throat. Bumper bit harder, dimly aware of Peaty's moans and his own blood seeping out of his shoulder. Well, at least he would take this fox's ear with him when he died.

Then everything changed.

The fox who had gashed his shoulder let out an agonised howl, which sent Bumper's hackles up even further. The howl was so loud and sudden that the fox who was trying to bite into Bumper's throat stopped struggling. Bumper took his chance and finally amputated the ear. He spat it out onto the snow and raised his right paw to swipe at the face of the fox. The fox ducked which was exactly what Bumper was hoping for; he planted his teeth into the fox's throat and swung his head from side to side. The fox gurgled and his hind legs beat a fast *thud-thud* on the snow and then he went limp. Bumper let go and turned to face the other foxes.

Oh Peaty, he thought as the turned. *You did just fine, youngun.*

But Peaty was still lying on the snow. His cyes were half-open but there was no way he could have done any damage to the fox who had been on Bumper's back. Bumper reared up and swivelled to face another pounce from whichever fox came first. Then the badger lowered himself down onto all fours again, his face a mixture of relief and disbelief.

Lying next to the dead fox Bumper could see that the other two were disabled, their rear legs twitching as they tried to overcome the ripped tendons there. Next to them, snout and forepaws covered in blood, stood a panting Beech.

Bumper began to speak and then decided that making sure the two injured foxes were dead was a better idea. He killed them quickly. Then, he said, "How...humph, how did you mana—"

"Let's see how the youngun is first," Beech said and padded across to Peaty.

Peaty had managed to get himself to a sitting position but he was breathing harshly, tentatively prodding the back of his head.

"Well, Peaty," Bumper said as he came alongside the young badger. "How is it?"

"Sore," Peaty told him, squeezing his eyes closed. "There's a big lump there as well as a lot of blood."

"Get your paws out of there, Peaty and let's have a look." Beech moved round the badger and looked. He carefully and gently moved the fur away from the wound, ignoring Peaty's 'oohs' and 'aahhs'.

"What's it look like?" Bumper asked.

"Pretty deep but it looks clean. It's the bump that's going to hurt the longest. He must've caught you with an elbow or his forehead. Typical, really," Beech said scornfully. "The more I see of them, the more I think we might have a chance against them. They can't aim, just barge in and expect the sight of them pouncing will do the job of a well-aimed swipe." He shook his head.

"Were did you spring from?" Bumper wanted to know as Peaty finally got himself onto all fours.

"I was out looking for you two," Beech told him. "I was following the creek when I heard those three. They were whispering and that seemed a bit off because there's so many of them in the forest, they think they own it and act how they like. Anyway, I got up a tree and followed them. They said something about badgers but they were going really careful and I didn't like that at all. I heard them muttering about somebody called Doggo and Denny and how they were sure it must've been a badger and getting to kill one in revenge was a good idea. I followed them and saw you two and it all clicked and...well, here we all are."

Bumper shook his head.

Here we all are? He takes on two foxes, saves Peaty and me, just sits there, and says here we all are? By the Lake, we've got a rare one here.

"Did those names, Denny and Doggo, mean anything to you? They were blaming a badger for whatever happened but I don't know anything about it."

Beech shook his head and then, before answering, rubbed blood of his paws and his snout. Then he raised his head and looked at Bumper in a way that made the badger wonder if he had made a mistake asking the question.

"Well," the squirrel said slowly, still staring at Bumper. "I heard from a squirrel who heard it from another who knows one of Chestnut's guards that two foxes were found dead. One was clawed and bitten but it was the other one that got the foxes all worked up. This one looked like a tree had fallen on him." He paused and cocked his head to the left, as if expecting some comment. When Bumper said nothing, Beech went on. "Anyway, the foxes who found the bodies had a snout round but could only smell badger and they reckoned no badger could claw one fox to death and bash in another's head. They had a go at their boss who had a go at Chestnut."

"What did he say?" Bumper asked. "If he wanted to keep the foxes sweet, he might decide to have a purge on squirrels and that could put your little group in trouble."

Beech nodded. "Yes but Chestnut just blew his top. He told the boss fox that if he ran his foxes the way Chestnut ran the squirrels, it wouldn't have happened and the fox wouldn't have been there whingeing at Chestnut."

Bumper's eyes widened. "He said that to a *fox*?" His voice was soft and disbelieving.

Beech nodded again. "That and more, probably. Anyway, so long as he leaves the squirrels alone, I couldn't give a hazelnut in the Lake. Except that, maybe..."

"Maybe you think I know something," Bumper said slowly, understanding now the look in the squirrel's eyes. "Even though I've already said I don't know anything."

"Maybe you didn't know what they were talking about," Beech said evenly. "But maybe you have an idea how the other fox died. Now you know the other fox *wasn't* bitten and clawed to death?"

"Humph, look, maybe I can but...well, I don't want to insult you, especially after what you did here, but it's not really up to me. You'll have to trust me for a couple of days. It's not too much to ask of a friend."

Beech settled on his haunches and gave Bumper another long look. Finally, he nodded. "Okay. I'll meet you by the lakeside, that big willow just west of your Hollow."

Peaty let out a sigh of relief. For a moment, he'd wondered if Beech might get annoyed at Bumper's hesitation. Now that the squirrel had agreed to wait, the thought of the dead foxes became more urgent to the young badger. "Don't you think we should...do something with these? If they're found then the fox leader might really push your Chief to do something. The foxes will smell squirrel as well as badger here."

Beech glanced at the bodies. "You're right, youngun. Let's see if we can push them over towards that drift by the trees. With luck, the snow will cover them and they won't be found till the thaw. Just one more thing," he said gently. "Chestnut's not my boss. I think of him the way you badgers do. He's that bloodydamn squirrel. Okay?"

Bumper chuckled. "Right you are, Beech. Now, let's see if we can hide these three."

It took them a good few minutes but they managed it well enough. Even before they left, the snow had covered the bloodstains and the bodies were becoming a part of the drift against the trees.

"I wish you'd stop muttering to yourself, Stripe," the turtle said. "Half the time, I don't if I'm supposed to be listening to you or not."

Stripe was scrabbling across the yard or so of ice and snow at the side of the lake. It was past midnight, a month since they had arrived at the witch's cottage. The turtle had brought Stripe back to this side of the lake so he could meet up with Bumper. The journey this time had been in pitch-blackness, made worse by the light snow blown by a harsh breeze. The waters of the lake had been choppy and the tough old badger had kept his eyes tightly closed all the way. Now, he was slipping and sliding, trying to get a grip to push himself onto solid ground again.

"Did you hear me?"

"Humph! Hear you? Probably the whole crew of bloody foxes heard you." Stripe grunted as his feet at last found decent ground.

"Well, answer me then."

"I'm muttering about all this sailing or swimming or whatever you call it. Might be wonderful for you and even some of the others in good weather but I don't like it and never will. Not now, not in sunshine, not ever."

"But we had to come so you can meet Bumper."

"Harumph. I know but it doesn't mean I have to *like* it. And I don't."

"Hush your grumbling you old grouch," Bumper said as he came out into the open. "The foxes won't have heard the turtle but your voice carries."

The turtle paddled up and down the shoreline for about fifty yards either way. He was keeping an eye out and an ear cocked and he knew that was a really stupid expression but that's what he was doing while the badgers talked and he wished they'd hurry up because he didn't like this hanging round when the foxes could be...ah, finally, they'd finished.

"So, how do things stand now," the turtle asked when he swam up onto the ice at the lake's edge.

Bumper explained about Beech and then Stripe asked the turtle what he thought about it all and about Beech's little resistance group.

"He sounds exactly what we're looking for. Him and his friends." The turtle ducked his head and made a bubbling sound in his throat. "Telling him about you, Stripe, and Chatter shouldn't be a problem. But I'm not sure about Blinkwink and I definitely don't think he should know about Rolf." He waited for Stripe's angry reaction and wasn't disappointed.

"What? Humph, why not? Knowing about Rolf would keep his and his mates heads up, just the sort of thing they need, eh? And Blinkwink? What's the problem?"

The turtle sighed; he knew why but he wasn't sure he could explain it in a way that Stripe would accept. Still, there was nothing for it but to try. "I think Chestnut's got a real fear of Blinkwink for some reason and the longer the owl stays 'dead' the better, I think. As for Rolf...well, he's not well yet and, let's be honest, he might not get well enough to cross the lake again. Now, if Beech and his friends know Rolf's alive, they'll expect him to lead them when the time comes. If he can't...it might do exactly the opposite to what you hope." He took a deep breath. "And while I'm sure Beech is solid and true and brave, maybe not all of the others are as brave? What if Beech knew everything and told just one or two of his mates and what if one of them got scared or caught? Chestnut could end up knowing everything. If Beech knew about the cottage and Chestnut somehow found out, how long before he organised things so the cottage was put under siege?"

Stripe grumbled but nodded; he knew the turtle was right.

"Yes," Bumper said. "Can't say I like it but you're right. I'll tell Beech about Stripe and the monkey and hope that satisfies him. It will quench his curiosity about the two dead foxes, at least." He glanced at Stripe and smiled; hearing Stripe tell *that* story was worth the cold and the snow. "Still, he'll know there's more and he'll not like that. Ah well. When shall we meet up next time, then?" He looked at Stripe and frowned. "What's up me old mate?"

"It's the snow and the wind and the bloody water and having to ride on the back of Mr Turtle. That's what's up."

Bumper understood how hard this must be for Stripe. It must be hard to have to face that sort of fear and know that there was no other way if you were to do your job properly. And Stripe would never pass the buck. Bumper looked at the turtle and saw something in his eyes and it took a moment for him to understand. Then realisation hit him like a falling branch. He looked back at Stripe and then took a breath.

"Well..." Bumper said and paused. He took another breath. "Why don't *I* come across to meet *you*?"

Stripe simply stared at his old friend, filled with something so big, a feeling so good and wholesome, he could not speak. Then the turtle did something that made both badgers gape at him and then laugh. The turtle clapped his front flippers together. Once, *slap*, back to the snow, once more, *slap* and back on the snow.

"A true friend," the turtle told Bumper. "Brave and intelligent."

"More likely, I'm just plain daft," Bumper said quietly.

Stripe nudged his friend just below the wound, now scabbing over, the fox had inflicted. "No, the turtle's right and thanks, friend. Anyway, time we got on back, all of us. Make it a fortnight from tonight, Bumper. The turtle will meet you here."

"Humph, fine, fine," Bumper said, still trying to come to terms with what he'd said and offered.

"Take care, Bumper," the turtle told him as he headed back to the water. "Don't worry, I'll keep you safe when I carry you back. You'll get to see Rolf and Blinkwink and the witch, eh?"

Bumper nodded and watched as Stripe eased himself onto the turtle's back before the turtle headed back towards the far side of the lake. Then he turned and made his way back to Badger Hollow.

*

Peaty stood silently next to Bumper who had just finished telling Beech as much as he felt he could. The younger badger's breath plumed out into the air; the night was as deeply cold as all the nights had been for what seemed like forever to Peaty. The cold made his head ache, particularly round the swelling where the fox had caught him. The bump pulsed with a dull ache and had done since it had happened. And Peaty was truly fed up with it.

"Well," Beech said slowly. "That explains the fox whose head was bashed in but it's not all. Is it, Bumper?"

Bumper shrugged. "No," he agreed. "No, but it's all I'm going to tell you."

"What happened to friendship?"

"We're still your friends, Beech and I hope you're still ours. We can't do much on our own and neither can you and your little band." Bumper could hear his own distaste for keeping back the knowledge of Rolf and Blinkwink.

Beech heard it, too. "I don't like this, Bumper and I can tell you don't, either. It's written all over your face and it's playing havoc with your voice. If it makes you feel so bad, how can it be right?"

The fact that Beech was right only made Bumper feel worse; he didn't like all this secrecy and having to sneak around, even if he did understand the need for it. Still, he had agreed and that was that. "Look," he said in a guttural whisper. "I've told you all I can and, no, I'm not happy about it but that's my problem. We still need each other but if your price for that friendship is me breaking a promise to my oldest friend, then maybe we should just go our separate ways. I might not like all this secret stuff but I understand the reasons and the need for it. I thought you would, too. Especially with you and your little band having to keep your heads down." He shrugged again. "Like it or lump it, Beech."

The squirrel and the older badger looked at each other for what, to Peaty, seemed a long time. The wait and the tension in that wait made his head ache worse than ever. Finally, Beech broke the silence and the tension.

"I'll have to like it, then. If that old groaner, Stripe, thinks it's necessary, he must have a good reason." Then he turned to Peaty. "How's the head, youngun?"

Peaty was a bit flummoxed by the sudden change but eventually found his voice. "Oh, well, it's still a lump and it gives me some terrible headaches." Then, so he didn't sound like a cry-baby, he added, "but the cuts are healing. I'll be okay."

Beech nodded. "Aye, well, next time you fight foxes, just use your head for thinking, eh?" The three animals were glad for the chance to laugh. Then Beech said, "Best be off. When are you meeting Stripe again?" Beech asked and shook his head once when Bumper threw him a sharp look. "Don't worry, I won't be following you. I was just thinking that it would be good to have some solid information to give him. Something he could think about in that cottage instead of just sitting round and waiting. I'll see what I can do." He turned to Peaty. "You sure you're okay, Peaty?"

"Mmm? Oh, humph, yes. Okay, okay. Take care now, Beech. Okay."

"Right," Beech said and watched the two badgers walk away.

It might have been the dark or the blowing snow or both distorting his vision but Beech thought the younger badger looked unsteady on his feet. Peaty seemed to take a sideways step for every two forward steps.

"Probably just tired and cold," Beech told himself but it didn't feel right to him. Still, Bumper was with Peaty and they were both safe from foxes, weren't they? Yes. Beech made his way back home.

Now that he was here, Slygo was even more convinced that his brain had been away on the downs when he had told Slink he wanted to go with him next time he met up with the Chief Squirrel. In fact, this wasn't really the 'next time' because Slink had been alone when he learned of the attack on Doggo and Denny. Slink had been so enraged by the description of how the two dead foxes had died, he had charged into the forest, found a lone squirrel and demanded to be taken to Chestnut. Outside Chestnut's drey, Sink had called for the 'double-dealing, sly nut-cracker' to come down and talk to him. Chestnut had listened to Slink and then had yelled at the fox for a good five minutes before turning his back on him.

Slink had watched the squirrel turn away and even then he could not quite bring himself to attack the nut-cruncher. Instead, he had galloped back to Slygo's den and told his old friend about it all.

Slygo had listened but, while he could understand the general opinion that it must have been a combined attack by badgers and squirrels, he thought there must have been more to it than that. The injuries were too strange. Still, the two foxes were dead, nothing would bring them back and there had been no other dead foxes. Gradually, the odd deaths of Doggo and Denny faded in everybody's mind and the daily round of hunting and killing and eating went on.

Now, here he was, standing in the freezing wind while big snowflakes fell on his fur, some melting and some sticking in his whiskers. Slygo's four paws had, apparently, become part of the frozen earth because he could not feel them.

You could be home, his mind told him. *Warm and dry and eating a leg or chewing on a shoulder bone. Or asleep and dreaming of summer and chicken runs. You could be doing anything but you're here waiting to see King Cruncher. What were you thinking of, volunteering for this little caper? This place is enough to give you the willies and you haven't even scented him yet. What's it going to be like when he finally gets here?*

"Oh shut up. You're here now. Stiffen up and try to look the part for coop's sake!"

Slink grunted and looked at him. "What?"

Slygo shook his head. "Nothing. It's the weather. I'm sick of it."

Slink nodded but he heard the lie in his old friend's voice and had a good idea what Slygo was thinking. The Lake knew, Slink had similar thoughts himself but things were the way they there and here was Chief Nut-cracker himself and the fact that neither of the foxes had even scented the squirrel was not a good thought. They looked at each other and both decided that the weather and their talking was the reason the squirrel had been able to appear as if he had materialised out of the air. Thinking anything else, like maybe the squirrel *had* simply materialised out of the air, was not a good idea.

"Ah, good, here already." Chestnut said cheerfully. "The less time we spend out in this weather, the better, eh Slink?"

Slygo heard that sweet, oh so sweet and cheerful voice and he had the feeling that his breakfast was about to heave itself up from his stomach.

"And you've brought a friend. You would be Slygo." Chestnut grinned but, when Slygo said nothing, the squirrel turned to Slink. "Now then, Slink, what's on your mind? I hope we're not going to start ranting and raving at each other again? I really don't think allies have any need for that sort of thing, do you?"

"I've got some news for you. Something to nibble on when you get tired of nibbling on nuts." Slink grinned. Slygo saw it and felt better.

"Oh good. I do get bored sometimes." Chestnut's voice was still sickly sweet.

"The owl, Blinkwink?"

"What? The owl?"

All the sweetness was gone from Chestnut's voice; this voice was hard and edged, as sharp as the biting wind. Slygo heard it and waited for his legs to collapse beneath him and his breakfast to finally vacate his stomach. He waited but it didn't happen. In fact, Slygo felt better because he wondered if, behind the sharp edge of the squirrel's voice, there wasn't something else? Maybe not fear but something close, something like concern or worry. Whatever it was, it gave Slygo the chance to see this squirrel as something less than all-powerful, something other than an animal who could not be hunted and killed and eaten if you were hungry.

"Ah, thought that might get your attention," Slink said, relishing this as much as he'd told Slygo he would that night when Slygo had asked to come to the next meeting. When Slink had ranted at Chestnut about the two dead foxes, he hadn't mentioned the owl and now he knew he had been right; this tasted much better than it would have tasted then. Now, it tasted just chicken-neck fine.

"The owl, what about the owl, Mister Fox?" Chestnut was really wound up tight now and the word 'mister' came out as an insult, came out like undigested food, like vomit. "Just *tell* me about the owl. If your stupid crew found him and lost him I'll—"

"Ggrrr."

Both foxes growled, a low, menacing sound that hung in the air like jaws and teeth.

"You'll what?" Slink demanded.

Chestnut breathed in slowly and composed himself. "Please," he said and that sickly sweetness was back. "Just tell me about the owl, Slink."

So Slink told him how the foxes had not only found and toyed with the owl for a good few minutes but that toying had inflicted such injury that the bird had fallen into the lake. "The cold probably killed it," Slink told Chestnut. "And if it didn't, it drowned. It never even surfaced once."

Slygo heard his friend's strong voice and, even in the grey light of the winter's day, he saw how Slink's eyes glinted and both things did Slygo's heart good and his legs no longer felt weak and liable to collapse under him. When he added this to the way the squirrel's voice seemed to be hiding something like concern, Slygo felt even better and glad that he'd come to this meeting after all.

Chestnut heard the sneer in the fox's voice and saw the contempt in those glinting eyes but it was okay, it was fine, no need to let it get to him. Chestnut could even understand the fox's need to strut a little and it was okay because everything was okay, everything was fine because Blinkwink was dead. Chestnut did not really understand *why* it was so important that the owl be dead and gone but it was and the owl was dead so everything was okay and fine.

Chestnut closed his eyes and saw the future. Not just the end of this wonderfully deep and cold winter and the spring that would follow, but all the winters and springs and summers and autumns to come. He saw far into those future seasons, where Chief Squirrel Chestnut reigned supreme over Moonrise Forest and everything and everybody in it. He would be Lord of the

Forest and of Sunset Lake, too. Yes, he could see that, could see his rule spreading out from Moonrise Forest, across the lake and into other lands, other forests. Oh, perhaps not by him but certainly by his heirs. Yes, Chief Squirrel Chestnut would sire a dynasty that would last forever.

"Gggrroy! Squirrel!"

Chestnut was dragged back from his glorious vision of the future by the harsh call from the fox. The fox had said something, perhaps had even asked a question and it would not do to have these foxes think that the Chief Squirrel was not always in total control.

"Excuse me, I was picturing the fall of the owl and it was such a good picture, I did not quite catch what you said."

"Yeah, it was a nice picture," Slink agreed. "What I want to know is why it was so important that the bird died?"

Slygo was watching the squirrel intently because he had the strongest feeling that *this* was why he had volunteered for this little outing with Slink. The squirrel did not move or speak for a moment but Slygo was sure there was something going on behind those beady black eyes, something Chestnut didn't want the foxes to see or know about. It was like...oh, what was it like? But before Slygo could pin it down, the squirrel shrugged his shoulders and let out what presumably passed for a laugh.

"Oh, we had a little difference of opinion," Chestnut said lightly. "He insulted me and I don't like being insulted. Bad for the dignity of the crown as you—" Chestnut stopped abruptly and looked surprised by what he had just said. Crown? Lake and Forest, his mind had jumped back, or was it forwards, to what he had been thinking about, to the dynasty. Not good, not good at all. "That is, it's bad for discipline. You know about that, Slink. You let one get away with it and the rest think they can, too. You're a strong leader, you know how it is." Chestnut smiled, happy at the way he had turned it round; puff the fox up about what a good leader he was and he wouldn't remember the odd slip of a word here and there. And as for the other fox, he was probably slow or stupid; he hadn't said a word all the time they'd been here.

"Oh aye," Slink agreed. "I know about the whingers. Yeah, me and you both know the score with them."

"Yes indeed," Chestnut said and nodded his head. "Now, I think we've been out in this weather long enough. I'm sure your friend will be glad to get back home in the warm. Won't you Slygo?" He looked at the slow or stupid fox who only stood there and said nothing; definitely stupid then. "Right, well, thank you for the news about the owl. I think our bargain is working well, don't you?"

"Oh, chicken-neck fine," Slink said and licked snow off his snout.

Chestnut nodded again and turned away from them and was soon lost amongst the trees.

"I hate that squirrel, Slygo. I hate that bushy-tailed, slick-tongued, shell-spitting squirrel. One day, Slygo, one day. Gggrr, break and bite! One day."

"One day," Slygo agreed but with less venom than his friend.

Back in his earth, chewing a bone he had saved from breakfast, Slygo thought about the meeting with Chestnut and he kept coming back to the look in the squirrel's eyes when Slink had asked why it was so important that the owl was dead. Oh, the answer they got seemed plausible enough but Slygo's first thought when the squirrel had given it had been *liar*. Slink was satisfied and why not? It was just the answer any leader would have given. But that look in Chestnut's eyes gnawed at Slygo the way he was gnawing at the bone between his paws.

Why?

Did it matter? The bird was dead so why worry about the reason the squirrel wanted it to happen?

True.

Of course it was true. What Slygo should be thinking about was the way he had felt when Chestnut had lost his sweet, sickly tone of voice because that was when Slygo had begun to see him as just another squirrel, a meal if he wanted it.

"But there's still something about that nut-cruncher that sends shivers down your back," Slygo muttered round the bone in his mouth.

And that was true, too. There was something...cold about that squirrel. As cold as the Lake. Well, colder actually. Colder than the wind and sharper than any barbed wire round a chicken run. Still, there was no doubting it—if Slygo had to kill Chestnut, he knew he could now. After the way the squirrel had lost it, Slygo knew he could kill him, that the squirrel was nothing special.

Oh? You sure, Slygo?

Slygo slurped his tongue round the bone and nodded once; yes, he was sure. At least, he thought he was...no, he was sure, definitely sure...

"Go to sleep," he told himself and, strangely enough, sleep came easier tonight than it had done for a while.

But he dreamed.

It was the same dream. The one where he stumbled across the strange aisle of trees and found the clearing that was full of contradictions but nevertheless made perfect sense. There was a difference this time, though; this time, the animal that came marching down the aisle towards him was not a huge squirrel but a bird. A bird that stopped marching and began to fly towards the fox. Everything else was the same; the terror Slygo felt and the terrible heat he could feel almost baking off the approaching bird and the whimpering that Slygo could not stop. The whimpering that evolved into a throat-ripping scream.

This time, when he came awake, Slygo knew the scream had stayed in his throat because he did not feel as frightened as that first time. Lying awake in his cosy, warm earth, Slygo thought he understood why; it all had to do with the way the squirrel had *needed* to know that the owl was dead. Slygo had gone round and round the mulberry bush with that and the dream had been an extension of that; the animal in the dream therefore became a bird. Simple and, since the owl was dead in the lake, there was no longer anything to worry about. Slygo had obviously failed to think that first dream through properly but now, with this second dream as a reference, he could see that the first dream had been about the squirrel. And he had dreamed *that* because he had got himself all worked up about the old squirrel

Slink had killed but could not eat; it had fretted at Slink and so Slygo had fretted about it and then dreamed about a squirrel. Simple.

Slygo went back to sleep with a big grin on his face.

The air was full of dreams that night as the cold deepened and the snow thickened over Moonrise Forest.

Chestnut dreamed but his dreams were merely extensions of what his mind dwelled on during most of his waking hours anyway; conquest and victories and the dynasty he would begin and the power and glory it would bring to his name. These were the things he thought about nearly all the time now that his position was secure. He had his guards to see to the daily ordering of his rule and he had his spies to make sure those guards remained loyal; 'safe' food was survival and bought anything he needed. Most of the spies were squirrels but he did have one or two other animals who spied for him. He met with his spies at a dead birch tree a hundred yards from his drey and the meetings were staggered so that they never met each other, never had the chance to compare notes. That would not be a good idea at all.

Everything was running smoothly and even the fact that he had no real control over the badgers did not ruffle Chestnut's fur. And, really, it did not matter at all because Bumper and the other one, the young, simple one, kept their watch and the fact that they seldom met with Chestnut mattered little now that Blinkwink was dead and gone. Besides, if and when he decided to do something about the badgers and the way they seemed to think they might almost be on a par with the Chief Squirrel, Chestnut would simply call on the foxes.

Ah yes, he liked that thought as he thought it in his dream that night. He liked the idea that his power was such that he could even order the foxes if he felt like doing so.

In his dream tonight, he smiled and his sleeping face smiled as he thought about how strong he was, how powerful and, the way things happen in dreams, he saw himself striking out against an animal and killing it. It did not matter that he could not see what sort of animal it was because it simply confirmed how powerful he was, the way it had been confirmed in reality at the beginning of his reign. Then, he had lashed out to show the others how strong he was and, oh there was no need to deny it was there, because he *liked* to maim and kill, almost *needed* to. He had learned to control the bloodlust over the weeks and months and no longer lashed out whenever the urge came on him. Still, he had also learned that he could not simply *stop* lashing out and maiming. And killing.

He had tried but found that if the bloodlust was denied too long, his mind began to turn on itself, to bombard him with questions he had no real answers to, to fill him with doubt. Whenever that happened, Chestnut found himself wandering the forest aimlessly, his head screaming with pain. When that happened, he always arrived home feeling ill, almost broken. And that was unacceptable. *Then* he would just let the bloodlust have its way in a welter of ripping claws and teeth. When it was over, he would order whatever was left of the body removed from his sight and then he would feel better and he could close his eyes and see the future.

Tonight, dreaming and smiling, he dreamed of killing and it felt as good as it did when he was awake. Tonight, he dreamed of killing Blinkwink, dreamed of the owl trying to escape and only succeeding in falling into the lake and drowning. When the last bubbles disappeared, Chestnut was already marching across the land and conquering more land and more animals. He smiled as he slept and dreamed.

Across the black and icy waters of Sunset Lake, the owl who was supposed to be dead beneath those waters, also dreamed.

Blinkwink was perched on the back of a chair close to the witch's blazing fire. His breathing was steady and deep, his feathers fluffed out. The witch had treated his injuries and he knew he was improving daily. This morning, during a lull in the blizzard, he had exercised for a full hour in the back garden and he knew he was not far off a full recovery; he had even caught his own dinner. The good feeling it gave him had still been with him when he settled down on the temporary perch on the back of the chair. He still had to sleep at the wrong times for an owl but he knew he had to be awake when the others were.

Now, warm and cosy, Blinkwink dreamed. It was nothing dramatic or even very vivid but, when he woke, he knew it had been important.

In the dream, there was the thundering sound of rushing water, overlaid by a high *cawing* note that filled him with a sense of freedom and open skies. The sun was bright in the dream but the light wasn't the golden light of summer. This was a pale, lemony sunlight that hinted at a winter that might be finally drawing to its close. And there was an enormous sense of height in the dream, the sort of height that the waking Blinkwink had occasionally come close to as he rode an unexpectedly strong thermal. But the height in the dream was not only of the sky; the dream-Blinkwink somehow knew that the *land* here was high, higher than any land he had ever seen. In the dream, the owl revelled in this height, it filled his mind with joy and he felt light and free. But when Blinkwink woke, he knew that the important thing to remember from the dream was that sound—that high, *caw caw* sound.

And Rolf.

After more than a month in the witch's care and whatever it was she added to the broth she fed him three times a day, Rolf found breathing easier. Oh, he was still ill and occasionally feverish but he was improving and talking was less of a trial. Still, no matter how hard he pressed, the witch would not put a time on when she thought he would completely well again.

The others took Rolf's persistent questions about his health as a sign of his eagerness to be about the business of sorting out, as Stripe put it, that bloodydamn squirrel.

The truth was a little more complex.

Rolf knew he *should* be eager to cross the lake and face Chestnut, at least eager to think of a way of repairing the damage caused by the renegade's treachery but, whenever he thought about it all, his mind refused to give it room. His mind fought against any idea that even sounded like *fighting back.*

Some part of Rolf's mind seemed to think that, since squirrels had allowed Chestnut to commit such vile acts, they deserved everything that happened to them. To that part of Rolf's mind, it seemed that all the squirrels had, however unconsciously, conspired in the betrayal of Moonrise Forest.

As the days went by, that small part of his brain seemed to be growing until, now, it seemed more and more right to Rolf that he should just leave the forest to its fate.

He had good friends inside this cottage and if and when he was fully recovered, perhaps he could explain how he felt and they would understand. Maybe they could all leave the forest behind, find another place where they could fit in and live in peace. Let Chestnut have what he wanted so badly that he had killed and turned against his own kind.

All this was in Rolf's mind during the day when they were all awake and he could, to a degree, control his voice and his actions. At night, when the cottage was quiet apart from the crackle of the fire and the sound of the others sleeping, things were different; his dreams would not leave him alone.

Tonight, as the fox Slygo dreamed of a giant bird (which was nothing to worry about), while Chestnut dreamed of conquest and dynasties (which were inevitable) and while Blinkwink dreamed of a high place where the sound of freedom was a *cawing* (and very important), Rolf also dreamed.

Rolf's dream was all floating faces and faceless voices that echoed and blended in a kind of mist that the dream-Rolf tried to push through so he could hear and see properly; so he could *understand.*

He was back in the forest at the place where he had seen Saltpepper's shade or whatever it had been. As then, Rolf was sick and in pain and he was very tired. He wanted to be left alone to rest, to sleep so he did not have to think about anything anymore.

He just wanted to be *left alone*. Was that too much to ask? He was sick and hurt and tired and all he wanted was to be left alone...

Alone! Oh and don't I know it? Alone and alone! By the Lake, Rolf, that's all I've heard from you and to tell the truth, I'm about sick of it!

...and that was Saltpepper's voice but hardly his old teacher's tone. This was no warm, kindly voice and, even when Rolf had seen Saltpepper lose his temper, he had never heard his teacher lose that essential gentleness. It didn't seem fair that Saltpepper should be talking like this, so harshly and unkindly, not when Rolf was hurt and sick and tired. No, it did not seem fair at all.

(In his sleep, Rolf grimaced as though he heard the whine in his dream-voice and didn't like it all).

Fair? Oh dear, it's not fair and he's poorly and everybody's picking on him and it's not fair. Oh dear, now he's upset because I'm picking on him, as well.

The dream-Rolf cringed at the mockery, almost contempt, he heard in Saltpepper's disembodied voice but it was still true, wasn't it? He *was* sick and he *was* being picked on.

Oh dear, he's still at it, not fair, not fair, not fair not fair not fair

It seemed like this voice (which was Saltpepper's but, somehow, also sounded a bit like Rolf's own voice), could go on and on forever, saying those two words. Rolf couldn't stand that, not even the idea of it.

"Shut up!"

Rolf's voice was very loud and it made him feel better, feel as if he wasn't being picked on so much. So he said it again.

"Shut up! Shut up! Just shut up!"

Rolf repeated the words, a little louder each time until the other voice could no longer be heard. When he stopped repeating the words, he expected the other voice to come back but it did not. Now, there were just the faces. More faces now, in fact.

So many faces he could not distinguish one from the other. He thought he saw his own once but it was there and gone so quickly he couldn't be positive. Then there seemed to be a fox face but it became, he thought, a monkey's face or a badger's or an owl's or another squirrel's face. For a few moments, Rolf almost felt as if he was enjoying this game of catch-me-if-you-can and he waited for another face to arrive in front of him, wondering what it would be. But no other face arrived.

Instead, a shape moved towards him, as if from a long way off. Slowly, the nebulous shape became the definite shape of a squirrel, a squirrel he recognised. Then there were the mottles of a furry coat, which he knew as well as he knew his own face in the calm waters of the lake during summer.

Rolf saw Saltpepper and immediately wanted to back away because he did not want to see the knowing look in the old squirrel's eyes and he did not want to hear that mocking tone, the edge that was almost contempt when Saltpepper spoke to him.

But Rolf could not back away and he could not wake up and now Saltpepper was standing in front of him and was about to speak. Rolf winced in anticipation and looked at his own paws on the ground.

There was no mockery in Saltpepper's voice as he said, "Well, young master Rolf, don't you remember your old teacher? Come on, look up. I won't bite."

Rolf looked up very slowly, very reluctantly but, finally, he was looking at the well-remembered, well-loved face. Rolf smiled.

"There, that's better," Saltpepper said and smiled. "Now then, Rolf, don't you think it's about time you got down to trying to sort all this out? Mmm?"

"But, Saltpepper," Rolf said and had to clear his throat. "I'm not...ready. Really. I'm not well and I'm not whingeing...well, maybe a little but it's still true. I'm really not well enough to..."

Saltpepper nodded, still smiling. "Yes, you're still ill but you're getting better. A little more each day. If you stopped fighting your own recovery, you'd be better a lot quicker. Even so, soon, you *will* be well enough and it would be as well to have some idea of what you're going to do. Don't you think?"

Rolf had had enough. Part of him knew this was probably a dream but it didn't matter; he'd had enough. Enough of being talked *at*, of feeling the expectant stares of the others in the cottage, of being expected to get better just so he could go back and risk everything again against Chestnut and the foxes and all the other mealy-mouthed animals who had let it happen in the first place. It didn't matter that Saltpepper was smiling at him, that the old squirrel's voice was its usual kind and gentle self, Rolf had had enough. Let them sort it out themselves and let him get on with his own life. Away from here and the forest, some place where the animals didn't betray each other. Let Moonrise Forest and all its animals sort themselves out and good riddance! He was out of the forest!

The dream-Rolf thought he only thought all of this but when Saltpepper said, "Feel better now? Mmm? Now that you've got it all off your chest, d'you feel better?" Rolf knew he had voiced all of it and he was glad and, yes, he did feel better.

"Yes," he told Saltpepper and then swallowed hard because he saw flint in his old teacher's eyes, glinting like thin ice under moonlight.

"Well, if it did you good, perhaps it was necessary," Saltpepper said. "Perhaps some of the sickness came out with the words. Even so, self-pity is something you can ill-afford, Rolf. Neither you nor the forest has time for you to go on feeling sorry for yourself. I'm dead. You remember that, don't you? You recall that I was killed? I was ripped apart by a fox. I heard my bones break and felt my flesh tear, felt fox-teeth in my neck. I'm sure you must remember that I was killed by a fox?" Saltpepper's voice was as hard and cold as a stone on the bottom of Sunset Lake and his eyes looked even harder and colder.

"I remember," Rolf said in a small voice. "Won't you stop it now, please?"

"Yes but you have to stop feeling sorry for yourself. Rolf, there are animals depending on you. Not just squirrels but the badgers and the birds and a certain monkey. You remember that monkey? He faced his own fears to help you and nearly died saving your life. And the turtle? The turtle who stays out of water longer than he should because he knows how important you are, the turtle who refused to return to his own shape because he wanted to help restore the order that Chestnut destroyed."

"Yes, I know but—"

Saltpepper raised his right paw and silenced Rolf effortlessly. "And the squirrels? Oh yes, some of them colluded with Chestnut but there are others who had no choice and even a few who risk their lives daily, doing what they can to fight that renegade. Aye, and one of them is an old friend of yours, Rolf. Beech leads the resistance. He doesn't know you are alive but he suspects and even if he doesn't, he will still stand against Chestnut until some way of removing him can be found. See, Rolf? Even those who think you dead believe your spirit is alive and it's that belief that keeps them strong in their opposition."

Rolf shook his head. "No, I don't think so. Your spirit, maybe. I was only your pupil and not a very good one."

"Ah, Rolf, you're not listening," Saltpepper said but a lot of the hardness was gone now. "They *know* I was killed. They saw the body and they know I am dead. They grieved but they still had you to believe in because your body was never found. I was old, Rolf but you were their future and they still want their future. You remember what I told you about the Autumn Red Squirrel? How the fire burned in him and how it was passed down to every Elder Squirrel but most of them only had a glimmer?"

"Yes but it was just a myth, Saltpepper. It was...symbolic."

"No, it was true then and it is true now. The flame is your heritage, Rolf. It burned in me but it *blazes* in you. It was no accident that you were my pupil. The flame burns in you, stronger than at any time since that Autumn Red Squirrel. It is banked now but even those in this cottage know it's there. They don't know what it is but they sensed it in you and saved you from the winter and certain death. So, young master Rolf, leave off your self-pity and let the flame burn strong. Take it out of this cottage when the time is right and let it burn away the cold evil Chestnut brought into your home. Take up the flame and let it burn, Rolf. Let it burn!"

The dream-Rolf took a breath to answer this nonsense, to rail against even the idea, to demand to be left alone, left in peace. He took the breath but found he could not let it out because Saltpepper was fading, his shape unravelling, becoming wisps of smoke, plucked by a breeze, taken away.

Rolf felt cheated; he hadn't been able to refuse, to tell Saltpepper he would do nothing, nothing at all. He looked at his paws and finally let out the breath and closed his eyes, aware for the first time in the dream that it was cold. He shivered and began to turn and leave and go...anywhere.

Rolf stopped and his eyes opened wide.

Deep inside himself, something seemed to turn over and he felt warm. No, not just warm, he felt *hot*. Deep inside there was a heat that felt like the sun in the middle of a summer's day. It burned. Rolf felt his whole body burn and he began to pant.

"No," he gasped. "No, I don't want..."

He could manage nothing else but his thoughts went on anyway.

He did not want this flame, this burning inside him, he wanted to be left alone, that was all and that was enough. Just to be left alone.

But the flame inside him refused to be denied and, as it raged, Saltpepper's voice rode on the waves of heat.

Take up the flame, Rolf. Take it up and let it burn!

Chapter Seven

Beech gnawed thoughtfully at a nut he had managed to filch from the small store Bushy had hidden beneath the few refugee leaves he'd gathered before the snow fell. And, lake and forest, it seemed so long since there had been a day before the snow fell, so long it seemed almost like a dream. Beech thought about Bushy as he gnawed.

Of all the squirrels who turned a shift for Chestnut, Bushy seemed the least likely. That was not to say Bushy was dead-set against Chestnut, but he seemed to take no delight in the way the forest was these days. He did his job and followed any orders he was given but he never took any pleasure in it as some of them did. Bushy followed orders because he was able to eat his pay and so he was able to survive.

Bushy knew Beech, had done since they were younguns and had often played with Beech and Rolf but Beech knew Bushy tried to make others believe he was sanguine about things these days. The few times he met and talked with Beech, Bushy passed the time of day and talked about 'safe' things like the weather and maybe settling down and having a family. Beech also knew that Bushy still felt close to him, mainly because Beech had not shunned him when things changed, even though Bushy knew what Beech thought about everything. Bushy showed his gratitude by giving Beech a little food now and then.

Beech sensed Bushy's discomfort with his job and he thought that, if push really did come to shove, Bushy might be persuaded to turn against Chestnut.

But that was for the future and in the meantime, Beech was happy to talk about the inconsequential things Bushy wanted to talk about, eating whatever Bushy offered and hoping that, soon, he might be able to get Bushy talking about Chestnut.

That was for the future, too because right now it was an hour or so past sunset and Beech was waiting inside the hollowed remains of a fallen bough, waiting for Bumper or Peaty or both. He had little to tell them but, as his auntie was always saying, every little helps; maybe they would have something to tell him.

"If they ever get here," he muttered to himself and found himself returning to what he had been thinking about before he had turned his thoughts to Bushy.

Time was getting on and the badgers had yet to arrive and, no matter how hard he argued against it meaning something had happened to them, it did no good; these days, if an animal did not arrive on time, it usually meant something *had* happened to them.

"Ffsst."

The sound made Beech draw back into the hollowed bough. His eyes, bugging out, searched the area in front of him, trying to make out anything beyond the shadows and the eerie blue/white of the snow under a bloated silver moon. His whole body was tensed and his heart thudded in his chest and ears and throat.

"Fffsst, Beech, you there?"

Beech relaxed and padded out into the open. "Here, Peaty. You're late."

"Sorry," Peaty said and stepped out from behind the wide bole of an ash tree.

"Why are you late? And where's Bumper?"

"Well, it's all tied up really, and, humph, we haven't got time here. Just come with me and you'll find out everything." The young badger did not even wait for a reply. He just turned his back on the squirrel and padded towards the lakeside.

Beech shrugged and followed, having to move quickly as Peaty was certainly in a hurry. As he followed him, Beech noticed how Peaty was still walking with that slight list to the side and Beech suddenly thought of the wound, the *lump* Peaty had received in the fight with the foxes. Beech paused and frowned but then got moving again because he wasn't sure what it meant and whatever was in the wind tonight was obviously important.

At the lake, Peaty stopped and waited for Beech to catch up. "Just a minute," he said. "I'll be back as soon as I can."

He was only gone a few minutes and then he told Beech to follow him again. A few yards up the lakeside, Beech finally saw the turtle in the chancy light of the moon and his mouth dropped open and stayed that way.

"Hello, Beech. Glad to meet you," the turtle said slowly.

Beech heard that voice and thought of the lake in the summer, slow and bubbling. "Er, yes," he said and nodded. "You too."

"Right then, you're supposed to meet Bumper tonight and you will. But you have to cross the lake, so..."

"*What*?" Beech almost shouted. "Why?" He looked from the turtle to Peaty.

"Because Bumper is on the far side, meeting with Stripe," the turtle explained. "Along with...one or two others."

"Oh. Right but...how?" Beech looked at Peaty again and saw that the young badger was trying very hard not to laugh. Beech frowned and looked back at the turtle.

"On my back," the turtle said.

"What? Oh no. No, definitely not. Oh no."

Peaty gave up trying to hide his laughter and let it out.

"What are you laughing at, you young pup? There's nothing funny here."

"That's...that's because you can't see your face," Peaty told him and giggled.

"Look," the turtle said. "That's where Bumper is and we, all of us over there, need to have you there. It's important. The night's quiet and the lake's calm and I'm very careful with my passengers. We have to go now because I've got to come back for Peaty. Beech?"

Beech looked hard at the turtle and then at Peaty and finally rolled his eyes and shrugged. "Oh, Lake and Forest, come on then."

As he climbed off the turtle's back and put his paws down, finally, on the ground again, Beech let out a long sigh.

"That wasn't too bad, eh?" The turtle did not wait for an answer. "Just wait here while I fetch Peaty and then we can go to the cottage."

About twenty yards from the cottage, Beech finally made out the moving shape he had been watching since cresting the small rise in the land. He could hear what the shape was saying, too.

"Oh my, oh dear, they're here now. Yes they are."

As he passed through the cottage door, Beech thought, *Yes, here we are,* and wondered why he did not feel even the least bit afraid. Then he was inside the cottage and felt the warmth amid the leaping shadows.

"Hello, Beech," Bumper said. "Since I'm the one who had you invited, I suppose, humph, I should introduce you. The turtle you've met and you know Chatter and Blinkwink and Stripe. This lady is a witch and it's her cottage."

Beech looked up at the woman and nodded. "Er, pleased to meet you."

"And you're very welcome," the witch said and smiled at the way the squirrel's eyes widened when he realised he could understand her and she him.

"Er, what is your name?"

"Oh, it's just a name. I think just witch will do."

"And hoo hoo here is somebody I'm sure you'll be glad to see again," Blinkwink told Beech and hopped to his right.

Beech blinked at the sight of Rolf, half-sitting, half-lying in a sort of cradle full of cloth. Beech crossed the room in three bounds and took his old friend's right paw in both of his front paws.

"Rolf! Lake and Forest, it's good to see you, Rolf. To see you *alive*!"

Rolf smiled. "Good to see you, my old friend. I hear you're standing up to Chestnut."

"Well," Beech said as he let go of Rolf's paw. "I don't know about standing up to him but there's a few of us who aren't lying down anyway. But what about you? You don't sound too good. How did you get sick? Why aren't you dead? I mean, I don't want you to be dead, er, oh, flick and flack, what happened?"

Rolf smiled again. "Sit down and I'll tell you." He looked at the witch. "I'm telling this for you, too. I made you a promise and I haven't forgotten."

The witch smiled. "I'll get some food and drink for everybody."

When she came back, Rolf told the whole story. When his voice coarsened, he passed the tale onto others. Beech listened with frank fascination and, as he listened and the night turned towards another winter's morning, he felt something growing inside him. Whatever it was, it warmed him in a way not even the huge, noisy fire could match. It was a warmth that made him feel clean and strong and it made him want to cross the lake again, *right now*, and burn the helplessness out of the other squirrels, to burn the evil out of the Chestnut, to burn the foxes out of Moonrise Forest.

Rolf told the last of the story in a voice weak but no longer rough. When he finished, it was the witch who spoke first.

"Though you owed me nothing, young Rolf, I'm glad to have heard it all." Then she looked at each animal in turn, holding their eyes for a moment before nodding once. "And now, I think there are things which need to be said before you can go on." She looked at Blinkwink.

There was a brief, thoughtful silence, finally broken when Blinkwink cooed twice and fluttered his wings.

"Last night, I had a dream," he told them all. "I didn't understand it boo boo but it's somehow very important and I know it has a bearing on all we have to do."

"Well, harumph, come on then," Stripe grumbled. "What was it? Eh? Come on then, tell us. What did you see, eh?"

"I...oo oo oh, I *saw* nothing," the owl said and shook his head. "It was all...sensations, feelings. I was high, very high and it wasn't just the height of an open sky. I felt there was land, too and the land was very high and it felt...felt...oh, what is the word?"

"Majestic?"

Blinkwink looked at the turtle and nodded his head. His eyes glittered in the firelight. "Yoo yoo yes! And I wanted to see it but it was nowhere that I could see. And the sounds! A roaring, a thundering rush, so there was water somewhere above me. But, even above the roaring of the water, there was another sound, a high, keening sound, a cawing sound. It...thrilled me for some reason and my heart went out to it because...oh, because I wanted to be with it. I *longed* to be with that sound and..." Blinkwink blinked and fluttered his wings again. "I *still* want to be with it, to join with it." He closed his eyes and took a long breath. When he opened his eyes, he was looking at the turtle. "Yoo you knew the word, turtle. D'you know what it was I dreamt about?"

The turtle looked at the witch but she only continued to smoke her pipe but he thought he saw a knowing light in her eyes. He turned back to the turtle. "Mountains, Blinkwink," he said and lowered his long neck in a nod. "Yes, you dreamed of mountains, I think."

"Moo moo mountains?"

"I can't think of anything else that could fill you with such a sense of height and freedom and majesty. Mountains soar and climb and reach so high they pass through the clouds. Yes, mountains are majestic but they're very dangerous, Blinkwink."

"And the water? Such a noise it made."

"Rivers start in the mountains," the turtle told him. "They carry snowmelt down to the lower ground, heading for the sea."

"Oh yoo yoo yes, I can see that. But the other sound, that cawing sound? What was it?"

"An eagle." This time, it was not the slow tones of the turtle, which answered Blinkwink; it was Chatter.

"What? Humph, what did you say, Chatter?" Stripe's voice, as always, was gruff but there was an edge to it that might have been worry; something in the way Chatter had said the word *eagle* had told the badger that Chatter was not too fond of whatever it was.

"Oh dear me, I think you heard an eagle, Blinkwink. Oh yes, I do. An eagle when he flies home after he's killed his food. Oh dear me, yes, an eagle."

The fire flared and popped importantly, hushing them all. The shadows waxed and waned. Chatter looked at the palms of his hands as they lay in his lap. The witch broke the heavy silence.

"Tell us about the eagle you knew, Chatter," she said and rocked back on her chair.

"In the circus," Chatter said, still looking at his hands. "A man had one and he trained it to fly from his hand and it always caught what it went after. It's claws...oh my, huge! And they curled and its beak was even bigger and he *never* missed what he went after."

"Humph, well, that's it then," Stripe said briskly. "You don't want to meet up with one of them, Blinkwink. No matter how the sound makes you long to. Humph, no, eh?"

"Well, well, little chatterbox," the witch said gently. "You certainly have a lot of tales, don't you? Still, I don't think you saw an eagle. It was probably a falcon or a merlin, some hawk. Not an eagle. But, even so, it's still a bird very like an owl," she finished and looked at Blinkwink.

"Yes, of course. That's why it called to me so much. And even if it is as big as the one Chatter knew, it will recognise me the same way."

"Yes," the witch agreed. "And eagle would recognise you but—"

"Humph, yes, I knew it. Something ba—" Stripe began.

"Hush and let her finish," Peaty told Stripe, amazing them both. Stripe was so amazed, he actually *did* stop speaking.

"Thank you, Peaty," the witch said and grinned and looked back at Blinkwink. "An eagle is something very different from a hawk or an owl. An eagle is massive, bigger than any of you, as big as a medium sized fox." She looked at Peaty as he gulped loudly. "Eagles live in the mountains but they fly far to find food and they ride the air the way the turtle rides through the water of the lake. The eyes of an eagle, so it is said, can see the night wind. So, Blinkwink, does your dream still fill you with longing?"

"Yes," the owl replied simply.

"What?" Stripe was flabbergasted. "It's *dangerous*! You should just leave it alone."

"Noo noo no, I cannot do that, Stripe. I told you, it's important to everything."

"Well," Bumper said from the corner by the ingle. "It lives in the mountains and I know *I* don't know where they are. Do you, Blinkwink?"

Blinkwink thought about it for a few moments and then shook his head sadly.

"Maybe it is important," Beech said, speaking for the first time. "But what I'm bothered about is the forest and Chestnut. I thought we were here to decide the how and the when about that?" He looked at Rolf.

"Yes, to all of that, Beech," Rolf agreed. "But I think Blinkwink's right and his dream, this eagle, is important."

"Maybe, but it can't be more important than clearing the foxes from the forest," the turtle said.

"Right!" Stripe's voice boomed around the room, glad that they seemed to be finally getting to the real point.

"Listen," the witch said softly and they all looked at her. "Clearing the forest *is* the most important thing and Rolf is healing well. Still, it will be a month or so before he can cross the lake and lead the battle." She looked at Rolf who nodded and she knew he had finally settled things in his own mind and this pleased her. "So," she went on. "I see no reason why Blinkwink should not look for the eagle of his dream. Perhaps there is a part for this eagle in all of this."

"Oh yes," Chatter bounced on his haunches. "Perhaps his part in all of this is to kill Blinkwink."

The witch chuckled. "Oh, I don't think it will come to that, Chatter. Whatever is in store for Blinkwink is here, not in the mountains."

"Yoo yoo you *see* that?" Blinkwink asked and was suddenly sorry he had.

"See? No but I feel it; your destiny is bound up with your home, Blinkwink."

Rolf coughed and eased himself up in the small bed she had made for him. He wondered if he should ask her what she *felt* about him. She seemed to sense his thought.

"No, young master Rolf. Your destiny is beyond my art. It is bound up with something much higher." She smiled and then spread her arms. "So, as I said, there is no reason why Blinkwink should not try to find his eagle."

"Boo boo but I don't know where to start."

"I can point you in the right direction. But you must be sure you are fit enough, Blinkwink. The mountains are a long way off and you will need all your strength and all of your flight feathers. The winds in the mountains will be far stronger and more dangerous than those you are used to."

Blinkwink closed his eyes; he wanted with all his heart and mind to say in a loud voice *of course I'm ready, of course!* but he knew she was right. He was almost back to his best but not quite. Finally, he opened his eyes and looked at her. "A week," he said and hated the words as they came out.

"Good," she said and stood up. "Now it's time I went to my bed and left you to consider your plans for when Rolf is ready to lead you against this renegade Chestnut. Goodnight."

"You won't stay to advise us?" Bumper asked and Peaty nodded his broad head eagerly.

The witch shook her head once at them and then smiled knowingly at the turtle and left them.

Stripe turned to the turtle and asked, "Humph, well, what was that about?"

"She knows it's our battle. Not hers. She gives us shelter while we need it and she can give Blinkwink directions but when Rolf is well enough, it is our battle and we have to decide what to do. And when." He closed his eyes and sighed; he was tired and wanted the water but he knew it would be some time yet before he could leave. He waited, like the others, for Rolf to begin his leadership by making their plan. It was time.

"It will be dangerous for you, Beech. You know that?" Rolf was very surprised at how strong his voice was; he had done most of the talking and had expected to feel ill shortly after opening the discussion but, the more he talked, the stronger he felt.

Beech shrugged. "The way things are in the forest, just waking up is dangerous." He smiled a bitter smile.

"Still," Rolf said. "It will mean taking the fight to the foxes for more than a month. Will you have enough squirrels to back you for that long?"

"Yes," Beech answered simply. Actually, he believed he could find enough squirrels to back him for twice that long. He was not sure why he felt this but he knew it had something to do with having talked to Rolf and having seen something in his old friend that had not been there before, something deep inside Rolf which was growing stronger. And, somehow, Rolf had transferred a little of that something to Beech; Beech felt sure he could pass a little of it on to other squirrels.

"Humph," Stripe grumbled. "A month's a long time. I'd be just as happy to get over there now and sort it out."

Beech nodded and grinned. "Yes, you old battle-grouch but it would only take one fox or a squirrel loyal to Chestnut to see you and that would be it. Chestnut is so jealous of his position that I imagine he worries every day that he might lose it. If he knew you were alive, he'd assume Blinkwink was and maybe even Rolf. We can't afford that, Stripe. Not yet."

Stripe grunted and reluctantly nodded his head.

"And the badgers?" Rolf asked. "No problems likely there?"

"There better not be," Peaty said loudly and then looked at Stripe and Bumper apologetically. The two older badgers only smiled at each other.

"Oh, but what about Blinkwink?" Chatter asked. "If he's away looking for eagles, he might not be back."

"I'll be here, little chatterbox. Don't you fret about that. And with Beech and Bumper getting my message to the other birds, they'll be ready when the time comes."

Rolf looked at them all and knew what they were all feeling. They were looking ahead and looking forward to what was going to happen. It was not as comfortable a feeling as, say, just sitting by the creek on a late-August afternoon and enjoying the feeling of rest and warmth. No, it could never be like that because there was fear in this expectancy but it was fear of something inevitable and because it was necessary, you knew that you would face it. And that was what made this feeling slightly uncomfortable but, at the same time, strangely satisfying.

Rolf knew this not simply because he felt it himself but because he was the true Elder Squirrel and, so, he was Moonrise

Forest; he had the flame and now he welcomed it, he embraced it; not happily but firmly.

"Whatever happens," the witch said as she sat in her chair. Nobody had heard her come back into the room, none of them had, apparently *seen* her. "It can't be said you have not thought it through. I just came in to say goodbye to Bumper and Peaty." She bent down and patted each animal on the head. "Well now, Peaty. It's been a long night and morning. How do you feel?"

"Erm, yes, yes it has. I suppose." Peaty was a bit flummoxed at the question; he felt fine, never better in fact. Well, apart from the headache and how, now and then, he felt he might be falling over but, as she had said, it had been a long night and morning.

"Good. Well, it's almost afternoon and I think you should have something to eat before you go. After you've eaten, it should be dark enough for the turtle to carry you back unnoticed. Now, if Stripe and Bumper would come with me to the kitchen, everything will soon be ready."

The two badgers looked at her quizzically but she only turned and left the room so they followed her. Their puzzlement grew when they saw that everything in the kitchen was already prepared.

"I needed to speak to you about Peaty," she explained. "What's wrong with him?"

Bumper blinked. "Nothing," he said slowly.

"Nothing to stop him being cheeky, anyway," Stripe agreed.

"There's something wrong with him," the witch said. "Has he hurt himself at all? His head? Recently?"

Stripe looked at Bumper who said, "Well...yes, actually. He was clouted by a fox in the fight we had when Beech helped us. He was cut on the head and there's still a lump there, I think. But the cut's healed fine."

"Ah." The witch nodded.

"Humph, what does that mean?" Stripe asked.

"I think he should stay here." It came out flat but her face was creased with concern.

"Stay here? Oh no! No I won't! I won't stay here, no!"

None of them had heard Peaty come into the doorway.

Stripe turned quickly. "What're you doing here, young whippersnapper? Nobody told you to come here."

"I just thought you might need some help."

"Humph! I'm beginning to think you think too much!" Stripe told him.

Peaty ignored him, looking directly at the witch. "I won't stay here. I'm going back with Beech and Bumper and help get everything ready for when Rolf crosses the lake. I *won't* stay!"

"Just till Rolf is ready," the witch said gently. "It's only a month."

She made as if to touch the youngster but the badger shook his head and then winced at the pain that shuddered through his body. He turned away and went back into the other room. Stripe muttered and began to go after him but the witch called him back.

"No, leave him. He won't stay now. Not for anything. Rolf's flame, as he calls it, has lit Peaty's own spark. He'll go back even if he has to trudge right round the lake to do it. All we can hope is that, in any fighting, he'll steer clear of any blows to his head." She sighed and looked at the floor.

"How bad is he?" Bumper's voice was thick and gruff.

"I don't know...that's the problem. You'll have to watch him carefully. If he looks as if he can't see properly or staggers as he walks or...perhaps he says strange things, you *must* bring him back here."

The three of them were so busy looking at each other, they failed to notice that Peaty was still in the doorway, hidden by the jamb.

Well, now that he knew what Bumper would be looking for, Peaty could make sure he saw nothing like it because Peaty had no intention of missing anything to do with clearing the foxes from the forest. Oh no, not at all. Besides, the witch didn't know everything; he'd be fine in a couple of days. Just fine.

Eating took longer than any of them would have expected. Or perhaps not; it was clear that they were all reluctant to be separated so soon after coming together. Still, it was time to go. It was well past evening now and the night was dark but the clouds had finally moved away. The sky was a billion points of light above them when they all stood at the cottage gate.

"A month," Rolf said. "No longer."

"We'll be ready," Beech assured him.

"Yes," Peaty agreed. "We'll *all* be ready." He looked pointedly at the witch.

The witch smiled and bent down to stroke the young badger's head. "Take care, Peaty. Goodbye," she said and looked at Beech and Bumper.

The turtle led them down towards the lake. The sound of the water beyond the ice was soft and soothing but also, somehow, implacable and inevitable; like their futures.

"You're sure, Mr Owl?"

"Hoo hoo how many more times? I'm sure, turtle. I'm fine. I can fly."

It was exactly a week since they had watched Bumper, Peaty and Beech leave the cottage. It was still bitterly cold but there had been no more snow and only two days when the sun had failed to shine. The owl had exercised every day, pushing himself and his wings to the limit. Yesterday, he had flown as far as the downs and back, catching a vole and eating it on the wing, feeling as good as he had ever felt.

"Well, Blinkwink," the witch said from the cottage's rear doorway. "Since you are positive, it's time I gave you directions to the mountains."

Inside, with the cottage doors having closed themselves as usual, Blinkwink hopped onto the small table where the witch had placed a globe of heavy glass on a satin cloth.

"Look at the globe, Blinkwink," the witch told him gently.

At first, he could only see the distorted reflection of himself and the room. He began to turn his head to look at the witch again and the globe clouded, like the sky in a sudden March shower. Blinkwink's eyes widened and his feathers riffled round his throat.

"Watch closely. Mark the way well, watch for landmarks."

Blinkwink nodded, still staring at the globe but aware of the way the fire suddenly crackled and popped and flared. The globe cleared completely and he saw land dotted with a few trees. Sunlight glared on the white mass of snow inside the globe. The scene shifted but not so fast that the owl could not follow. Blinkwink saw a huge, solitary oak, a narrow gully through which a stream ran in glittering sparkles. The land rose slowly and, as it did, it became rockier, the snow frozen and packed. The stream broadened and then became a river. Then, suddenly, the land stopped rising slowly and began to jut upwards in large crags where pine trees clung precariously to their sides.

Then Blinkwink heard what he had heard in his dream.

Water crashed and roared somewhere the globe could not show him, over harsh and cruel rocks, pounding down to the river. He saw the water flung upwards in huge white sprays, turning the inside of the globe into rainbows. Then it was gone and the globe became cloudy again and he drew back reluctantly.

"You saw enough to know the way?"

"Yoo yoo yes," Blinkwink replied

"You heard the waterfall?"

Blinkwink nodded.

Two hours later, they all gathered in the rear garden, looking out across a moonlit snowscape which blinked with tiny pinpoints of ice, imitating the stars in the cloudless sky. After eating, Blinkwink had slept and woke refreshed and eager to be on his way; he had never felt so alive.

"Oh Blinkwink, dear me but you'll be careful? Won't you?" Chatter hopped from one leg to the other.

The owl swivelled his head. "Surely, little chatterbox."

"Humph, and make sure you're back when we cross over to sort out that bloodydamn squirrel."

"I will, Stripe, I promise. Now, let me get on." He beat his wings and raised himself off the threshold and into the night. The sound of his wings—*thwap thwap*—reminding Chatter of the circus tent in a breeze. Then Blinkwink was off, heading towards the mountains.

"Will he be alright?" Rolf asked the witch.

She smiled and they all felt their hearts lighten. "I believe so and I believe he will return to add more than just his own strength and wisdom to your battle," she said and then went inside.

They followed one by one until only the turtle was left on the back step. Nobody heard him as he spoke to the fast-disappearing dot in the winter moonlight.

"Oh, Blinkwink, I will miss you. Be careful and be quick. And remember that eagles are only *like* owls. They're not owls. Remember that, Mr Owl."

He went inside then and the back door, knowing its place as well as did the cottage's front door, closed itself with a whispered *click.*

Chapter Eight

"It's good to feel the sun on your back," Slygo said and went back to chewing on the bone between his paws.

Slink nodded and they were both silent again, content to feel the thin warmth of the sun, happy to stay here on the edge of the forest for as long as the sun continued to shine.

They were to be disappointed.

Ten yards from where they were lying, the forest came alive. The branches shook and frozen snow fell from them with dull thuds. Fox voices rose over this sound, rising and falling in yelps and yips and one long, pain-wracked howl.

"What the..." Slink scrambled to his feet.

"Chickencoopslime! Sounds like murder in there!" Slygo was already galloping towards the forest.

Both foxes broke through the skeletal branches into a small clearing and what they saw brought them to a sliding halt.

There were two foxes lying on their sides, the snow around them spotted with blood. Another fox was licking himself with a foam-and-blood-speckled tongue. Another fox was obviously dead, his unseeing eyes barely in their sockets any more. His muzzle was split and there was a deep gouge in his throat.

Slink moved among the others, asking questions but not getting any coherent answers. The injured foxes were not badly injured; it seemed to be mostly shock. Why not? From the little Slink could make out, all this damage had been done by birds. The small group of foxes had been heading back from deeper in the forest and they were attacked by a flock of birds. Twenty or more it seemed. It was impossible but, as the dead fox proved, it was also true.

Slink shook his head. "Birds? Birds!"

"What?" Slygo had managed to control the urge to vomit up the food he had recently eaten but what Slink said forced him to swallow hard again.

"They reckon it was birds," Slink told him and then he let out a long howl, which went on for minutes.

Slygo let him howl. He let him because Slygo was afraid. He shuddered as his memory unerringly went to the dream he had had about the huge, hot owl.

Knock it off! You sorted that dream out the other night so knock it off! Right now!

When Slink had finally howled himself almost hoarse, he looked at Slygo and told him to have the vixens and the younguns rounded up and seen back to the earths. Slygo nodded and told one of the other foxes to see to it.

"What about that one?" Slygo asked Slink and nodded to the dead fox.

"He's dead," Slink said coldly. He growled and the urge to howl was building inside him but he bore down on it and took a long breath. "Somebody's going to pay for this. *Hard*!"

"How? It was birds. How are we going to get back at them?"

"Somehow."

"Yeah, well, I'm more concerned about why they did it," Slygo said. "Why now all of a sudden? Birds?"

"Right," Slink agreed. "Let's go and find that nut-cruncher. Now."

Slygo was about to ask why, what was the point in seeing a squirrel when birds had done this and then he realised that, like Slink, his own mind had decided that Chestnut was the one to see after all.

Inside his drey, Chestnut had heard the bone-freezing howl and his whiskers and tail had quivered violently. When the howl faded and then was gone, he decided that he would go and find out who had howled and why. Outside, he told the guards to stay where they were and set off.

They met at the same place as the last time, the only difference was that the snow was not falling and, thin though it was, the sun's warmth felt good. But that was all that was good about this meeting.

Chestnut listened to what the foxes told him. He made no comment, simply sat on his haunches and listened. While Slink did most of the talking, Slygo watched the squirrel and here was something else that was different to the last time the three of them had met.

Last time, Slygo admitted to himself, he had been scared silly. This time he felt mostly calm. Only when Slink mentioned the dead fox did he really feel anything and that was only a dull anger. He watched the squirrel but saw nothing that hinted that Chestnut knew anything about the bird attack or the reason for it.

"Well?" Slink said when he had finished telling everything. "What're you gonna do about it?"

"Me? What d'you think I can do? They were birds. Do I look like a bird?"

Slygo felt his anger rise at the slimy-sweet voice and the impassive face of the squirrel. "You're supposed to be running this forest," he said in a thin, dangerous voice. "These birds live in the forest and that makes it your responsibility!"

Chestnut did not even flinch. "Well, I'm responsible for the squirrels and I have a certain influence with the badgers but the birds? Well, they're pretty much on their own aren't they? I mean I can't round them up and ask for the guilty ones to own up."

Both foxes knew that what he said was the bare-boned truth but, even so, they felt he should be able to do *something*.

"Yeah, well, maybe you can lay it off on them this time but it better be a one-off. If anything like this happens again," Slink told the squirrel and his eyes blazed. "Then I'm coming looking for you and you better remember that you're King

Cruncher mainly because I back you. We've kept our end of the bargain and you better get your house in order or the bargain's off. You got that?"

Slygo felt like cheering even if the threats did have a hollow ring; just to hear Slink talk to the squirrel as if he was not afraid of him was worth a cheer.

"Oh, I've got it, fox," Chestnut said and there was something in his voice that put a stop to any idea of cheering on Slygo's part. Oh yes, there was still something very definitely un-squirrel-like about this squirrel. "And I'll tell you what," Chestnut went on. "Your foxes will have no trouble from my squirrels and I can virtually guarantee no trouble from the badgers because I'll make sure they stay out of your way. As for birds, well, they've got *nothing* to do with me. You and yours are eating well and that's down to me so don't threaten me. Right? You have any problems with the animals I control, let me know. Any other problems, sort them out yourself."

And the squirrel turned his back, just like last time, and headed back the way he had come.

"One day, goofy-gob, I'll eat your stinking guts and you'll watch," Slink muttered.

Slygo did not say anything but he hoped that that day would come soon.

Because the longer it goes with that squirrel, the worse it's going to get. He's as mad as a farm-dog chained up when the foxes are in the coop.

Chestnut took his time going home. He wanted to enjoy the pale sunlight because, now that everything was running smoothly, he was just as glad not to have the snow falling as he had been when he had called on it to fall. The snow had done its job and locked the forest while he established his reign but the sun meant that spring was not that far away and the spring would bring even more power to Chief Chestnut, Lord of Moonrise Forest.

Running smoothly? Really? If it's all going so smoothly, how come a lot of flittering birds kept four foxes at bay and managed to kill one?

And, of course, this was the *real* reason he was taking his sweet time walking home; he needed to consider this strange event. Birds *attacking* foxes, not just defending themselves but actually setting upon a group of foxes. It seemed beyond belief but Chestnut had heard that howl and knew Slink was telling the truth.

Now, if that crafty owl Blinkwink were still around, Chestnut would probably have laid the blame squarely at the owl's door. But the owl was dead and in a watery grave. So, if not Blinkwink, who?

The truth was, he hadn't the faintest idea and, really, did it matter? What Chestnut had told Slink was true; where the Chief Squirrel ruled, there was absolute authority. Even the badgers followed his lead for the most part. Everything was running smoothly and to plan

"I am Chief Squirrel Chestnut and this forest is mine."

Saying it aloud gave it substance and therefore made it true.

Chestnut paused; his mind had made one of this annoying little twitters that usually meant it was about to ask some probing question or other. He waited but it did not twitter again.

"There. Everything is going smoothly and to plan."

He grinned and then, for no apparent reason, he reared up on his hind legs and pawed frantically at the air before thumping his chest twice. Then he walked on, unaware that he had finally crossed the line he had been walking since that long-ago night in his drey when he had seen his opportunity to become Lord of Moonrise Forest. Chestnut crossed that line by refusing to allow that mind-twitter to become a probing question.

He grinned again and a brief ray from the dying sun glinted redly on his two, long front teeth. It looked as if his teeth were covered in blood.

"Birds?" Beech hoped his voice sounded suitably amazed and that his face looked as surprised as it needed to for Bushy to continue.

"That's right," Bushy said. "They attacked a group of foxes and killed one. Chestnut went on one of his 'alone' walks and when he came back, he was full of it. And laughing. He heard it straight from their leader who was really mad about." He looked up at Beech who nodded. "And that was what Chestnut found the funniest. Took him all his time to tell me that the fox wanted him to do something about it. Chestnut just kept laughing. Anyway, he told the fox that he couldn't do anything about birds but if had trouble with...us or even badgers, he could probably help." He dropped his eyes and looked at his paws.

Beech understood. It hurt Bushy to talk about the way Chestnut was willing to sacrifice his own to maintain his position. It hurt even though Bushy was one of his guards.

"Well," Beech said quietly. "I don't know what to think about all this."

"Don't you?" Bushy asked but his voice was almost flat and he didn't look up from his paws.

"What's that supposed to mean?"

Bushy finally looked at Beech. "Come on, Beech. This is me. We've known each a long time and I know how much you hate Chestnut. Probably more than you hate the foxes. I'm not stupid and I think you know something about this bird thing."

Beech frowned. "What's this about? Is it my turn? Has Chestnut decided it's my time for some...*discipline*? Is that it? And you're the messenger? We used to be friends."

"Yes we did," Bushy agreed. "This has nothing to do with Chestnut. This is just because...because..."

"What?" Beech's voice was edged but, from being prepared to fight and then to find a place to hide from Chestnut's anger, he was now hoping that the stricken look on his old friend's face meant something much better.

"Oh Moon and Lake! I'm sick of it! Sick to my stomach," Bushy said and thumped the side of Beech's drey with his tail. "And I'll tell you something else. When he got back from seeing that fox, he...Chestnut looked crazy. It scared me half to death." He shook his head. "Just talking about it gives me the willies!"

Beech felt hope like a burning flame but he had to be sure. "I still don't see what Chestnut being mad's got to do with this bird thing. He's been mad for a long time as far as I'm concerned."

"It's got everything to do with this bird thing! You know it and I know it. Chestnut's that far gone, he's liable to do anything. He can't catch any birds but you'd better believe that if the foxes have a problem with us or the badgers, he's going to go berserk." He took a long breath and let it out. "The snow in this forest won't be white for long if that happens, Beech."

"Bushy, I don't—"

Bushy waved a paw at him. "Oh, stop it. What I'm saying is, birds are okay but keep the squirrels out of whatever you've got planned. You're a rebel, Beech and you're not the only one." His voice cracked and he shook his head again. "Look, I hate what's going on but I also hate the idea of dying. Okay?"

Beech nodded but said, "Sorry, old mate, it's not that easy. Yes, I'm a rebel and, deep down, you know things have reached the point where if you're not with us, you're against us. Time to choose, Bushy. You've just slipped off the branch. Which side are you going to come down on?"

Inside the drey, it was quiet. Outside, the sun was shining again and, in the quiet, the sound of the breeze was a soft, intimate sound, like a sigh. Or a secret.

"Your side."

It was said so quietly that, for a moment, Beech thought it might just have been his own wishful thinking. "Bushy?"

"Your side. Yours!" Bushy's voice was strident. Then he looked at his paws again and his voice softened. "And the High Ones help us all."

"Yes," Beech agreed. "We're going to need it. Come on my old mate, cheer up. It's the right side and you know it. Now, listen to me and see if you don't feel better when I've finished."

Bushy listened while Beech talked. He listened for a long time. Then, towards the end, he felt something stir inside and it felt good. It felt strong and right. It also felt warm.

Blinkwink had reached the waterfall and was perched on a pine branch a little to the left of where the water hit the ground. The sun was low and smoky, almost gone beyond the horizon. Its rays were broad and flat and shone in dazzling rainbows through the crashing water. The owl was mesmerised; seeing this in the witch's globe was one thing but seeing it for real was something else again. The colours and the way they changed held Blinkwink's gaze easily and he was loath to leave this joyous sight until the last of the sunlight bid goodbye to the waterfall.

The journey so far had been uneventful but the owl had loved every second of it after his forced confinement in the cottage. The hardest part had been pacing himself; he needed to fly fast but he needed to conserve his energy for the trip back to his friends and the battle to come.

Now, here he was at the waterfall. As the shimmering rainbow dazzled his eyes and touched his heart, he knew that he was at the mountains and that, somewhere, he would meet the eagle of his dream.

Suddenly, the sun was gone and, with it, the dancing colours in the waterfall. The water became only water again and, as it did, Blinkwink realised something; this fall roared and rushed but it was only a baby. Now, as winter still gripped this place (but not for much longer, he knew), the owl knew that it was only a trickle compared to what it would be like come spring. When spring flexed its muscles and yawned itself awake, ah what a sight this fall would be and if he saw it then, how could he not burst with the beauty of it?

Blinkwink sighed and raised his blinking eyes to the soaring peaks above him. The turtle had been right; these mountains were magnificent and majestic and they soared even higher than they had seemed to in the witch's globe or even in his dream. It was time to see if he could meet his eagle.

He flew upwards, his ears primed for the sound of the eagle, that *cawing* which had filled him with a sense of freedom. As he flew higher, the wind sharpened and buffeted him and the effort he had to put into the flight made him tired. He looked at the rock face as he flew but there seemed to be nowhere he could land or perch, not even a single tree. For the first time since setting off on this journey, the owl began to feel worry fret at him; falling into Sunset Lake would be as nothing compared to plummeting down into the roaring waterfall. Then, just as he thought that the witch had been mistaken and his fate was to die here, he saw something he had first thought was a shadow but, he now saw, was a cleft in the rock face.

Blinkwink thanked the High Ones and dipped his wings towards the gap and came to rest on the ledge of the fissure. It was about twice his height and he sensed that it went back at least four times that distance. He turned and looked out on the sky where the early stars blinked and winked in the deep blue.

He looked down, expecting to see the foaming pool where the water crashed to earth and saw nothing but mountain. It seemed impossible that he had flown so far and yet seemed no nearer reaching the summit of this mountain. He shook his head once and hopped into the crevice and out of the searching wind.

What he needed, he told himself, was a rest. He needed all his strength if he was ever to reach the peak of this huge mass of rock. A loud and long gust of wind found its way inside and rocked him on his feet, riffling his feathers like a rude paw or talon and it convinced him to move deeper inside this crack in the rock.

The fissure turned to his left bare inches from where he was and, beyond the curve, the wind could not reach him and the air even felt quite warm. He settled on his feet and puffed out his feathers and closed his eyes. Just a short rest, out of the wind and the cold, and he would start again trying to fly to the top of the mountain. Just five minutes perhaps, maybe ten.

Light woke him, pushing at his eyelids, stirring him from a deep and dreamless sleep, though he did not know that when he first opened his eyes. Seeing his shadow on the wall of rock, Blinkwink assumed that the moon had simply travelled across the sky and was now shining into the gap.

"Time to go, Blinkwink," he told himself and turned the bend.

He was momentarily blinded; this was no pale moonlight but the full glare of the sun.

"Oh, you stupid owl! You've slept the night away. Yoo yoo you should be perched among the peaks and meeting an eagle by now. Instead, you're still in this crack, blinking stupidly in the sunlight."

He hopped towards the opening, looking at his feet, his eyes still half-blinded by the dazzling sunlight. When he was still a yard from the ledge, he realised what else had happened while he slept.

The wind was wild, blowing directly towards him, knocking him backwards. He steadied himself and waited for the gust to blow itself out but, after three minutes, he had to admit that this was no small if strong gust; the wind was blowing hard and cold and seemed set to blow for the rest of the day. Blinkwink chided himself again for falling asleep and turned the corner again where the wind could not reach him except with its howling noise.

Out of the wind, he began to chastise himself again and then stopped, a look of wide-eyed realisation on his face.

"If I had been out there," he murmured slowly. "I would have been caught in that gale."

Yes, and he would not have been able to ride it out and if there had been no more convenient fissures, he could well have been smashed against the sheer cliff-face and then thrown down to the ground so far below.

Blinkwink nodded in relief and then shook his head because he had no idea how long this wind, this terrible gale might blow. A week? A month? What if he was stuck in this crack in the mountain for such a time? He would never get back home in time to help his friends in their battle against Chestnut and the foxes. On the heels of this came the thought of food.

What did he do for food if he were to be stuck here for any length of time?

Blinkwink dared a peep round the curve of rock and was rewarded by being pushed backwards by the wind and being half-blinded again by the sunlight. No, there was no way out in that direction.

"Well," he told himself when he was back in the relative calm and safety of the place he had slept the night away. "You were tired, owl, but you've paid the price. So, you're supposed to be wise, it's time to prove it. So, think."

He closed his eyes for a moment and, when he reopened them, he was already beginning to move forwards, having made up his mind.

He had to assume that the wind was going to blow for a considerable time so what did that leave him? Well, the crack was deep but he still might end up banging his head against solid rock but the alternative was to stay where he was and starve to death.

As he moved deeper into the mountain, the thought that he might run out of breathable air prodded the back of his mind but that was where he kept it. He watched his shadow on the rock instead and, the further he went, the less defined it became so that, after a while, he was walking in darkness. Only the fact that it was not complete darkness cheered him; light from somewhere was leaking in and that must mean that there was another way out of the mountain. He lost track of real time, though, in that darkness. Once his shadow was gone completely, he tried to measure time by comparing the number of steps he took against his heartbeat but, after a while, time became subjective; as long or as short as he wanted to think it. After what seemed, subjectively, to be an age, he heard it.

Plink plink plonk.

Blinkwink stopped, all his senses were turned up to their highest point. Now that it was loud enough to make him stop, he realised that he had, in fact, been hearing it for some time.

Plink plink plink plonk.

Water. Dripping water. Not rain but water dripping into more water. Slowly but continuously.

Blinkwink hopped forward eagerly. And bumped his beak against solid rock. He hopped back, puzzled. He knew that the crack in the mountain went on beyond this point because he could feel a broad breath of air pushing at him. Then he understood.

The fissure had not stopped or been blocked. It simply curved again as it did when it first began at the rock-face. He chuckled softly and moved to his right some five steps and was forced to stop again. Not because the crevice bent again but simply because what he was looking at stopped him as efficiently as a blank wall.

This was where the water dripped into a pool of water, like it did after a heavy shower in the forest when water dripped from leaves into some puddle next to the tree. But that was where the similarity ended. Here, the water dripped from the curved roof of a cavern rather than the crevice down which he had walked for so long. There were things similar to trees here but like no trees Blinkwink had ever seen or even imagined.

The water had formed crusted growths that were broad at their bases and tapered as they reached up towards the roof of the cavern. The sight was enough to make the owl stop but it was really the colours that forced him to simply stand and stare.

The colours were not as many or as ethereal as those in the waterfall before the sun finally set but they did have their own beauty and they shone with a light that seemed to throb from within those strange water-trees. There were blues like the colour of Sunset Lake in summer but which seemed to tremble and oranges that seemed to burn like a sunset in deep winter, greens like the meadows in spring and whites that actually glittered.

It was the colours that finally brought Blinkwink's mind back to itself. For there to be colours, there must be strong light somewhere. He raised his eyes from the water-trees and looked beyond them and the pool.

There, he saw the hole in the mountain. So much larger than the one where he had entered the previous night. Through it, light glared but it was not the light from a sun that had travelled over the mountain as the day wore on. This was reflected light that blazed off the side of another mountain where ice had gripped the rock in huge sheets. The light, strong though it was, did not blind the owl because it was being reflected at an angle and he could see that the mountain he was looking at was not as steep as this one, and that it had many cracks and fissures and even two clumps of bush.

"Oo oo oh, Blinkwink, what a story you'll have to tell them when you get home," he said in a light voice. "Of course, you have to find your eagle first."

He walked towards the pool of water and dipped his beak into it but quickly withdrew it; whatever was in the water to grow the water-trees and to make such colours was something that rendered the water unfit to drink. He wondered if that substance might be poisonous enough to burn his feet when he tried to walk through it but, really, he had no choice; there was not enough room to fly across.

The water was only wet and he crossed it in three hops. Then he was standing on the edge of the cavern, looking out on the daylight, feeling the tug of a wind, which, though strong, was not as vicious as the one that had forced him through the mountain. The air smelled and even tasted fresh and sweet, almost brand-new.

Blinkwink looked down and saw a long, wide, snow-filled valley between the two mountains. He looked across and up again, preparing to push off and out, to continue his journey, his search for the eagle of his dreams.

His eye was caught by something on the opposite mountain, away to his right. He scanned it hard, not really needing to because he knew what he was looking at; small branches and twigs, twined with long and short stems of grass and packed with dark bracken.

"A nest?" Blinkwink wondered aloud.

His heart skipped a double beat and his ears strained for the sound of that *cawing* from his dream but all he heard was the rush of the wind against the rock. Still, his heart ruled his head and he really believed that he was close to realising his dream.

Rather than set off, Blinkwink stepped back inside the cavern and settled on his feet, feathers puffed out, eyes focused on the jutting crag directly opposite him on the other mountain, seeking the groove in his mind that he had last used when trying to fathom how the forest had fallen to that renegade Chestnut. In this state, he knew he his third eye, the wise far-seeing eye of his mind, would see the bird that lived in the nest long before it finally arrived. And the owl would be ready.

Blinkwink waited, knowing already that it would not be a long wait.

Blinkwink's inner-eye saw the eagle approaching from the left just as the light reflecting off the opposite cliff-face dimmed with the setting sun. The owl shifted on his feet and his feathers settled back against his body. He stood up and stepped carefully to the edge of the cavern.

Blinkwink looked to his left and upwards and saw the eagle as it came down towards its nest. It tilted on a downdraught and settled on the air again with its wings spread. Blinkwink stared at this graceful flight that gave no hint of the unimaginable power needed to keep those massive wings always at the correct angle to the air and the thermals the bird rode. It was seeing those huge wings and understanding the enormous strength needed for the eagle to fly that made the owl realise why only the mountain could be a suitable place for the eagle to live.

The eagle suddenly plummeted, like a stone dropped from the top of the tallest tree in Moonrise Forest and Blinkwink gasped a split-second before his mind told him that this fall was nothing like his own fall into Sunset Lake. The eagle was always in control and this was proved as the eagle again opened its incredible wings to catch another thermal before descending towards its nest. The huge bird was almost within calling distance now and Blinkwink could see how its feathers twitched minutely all the time as it flew closer to the nest, could even see how powerful the legs were and how the talons opened up from their curling position as the bird stalled on the air and lowered itself down among the twigs and bracken and grass of its home.

Just watching the eagle arrive and make its graceful way home filled Blinkwink with a desire, an almost insurmountable urge to take flight himself. His heart swelled, his muscles strained and his own wings opened, longing for flight. Then he relaxed his body and only sighed because what he had just witnessed was not flying the way Blinkwink and the birds he knew thought of when they used the word. No, what they did was ride the air and, yes, they did it well but what the eagle did was...was...

"He flies true," Blinkwink murmured and his voice was filled with admiration and awe, tinged with envy.

True flight. The phrase was the only one suitable because the eagle flew true. Blinkwink nodded and then drew in his breath, his heart pulsing with excitement because he finally heard for real what he had heard in his dream.

As the eagle settled into its home, it called out into the dying light of the setting sun and the sound carried on the clear air of the mountaintop.

Caw caw caw caaaww!

Blinkwink stood at the lip of the cavern for five minutes, staring up towards the eagle's nest but only seeing the bracken and twigs and grass; the eagle was settled back into his home and was invisible to the owl. As he stood there, the last of the light flashed off the opposite mountain and the twilight lowered itself into the defile, turning everything a dark blue and then, finally, a deep purple.

Blinkwink began to wonder how he could make contact with the eagle. There had to be a way. It was why he had come, after all.

Dawn was a pale lemon line on the hem of the sky somewhere behind Blinkwink's mountain. The night had been so silent that the owl wondered if the world had simply stopped. Even the wind had died.

Blinkwink ruffled his feathers and tried to shake some of the tiredness out his body. And the hunger.

"Coo coo come on, bird," he told himself as he moved back to the opening of the cavern again. "You have to try to make some sort of contact with the eagle today. Right now."

He had wondered if he should just fly up towards the eagle's nest but reluctantly decided against that because the eagle, taken by surprise, might simply attack. If that happened, Blinkwink knew he would die without ever getting the chance to explain why he was there; having seen the size of the talons and the way the eagle flew told the owl that much. So, all that was really left was for Blinkwink to try to call out loud enough for his voice to carry across the distance between here and there and attract the eagle's attention.

Blinkwink called out in the ancient tongue of his kind, remembering the cawing of the eagle as it had come home the previous night. The high pitch of the call sounded harsh and even cruel but it rose and fell like normal, everyday language and, the most important thing, it *carried.* As he called, the owl realised that this ancient communication must have been designed for places such as these mountains; the sound would carry across the defiles and the crags and even be heard above a shrieking wind.

Yet, it brought no response. For five minutes, Blinkwink called and, each time, his voice and its call was louder, stronger, seeming to gain strength from usage. And still it brought no response, no movement from the eagle's nest on the next peak. Blinkwink wondered if the eagle had flown off during the time the owl had dozed.

Blinkwink closed his eyes and drew in another long breath. He opened his eyes and looked at his feet, gathering his strength for another, longer call.

The world exploded in a rising clamour of sound.

Blinkwink's heart staggered in his chest and, for a terrifying moment, he could not breathe. His head came up with a snap and his eyes strained painfully. The noise filled the gap between the mountains, filled the sky, the whole world. It screeched and cawed and the air seemed to vibrate so that Blinkwink was sure it must finally crack the rock walls of the cavern and perhaps even bring the entire mountain down on his head.

Then, mercifully, the screeching and cawing ceased only to be replaced by the thunderous sound of beating wings and Blinkwink saw the eagle flying towards him from across the defile. Instinctively, the owl stepped back inside the cavern.

The eagle landed and closed his huge wings behind him. His eyes sparkled like the stars that had filled the sky last night.

His head was broad and high and the beak looked almost as big as the turtle's whole head. The eagle filled the opening of the cavern and blocked out everything behind it, so that Blinkwink stood in deep shadow. For the first time in his life, the owl was truly afraid.

For five heartbeats, silence returned to the world before the eagle spoke and, again, the owl feared for the rock.

Blinkwink recognised the sound the eagle made as the ancient tongue but it seemed different, perhaps even older than the one the owl knew. Blinkwink waited, hoping for a chance to speak before he was ripped to pieces by that enormous beak.

The eagle paused in his questions and put its head to one side. The eyes still sparkled with intent but there seemed little malice in that sparkle. Blinkwink took the opportunity to speak.

He told the eagle who and what he was, dredging his mind for the right words in the old language. He finished by asking, politely, if the eagle knew the common language of animals. Then Blinkwink stopped talking and waited for the swipe of the talons or the sharp peck of the beak.

"Yes," the eagle replied. "Some. Slowly."

Blinkwink let out the breath he had been holding. "The High Ones be thanked."

The eagle's eyes blinked slowly. "You know the High Ones? What did you...say...you were called?"

"Blinkwink," the owl told him and, when the eagle shook his head, went on quickly. "Oh, yes, an owl. I am an owl."

The eagle closed his eyes, obviously thinking. When he reopened them, Blinkwink finally relaxed; the glint in the eagle's eyes was less sharp now and he had settled down on his feet rather than standing on them.

"Owl. Yes, owl is a name I have... know. You prey. Yes, you do."

"Soo soo sorry? I don't know what you mean."

"Prey," the eagle repeated and then shook his head. "Ah, you...search? No, no...*hunt*. Yes, you hunt for your food."

"Ah. Yes, yes, I do."

"Good. How are you here? Here in the..." The sound was ancient-tongue.

"Er, the mountains?"

The eagle closed its eyes again. "Yes, so they are called now but my calling is better. A truer calling. Still...how are you here?"

Blinkwink began to try to sort it all out in his mind, where to start, how to continue. Of course, the ending was easy—will you, eagle, help? But, before he could even begin to talk, the eagle was speaking again.

"Wait. Owls...hunt in the moontime, yes? You did not hunt last moontime. I did not feel you on the..." Another sound as old as the mountains themselves.

"Wind," Blinkwink. "We call it the wind."

"Ah, good. A good word. Well, do you need food?"

Suddenly, Blinkwink was famished and nodded his head.

"Food first," the eagle said and turned his back to the owl. "You call your ways to me later, after food. Fly after me to my eyrie."

"Eyrie?"

"You call it nest," the eagle said and then he was gone, out into space, flying across the air without any apparent effort.

Blinkwink followed but with enormous effort. Still, when he finally alighted in the eyrie, he felt he had flown quite well. What the eagle said as he landed filled the owl with a mixture of pride and deflation.

"You fly good. Fly well. Not true. Not yet. But can learn soon."

Breakfast had never tasted better.

The sun was bright but gave no real warmth at this height. Wisps of cloud drifted across the sky and the peaks and Blinkwink knew that, down in Moonrise Forest, the day would be clear and bright, probably a little warmer than it had been for a long time; spring was not far away, not really.

The eagle had shared some of Blinkwink's food but not much, only enough to be sociable. Now, they were both backed into the cleft of rock where the eagle had built this nest he called an eyrie. They looked out and Blinkwink, for the first time, was able to see and appreciate the majestic sweep of the mountains but he knew that the eagle was impatient to hear the full tale so he turned away from the sweep and soar of the mountains and told the eagle everything. By the time the story reached the waterfall, the sky had darkened to a lovely purple and the air was very cold.

The eagle listened but made no comment except for a sharp caw when the owl told of his meeting with the squirrel who had incurred Chestnut's wrath but had struggled to tell Blinkwink everything he could.

"I made my way up from the bottom of the waterfall," Blinkwink said and then had to pause to dip his beak in the trickle of water that glistened in a crack behind the nest; talking at this height was thirsty work. "I made it to the crevice and I...well, I was tired and slept. When I woke, the wind was too strong for me to fly to the top of the other mountain so I made my way through to the place where you found me." He blinked and cocked his head to the side when he heard a soft chuckle from the eagle. "Poo poo pardon me, but if there is something funny in what I've told you, I would like to know."

The eagle shook his head once. "No no, not in the...story. No, but in saying the...wind?...yes, the wind was too strong. That is funny."

"Boo boo, but the wind yesterday would have killed me."

"Yes," the eagle agreed. "But because you do not know how to fly true. Soon, you can learn to know the wind and fly true."

Blinkwink felt excitement bubble in him; yes, he would love to learn how to fly like the eagle. But it would take time and time was something he did not have. He said as much to the eagle who only shook his head.

"Ach," the eagle said and gave the owl a long, slow look that Blinkwink could not read. "Time? A trick. I have to take time to...think? Yes, to think about what you have talked...told me in your bad story. While I think, you have same time to learn to fly true."

"But I have to be back at the cotta—"

"Yes, but, how did you call him? Rolf? This Rolf is not ready, no? See? Time is not all the same for everybody. You learn the wind and I will look...ach, think about your story."

Blinkwink thought of objecting again but then he understood what the eagle meant and that he was at least partly right. How often had Blinkwink felt minutes fly by when he was busy and how hours could seem to last days? Yet time was constant, time continued in its course; a day was a day and a night a night. Time went on. It was perhaps, and despite the witch in her cottage, the only real magic.

“Yoo yoo you are right,” he told the eagle. “Wiser than I who am supposed to be wise. Yes, I will try to learn the wind and how to fly true. If you can teach me only a little, I will owe you more than I could ever repay.”

“Oh, owl, you will learn but it will be...hard. Yes and you will not like me, I think. But you will learn the wind and while you learn, I will try to...think why you saw me in the globe.”

At the cottage, the animals spent long hours going over the plan, talking about it and refining it but all of them knew that, however many times they went over it, the result would be the same; when the time came to cross the lake, what happened after they entered the forest was bound to be the same. They would have to fight a vicious battle against the foxes, perhaps against squirrels, too. It was not a good thought.

Still, despite the darkness of that thought, all their spirits were rising steadily as the sun became a little warmer each day. They woke early and spent much of the day in the back field behind the cottage and, by unspoken agreement, left their discussions until the evening beside the roaring fire.

The witch left them alone as she did her chores and, when they settled to their talks, she sat in her rocking chair with her pipe in her mouth, blowing the occasional smoke-ring, the chair squeaking gently, never grating. When they began to repeat themselves, the squeaking became faster but still gentle and it soothed them to sleep; it was how she stopped them from becoming frustrated and impatient.

The turtle often left them, and swam in the lake, thinking his own thoughts. He thought back over all that had happened and soon realised that there was nothing he had done or could have done that would have stopped anything or changed anything. There had been an implacable momentum to all that had taken place and the turtle understood that if he had not brought Chatter the monkey to the forest, Chatter would have found his own way there. What had happened was, simply, meant to happen; they were all being moved and used by something, some power or Power, for reasons of its own.

Stripe and Chatter grew closer as the time passed, developing something very close to telepathy that they accepted easily and happily; they had fought alongside each other and had won. They knew that they would have to fight alongside each other again and that, this time, it was possible that the fight would end their friendship permanently. It was the sort of knowledge to forge strong bonds.

Rolf watched his friends and was filled with a mixture of joy and sorrow which, at times, was almost overwhelming. The flame burned within him and he knew that the flame had lit a small but strong spark in each of his friends. This was the joy he felt because that spark made them more than friends. The sorrow was because he realised that the flame within him might burn his friends to death. Still, there was no other way and he felt the dilemma all leaders come to know. He found that exercise helped him damp down the sorrow and he pushed his body as often and for as long as it would let him and, the more he pushed, the stronger he felt and the more powerful the flame burned within him. When the time came, he would be ready to lead the battle whatever the outcome. Besides, he had debts to pay and promises to keep.

The month was almost up. They had three days before they left the cottage.

Somewhere, high in the mountains, Blinkwink could almost fly true.

In the forest, the foxes continued to be angry and confused.

"How the coop should I know?" Slink's voice was low but the anger was barely contained. He was talking to a group of foxes who wanted to know whether he knew where all the squirrels were, the ones they had been expecting to eat nightly.

"We thought you and the Chief Squirrel might've changed the agreement."

"Ggrra, *think*? That's the problem, you *don't* think. You really expect me to agree *not* to eat squirrels? Do me a favour! Nothing's changed. If you see a squirrel, eat it! Now get out of my sight!"

The foxes left. All apart from Slygo who sat on his haunches and waited; he knew Slink would get round to it eventually.

"Ah, they get right up my snout but they're half-right," Slink said, the anger gone now, replaced by a low, thoughtful tone. "It's bloody odd the way the squirrels seem to vanish just when it's time to eat."

"There's something else," Slygo said. "It started just after that bird attack. You go and see King Cruncher and tell him we won't take any coop-muck from any squirrels and suddenly, no squirrels."

"Yeah," Slink agreed. "That's right." He settled on his haunches and put his snout on his front paws and thought about it all.

Slygo did the same but he wasn't really thinking about it all because he had already thought about it. Now, he wanted Slink to think about it, to see if he could come up with anything to make it all fit but what Slygo wanted most was for Slink to get himself so worked up that he would go after the Chief Squirrel. Slygo wanted Slink to get so angry that he went looking for that honey-tongued nut-cruncher and really get down to it. Slygo wanted Slink to do what Slink had said he intended doing someday; kill that squirrel. Kill that squirrel soon. Slygo wanted this very badly because he felt that it *needed* doing. Slygo did not question this feeling; too often over the past months, his mind had squirmed with questions about things that did not seem right and he was fed up with it. Right now, he wanted Slink to find the squirrel and kill him.

"Maybe," Slink said slowly but Slygo saw the glint of anger in the eyes. "Maybe that goofy-gob told all his friends to lie low. Maybe he thinks it's a good way to get at me, make me look like an idiot in front of the foxes. Yeah, it's the sort of thing he'd do. Thinks he's something special but he'll break and bleed just like any other squirrel." He got onto all fours and grinned at his old friend. "Come on, Slygo, let's pay old Boss Cruncher a visit."

Bushy was on duty outside Chestnut's drey, the place where he spent his days when he wasn't inside his own drey. It did not really matter where Beech's old fiend and, now, fellow-rebel, spent his time—his state of mind was the same; a feeling of such high-tension that was so exhilarating and frightening that it left him drained and tired.

When he had begun his new career as an undercover rebel, Bushy was convinced that Chestnut would somehow smell it on him and quickly put an end to Bushy's new career with a swipe at the throat. After a week, Bushy realised that Chestnut was so convinced of his own invincibility that he was effectively blinded by it so that Bushy was as safe (if that was the right word) as he had ever been.

He had been able to pass on some fairly useful information to Beech. Especially the names of some of the spies. Chestnut had, apparently for the same reason he was unaware of Bushy's new career, decided there was no reason now for seeing his spies away from the guards. Bushy had seen one tatty bird, a hare he was sure lived outside the forest, a mole who knew a lot about badgers and two squirrels who had been so full of themselves that it had taken Bushy all his time not to swipe them as they walked away. When he told Beech about these spies, he had wondered at why they would so willingly fall in with Chestnut. Beech had told him that it seemed, apart from the squirrels, that the other animals sounded like outcasts, ones so bitter that helping Chestnut probably looked like the ideal way of 'getting their own back'. When Bushy told Beech that the spies had not mentioned the way the squirrels seemed to have stopped being out and about at night, Beech had explained that there were squirrels out there, himself included. All they did was lead the foxes and any other animal who saw them, a merry dance, showing themselves before taking off into well-prepared hiding places. This way, the spies would see no reason to report what they thought of as a natural caution on the squirrels' part.

Today, three days before Rolf would cross the lake, Bushy was about to find out that somebody had noticed the way squirrels seemed to have stopped going abroad at night. And that Chestnut would finally know that not everybody was following his orders.

It was late morning and the sky a cloudless blue. The snow still lay thick all around but Bushy could sense the slow change in the air and feel the stronger warmth of the sun. His fellow guard today was called Acorn, a dour, close-mouthed animal who obviously thought of his job as nothing more than an easier way of getting food and staying alive. Acorn did what he was told and gave no indication of having deep feelings for or against Chestnut. This suited Bushy.

They both stood silently outside Chestnut's drey, listening out for the sound of his voice or the sound of anything else approaching the tree. Bushy heard them before he smelled them but said nothing. Acorn spoke first.

"Two by the sound and smell. Oh Lake and Forest, what's going to happen?"

Bushy's calm reply surprised even himself. "Easy, lad. We're guarding the Chief Squirrel. No fox is going to bother us." He turned to face the entrance to Chestnut's drey. "Two foxes, sir."

"Grraah, that's right, you nut-cruncher. Two foxes. Slink and Slygo. Come out where we can see you."

"I'll come down," Chestnut replied and made his way down the inside of the tree to the ground. He was amused by the tone of the fox's voice and rather curious.

Bushy waited until he saw Chestnut pad outside the base of the tree and then moved slowly to the edge of the branch. He was not worried about Acorn; the sight and sound of the foxes had virtually paralysed him.

"Grrack! It smells here, Slygo," Slink said when Chestnut settled himself on his four paws and looked at him. "It really reeks."

"Really?" Chestnut asked quietly. "It's strange because I smelt nothing at all until you arrived. Now, though, I think you might be right."

"All right," Slink said and his voice was less contemptuous. "That's the formalities out of the way. Let's get down to it."

"You obviously have something on your mind. If it will make you feel better, by all means, tell me."

Slygo heard a cold amusement in the squirrel's voice and saw it matched by a glint in the black eyes; Lake and Forest, he wished Slink would just rip the bugger's neck open. But Slygo knew that was not going to happen, any more than Slygo himself would rip open the squirrel's throat.

Above them, Bushy listened as they talked. His face remained impassive and Acorn merely stared ahead as he always did, his fear of the foxes coming off him in waves. As he listened and concentrated, Bushy knew that this was what he had been waiting for since crossing the line to the rebel's side—to the right side.

When the two foxes left, the leader was still grumbling at Chestnut.

"Bbraack, you better, you just better. Last chance, nut-cruncher."

The other fox was silent but Bushy could see him as he looked at Chestnut and the look in that fox's eyes seemed a lot more threatening than all the guttural threats from the leader. Still, Bushy didn't care about that, especially when Chestnut climbed back into his drey and stepped out onto the branch where the two guards stood.

"Tomorrow," Chestnut said without preamble. "I want everybody, no excuses, *everybody*, here. Down below. Before the sun gets too high."

As he turned, his eye was caught by a flash of sunlight on a long icicle that hung from a branch to his left. He squinted. He looked from the icicle to the sky and at the sun, which was partly obscured by a thin, scudding mist. The pale disc had a glimmer of colours surrounding it and its heat was as thin as the light it cast. But Chestnut suddenly felt the heat of summer arrow down from the sun and it made the skin beneath his fur prickle. He felt the beginning of a headache behind his eyes. He shook his head and almost stumbled into his drey. Chestnut no longer found any enjoyment in the sunlight as he had the day the foxes had told him of the bird attack.

Neither Bushy nor Acorn noticed the way the sun had seemed to affect their leader. Acorn simply stared ahead, the fear of the foxes only slowly leaving him. Bushy just wanted Chestnut to get inside and for the shift to be over; he had a lot to tell Beech.

Half an hour later, Bushy and Acorn were relieved and Bushy almost galloped to his drey. He was dry-mouthed but not with that high-tension feeling of excitement. This time, most of it was fear; something told him that the early morning gathering would hold nothing good for squirrels.

In his drey, Chestnut tried to sleep but it was impossible. Each time he closed his eyes, he saw the sun and had to open his eyes quickly. He kept telling himself that it was just anticipation of the morning's gathering and the way he was going to prove his power once more. He kept telling himself and kept telling himself and, eventually, it worked enough for him to find two hours sleep before a new morning's sun prodded him awake.

"No idea what it's about, what he's planning?" Beech asked.

When Bushy told him what had happened earlier, Beech was excited at the thought that perhaps the agreement between Chestnut and the foxes might no longer be as solid as it had been; with Rolf's imminent return, it looked like things might be turning in their favour. When Bushy told him about the gathering early the next morning, Beech felt the excitement leave him in a rush and it was replaced by a dull but undeniable sense of unease; what was that bloodydamn squirrel planning this time?

Bushy shook his head. "Just that everybody's got to be there. I can't see it being anything good, Beech. Not if it's got to do with the foxes."

Beech nodded, thinking. He imagined it was another show of power from Chestnut but what did the foxes have to do with it? Beech wouldn't put it past Chestnut to hand over a squirrel to the foxes, some sort of sop, an apology for the fact that there weren't so many squirrels out and about for them to eat. Still, Beech just could not see how the sacrifice of one squirrel, or even two or three would satisfy the foxes.

Then a really horrible possibility occurred to Beech, one that poured through his mind like a splash of cold water from the lake. It was such a terrible thought, it must have shown on his face because Bushy almost shouted out his next question.

"Beech? Beech, what've you just thought of?"

Beech had to take a long breath and let it out slowly to calm the tremble in his voice before he answered. Even so, his voice wavered when he said, "I think...I think maybe that black-hearted renegade might let the foxes run loose on us. Giving them a feast they don't even have to hunt for."

Bushy blinked, swallowed hard and then said, "But...I mean, not even Chest...he couldn't...Oh, Lake and Forest, that's horrible!"

"Yes," Beech agreed. "But he's mad now, he's capable of anything."

Bushy closed his eyes and rubbed at his teeth. Then he looked up at Beech. "But..."

"What?"

"If he did that, just let them loose and they killed us all or nearly all...well, who'd he have left to lord it over?"

Beech shrugged. "Does it matter? I don't think it matters to him. He's mad."

"No, no," Bushy said and was sure he was right. "You haven't stood outside his drey with your paws feeling like they've left home because they're so cold you can't feel them. You haven't had to stand there and listen to him talking to himself about how great he is, how clever and strong and how nothing can stop him. You haven't heard him talking to the inside of his drey like it was another squirrel, talking to it and telling it how he's going to rule Moonrise Forest and then he's going to send his subjects out to battle and win other forests so his children and their children can rule everywhere. It's the way he sees himself living forever." He took a breath. "He can't just let the foxes howl and mangle us because he needs squirrels to do what he really thinks he's meant to do. Can't you see that?"

"Well..." Beech thought about it hard because it was vital; there was no way of getting Rolf over tonight so there was no way of getting everybody on this side of the lake ready by the morning. Ah, but...yes, wait a minute. Bush was probably right and, in that case...

"I think you're right, Bushy. Yeah and I think maybe the foxes won't be there in the morning. Oh, I don't doubt it's something like I thought, maybe even worse but not tomorrow. But that's not the point now. See, the foxes will have to be told, won't they? And the only way for them all to be told, is when they're back in their stinking dens."

"So?" Bushy had thought he knew where Beech was going with this but now he wasn't sure.

"If we could get close enough to hear what their leader tells them..." Beech grinned.

"Oh yes, you and me just stroll up to the downs and ask if we can sit on their meeting please? Great idea, Beech."

"We couldn't but a badger might, don't you think? With them all growling or cheering or whatever and with no wind, a badger might."

"I suppose. And I suppose you know a badger who'd do it, too?"

"Oh, I might. Anyway, I'll get off and see what I can do. You get some sleep. I'll try to see you before the gathering but if I don't get back in time, don't wait for me."

Bushy watched him leave and then settled back and closed his eyes, muttering to himself.

"It feels like it's getting away from us," he mumbled and then shook his head. "No, that's the way it *should* feel but it feels like it's all *coming together."*

And it did. Daft but true. Anyway, he better try to get some sleep. Hah! Fat chance.

But he did sleep, deeply and without dreaming.

Beech found Bumper not far from the ridge of the Hollow, snuffling out grubs. The badger heard Beech before he reached him and Bumper led him over to a deadfall that gave enough cover for both of them.

Beech told the story quickly and Bumper was as horrified as the two squirrels had been. The badger eagerly agreed to do what Beech asked and began to move out of the cover.

"Where's Peaty?" Beech asked. "How is he?"

"He's at home. I got him something to eat and left him in the warm," Bumper explained. He thought about telling Beech that young Peaty was still not really well, that he still seemed to lurch slightly when he walked. But that would take time and time was something they did not have a lot of so he left it at that and then left the squirrel. Beech settled down to wait for Bumper to return.

It took Slink and Slygo most of the rest of the day to get all the foxes together. While they were being found and called home, Slink and Slygo talked over Boss Cruncher's plan and decided that it was as good as it was going to get. The hard part was convincing the rest of the foxes that when it happened, they would need to keep back as much of the food as they could; it was a new idea, saving food but there had been a lot of new ideas this winter.

Now, having told them, Slink had to go over it again to make sure they all understood.

"One last time and listen for coop's sake! You don't eat everything all at once. You've got to make it last a bit."

And, again, the muttering began—*why? what for? how long?*

Bumper had arrived when the meeting was already half-over and, though was enjoying the confusion, he still didn't know what he needed to know. What exactly was Chestnut's plan? He was beginning to think he'd wasted his time when the fox leader made him and most of the foxes jump with a deep, long growl that was almost a howl.

"Gggrrrowl! Shut up! I'm telling you to save it and that's good enough!"

Slygo stood next to Slink but he'd said nothing. Mainly because it wasn't his place but also because he was troubled about the whole thing. He understood the need to save food but what about afterwards? Was that squirrel going to do this sort of thing at intervals or what? If that *was* his plan, wouldn't the other squirrels just fade away, slip out of the forest and find some other place to live? Looking at old goofy-gob gave Slygo the heebie-jeebies so how did other squirrels feel about him? No,

Slygo just couldn't come to terms with the idea that everything after this would be hunky-dory.

"Ggrright, that's better," Slink said. "Now get off and make sure anybody who isn't here knows it's the day after tomorrow, just before the sun dips into the lake."

Bumper waited for five minutes and then made his way back to the deadfall and Beech. He was happy he had finally heard the important thing, the *when* but there was something about it, about all of this that made him feel...well, almost scared; just how much control did he and his friends have over things? He shook his broad, flat head as he padded through the trees. Did it matter? Probably not. The important thing was that he had the information.

And how did you get that information?

By listening to the foxes.

And why did you do that?

So we would have a chance.

Yes, exactly. You took a chance to have a chance. You decided to risk your life so that you and your friends and the forest could have a chance. Things might be turning your way a little but all of you took chances to make things turn.

Fate?

No. Balance. Things are balanced. You do something and it tilts your way, you don't do something and it tilts the other way. It is always up to you. You always have a choice and you always have to make that choice.

Bumper stopped and looked around; what had that been? At first, it had just seemed to be his mind, thinking things through but at the end, it had felt like a conversation he was having with somebody else.

Still, whatever it had been, it had gone and, Bumper realised suddenly, the unease, the almost-fear he had felt, had gone with it. Now, he was just excited that he had the information and here was the deadfall where he would tell Beech.

It was late afternoon, almost twilight and, while Beech waited impatiently for Bumper to return with the information they all needed, Rolf was on the back step of the cottage. The others were inside, sitting by the fire, eating and talking. Rolf had stayed for a last look at the back field, to watch the sun finally give up its thin hold on the day. Tomorrow, probably at about this same time, he would cross the lake.

The thought filled him the way food filled his stomach but it did not give him the same satisfaction. Oh, there was no doubt anymore in his mind about the need to do what was going to be done; all that was settled and he was sanguine about that. It was the thought that it might still all come to nothing; plots and plans were all very well but none of them came with any guarantees. They could all end up dead and Chestnut and the foxes could still rule the forest. Worse, Rolf felt that some of his friends *would* die. He felt it very strongly. Several times, he had come close to telling the others, telling them and asking them what right he had to expect death of them. He said nothing of course because he knew, just by looking at them, what answer they would give him. Instead, he asked the question of himself and he always got the same answer.

He had no right. None at all. Nothing gave him the right to ask badgers and birds and Chatter and the turtle to fight and possibly to die. Perhaps he had a tenuous right to ask it of the squirrels but not of the others. Yet they would follow him across the lake without a word, a sideways glance.

"...definitely warmer..."

"Oh my, yes, you can feel it and..."

Fragments of the others' conversation drifted out to him through the open back door of the cottage; not everybody was indoors so the door, which knew its place, had not closed itself yet.

"You'll only give yourself a headache, Rolf."

Rolf started and he turned to see the witch standing in the doorway. She bent down and sat alongside him, her knees almost touching her chin. She looked into his eyes.

"Oh, I'm just tasting the air," Rolf told her. "And smelling the snow. It's nice." He looked at his paws as he spoke because you could not look into the witch's eyes for long without finally telling her everything that was on your mind.

"Yes, it's nice," she agreed softly. "The snow smells clean and sharp but the air tastes of the warmer days to come and they're not far off now. Still, that was not what I meant when I said it would make your head ache. Do you want to talk about it? Sometimes, it helps." She smiled.

"Not much left to say now," Rolf said and then told her everything anyway.

When he had finished, he opened his eyes, half-expecting the witch to have left him, satisfied that she had got him to get it off his chest. But she was still there, smiling at him through the perfect smoke-rings she had blown.

"What d'you think?" Rolf asked.

"I think you won't have a headache now," she replied and chuckled. "But that's not enough, is it, young Master Rolf?"

The phrase suddenly brought images of Saltpepper to his mind and he felt the memory like a thorn to the heart. "No, not really."

"Well, I don't know how it will all end," the witch said gently. "That is hidden from me. All I can tell you is what you already know. You have to return to the forest and those inside my cottage now will follow you. Not because you ask them but because they have to. None of you have any rights in that sense. But, rather than let it upset you, you should welcome it. They are your friends and that fact gives you the right to lead them as it gives them the right to follow you. If it were Blinkwink, say, who had your flame, you would follow him, would you not?" Rolf nodded and she nodded in return. "And there is something else. If it has to be done, then it is surely better to fight and, if necessary, to die, alongside your friends than to die alone." She said it quietly and then left him alone on the back step.

Rolf raised himself slowly from the lying position in which he had laid bare his heart. He took one glance at the setting sun. It was very low now and it looked inflamed as it turned the sky a dark red. Like blood.

"Yes," Rolf said and turned toward the door. "Better than alone."

The door waited until he was inside before closing itself against the bloody sunset.

Chapter Nine

Blinkwink had been away from the cottage for two weeks. In a week, Rolf was due to cross the lake. Blinkwink knew that it was time to leave the mountains and the eagle. Oh but he wanted so much to stay.

He had listened hard to the eagle and watched intently and then he had practised and practised. At first, he had feared the wind as it blew around and through and above the peaks but, as he practised, he moved from fear to respect and then, finally, to testing the wind as he tested himself. He learned to feel the different currents in the air and to gauge when they would change so that he was always in the right place to take advantage.

"You cannot bend the wind, owl," the eagle told him. "The wind is what it is. You have to move. A little, a middle, a lot. Remember that well. Wind will carry you if you move right. Try to move the wind and the..."

Here, the eagle had used a word in the ancient tongue to describe the different currents of air. Blinkwink had his own word; feeling the way the air moved through his feathers as he flew, he had been reminded of the witch, moving through his feathers when he first arrived at the cottage, using her fingers. The currents of the air and the wind reminded the owl of those fingers and he explained it to the eagle who nodded and said he liked that word.

"If you try to move the wind, the fingers will close around you and drop you like raindrops. Know it good, owl."

And Blinkwink had known it good. He learned the lesson well so that, now, he knew how close he was to flying true. But he knew something else, too and, though it hurt to admit it, it needed saying.

They were in the eagle's eyrie, watching the last of the day's light glimmer on the snow and ice of the peaks. Blinkwink sighed and turned to the eagle.

"I have to leave soon," the owl said. "My friends will be looking for me. Too too tomorrow, maybe."

The eagle was looking to the sky, away from the dying sun, watching the thin clouds there. Clouds that had been gathering all day.

"Eagle, I want to thank—"

"Hush!"

It was an imperative and the owl blinked his big eyes; he had never heard this tone in the eagle's voice before. Blinkwink was silent and looked up to where the eagle was looking.

"Since you flew here," the eagle said as he turned to look at Blinkwink. "Since you said...ach, *told*, your story, I wonder why you hear me in your globe. I...live here. In the mountains. I am here, not in forest. I don't see forest in me and don't see me in forest." He blinked slowly and lowered his great head. "I cannot come with you to the forest. This I know you have been hoping, yes?"

Blinkwink nodded sadly; he had been hoping but, with each day's passing, he knew in his heart that it would not be so.

"But still, there must be reason for me in the globe. So, I learn you some flight and while you try to fly true, I wonder. I think. Nothing comes to me, to my mind." He looked back towards the thickening bank of clouds away in the east. "Till now."

"I don't—"

"Growing. Like wings. Watch them, the clouds. Dark at their feet and grey at their beak." The eagle nodded again, looking at the owl. There was a flickering in his eyes that Blinkwink could not read. "Yes, you go tomorrow. But, now, one more flight. Fly with me. Come now, owl."

The eagle was aloft with a thundering of wings. Blinkwink waited until the trembling air settled and then he took to the air and climbed after the eagle. The owl flew as true as he could and it was well indeed yet he worked furiously to use the fingers of the wind while the eagle seemed to merely hang and drift without any effort at all. When he reached the same plane as the eagle, the eagle nodded.

"Now, fly with me. Feel the fingers and know them well. Do not think about flying or where we fly, just fly. Know the fingers in the air."

They flew for what seemed like an age and the owl did as the eagle had bid him. He concentrated only on his body and the air and, soon, he was simply flying true and knowing nothing but the joy of that and the even greater joy of flying with the eagle. They rode the wind, tilting and banking and soaring yet feeling as if they were still on the air while the mountains seemed to fly beneath them. Peak gave way to snow-capped peak and the last of the sunlight flashed on ice or cast thick shadows on the grey crags or in the deep valleys. The two birds flew as one and Blinkwink, knowing he had to go home to the forest, still only wanted it to last forever.

Finally, the eagle banked to the right and dropped through the air. Blinkwink, feeling almost tied to the eagle's tail, followed him down to a bare outcrop of rock.

"I had not recalled it for a long time. It feels good."

Blinkwink, still full of the joy of the flight, shook his head. "Soo soo sorry?"

"Flight with another. It is long since I did it." The eagle made an odd sound and dropped his head. "She left the wind behind long ago."

"You mean...you had a mate?" Blinkwink was suddenly overwhelmed by the knowledge that, until now, he had not thought of the eagle as anything but solitary.

"Yes. We flew together a long, long time. But she left the wind behind a long time ago. She went to the High Ones." The eagle closed his eyes and said nothing for almost two minutes. Then he raised his head and said, "Look," he told the owl. "Watch and hear the clouds, owl."

Blinkwink listened and watched but he still saw only clouds. "Sorry, I don't understand."

"Clouds not full of snow now," the eagle said. "Full of...snow not frozen. Ach! Not snow...Wet! Wet! Rain!"

Blinkwink was about to ask *so what?* and then his mind made a jump, a nimble leap from this outcrop of rock high in the mountains to the waterfall where he had been mesmerised by the dancing colours. The waterfall that fell into the meandering loop of stream whose top was rimed with a thin scrim of ice.

The frozen stream that would become a river when that ice went out of it.

From the waterfall and the iced-stream, Blinkwink's mind took him to Sunset Lake and he saw it the way he had seen it the day he had left, winter-cold but calm.

Then Blinkwink saw it all.

He saw the waterfall when it was no longer a baby but when it pounded down its huge weight of water and turned the stream into a raging river that would charge down the low hills and across the flat land and empty itself into Sunset Lake before finding its way out again in its eternal search for the sea. All that water, full of snowmelt. And rain.

"All that water," Blinkwink murmured and then flapped his wings. "All that water! Yes! Oh yes!"

The eagle nodded. "Good, you see it. It will be a friend...ach! Not friend! It will...help?"

"I'm not sure," admitted Blinkwink. "But it will be unexpected and that might help. Doo doo do you know how long?"

"Not long. Begin tonight maybe. You hear the water?"

Now that he knew what he was listening for, Blinkwink could hear it; the faint, silvery tinkle of dripping water. He looked around but could not see where the sound was coming from.

"Deep in the mountain but high, by the peak. Runs to the fall you watched when you came first. Here clouds collect. See?"

"A storm."

"Storm. Hard wind and lots of...sound. Sun inside cloud like branches."

"Thunder and lightning," Blinkwink said and flapped his wings again.

"Here now but not at eyrie. We go back and you rest. Go home tomorrow. Fly fast and know the wind. Learn it as you fly. Learn it well."

That night, Blinkwink tried to rest, to remain calm but his mind was sifting everything he had seen and heard and done since arriving at the mountain. The eagle tried to help him keep calm by repeating *'know the wind, learn it well, know the fingers well.'* but it only worked for a few minutes at a time before a glazed look appeared in the owl's eyes. The eagle knew that Blinkwink was already flying, flying home, back to his friends.

As the night deepened, the sound of the storm building was a low mutter in the distance. Outside the eyrie, the sky was still hard and clear, studded with stars, only an occasional thin wisp of cloud to hint at what was to come. Yet they could feel the change in the air which, though still sharp, seemed to be rounding its edges, becoming softer by minute degrees. With that slow but implacable change, Blinkwink could feel his excitement and eagerness grow and he knew he needed to bank it or it would tire him out so much that, come the morning, he would not be able to fly true and might even be forced to wait out the storm and that would be no good at all; better not to come at all than to come too late back at the cottage.

"Coo coo could you tell me about your...your life and..."

"My mate? Yes, the time to talk of that is now. To talk of when I was young, yes."

Blinkwink nodded but he found it hard to imagine the eagle as ever having been young. "Yes," he said.

The eagle's story filled Blinkwink with a sense of wonder and long years that made him feel insignificant. So many days the eagle had lived, a life so long and so filled with danger and excitement. And he heard of the eagle's mate and of the love they had shared. The tale soared and swooped as the eagles must have soared and swooped together and Blinkwink found himself loving the eagle who had left the wind behind long before the owl had been born. It was the same love Blinkwink felt for his friends, for Rolf and the chatterbox of a monkey and the turtle and old grumpy Stripe. It was a love so deep and natural that it went unquestioned without any need for it to be explained; it was love and it was enough.

When the eagle finally finished his story, the sky was no longer full of stars; dawn was breaking somewhere to the east but the sky was leaden grey now and the air itself actually smelled of water. The thunder was no longer a mutter but a deep booming, coming fast now. It was time to leave.

"I don't know what to say," Blinkwink told the eagle. "Thank you seems so...inadequate."

"Nothing to speak," the eagle said gently. "And thank you is all that is needed when spoken true. I was glad to have you and to learn you to know the fingers. Time to leave and to win your home back."

Blinkwink nodded. "Yes. And if they know the lake will be full it could help them." He took a long breath and let it out slowly. "Eagle, if...when the forest is...I mean, if I still live when it is all over, may I come back? To learn the final secrets of the wind and learn to fly true like you?"

The eagle cocked his marvellous head and even in the pre-dawn light, Blinkwink could see the glint in the incredible eyes. "Yes. Oh yes, owl. You fly and know the wind and stay with the wind. Stay alive and come back and I will be glad to see you. Come back soon, owl."

Blinkwink riffled his feathers and felt the fingers of the air. He looked at the sky and began to prepare to leave the eyrie, to begin his long flight home. Then a thought struck him so forcefully that he almost called out in alarm.

"I doo doo do not know your name." He shook his head and flapped his wings angrily. "I never asked!"

A subtle change in the eagle's features told Blinkwink that he was amused. Then the eagle gave him his name in the old tongue and it was long and full of the dignity and majesty of the mountains where he lived.

"In the common tongue," the eagle told Blinkwink. "It is not told so true but, like your word, wind, it is close. My name is Melringador."

"Melringador," the owl repeated slowly. "Yes, it is almost a true-telling." Then, before he found another reason to delay his leaving, the owl raised his wings, felt the fingers of the wind and took to the air.

As he banked to his right, Blinkwink heard the eagle Melringador call out a farewell from his eyrie. The owl called out his own farewell and then headed home. It was five days before Rolf planned to cross the lake and that was not very long at all. Still, Blinkwink the owl, feeling the fingers in his feathers, thought he knew the wind well enough now to make it home on time.

Beech had finished giving Bushy the news about how the foxes fitted into Chestnut's plan for the gathering. Dawn was an hour away. To the northeast, Blinkwink was flying ahead of the storm.

"Tomorrow? But that's when—"

"Yes, when Rolf crosses the lake and," Beech said stiffly. "He won't cross until the afternoon and that's going to be too late."

"There's no way of getting the news to him sooner? So he can come sooner?"

Beech shook his head. "The turtle won't be at the lakeside until the set time."

Both squirrels looked around Bushy's drey, the knowledge that it seemed to be going horribly wrong was like something heavy and solid in the air. Then a hollow knocking sound came from the outside of the tree and they both stiffened, their whole bodies tensing painfully.

It came again. *Thock thock thock.*

Bushy looked at Beech and his fears were written all over his face; they had been caught. There was nothing to do but ask who was outside the drey.

"Who is it?" Bushy asked as calmly as he could. "I'm not due on shift for another hour."

"Beech?"

Beech darted a glance at Bushy; why would anybody expect to find Beech here?

"You've got the wrong tree. I'm Bushy."

"Yes, I know but I want Beech. Oh, Lake and Forest, I'm a bird. Grassear's my name. Beech knows me."

Beech let out a breath and nodded.

"Okay," Bushy said.

There was a flurry of shadowy feathers and the bird was inside. He was dark, almost black, his beak a dull yellow, a little glint of light in his eyes. Beech knew him well; he was the bird who had led the attack on the foxes.

"Bit of a risk for Bushy," Beech told the bird.

"Nobody knows I'm here. Listen, I've just heard about this gathering Chestnut's called and I don't like the sound of it."

"How did you hear about it?" Bushy asked.

"From Acorn. If it matters. He was talking to another squirrel and they both sounded scared to death. So, what's it all about?"

Beech gave him a quick account of everything that had happened and finishing with the problem of Rolf not arriving until after the gathering.

"If we could get a message to Rolf, he might be able to hurry things along. But the lake's in the way." Beech said shook his head.

Grassear looked at them both as if they were mad. "What d'you mean, the lake's in the way?"

"Well it's too bloody cold to swim it," Bushy said testily. "Even if I was that good a swimmer."

"Who needs to swim?" Grassear asked.

The squirrels looked at the bird and then at each and then made loud tutting noises; it was so obvious, so simple, so the first-thing-you'd-think-of, that neither of them had even considered it. Then they both started to babble instructions at the bird.

"Look," Grassear said impatiently. "I don't need any directions. I know how to get there and I know Blinkwink and I know what to tell them. So, if you two idiots don't mind, I'll get on with it, shall I? If I have to stay and listen to you two going on like a couple of nutty nut-hatches, I'll end up thinking I've joined up with the wrong side."

Then he was gone, leaving the two squirrels looking at the space where he had been.

"Well," Beech said slowly, chuckling. "Let's get ready for our beloved leader."

Blinkwink flew ahead of the storm but not by much. He needed to get to the cottage and tell them about the water that was already rushing towards the lake; with that extra water, who knew what problems it could cause them? Only the turtle would know and so Blinkwink had to get the information to him.

Rolf was awake. His mind was calm and clear. Tomorrow, he would return to Moonrise Forest with his friends. To fight. To live or to die with his friends. The others were asleep. Stripe snored and Chatter's breath came out in a high whistling sound through his half-open mouth. The turtle was somewhere in the lake, close to the shoreline.

Rolf crossed the room, thinking he might watch the sunrise. If it rose. He had barely nudged his snout to the back door when he heard a knocking sound at the front door.

Thock thock thock.

Rolf stiffened and almost called out but then the witch was there, seeming to glide across the floor, her skirt *whishting* as she passed him. "A bird, I think," she told them; Chatter and

Stripe had come awake with the sound of the knocking. She opened the door.

The bird hopped inside the cottage, all fluttering feathers and darting head, for all the world as if he belonged there.

"Blinkwink?"

"He's away just now," the witch told him. "And you are?"

"Grassear. I'm a friend of the owl's and I've come with an urgent message for Rolf."

"Well," Rolf said, relaxing. "Here I am. What it is it?"

"Humph, get on with it, then," Stripe muttered.

"Well, I was hoping Blinkwink would be here but..."

Grassear told them everything he knew and told them as quickly as he could. Even so, dawn was a reality by the time he had finished. The sun had not shown its face but the sky was lighter. And heavy with cloud.

"So we think it would be best if you could get across sooner," Grassear finished.

Rolf nodded and the bird left through the opened front door.

Rolf wondered what Chestnut was planning.

Chestnut was awake and looking up at the dark, cloudy sky. He smiled; no sun to itch at him or make his head ache. He felt strong and clear-headed. He rubbed his front teeth and said, "Today, Chief Squirrel Chestnut will show his subjects and all animals within and without Moonrise Forest the depth and breadth of his power. Today and forever, they will all know their place in my scheme of things. Dynasties and dynasties."

Chestnut grinned and prepared to leave his drey to address the gathering.

Blinkwink could see the lake now. He was still some way off but high enough to be able to see how the wind was pulling the water this way and that. Even in the dim light of this early morning, he could see the white flecks on the surface of the water.

A quarter of a mile further on, the owl's heart beat a sudden, joyful thump as he saw the trees at the edge of the forest, the edge of his home. He banked to the left, feeling the fingers of the wind and using them, gliding down towards the cottage. As he stalled his drop, the door of the cottage, which had always known its place, opened for him. Blinkwink glided inside and was met by a clamour of voices.

For a full minute, the four animals who were arguing with each other inside the cottage were unaware of Blinkwink's arrival. Blinkwink waited but finally grew impatient.

"Foo foo fine welcome home, this is," he said loudly and nodded as his words finally made them all stop talking and look at him. They stared at him for a long moment and then the babble began again. Blinkwink fluttered his wings. "Stop! Stop!"

They stopped. The witch crossed the room and squatted down so she was able to look in the bird's eyes. She smiled and smoothed his feathers behind his right ear. "Welcome back, Blinkwink," she said. "You'll have to excuse your friends. Things seem to be running together rather too fast for their liking. You perch on my chair and I will listen while you tell me everything. These four can hear your story when they've finished shouting at each other."

"Harumph, now, humph, just a minute," Stripe said. "We all want to know what happened but—"

"Oh yes," Chatter interrupted. "Dear me, yes but we have to get ready to cross the lake later today and—"

"*What*?" Blinkwink demanded and fluttered his wings. "Boo boo but it's supposed to be tomorrow!"

"No," Rolf told him quietly. "We have to cross today. This afternoon. Because..."

So Blinkwink perched on the back of the witch's chair and heard everything. As he listened, he thought of what the eagle, Melringador had said about time. When Rolf had finished, Blinkwink nodded his head.

"Well, perhaps it's just as well."

"Humph, what? What d'you mean, just as well? Eh? Doesn't sound well to me," Stripe grumbled.

"I've flown here ahead of the biggest, most violent storm I've ever heard," Blinkwink explained. "It will probably arrive in earnest tomorrow but the first wind and spots of rain will probably arrive tonight. The lake is beginning to move already."

"Harumph, oh bloodydamn! That's all I need. The lake churning up. Harumph!" Stripe shook his broad head.

"There's something more," Blinkwink said, looking at the turtle. "The rain will be...oh, the waterfall and the river and the snow melting..." He blinked, shook himself and began again. He told them of his journey and of his meeting with Melringador, of learning to know the wind. Then he told them of how the storm began high in the mountains and described the waterfall and the river. "The weather is changing, spring is on its way and with all that water...the level of Sunset Lake will rise. A lot."

"Oh, bloodydamn, bloodydamn!" Stripe moaned.

"Cheer up, you old battler," the turtle burbled and grinned his odd grin at the badger. "Yes, the water will rise but it means more than that. Oh, it means so much more than that my friends."

"Nothing good, I bet," Stripe said.

"Oh it is. It *will* be good for us," the turtle said and the joyful sound of his voice made Chatter shiver; it did not seem right to hear joy in something which, to the monkey, sounded like something bad. "Listen," the turtle continued. "Come closer to me and listen."

“Everybody here?” Chestnut boomed in his best Chief Squirrel voice and then he laughed; a cold, humourless, chilling laugh. “Oh, yes, everybody’s here. Aren’t they? They all know better than to ignore a command from their Chief Squirrel.”

They *were* all there; the old and the young, even the sickly but none of them said anything. A sense of dreadful expectation hovered over them like a cloud, as dark and threatening as the real clouds above them.

Beech was at the back, well hidden by other squirrels but Bushy had to stand to attention beside Chestnut. Bushy's throat was tight and hot with a mixture of fear and excitement. Sprinkled through the gathering, like dandelion seeds on a warm summer's day, were the other rebel squirrels whose job was to make sure the squirrels knew that Rolf was alive, that there would be a second gathering soon after this one and that they would learn that it was not all over. Not yet.

It had been a hectic hour for Beech and Grassear, going round and passing the word to the animals who needed to know and who would not be at the squirrel gathering but they had managed it and now Beech stood like any other squirrel, waiting for his Chief to tell them why they were all here. As he stood and waited, Beech looked around and nodded to himself; whatever Chestnut said this morning would, he hoped and expected, serve the rebel cause well. That cloud of fear was almost palpable and anything that heightened that fear would make the thought of Rolf and fighting back a much better proposition. Then Beech stopped looking round and listened to what Chestnut was saying.

"The new season is coming and it will rejuvenate the forest. The forest and everything, every animal in it. Your Chief Squirrel feels that such rejuvenation is needed amongst his subjects."

Subjects? Did he really say subjects? Beech thought. He glanced at the squirrel next to him and could tell by the look of disbelief on the squirrel's face that, yes, Chestnut had used the word.

"To ensure this rejuvenation happens," Chestnut continued. "Certain...ahem, measures, will need to be taken. Soon. Tomorrow, in fact."

Here it comes, Beech thought. *How bad is it going to be?*

"Before I explain exactly what those measures are, I want to explain why they are necessary. You need to understand why they must happen, why they are so important for my dynasties…" Chestnut paused, as if he suddenly remembered where he was and who was listening. "That is, for my subjects…for *us* to all survive. Survive even the harshest of seasons and conditions. My measures will ensure that this happens. They will ensure that the squirrels who serve me, serve Chief Squirrel Chestnut will, when I deem the time right, carry the blood of the squirrels of Moonrise Forest to new forests, distant horizons. The squirrels of Chestnut Forest…"

What? This is Moonrise Forest. Beech shook his head slowly, seeing the same confusion in every squirrel's face and, more importantly, some raised hackles.

"…the squirrels from Chestnut Forest will spread to cover the world. *The world!"* Chestnut's voice rose and he was no longer really there. In his mind, he was already abroad, leading his dynasties.

Standing next to Chestnut, Bushy could see the fear and astonishment on every face but, like Beech, he could also see the anger rising in more and more of the gathered squirrels. He could also tell by the odd, glazed look in Chestnut's eyes, that the Chief Squirrel had no idea of that building anger.

"...so, a cull. Those not fit enough to be part of my great plan will be necessarily removed. This will be done tomorrow. You will know yourselves those among you who are not fit. You will have friends and relatives and neighbours who are nearing their ending. You will know others who are young but sickly, those who have not coped well with the hard winter now passing and who are not fit to be part of my plan or of the future. These squirrels will gather tomorrow, close to the Midge Marsh. In the afternoon, the cull will begin. Since I am a sensitive ruler and understand that it will be too upsetting for you to carry out the cull yourselves…"

Upsetting? To kill your father or mother, your siblings or your children? Upsetting? Beech felt sick to his stomach, appalled to a degree that overrode his knowledge that, now, the squirrels would do anything to overthrow this black-hearted renegade. The sheer callous way Chestnut talked of massacre went beyond Beech's worst expectations.

"…I have arranged for certain other animals to carry out the cull on your behalf. This will also show you how strong your leader is. Strong enough to command such favours from animals who have always considered themselves our betters and natural enemies. Your ruler has a very long reach." Chestnut nodded, agreeing with himself. "Yes, indeed. So, tomorrow, after midday, you will arrange for those chosen to be gathered at the marsh. Those of you not required for the cull will, nevertheless, be required to witness it so that you may see how the foxes follow my orders. And remember, I have a good idea of the number of squirrels who should be culled so nobody should think of trying to fool me." He turned and swept away, head high, his bush a showy fan behind him as he moved with a cheery, bouncy step.

The squirrels stood, unable to move, trying to take in what they had just heard. Finally, Beech nodded to his fellow-rebels and they began to tell the rest the where and the when of the second gathering that day. Beech didn't worry about any guards or spies; all they would hear would be what sounded like disgruntled mumblings and that would not be any surprise after what had just happened. The most likely tale any would take back to Chestnut would be that the arguments about who were to be culled had begun in earnest.

Gradually, the squirrels broke up the gathering and Beech made his way to the place where he would meet with Rolf and the others. He would meet up with Bumper and Peaty on the way.

"D'you think it will rain hard, Bumper?"

Bumper watched Peaty cock his head to the side to look at the heavy, overcast sky. The older badger frowned as he saw the scar where the fox had wounded Peaty. The scar twisted down towards Peaty's ear and it was still a sullen red, almost angry. Bumper thought of the witch telling him to keep an eye on Peaty, to watch for anything unusual in his actions or what he said. Bumper had done this but he hadn't noticed anything odd about the way Peaty talked although, he had to admit, occasionally, the younger badge seemed to move sideways when he walked. Still, there did not seem to be any real problems and Bumper had felt a little easier in his mind as each day passed.

"Oh, when it comes," Bumper replied. "It's going to come down hard alright. I don't think we need look for it just yet, though. Tonight maybe or early in the morning. Anyway, leave off looking at the clouds youngun, we've got things to do. The clouds will look after themselves."

Peaty smiled at Bumper. A real smile that made his eyes shine. "Yes, and we'll take care of that bloodydamn squirrel at last."

Bumper smiled back and nodded at the thought of sorting out Chestnut but, as much as that, he was looking forward to having Stripe and the others back on this side of the lake; it would start to feel like home again then. "Come on, Peaty, let's meet Beech."

They arrived a few minutes after Beech who was obviously excited. The squirrel was darting glances all round, leaning back on his haunches and rubbing his teeth. When he saw the two badgers, he almost galloped towards them.

"Good, good! Come on, let's go," Beech told them and turned towards the lake.

"Hang on, Beech, what's got you all worked up?" Bumper asked. "I know we've got things to do but we've got all day. Hey, hang on!"

But Beech was already a good twenty yards away and the two badgers had to hurry to catch him. As they followed, Peaty was glad he was slightly behind the older badger; each time Peaty put his paws down on the ground, he felt the vibration all the way up to his head and it made him wince.

"Come on," Beech called over his shoulder. "I'll tell you as we go but hurry!"

"Oh," Peaty mumbled. "Fine, fine, just slow down a bit. I'm not awake properly at this sunshine shower." He winced, aware that he had said something but not what, only that it hadn't felt right. He slowed a little and tried to think but it only made his head ache and, in the end, he was just glad the other two hadn't heard him. He promised himself, though, that he would not say anything unless asked a direct question and would try to only say 'yes' or 'no' even then.

By the time they reached the holly bushes where the turtle had suggested Blinkwink rest when he had rescued him from the lake all those weeks and months ago, all three animals were quiet and thoughtful. Beech had told the two badgers what Chestnut had planned, virtually word for word. Beech had told them calmly, much more calmly than he had expected to be able to tell it. It seemed that the more distance he put between the gathering this morning, the easier it was to control the anger that had threatened to boil over inside him.

Bumper and Peaty had listened as the squirrel told them about the cull and found that there were no words either of them could use to encompass the horror they felt at the enormity of Chestnut's madness. There were no words so they kept their silence, even after they reached the holly bushes and settled down to wait for Rolf and the others to arrive.

"Time to go, Stripe," the turtle burbled cheerfully. He looked at Stripe who muttered something and kept staring at the lake. The turtle knew what Stripe was feeling; despite what Blinkwink had said about the coming storm and what the turtle had said about the rise in the water level of the lake, Stripe still did not like the idea of crossing the water. Still, it had to be done. "Stripe, look, I promise, you'll be fine. I'm not saying it will be easy..."

"No," Stripe said and shook his broad head. "No, don't try to tell me that."

"No, but I *will* get you across safely. I'm taking you first because I know how you feel about it and, I won't lie, because the way the water is now is as good as it's going to be. The wind's picking up. Stripe, we have to go now."

Stripe finally looked away from the lake and at the turtle. His face was a mixture of emotions; doubt, screwed-up determination and stubbornness but his eyes were clouded with hateful fear. Stripe hated that fear but the sound of the lake, a slap and gurgle of moving water, seemed to be the only sound in the world. "No other way?" His voice was almost mournful.

The turtle slowly shook his head, blinking slowly.

"Humph, no," Stripe said. "Ahh, let's go then."

Rolf and Chatter watched them as they slid down across the now thinning and cracking scrim of ice round the lake, both of them expecting the badger to 'humph' once more and then simply turn round and come back. But Stripe did not turn and come back. He clambered on top of the turtle and then they were in the water, moving away, towards the forest.

Blinkwink hopped down from the cottage roof. "I'll fly above them," he said and took off.

Rolf and Chatter watched the owl as he climbed and their eyes were full of a soft wonder at the beauty of the rise and the following flight; it was a beautiful sight.

"He learned a lot," Rolf said quietly.

"Oh yes," Chatter agreed, still watching the diminishing shape of the owl with round eyes.

"Yes, he learned a lot but he learned much more than just the ways of the wind," the witch said. She was standing behind them, breaking her silence for the first time since the turtle had told them to come close and listen. She was wrapped in a black shawl and a cloak. The cloak was white, held at the throat by a round brooch made of something that glinted even in the overcast. In the centre of the brooch was a stone of deep green which shimmered at its centre with an eerie orange flicker.

"What else did he learn?" Rolf asked, his eyes fixed on that orange glimmer.

"Ah, that is his tale to tell. And he will tell it when the time is right."

"Oh dear," Chatter said and looked at her. "Yes, I'm sure but…well, we might not be…dear me, not all of us…and…" He broke off, aghast at what he had almost said.

"Don't worry, Chatter," Rolf said gently. "We've all been thinking the same thing. We're all going into this with our eyes open. It's the only way to do it. It's not going to be easy and maybe that's right. Maybe it shouldn't be easy. But we have to do it, no matter what the cost. Knowing that will make us more careful."

Chatter had almost been in tears after coming so close to saying what was on his mind but, listening to Rolf, he felt better. Following Rolf would be easy even if the job was a hard one. The monkey nodded and then settled down to wait for the turtle to return.

Blinkwink arrived back first but he would only say that Stripe had crossed to the far side safely. Even when Chatter pressed for more, the owl only repeated that Stripe was safe on the other side.

Stripe *was* on the other side and safe but the journey had been hard on him. His feet had not been just wet but drenched half way up his legs. The lake moved in swells and the rocking movement made him feel queasy and the wind made his eyes water even though they were tightly closed.

When he finally made shore, the badger felt like a day old pup. His legs wobbled and tried to sit him on his backside as he scrambled up towards solid ground. When he reached the waiting Bumper, he didn't even have enough breath left to say hello.

Back at the cottage, the turtle only came up the rise far enough to call for Rolf to hurry.

Rolf turned to the witch. "I can only say thank you and it isn't enough. You saved my life so how can thank you be enough?"

"It is always enough if it is meant and I know it is. I was glad to do what I could but you did as much for yourself." She bent and laid her hand on Rolf's head. "Goodbye young master Rolf. Go with strength and with your flame burning bright. Do what you must do and remember, they are your friends and follow you because of that. Think no more of 'what right?', only of what has to be done. Go with your flame fanned by hope and the trust of good friends."

Rolf nodded but said, “You still cannot see more than hope?”

“No, but I know that spring always comes. Even after the harshest winter.”

“I will hope to see you in the spring, then. I can come back, if I am able?”

She smiled. “You have not seen the sunlight on the flowers in my back fields so, yes, you must.”

Rolf saw the tremor at the edge of her smile even through the prism of his own tears. He turned away and padded down to the lake. Blinkwink flew above the squirrel.

“So, little chatterbox, it is just you and I. For a little while. How do you feel?”

“I feel…strange. Happy and excited and, oh my yes, scared a bit, too.”

“That’s not strange,” the witch told him. “You are not going to a picnic.”

“Oh no, deary me no but, still, I feel excited about it. About the fighting, I mean. It’s because I feel excited about it that I feel scared. Oh, I mean, I should feel scared about fighting but I feel excited so I feel scared because I feel exc…oh dear.” He ran his paws across his face distractedly.

“I know. Tell me, Chatter, are you worried that you might die over there?”

She said it in a way that made it seem more important than he knew it was anyway so he thought about it carefully. Finally, he said, “Not really. What worries me most is that it might not be enough. Oh dear me, it might not be enough to sort out that bloodydamn squirrel. And those horrible foxes."

"Well, I can see I don't need to worry about you too much," she said and smiled.

The monkey did not really understand what she meant but he had no words to express this so he said nothing. The witch beckoned him and he followed her down to the lakeside. Blinkwink returned shortly after they reached the water's edge and, two minutes later, the turtle waddled out of the water.

"Is Stripe all right?" Chatter asked.

The turtle smiled at the concern in the monkey's voice. "Oh yes. He's fine, now. Rolf is fine, too." He looked at the owl.

"Woo woo well, yes he is. In fact, it was almost as if he didn't notice the crossing at all. The wind is building fast and the water is rising and heaving but Rolf just stood on the turtle's back, staring straight ahead. It was like…like he…"

"Like he was already on the other side," the witch said and looked towards the lake. "Well, perhaps he was." She looked at the animals again. "Now, the day draws on and you should be off."

"Yes," Blinkwink agreed. "It is time, witch." He shook his head. "I still do not like using that word. Will you not tell us your name now?"

"Oh yes, oh dear yes."

She smiled but shook her head. "No. If we meet again, there will be time for names. Now, it's time for you to go."

"Thank you," the turtle said. "It does not seem enough but it is all there is, I think. I will not say goodbye, though."

"I understand. Watch out for each other over there. Oh, and Chatter?"

The monkey turned back to look at her, his eyes wide. "Yes?"

"Remember how good it felt to heft that branch in your hands?"

"What? Oh...oh my yes. Yes!" He grinned and did a back-flip.

She watched the three animals leave until, finally, she stood alone at the lakeside. The wind had blown the hood from her head and her hair blew back from her face. Her face showed the concern she felt but she was also filled with a curious blend of pain and love. She knew that at least one of them would not return alive when spring finally made the flowers in her field bloom again. At least one but she did not know which of them.

"Ah, time is the only thing that sees all," she said and watched until she could see the turtle and the monkey and the owl no longer. Then she walked slowly back home to her cottage. She entered through the open front door and heard the soft whisper as it closed itself behind her. Then there was the faintest squeak and she turned to look at the door.

"A sound other than a whisper? Well, well, well." She shook her head and then sat in her chair. Soon, there were smoke-rings in the air as she rocked gently.

Bumper, Peaty and Beech looked at each other, at the turtle and then at each other again; they were totally nonplussed. They had just finished explaining what Chestnut had in mind for the following day but, rather than being angry and appalled, the turtle was chuckling and moving his head from side to side on his long neck.

"Harumph," Stripe said. "I can't see anything funny in this, turtle."

"I know and you're right but, you see, the Marsh is perfect for us." The turtle looked at Beech. "You're positive he said at the Marsh's edge?"

Beech nodded, still waiting for an explanation he could understand.

"Don't worry, Beech," Rolf told him. "The turtle hasn't gone mad. Now, turtle, explain yourself and put them out of their misery. I want everything and everybody to be ready when I meet with the rest of the squirrels and Beech will have a lot to do. Bumper and Peaty need to get the badgers organised, too."

The turtle hitched in a few gulps of air and got himself under control. "Right," he said slowly. "Now then, you three…"

The day drew on. Morning passed into afternoon with no change in the dim light; the sky was solidly grey and hung as low and threatening as it had at dawn. Sunset Lake was the same colour as the sky except where the wavelets rose as the wind blew harder.

The forest was quiet but not silent; there were pockets of noise blended with the *whisssht* of the rising wind. Squirrels talked and listened and knew enough to keep the noise below the sound of the wind.

In the high branches of Moonrise Forest, birds watched the sky above them and the forest below. In the way they had, they knew that *their* hope had also returned to the forest. The birds made no noise, content to wait until the time was right; *then* they would make plenty of noise.

No guards stood watch outside Chestnut's drey. The Chief Squirrel knew he was safe because his power was almost total. After tomorrow, after the cull, it would be complete and not just over squirrels. The foxes, too, would understand that Chief…no, *King* Chestnut was ruler of all without doubt. Inside his drey, Chestnut dreamed of blood and dynasties.

On the eastern edge of the forest, the foxes spent most of that day as they spent most of their days; they played, they hunted and they slept. They never went close to the edge of the Marsh, knowing that tomorrow would be soon enough. A few foxes, returning from the downs, noticed that the packed ice and snow made more noise than it had when they padded over it but it was nothing to worry about. In their earths that night, some others thought they could hear, faintly, the sound of dripping water but that was nothing to worry about, either.

Afternoon became twilight and then night.

The squirrels were in their dreys, awake and knowing what Chatter had meant when he told the witch he was both scared and excited. The squirrels had seen a miracle earlier in the day and not even the thought that some of them might not live beyond tomorrow could dampen the thrill of knowing that Rolf was alive and had returned to Moonrise Forest.

In the cramped space between the holly bushes, a squirrel, a badger, an owl and a monkey huddled in companionable silence. In the water, within calling distance, a turtle swam slowly up and down. All of them shared the same thoughts.

An hour before dawn, the sky finally began to give up its heavy burden. It was only a faint drizzle, close to mist, but it was real and it was going to become heavier and harder.

Slygo was asleep when the drizzle began. He was dreaming. It was the dream that had plagued him, on and off, all winter. Tonight, though, it was not so vivid but, somehow, more frightening.

There was no clearing without snow, no huge, hot-squirrel or huge, hot-bird. This time, there was heat all around him and this was strange because he could hear the sound of falling rain. And there was a noise that he could feel through his feet as well as his ears; a rumbling that rolled round the sky and in the air.

In his dream, Slygo knew he was dreaming but he was still afraid and struggled to wake up, pushing up through the dream towards wakefulness. As he came close to opening his eyes, the rumbling he had been hearing throughout the dream gathered and then crashed with an ear-splitting roar and his eyes were filled with a terrifying, stark white light. Still enmeshed in the dream, Slygo knew that this terrible light would burn him and anything else it touched.

It brought him awake, whimpering. Tremors ran through his body and forced his teeth together in a loud click. He pushed out of his den and into the fresh air. The drizzle soaked him within minutes and he shivered but it was a much better feeling than that of being burned alive by that awful white light.

Slink slept peacefully. His dreams were filled with biting and snapping and ripping and the visions made him grin and made his paws twitch, even as he slept.

Chapter Ten

"Ah, good," Chestnut said. "I see you have understood my reasons for the cull. Indeed, I see by the numbers here that your understanding is great. I am pleased. Very pleased indeed." He let his eyes roam over the gathered squirrels and nodded his head magnanimously. Beads of drizzle covered his fur.

In among the selected group for the cull were some of Beech's original rebels. They were feigning illness or injury and this was not easy since all of them were almost bursting to attack Chestnut. Still, they had to bank their anger because Rolf wanted Chestnut and the foxes together.

I want to rid the forest of them all if I can. I don't want to lose Chestnut, though. He's the most important thing.

That was what Rolf had said and so they had to keep their anger banked for a little while longer yet.

Beech was there. He knew it was a risk that Chestnut might spot him, but it was one worth taking; until Rolf and the others joined them, the squirrels needed a leader and Beech was that leader. Listening to Chestnut now, Beech realised that he need not have worried. The black-hearted renegade was barely aware of the squirrels; they were clearly already dead as far as he was concerned. Chestnut was talking to those who would be left after the cull, to his subjects, the ones who would perpetuate his line and, in his eyes, his legend.

Beech stopped listening and looked around, nodding and smiling, shoring up the others' courage. It would not be long now, those nods and smiles were saying. Remember what's at stake.

"Very well," Chestnut said finally. "Follow me." His voice was soft, almost kindly.

"The foxes must've been told to wait until all the squirrels were in place," Bumper said.

"All our badgers are ready, old friend?" Stripe asked and smiled.

"Just like you wanted. When the foxes move in, our lot will spread out behind them and cut them off. No fox is going to get out of this easily." Bumper thumped his tail on the ground twice.

"Well, Mr Turtle," Rolf said. "Time for you to go, I think. I'll look forward to seeing you again."

The turtle said nothing but something, which might have been sadness, crossed his crinkled face. He turned and waddled to the lake. Chatter followed him.

"Woo woo where's Chatter going?" Blinkwink asked.

"I don't know. Maybe he has things to say. They've known each other longer than they've known us," Rolf said.

"Harumph, or maybe he's looking for something," Stripe said in a way that made it seem to the others that he knew what the monkey might be looking for.

"Well, I'm sure he'll be back. Anyway, it's time we made a move. Blinkwink, you'll be careful up there?" Rolf asked.

"Yoo yoo you don't have to worry about me, Rolf. When it comes, I will be in front of it. Listen for my call." The owl left the holly bushes and took to the air.

Rolf sighed. "Let's go," he told the badgers.

They followed him out and saw Chatter waiting. He held something in his right front paw. Rolf laughed.

"Well, little chatterbox, it looks like you mean business."

The monkey hefted the branch in both paws and grinned, showing all of his teeth. "Oh yes," he said through those teeth. "Oh dear me, yes. I mean business."

"Humph! You stay by me and any fox is going to think twice about trying to get past us," Stripe said.

They headed towards Midge Marsh. The rain fell harder and the wind blew in gusts.

"Ggrrack! Coopin rain! I prefer the cold and the sunshine," Slink told Slygo who said nothing. Slink looked at his old friend and second-in-command. Slygo's eyes were darting from side to side and he was wagging his brush agitatedly, flicking his tongue out to lick at the falling drops of rain. "You alright me old mate? You look as if you just smelled something bad in the hen-coop."

Slygo shot a glance at Slink and the fox-leader flinched; there was so much…what? *Something.* But Slink didn't know what it was, only that he didn't like that look in Slygo's eyes.

"What?" Slygo said. "Bad? No…no, nothing like that. I don't know, maybe it's the rain." He turned to the foxes behind him. "Come on you lot, we're off."

"Right, that's fine. Those selected for the cull make your way across the small rise and down into the Marsh. Go. And remember that your friends and relatives will be all the stronger for what happens today. You are giving them a glorious future." Chestnut urged them on to their fate with a small grin. "Now, those of you chosen to be part of my fabulous dynasty must watch so that you will always remember the sacrifice made on your behalf. And so that you will remember the wonderful opportunity given you by your King."

Those selected for the cull made their way towards the Marsh slowly, their heads and tails down. The others waited atop the rise. Chestnut stood in front of them, his head and tail held high and proud. If he was aware of the way the squirrels standing with him began to fan out to the sides in a half-circle, he made no sign. He was waiting for the foxes. He had a few words for their leader, words to show everybody, squirrel and fox and any other animal within hearing distance, just who was King of Moonrise Forest.

The rain was falling harder and louder, drops as big as berries bouncing off branches and forcing the melting snow to give up its hold. Across the Marsh, the sound of approaching animals could be heard and, soon, Slink and Slygo led the foxes to the opposite rise above the Marsh. The foxes behind the two leaders were close together, their tongues lolling from the sides of their mouths. Even above the sound of the rain, the smacking of lips was audible.

The squirrels in the Marsh saw the foxes and some made mournful sounds in their throats. Beech whispered what comfort he could. In the trees, the birds watched silently.

"Fox! I see a fox!" Chestnut boomed. "Well, here they are. As I told you. Now you see how strong I am. Those selected are here at my command and these others will watch. And they will know, as will *all* animals in the forest, who controls this forest.

"I, Chestnut, am King of Moonrise Forest. King over all animals who live or move in or through Moonrise Forest. Yes, even you, fox! You will take only when I give and you will support me in my rule!"

Slygo glared at Slink. "What the coop is all this?"

"Wait, just wait, Slygo. Wait and watch. Let him have his moment and don't worry. My time is coming," Slink muttered, his eyes fixed on Chestnut.

Slygo took a closer look at his leader and friend and saw the hard glint in the eyes, the way Slink's body was relaxed but the ears pricked and the brush high, moving gently from side to side. Well, maybe this was the time, after all. Perhaps this was the time when Slink would finally make good on his promise to rid the world of old goofy-gob. Slygo hoped so, he really did because…and, suddenly, the dream invaded his waking mind and the fear was like a chicken bone stuck in his throat. Then the dream was gone but a fragment of the fear remained as he heard something other than the drumming of the falling rain. This new sound was muffled but it was there. He was about to ask Slink what he thought it was but Slink was already yelling to the squirrel.

"Ggrraah, shut your mouth, goofy-gob and get on with it!"

Chestnut grinned, showing long, sharp teeth. "Indeed. By all means." He waved his left forepaw across his chest, taking in the squirrels below in the Marsh. "Take them, they are yours."

Slink barked and led the foxes down the rise towards the cowering squirrels.

Slygo made to move off and then stopped. That muffled noise was louder now.

Behind the foxes, badgers broke their cover and began to move up the rise.

Suddenly, the sky cracked and boomed with ground-shuddering force. Foxes and squirrels yelped and squealed. The rain fell in a torrent.

Slygo felt the strength drain from his legs.

Thunder boomed again and the trees shook as the foxes poured into the Marsh, anxious to catch food before the storm reached its height.

The badgers reached the top of the rise.

Slygo howled and it gave his legs enough strength to propel him downwards. He did not really know what he was going to do when he arrived but just moving was enough for now because it meant he could not think about anything else. He soon caught up with Slink who was almost strolling, completely unconcerned with everything going on around him.

Then the rain stopped so suddenly that it made all the animals pause in surprise. For a split-second, there was total, perfect silence, as if the whole world was holding its breath. Then, the silence was broken by another long, rolling boom of thunder and huge hailstones pounded everything and everybody.

Slygo looked up at the sky, watching the rolling clouds as they crashed into each other. The hail hurt but he was only aware of…

Hot. It's hot. Oh coop and cowpat! It's getting hot, like in the dream! It's here! We've got to get away right now!

The heat was suddenly everywhere and he tried to call out to Slink but all that emerged from his open mouth was a thin whistle.

It was mayhem now. The foxes who had reached the Marsh found that, instead of squirrels meekly surrendering to the inevitable, these were squirrels fighting for their lives.

The attack was so sudden and so unexpected, so vicious, that seven foxes were disabled without so much as managing a return swipe. The next group of foxes, seeing what was happening, arrived more cautiously and the battle was joined in earnest.

Chestnut stood above it all, his eyes riveted on the fox-leader. Chestnut nodded and waited patiently for Slink to arrive.

The storm raged but the animals were no longer really aware of the noise and the hail. Their attention was taken by the need to survive. One howling fox who landed on them with all four paws killed two older squirrels. Slygo's friend, Rusty, paused half-way down the slope, still trying to take everything in. He saw two of his oldest friends attacked by five squirrels who looked far from old or sick as the foxes had been led to believe. The two foxes were overwhelmed, an eye gashed out, a hamstring torn, a snout ripped open. Rusty growled deep in his throat and tensed to pounce.

Slygo galloped past Rusty. Slygo's eyes were wide and crazed and spittle flew from his open mouth. Rusty took off after him, not really understanding why he should follow his old friend, only knowing he must.

Blood stained the melting snow now. The hailstones were not so huge, though they still hurt where they struck, but there were much more serious injuries to worry about now. This new pain meant that an animal would be maimed and would hurt for the rest of its life. Or the pain was mortal. All the foxes were in the Marsh now, eagerly attacking the squirrels who had baited the trap.

Beech darted between legs, nipping and clawing, leaving the foxes he had wounded to turn and, in some cases, to bite or rip at one of their own. After biting down hard on a waving brush, he darted away and looked around to see how the battle was going. What he saw was not all good. The foxes had regained some order after the initial surprise and were now forcing the squirrels back towards the side of the Marsh closest to the forest. They needed help down here. They needed the badgers. Beech began to turn when movement seen from the corner of his eye made him react instinctively.

He ducked and leaped to his left, feeling the wind of a paw-swipe close to his right ear. He turned and saw a fox already in the air, claws extended. Beech darted forward and then stopped, waiting for the right moment. The fox was on the downward arc and Beech leaned back onto his haunches and pushed. His front claws dug into the fox's belly and the fox's own weight ripped open the flesh along the barbs of Beech's claws. The fox fell to the ground, already dying. His front three-quarters fell on the ground but his rear end fell on the squirrel.

Beech was stuck, pinned to the gory ground, lying in the blood and entrails of the fox he had gutted. He struggled and squirmed, trying to get out from under the dead weight but it seemed impossible. He looked from left to right and saw two foxes looking at him. Their mouths were wide open and their tongues flicked from side to side, already tasting the squirrel pinned beneath the dying fox.

Bushy had opened the snouts of three surprised foxes and was making towards the black-flecked brush of another when he saw Beech push his claws into the belly of the pouncing fox above him. Bushy grinned at the sight but the grin faded when he realised that his friend was not going to escape from the falling fox. At the same time, Bushy became aware of the two foxes watching Beech and all thought of the speckled brush in front of him vanished.

Bushy bounded to Beech's aid. He jumped nimbly on the fox closest to him and raked the fox's cheek.

The fox forgot all about the squirrel pinned by the now dead fox. Howling, he went down, shaking his head madly, trying to drive out the searing pain in his cheek. Bushy dropped down onto the ground and darted between the other fox's front legs. He bit hard behind the lower joint and this fox, too, collapsed howling.

Beech didn't waste time waiting for Bushy to try to help him further. Taking in a long breath, almost gagging on the acrid-sweet smell of the blood, he shouted.

"Now! Hurry before the tide turns! All together!"

Bushy had no idea what Beech yelled because, while the second fox could not get back to his feet, the first fox was now up on all fours again and he was looking for the squirrel who had ripped open his cheek.

Beech had been yelling at the squirrels standing behind and to both sides of Chestnut on the rise. They came at his call, running and leaping down the slope into the battle in the dip of the Marsh. They used the elevation of the rise to great effect, taking off halfway down the slope and leaping at or onto foxes. The foxes had no idea what was happening when they found themselves being attacked, apparently from the sky.

The fox facing Bushy was aware of the new attack and decided he wasn't even going to try to work out where they came from. He leapt at Bushy and knocked the squirrel down. With one lazy swipe of a paw, the fox tore a large gash across Bushy's back. The fox opened his mouth in a long, triumphant howl and then bent his head, his eyes fixed on the pulsing beat beneath the squirrel's white bib, just below its chin. The fox savoured the moment when he would taste the hot, bitter blood as that pulse burst out of the squirrel's throat. And then the fox's back legs simply collapsed beneath him.

Two of the new wave of squirrels had landed close to the fox and had seen what had been done to Bushy. They wasted no time. Moving together as if it had been pre-planned, they bit into the taut tendons behind the fox's rear legs. As the fox collapsed, they turned their attention to Bushy.

"Where did he get..." the large squirrel began to ask and then stopped; it was obvious where Bushy had been wounded.

Bushy lay on the ground, panting and blinking rapidly as he tried to stay conscious. "Beech," he gasped. "See to Beech. He's…stuck under…get him out."

"What about..."

"Later. I'll…try to get up. Just…go."

The Marsh was a bloody quagmire now. Bodies lay everywhere, alone or locked in a final death-embrace. Thunder boomed and the hail continued to fall.

Even with the fresh impetus of the second wave of squirrels, the battle was still finely balanced as the foxes adjusted to the change. Although the squirrels were smaller and could move more easily on the churned ground, the foxes' weight and strength was still a winning factor.

In the trees, Grassear called for the birds to finally join the battle and the sky was filled with what seemed to be hundreds of dark leaves. Grassear led them in a V formation and they arrowed down into the gully. The sound of hundreds of beating wings forced the foxes to look up and it cost many of them eyes and snouts. The birds dived into the battle, pecking and flying, stabbing at any part of fox they could see or land on.

At first, the birds were totally successful but, as with the second wave of squirrels, the foxes learned to cope, ducking below the aerial attack and then catching the birds with vicious swipes or actually leaping up and bringing down two or three birds at a time.

When the battle began, Blinkwink had seemed to hang motionless above Sunset Lake, feeling the wind's fingers and adjusting his angle to them continually so that the wind buoyed him rather than driving him down. He could hear the sounds of the battle and longed to be a part of it but he knew what he was doing was as important as fighting.

"Soo soo soon," he pleaded with the main body of the storm still on the far side of the lake.

Below the owl, where the rising waters of the lake had eroded the banks, the turtle sat in the swelling water. The ice around the lake had cracked or broken completely and the waves rose and fell around him, rubbing away a little bit more land each time. Occasionally, the turtle would glance up to see if the owl had changed his position. The noise of the battle came to him even above the sound of the churning lake.

Rolf had held Stripe and Chatter back by sheer force of will. They had both wanted to charge into battle when they saw the first squirrel fall. But Rolf was waiting for something he was sure would come. He was waiting for the flash of blinding light to show itself in the boiling sky above. He had been waiting for it ever since the thunder and hail began ten minutes ago. The deep thrumming of the thunder was continuous and the hail, though smaller, still poured down but the flash was not here yet.

"Humph! Listen, Rolf, let's get down there, eh?"

"Oh yes, oh dear me yes!" Chatter agreed, hefting the thick branch in both hands.

Rolf looked up once more and still the sky refused to light up. He looked down from the blasted elm where they stood and saw the foxes beginning to regain their order and that could only mean that, soon, they would gain the advantage. He nodded once.

"You're right, let's go."

"Humph, finally," Stripe grumbled as he moved out from behind the tree.

"Oh look out, foxes! This monkey's got a big stick!"

Chestnut looked down on the bloody bedlam below and felt nothing but the deep calm he had felt ever since waving the foxes into the Marsh. He could see everything clearly, hear all the sounds as separate things, each howl of anger and every squeal of pain or death. He was almost sure that he could hear each separate hailstone splatter as it hit the ground or a tree or a body. Of course, he understood now, this was all part of his greatness, this ability to hear and see and know everything. The knowledge made him serene.

His face broke into a horrible grin, as cold and hard as the pounding hail.

Slink strolled across the Marsh and its mayhem, looking almost as serene as Chestnut felt. No squirrel or bird appeared to notice Slink as he ambled through the squelching mess beneath his feet. The fox was grinning, too.

Slink *did* feel calm; it was here at last, the time when he would finally rip open the squirrel's belly and feast on the steaming guts of that goofy-gob. And old Boss Cruncher was going to watch it happen. Slink ignored the chaos and the screams, the blood and the noise all around him. All that mattered was eating the squirrel's guts.

Slink kept his eyes fixed on the top of the rise above the Marsh and nodded once as he saw that Chestnut was watching him. The squirrel returned his nod and Slink grinned.

Slygo felt the heat all around him but some deep sense told him that this heat was only a forerunner of the main heat, the heat of the dream. He had to catch up with Slink before that happened, had to make Slink understand that the foxes needed to get out of here, needed to organise some sort of fighting retreat before the main heat arrived.

He crashed through the Marsh at an almost suicidal pace, banging into three squirrels and all three went down in a tangle of paws, their breath knocked out of them. Slygo growled and bit at them but only in passing, never thinking about eating them, only intent on catching Slink. The bites did not kill the three squirrels but Slygo's four paws galloping over them left them dying.

Slygo reached the bottom of the slope on the far side when the birds attacked but he ignored them and scrambled halfway up the slope where he paused to check on Slink's position. He saw him and let out a long howl.

"Slink! Stop now! It's here! The heat is back! Can't you feel it for coop's sake!"

Slygo panted, recovering his breath and saw that Slink was still calmly making his way up the slope, oblivious to everything around him, oblivious to the plea from his second-in-command.

Slink heard Slygo but only dimly, from far away but, even so, he answered him in his mind.

Heat? No, me old mate. I can only feel that squirrel and he's freezing cold but I bet his guts are hot oh I just bet they are.

Slink continued his unhurried walk up the slope, still watching Chestnut. He grinned again when he saw that the squirrel was still watching him. Good.

Bumper and Peaty stood on the ridge the foxes had recently stood on. Bumper's eye narrowed as he tried to judge how the battle was going. Peaty stood next to him.

When they had broken cover minutes ago, the younger badger had been filled with the expectant thrill of coming battle but that had faded when the thunder began. Each rumble and crash arrowed into Peaty's head so it ached with a sickening pulse. The pain was a gripping thing and it had left small patches of the young badger's cheek numb.

When the birds attacked, Bumper had looked across the Marsh, looking for Rolf and Stripe and Chatter to join the fight but still Rolf did not leave his place. Bumper began to wonder if he should just lead the badgers down anyway but all thought was driven out by the next huge crash of thunder. He winced and closed his eyes and did not hear Peaty in the tumult.

"Going now Treebranch for sunlight?" Peaty looked at Bumper but the older badger had his eyes closed. "Time's up for the leaves, eh?"

Another clap of thunder shook the ground and Bumper opened his eyes and looked at the opposite rise.

"About time," Bumper said as he saw Rolf and Stripe and Chatter finally begin to make their way towards the battle. "Come on badgers! For the Hollow! Stripe is here! Follow me!"

Peaty smiled dreamily and followed Bumper. Bumper did not notice how the young badger made his way down the slope sideways but, then, neither did Peaty himself.

The foxes were beginning to cut a swath through the squirrel ranks now and the birds' tactic of peck-and-fly was not as successful as before. Grassear knew the battle was being lost. He flew to a branch and looked around. He saw the badgers finally begin to pad down into the Marsh and said, "At last." He looked to the sky. "Wish you'd hurry, Blinkwink. It's past time old friend."

And there, across the length of the Marsh, towards the lake and above the trees, Blinkwink soared.

Blinkwink had watched the river and the lake for what felt like an age, seeing the waters rise but knowing it was not time yet. Then, off in the direction of the unseen mountains, he had seen the flash light up the sky and the torrent finally came, making the river swell and rush to the lake.

"Hoo hoo here it comes," he murmured softly and then changed his shape and dipped down. The wind's fingers pushed him with eager speed and he swooped to within feet of the surface of the lake. "It's here, Mr Turtle! Noo noo now it comes!"

The owl changed his shape again and the wind lifted him up above the lake and he called out in the ancient tongue, his mind filled with visions of the eagle Melringador. The call built and built until it overrode the thunder and the hail.

Rolf walked with a grace and sureness that kept him upright without any real effort on his part. He walked in front of Stripe and Chatter, aware and not aware of the turmoil around him. He was looking for Chestnut.

And there he was, standing above it all, unconcerned. Good. Ah, but wait. There was another animal moving towards the renegade squirrel. A fox.

For a moment, Rolf felt disappointed; he had wanted Chestnut for himself but the fox was closer, bound to arrive first. Well, never mind; if it were meant to be so, it would be so. Right now, he needed to concentrate on getting through the quagmire and the fighting.

Behind Rolf, Stripe was grim and grunted with each step he took and then grunted with each swipe he made at each fox he encountered. Two foxes felt their flanks burn with flaring pain and they turned to fight but the badger had already moved on, knowing they were no longer any sort of threat. A fox brush caught Stripe's eye and he swiped at it viciously, almost ripping it completely away from its body. He grunted and made to move on but his claws were caught in flesh and he paused. Almost casually, he began to untangle his claws. He felt the wind of something *whoosh* past his face and watched with a comical look on his face as the fox, which had turned to kill whatever had torn its brush, fell to the ground, making a big splash in the mud and slush. Stripe glanced over his shoulder.

"Oh dear me, Stripe," Chatter said cheerfully through his grin. "Almost got clouted there, yes you did." He put the branch back over his shoulder.

Stripe nodded and looked at the felled fox. The fox's head was crushed on its left side, showing bone and brain in the wound. The badger 'humphed', nodded once more and then moved on.

The foxes, so recently believing that they were winning, now faced badgers as well as squirrels and birds but that was not the worst of it, not at all. All of them, whether fallen or dying or preparing to kill, felt a sudden, deep and uncontrollable fear envelop them. They felt heat, gathering off to their left but coming towards them, pulsing and throbbing and implacable.

Every fox stopped in mid-bite or –swipe and simply waited.

Rusty reached the bottom of the slope, still making for Slygo, when he felt the heat. He had killed five squirrels on his way to this spot and one of his forepaws had been lacerated by one of them before Rusty had ripped the squirrel's throat open. The pain of his wounded paw had caused him to limp but it was nothing compared to the terror he felt now, the terror that came with the heat. Hadn't Slygo been yelling something about heat as he had galloped past?

Rusty looked around, seeking the source of the heat but saw nothing new, only the dead or the dying or the fighting. He looked back at Slygo and saw that his friend, too, had stopped running. Rusty shook himself and forced his reluctant legs to carry him towards Slygo.

Beech was up again. The two squirrels who had saved his life had called on another three squirrels and the five of them had managed to push the dead fox off Beech.

Beech was relieved to find that his legs still worked and he was now back in the fighting, though the speed of his hit-and-run tactics was slowed a good deal. Now, having helped three squirrels bring down another fox, Beech was clear of the worst of the melee and he looked up towards where Chestnut stood. He saw Chestnut and he saw the fox, too. Well, Beech meant to kill Chestnut; if that meant killing rather than maiming a fox, or dying in the attempt, so be it

The badgers swarmed into the Marsh, grunting and growling. Bumper led them the way the turtle swam; head down and close to the ground. His shoulder muscles rippled as he pushed through the dead and fighting bodies. Foxes fell to the side, gashed and bleeding, to be finished off by the badgers following their second-in-command.

Peaty swiped at three foxes and, for the first time in a long time, the pain in his head was bearable. The feel of tearing fox-flesh and the sound of their agonised howls did not hurt his head at all. He was shouting as he followed Bumper.

"Come on to the mountain fall! Watch me click! Who needs the rainbow and the hailing claws!"

Bumper heard this and paused in his march. He glanced at Peaty sharply and frowned; the young badger was swiping at foxes as if they were late-summer flies and nothing but an annoyance. Peaty's face was full of life but Bumper's frown deepened when he saw what looked like a dark caul over the young badger's right eye. Bumper wanted to stop and take a good long look at that eye but that was when Blinkwink called out in the ancient tongue and the foxes all seemed to stop moving at once. When the foxes began to howl in unison, Bumper knew there was no time to check on Peaty. The owl was signalling what the turtle had told them to expect.

Rusty was on his back. The squirrel's attack had been so unexpected that the fox thought it was the source of the heat that had hit him at last. Now, the squirrel was on Rusty's chest, trying to get a good bite in with those two sharp teeth.

The fox rolled right and left in an attempt to dislodge the squirrel but the squirrel's claws had a good grip in Rusty's fur and refused to be moved. In a way, this was a relief because, while he fought the squirrel, Rusty did not have time to think about the heat.

Beech was getting bites in and his claws were drawing blood but he knew the fox was bound to shake him off eventually. Even now, the fox's rear paws had found a decent patch of ground and were beginning to push him up again. Beech knew that if he didn't manage to disable the fox *right now*, the fox would toss him into the air. With a huge effort, the squirrel dug in with his claws and raised his head.

Rusty saw the squirrel's teeth and knew that they were aimed directly for the soft flesh beneath his chin. The fox struggled for a better foothold but it was too late. The squirrel's head was already darting down and the teeth looked very sharp indeed.

Beech bit down and was rewarded with the feel of warm blood on his lips. He bit harder and the blood fountained out of the fox's neck. Beech relaxed and began to move his head away from the fox's throat.

And his neck blazed with agony. And then he was lying face down in the bloodied slush next to the dying fox.

"Got him Rusty! Got him!" Slygo howled. "Too late for you and maybe too late for us all but I got this one!"

Slygo had given up chasing Slink when he sensed the other foxes stop as they all felt the terrible heat in the Marsh. He had turned to see if the huge, hot-squirrel or hot-owl from his dream was behind him and had seen Rusty struggling with the squirrel. He had pounded across the ten yards of ground, deciding that he would kill one more squirrel before the hot-squirrel or the hot-owl arrived. Now, Rusty was dying or already dead but the squirrel was still alive. Slygo growled deep in his throat and bent his head.

Beech's eyes were open and saw death coming down from the sky but he felt no fear because he had heard what the fox had howled after swiping him onto the ground. Beech knew that it was almost over now and, though he would not see it, he knew that Moonrise Forest would be saved after all.

And that's well worth dying for, isn't it?

"Yeah, it is," the squirrel murmured and smiled.

The foxes heard Blinkwink's call and at last found a reference point for their fear. They turned and tried to make their way back towards the far ridge of the Marsh. The badgers were already there and the fighting was terrible and merciless.

Bumper led the badgers through the retreating foxes, not pausing to see how many foxes his claws had killed, simply swiping and moving forward. Peaty was alongside him now, still merrily swatting foxes and still shouting nonsense. Not one fox managed to touch the young badger, though many died trying.

Finally, Bumper stopped and Peaty stopped beside him as Rolf, Stripe and Chatter reached them.

"Oh dear me," Chatter said happily. "Foxes bashed to bits! Oh dear me yes."

"I'm going to get Ches—" Rolf began but Peaty's shout cut him short.

"It's all up for the rainbowmountain now! Wave and wilt, Rolf! Coming down like the owl in the waterfall!"

Bumper stared at Peaty and saw the dark cloud where the young badger's right eye used to be. Stripe blinked and made towards Peaty but suddenly, there were foxes among them and they had to fight.

Rolf ducked beneath the paw of one fox and then leapt up, gripping the fox's ear with his teeth. The fox shook his head but Rolf held on, biting deeper.

The fox howled but not because of the pain in his ear; the fox knew where the heat had come from now, oh yes he did. The fox felt as if his whole body had been set afire. The heat from that fire raged through his body and killed him in seconds. Rolf let go and looked around but he could see that the others needed no help.

Stripe almost amputated a fox's rear leg and killed him by burying his teeth into the collapsed fox's belly. Chatter swung his branch with both hands and knocked the third fox onto the ground. Before the fox knew what had hit him, the monkey wrenched up the fox's head and pulled. Chatter's arms were sinewy, immensely powerful, and he pulled back on the fox's chin until he heard the snap of a broken neck. Chatter let the dead fox drop and picked up his branch again.

Bumper had not even attempted to defend himself but had only suffered a minor scrape along his right flank. Bumper was more interested in the younger badger and he bent down to peer at Peaty's right eye, his mind screaming in his head.

Not now, Peaty! Not now it's so close to being over. Not now!

Bumper was about to ask Peaty how he felt, if his head hurt, when the wind went out of him in a painful rush. He turned his head and saw the mad eyes of a salivating fox. The fox's head was rushing towards the badger and Bumper had time to wonder if he would feel the pain before he died.

"Look out in the cottage field!" Peaty yelled and rose up on his haunches. He flung his right forepaw out and his wickedly sharp claws raked across the fox's face.

The fox rolled as the pain tore into him. He hit the ground and tried to blink away the blood but it was no good, he was blinded. And then it did not matter anymore. There was another brief flash of pain in his belly and then nothing but darkness and silence.

Peaty lifted his head, licking at the blood on his lips and turned to find another fox to kill. And the pain in his head flared, making him stagger, making him groan, making him totter onto his flank, panting.

Then the pain faded and a soft, blissful greyness enveloped him

The lake overflowed just as it had done all those generations ago. The towering, white-crested wave lifted the turtle like a pebble on a shore. It bore him along the now water-filled path that led to the Marsh. He could feel the immense surge of power behind as the lake filled with rain and with the snowmelt that had begun in the mountains days ago. It carried him effortlessly towards the battle and he called out as loud as he could as it carried him.

"Water! Millions of gallons of it! Get clear of the Marsh if you can!"

The turtle had no idea if he could be heard and it didn't matter; he was simply giving voice to the joy he felt at being proved right in what he had promised the others about the lake.

Blinkwink heard him and watched as the torrent of water carried the turtle towards the Marsh. Then the owl flew to the forest, calling his own warning. He overflew the battle and, when he judged the water was about to crash into the gully, he changed his shape and dropped down from the sky.

Blinkwink stalled his dive and levelled out, feeling the wind's fingers lifting his feathers, keeping him in the air. He saw the brush of a young fox and let out another long call in the ancient tongue as he dug his talons into the fox's back, gripping at the base of the neck. He lifted the young fox effortlessly into the air and carried it out over Sunset Lake.

"Woo woo one for the owl!" Blinkwink shouted and let go of the fox, which tumbled down into the raging waters of the lake.

Blinkwink's warning was heeded by all the forest animals and they ceased fighting to hurry to higher ground. Rolf turned to the others when the owl called out his warning.

"I'm going for Chestnut," he told them.

"Oh yes," Chatter agreed and patted his left palm with branch. "Time to get up that slope and get that bloodydamn squirrel. Oh dear me yes."

Rolf shook his head. "No. This part is for me alone. You need to get on higher ground and you need to get there fast. Go on now, go."

"Harumph," Stripe grunted. "Well, maybe he's right this time." He looked at Bumper but his old friend said nothing, he only looked down at the prone Peaty.

Rolf saw where the badger was looking and closed his eyes slowly, letting out a long breath. Then he lifted his head and nodded at them. He began to pad towards the bottom of the slope.

Slink had breasted the slope and now stood foursquare on the ground, facing Chestnut.

"Ah," the squirrel said. "A fox. A sharp, clever fox. Well, Slink, what's on your mind this time?" Chestnut's voice was quiet and he looked peaceful.

Slink grinned. "We have business to finish, I think. Don't you?"

There was a long pause in which both animals grinned at each other.

Finally, Chestnut nodded. "Yes, I believe we do."

"Gggrright! Let's get down to it."

Slygo braced all four paws on the ground and faced the squirrel. There was a terrible, baking heat coming off the squirrel in waves, crossing the small gap between them. But Slygo did not care now, not any longer; the battle was lost and Slygo just wanted to go home. Besides, this was probably just another of those dreams and, if it was, he could just walk past the squirrel because it wasn't real.

"I'm going home now, squirrel," the fox said amiably. "You're just a dream and I'll wake up when I walk past you so you might just as well vanish now." Slygo began to walk into the pulsating heat,

"I'm no dream, fox," Rolf said. "I'm real and you're not just going to wake up. You can try to walk past me but I'll stop if you I can. And I think I can."

Slygo grinned and shook his head slowly. "Just a dream," he said and padded towards Rolf.

Rolf waited until the fox was only a foot away and then he rose on his rear legs, lifting his right forepaw in front of his face. As the fox reached him, still obviously believing in the dream rather than the reality, Rolf brought his claws down and across the fox's snout.

Slygo blinked and automatically licked at his bleeding snout. There wasn't much pain at first and Slygo was still willing to believe in the dream and then the heat hit him.

It began in the cut on his snout and then raged through his body the way the water from the lake was raging through the Marsh below them. Slygo howled, the reality finally coming home to him with the burning heat. He rolled on the ground, his paws swiping at his body in a wild attempt to kill the heat but the heat would not die. Instead, it increased and the fox howled louder and rolled faster until his momentum carried him over the lip of the ridge and down into the water-filled Marsh. And, even in the churning coldness of the flooded marsh, the heat continued to burn its way through Slygo's agonised body.

Rolf padded forward without a backward glance.

The turtle arrived in the Marsh at the head of the booming, raging water. He paddled hard, trying to maintain position until he felt the force of the water slacken. When he knew that the water had levelled off, he began to search for any fox still alive. Where he found them, he pushed them down below the surface of the water and held them there until their panicked struggles ceased. He came across many dead birds and squirrels and he pushed as many of these as he could towards the banks of the flooded Marsh. As he made another slow circuit of the small lake that had once been Midge Marsh, he saw Bumper.

"Bumper! Bumper, are you alright?"

Bumper turned at the sound of his name and saw the turtle stroking towards the bank where Stripe and Chatter stood beside another badger who was lying on the sodden ground.

"We're fine," Bumper told the turtle in a small voice. "Peaty isn't. He's...dead, I think. But we can't get him any further up the bank. It's too..."

The turtle swallowed and closed his eyes for a moment. Then he said, "Get him onto my back and I'll take him across to the lower bank. You can meet me round there."

Chestnut and Slink were fighting and Slink was losing.

The fox could not understand it; it was like fighting a shadow. Every time he thought he had a killing grip, he found his paws simply pulling free of the squirrel's fur. He had managed to bite a few good pieces of flesh from the thing but it did not seem to worry it at all. The cooping squirrel, if squirrel it was, just kept on fighting, not even making any noise as he fought. And, with each attempt at ripping the thing apart, with each bite, Slink could feel the coldness of the squirrel deepening.

Chestnut moved like a breeze. He did not feel his wounds, only his own glorious strength. He was a shadow, a shade, a breeze. He was King Squirrel Chestnut, Lord of Moonrise Forest, begetter of dynasties and he was unbeatable. His claws were like Blinkwink's talons, ripping the fox's left ear to shreds, his teeth were like the fox's own, sharp and strong and had already opened a deep gash in the fox's snout. Chestnut fought and felt nothing but the bloodlust as it thrummed inside him, cleansing his mind and his body like an icy wind blowing through him. With each bite, his mouth was filled with blood and the blood tasted sweet.

Slink was dying. He could feel his life ebbing away in implacable waves. He struggled, a frenzy of howls and growls as he tried to make the one bite or the one swipe that would kill this squirrel, kill this silent thing with its icy aura and its wickedly sharp teeth. The idea that he would make old Boss Cruncher watch as his guts were ripped and eaten had long-since faded from Slink's mind; just to kill the cooping thing would be enough.

Chestnut dodged the last desperate, questing swipe and lunged for the fox's throat. He bit down and tasted more blood.

He whipped his head from side to side, the way he had seen the foxes deliver the killing shake to a dying squirrel.

Slink felt his throat ripped open and howled. All that emerged was a long, blood-choked gurgle and he knew he was going to die, finally to die at the paw of this cold, cold nut-cruncher who had never really felt like a squirrel. Then the darkness seemed to fly towards him from every side and Slink embraced it eagerly.

Chestnut stepped back and leaned against the bole of a young elm. He looked up at the sky, at the clouds as they swirled above him. The thunder had stopped but the rain still fell and he opened his mouth and let the water rinse it clean, happy to lose the taste of blood because it was over now; the future was his and his alone. He closed his eyes and let the refreshing coolness of the rain rinse his mouth and cool the skin beneath his fur.

Then he felt the heat and his eyes flew open. He saw Rolf.

"Ah, Rolf," Chestnut said calmly. "Of course. How...inevitable. Well, come if you must. You will soon join the fox. I am beyond your reach. Come, Rolf, feel the ice and let it embrace you."

Rolf said nothing. He simply walked slowly toward Chestnut.

If it is meant that I should die, so be it, Rolf thought. *Perhaps it is the last of my promises to keep.*

As he walked, Rolf reached down inside himself and let his flame have its way with him totally.

Blinkwink landed next to Bumper and looked at the body of Peaty. Stripe nodded at the owl while Chatter raised his bloodied branch in greeting. Bushy, his wound still bleeding but not so heavily, lay on his side, breathing heavily.

"Where's Rolf?" Stripe asked the owl.

Blinkwink looked up. "He's facing Chestnut," he told them and then looked sadly at the body of the young badger. "Noo noo now, it is time for us to wait."

The turtle moved up from the water and inched his way to his friends. "Yes," he burbled slowly. "It is Rolf's moment. For better or for worse."

Chestnut raised his right paw as Rolf approached. The rain stopped and a silence, so perfect it hurt the ears, fell over Moonrise Forest. Both squirrels looked at the sky.

They were only a couple of feet apart now and one quick attack would have ended it all there and then but neither squirrel moved. They continued to watch the sky and, even when the first flash lit up the sky, they continued to look up.

The second flash was even brighter and the thunder boomed immediately. A searing blue/white bolt of lightning streaked out of the roiling sky and hurtled down. It seemed to scream as it came, its jagged length aimed at Chestnut. It came deliberately, unerringly.

Chestnut screamed. A long, nerve-shredding scream that was louder even than the thunder.

"*No! I am King of Moonrise Forest! You cannot do this! I forbid you to do this! Nooooo*!"

The bolt tore over Chestnut's head, singeing the fur of his head, and blasted into the tree behind him. Chestnut seemed to be picked up by something invisible and he was hurled back against the burning tree. He bounced off the tree and lay at Rolf's feet.

Rolf bent down unconcerned by the heat from the burning tree; it was not as hot as the heat inside himself. As his face came close to Chestnut, the dying squirrel opened his eyes.

"Chestnut?" Rolf asked sadly.

"I…dead? Yes…but I think…think I have…come home again. At last. Yes?"

Rolf nodded. "Yes, at last." He looked at Chestnut and sighed as the other squirrel breathed in and did not breathe out again.

It was over.

Rolf reached out with his right forepaw and gently touched the blackened fur on Chestnut's head. Chestnut had been evil but Rolf did not think it had all been Chestnut's fault; something had entered him and used him and had now fled the dead squirrel's body. And that was what he was looking at now, a dead squirrel.

"And he at least died as a squirrel. One who had finally come home."

Rolf turned and made his way to his friends.

SPRING

The back door of the cottage stood open and a warm, scented breeze blew across the back porch.

Spring had arrived the morning after the thunderous rainstorm that had changed Moonrise Forest and claimed the lives of so many animals. The sun that arrived with the new season was almost as warm as a summer sun and now the field behind the witch's cottage was a riot of colour. The day was gently arcing towards sunset and blossom from the one tree close to the porch lay on the ground like snow.

Bumper was talking to all of them but he was looking at the witch whose name, she had finally told them, was Lynora.

"When we got him safely above the water," Bumper said slowly. "Peaty opened his eyes. Well, he opened his one clear eye, the one without the caul of blood. I thanked the High Ones, believing he would live after all. I tried to raise his head off the ground but he winced so I lowered it again. He said, 'Just tell me it went well.' I did and he smiled a small smile and closed his eyes again and I knew he was really dying. I began to turn away when he spoke again. 'If she'll allow it, I'd like to be buried in the field behind her cottage.'" Bumper choked back a sob. "Then he died. Just a long breath out and he was gone. He was himself at the end, though. I mean, he could speak normally. Not like just before he saved my life."

Nobody spoke until, after a long few moments, Lynora said, "We'll do it now, as the sun sets."

When it was done, they returned to the porch and the witch asked the owl if he was ready.

"Yoo yoo yes," Blinkwink told her. "Tomorrow, I leave for the mountains. I will tell Melringador all that has happened and then I will learn all he is willing to teach me" He turned and hopped inside the cottage where Stripe was sitting by the hearth and sobbing deeply.

"And you, young Master Rolf?" Lynora asked.

"Yes, I return tomorrow as well. There are no foxes left now. Those that weren't killed in the battle have left the forest and they will never return. The Marsh, part of the lake as it has become, will be a barrier of death for them now. With Beech…" Rolf paused and blinked away another tear. "Beech would have been my lieutenant but he is dead so I had to leave Bushy in charge while I came to say farewell to Peaty. But all Bushy wants is to be allowed to be an ordinary squirrel again. I will go home and do what Saltpepper trained me to do." He looked at the field and then beyond it to the glinting waters of Sunset Lake. The sunset was a glorious fiery gold that, somehow, turned the sky a pastel green, tinged at its edges with a deep and lovely red/purple. "It *is* beautiful. The sunset over your field soothes me."

"Oh dear me, yes," Chatter said and then, realising that what he really wanted to do was to comfort his friend Stripe, left the porch and went inside the cottage.

Lynora turned to the turtle. "What of you? Will you leave the forest and the lake to look after themselves? Are you ready to be yourself again?"

"Yes, I am ready. I will take my friends back across the lake one more time and then I will come back here. And you and I can talk of many things."

They nodded at each other and the turtle went inside the cottage to join the others.

Rolf watched as the lake finally swallowed the sun. As the sun set, the last of its light beat a golden, shimmering path across the water and into his heart. There was one last, flaring flash of red, like a flame and it seemed to say, '*Until tomorrow*', and then sunset melted into twilight.

"What a beautiful sight," Rolf said and sighed. "I wish Saltpepper and Beech and Peaty could have seen it."

"Perhaps they do," Lynora said quietly, almost to herself. "Yes, I think perhaps they do," she finished and then left him alone on the porch.

Rolf sighed again and blinked back a tear. "Yes, I think so, too," he murmured. As he turned towards the cottage, he caught a last whiff of the secret scent of the blossoms and he looked at the deepening blue of the sky where the first stars waited to blink and wink. Rolf smiled. "Yes," he repeated. "Nothing is ever lost forever and the stars will always shine." He went inside.

A pale benevolent moon rose over Moonrise Forest.

The cottage door waited until Rolf was safely inside and then it whispered closed behind him.

The cottage doors had always known their place.

THE END

WALLASEY
December 2007

www.ingramcontent.com/pod-product-compliance
Lightning Source LLC
Chambersburg PA
CBHW020638030726
47498CB00002B/265
* 9 7 8 0 9 5 5 6 9 0 1 0 5 *